SPE

"I—I think I'd better go back," Marianne forced herself to say.

Nick blocked her escape. "Not yet," he said. "Stay and look at the mountain with me."

His voice proved more compelling than even the moon-dressed peak. His silver-gray eyes were more of a lure than the glittering snow. Marianne tried to pull away as Nick drew her into his arms.

"No . . ." she said, shaking her head. But he had already cupped her chin with one hand to hold it firm, allowing his tongue to slowly trace the shape of her lips.

She wanted to protest! She wanted to cry out against the way her body was flaming at his touch. She wanted to shout for him to stop, but when she opened her mouth to speak, just one word formed on her lips in a breathless moan. "Nick. . . ."

FORTUNE'S LADY

Robin LeAnne Wiete

AN ONYX BOOK

NEW AMERICAN LIBRARY

A DIVISION OF PENGUIN BOOKS USA INC.

NAL BOOKS ARE AVAILABLE AT QUANTITY DISCOUNTS WHEN USED TO PROMOTE
PRODUCTS OR SERVICES. FOR INFORMATION PLEASE WRITE TO PREMIUM MARKET-
ING DIVISION, NEW AMERICAN LIBRARY, 1633 BROADWAY, NEW YORK, NEW
YORK 10019.

ONYX TRADEMARK REG. U.S. PAT. OFF. AND FOREIGN COUNTRIES
REGISTERED TRADEMARK—MARCA REGISTRADA
HECHO EN DRESDEN, TN, U.S.A.

SIGNET, SIGNET CLASSIC, MENTOR, ONYX, PLUME, MERIDIAN
and NAL BOOKS are published by New American Library, a division of
Penguin Books USA Inc., 1633 Broadway, New York, New York 10019

First Printing, February, 1990

1 2 3 4 5 6 7 8 9

PRINTED IN THE UNITED STATES OF AMERICA

To all my writing friends, Eileen, Michelle, Alyson, Bonnie, Peggy, Deb, Dottie, and especially Nancy, for their many contributions of time and talent; I couldn't have done this without you.

And to Mark, because this wouldn't mean anything without you.

PROLOGUE

1888

Marianne Blakemore tightened the sash of her silk
wrapper, clutching it primly around her neck as she
slipped unerringly through the silent house. At first
the blackness was welcome, enveloping her with the
sense of comfort—of rightness—that came with knowing one's way in the dark. A table here, a chair placed
just so; all were the familiar pieces of a life rarely
straying from its predetermined path. And that, Marianne thought, was just the way she wanted it.

And yet, she could not shake the feeling that something was wrong. She wasn't sure what had awakened
her, or whether she'd even been completely asleep.
Her troubled thoughts of the past few days had not
allowed for much rest, and that was likely the case
now.

The mantel clock in the parlor chimed twice, causing her to glance in the direction of those doors. She
caught sight of her reflection in the gilt-framed mirror
on the opposite wall and gasped out loud, startled by
the silver-white image of herself in the instant before
recognition dawned. Her pale hair and white dressing
gown were visible even in the moon's feeble light,
shimmering like a spectre on the far side of the room.

Marianne smiled at her own skittishness. She wasn't
usually the timid sort, for that kind of behavior had
been discouraged in the orphanage where she was
raised. Vapors and nerves were fine for the wealthy
and spoiled who had nothing better to do, Mrs. Kendall had always said, but not for those who worked for

their living. She supposed that if the headmistress could see her now, the old woman would sniff her nose and jerk her chin knowingly, but Marianne had not yet succumbed to the habits of the idle rich. At least not until tonight.

She sighed a little, watching the slender figure in the mirror tremble at the slight movement. If she was jumpy, she reasoned silently, she had good cause.

Turning toward the kitchen once again, Marianne moved on, listening now to the telltale signs of the city just beyond the mansion's walls. Despite the hour, carriage wheels clattered through the brick-paved streets to the accompanying barks of stray dogs. When she reached the foyer at the center of the house, pale yellow rays from the gaslight outside filtered through the mullioned panes on either side of the door. They cast an eerie hue across the polished floor, adding to her unease. In the three years since her uncle Matthew had found her in the orphanage and brought her to live with him, Marianne had never grown accustomed to the clamor and bustle of New York. There'd been plenty of noise in Boston, too, but here it was relentless.

She clutched her robe a little tighter and stepped forward, then stopped short as the sound of voices drifted over her like a chilling mist. They came from Uncle Matt's study, and her feet moved in that direction as if they had a will of their own. Marianne realized she was about to eavesdrop but was helpless to stop herself, for in the midst of all the unintelligible words that floated through the air like dry leaves, she'd caught one name that was familiar—her own.

"She needs more time, Adam," Matthew Blakemore was saying, his voice growing clearer as she neared the study door. It hung open by a few inches; not only could she hear everything said, but if she dared take a step closer, she would have a clear view of the interior as well.

"You've had three years, Blakemore. That's quite enough for you both."

Though Adam Pemberton's response was muffled, Marianne sensed the anger lacing his words. That in itself was enough to make her wonder, for her uncle's business partner usually comported himself with meticulous control. This was the first time he'd ever raised his voice in her presence—whether he was aware of it or not. Adam had been a fixture in her life since she was fifteen, but she didn't know him any better than she knew the man who daily delivered fresh vegetables to the kitchen.

Which was why the events of the past few days left her feeling troubled and uncertain, she thought dejectedly. Adam Pemberton—wealthy, sophisticated, handsome—had proposed to her, and she'd been unable to summon any emotion stronger than disbelief.

The emotions of the men in the room, however, were far more powerful, and therefore more compelling. Sidling closer, Marianne peeked through the wide crack.

"She didn't refuse, you know," Matthew said pleadingly, his hand trembling around a tumbler of bourbon, the amber liquid sloshing over his fingers as he raised the glass to his lips.

"And she won't," Pemberton replied.

Marianne saw him lean forward over the desk, his broad back momentarily blocking her view of Matthew. His blond hair, oiled so that it lay flat against his head, glistened in the half-dark room. She didn't stop to wonder why the men had not bothered to light another lamp; the shadows lent an aura of mystery to the scene that matched the confusion in her mind.

"Our agreement was clear," Adam said, straightening so that she could once again see her uncle's face, blotched and strained. "I've paid for her, and now I want her. It's as simple as that. She'll agree, if you but inform her of the alternative."

"That," Matthew stated, slamming his empty glass to the table in a show of bravado that fooled no one, "is a choice she'll not have to make. The agreement is off, Pemberton. You can't have her."

"But you'll go to jail!"

Marianne heard the incredulous note in Adam's voice, but its meaning was masked by her own shock. To hear them talk, one could almost believe Uncle Matt had sold her! How long, she wondered, had they been plotting her future? Her senses numb, she listened as Matthew answered her unspoken question.

"I should have done that three years ago, rather than let you talk me into this farce of a partnership. My good name and the doors I could open for you in return for all the cash I needed. When you said you wanted my niece as well, I thought you meant to be allowed to court her."

"And what do you call all this?" Adam asked, hissing.

Marianne could not see his face, but his broadcloth coat grew taut across his shoulders as he tensed his muscles. It was Matthew's expression that jolted her stunned senses to sickening fear. His eyes widened, his mouth grew slack, and his arm flopped helplessly across his wide belly.

"It's not important anymore. Not to me, and not to Marianne," he whispered. "Take it away from us if you must, but remember that I can break you as easily as you can destroy me."

"Brave words, coming from a man who once begged for my help, eh, Blakemore?" Adam's voice had returned to its normal level, but the evil that sharpened his words to razor points was anything but natural. "You won't ever have that chance. I've worked too hard to have you go soft on me now."

Marianne's heart skidded to a halt as he pivoted halfway around, a quicksilver flash drawing her frightened glance. Before she could move, before she could even suck in a breath to scream, the gleaming metal spun toward Matthew, sinking into his chest with a sickening thud.

Her uncle looked up at her then, his eyes beseeching as he clutched the bloody hilt with one hand, the other outstretched toward the man he had once called his friend. While his fingers fumbled with the knife and his lips struggled to form a warning—and his mind grappled with the truth of his mortality—Matthew Blakemore found the strength to utter a single word.

"Go. . . ."

Paralyzed, Marianne stood rooted to the floor, her own gaze riveted on Adam's expression as he turned to her. His features were as calm as ever—cool, remote, untouched by what he had just done—but in his eyes glittered some things she had never seen there before. Passion, triumph . . . and something akin to pleasure.

Pressing the back of her fist against her open mouth, Marianne shuddered as fear shimmied through her, its impact rocking her like a blast of icy wind.

Only then could she turn and run.

Chapter 1

As the *Tacoma Flyer* rocked to a screeching, hissing halt, Marianne pressed her face to the window and peered into the dusk. Though she strained to see, billows of steam obscured her view of the immense engine, which had stopped along a great, curved piece of track in the foothills of the Cascade Mountains.

What she could make out was dim in the waning evening light, but even so the impression of an endless wilderness of trees embedded itself on her brain. A thick blanket of evergreen spread down the mountainside as far as the eye could see, the triangular spikes so close together, it was hard to tell one from another. The few that edged the track towered high above, their tops stretching far beyond her vision. Their brooding darkness made her glad for the familiar comfort of the railroad car. She'd read about the tall trees, but had never expected to see them up close. But then, nothing was turning out quite as she'd planned, including the train's sudden halt.

After nearly two weeks of traveling, it seemed odd to be unexpectedly still, deep in the wilds of the Washington Territory. The steady clackety-clack of the rails had filled Marianne with mixed emotions. On the one hand, every mile crossed was a mile further away from danger; on the other, each day brought her closer to the end of the line. Now that the huge pistons of the iron horse were silent, she felt suspended in time; afraid to go forward, unable to go back.

It was much the same indecision that had led her

this far, Marianne recalled dismally. If only she had gone straight to the police on the night of Uncle Matt's murder, instead of allowing Adam Pemberton the chance to prevent her escape.

In a blind panic, she had run to her room, screaming for the servants as she fled through the wide corridors of the mansion. Adam had followed, though not to silence her as she had feared. After bolting her door from the outside, he had calmly informed her that they would be married within the week, and that she would not, under any circumstances, reveal what she knew about her uncle's death.

"You must be mad!" she'd shouted, forgetting that she was completely at his mercy, despite the door between them.

"Control yourself, my dear," he had crooned menacingly. "You've nothing to fear. It was a *burglar* who killed Matthew, and I can *prove* it. Don't ruin everything now."

By the time Marianne had summoned enough breath to answer, he was gone, leaving her trapped and quivering from delayed shock. That condition, however, had lasted only a short while. Adam had forgotten—or perhaps had never known—that her bedroom had once been part of a suite. Hidden behind a chest of drawers was another door leading to an adjoining upstairs parlor. It was through this secret portal that she'd made her escape. . . .

"Why have we stopped? Can you see anything?" Leaning forward anxiously, another passenger squinted at the darkening summer sky from the other side of the wide seat. "What in the world could be going on?"

After glancing once more at her reflection in the window, Marianne turned to her new friend, shaking her head. "I've no idea, but I expect the conductor will tell us if we'll be long."

"Lord, I don't think I can stand another delay!"

Marianne smiled kindly at her seatmate, knowing that Mary Cooper had good reason to be anxious for the end of their journey. Mary, who was only a few years older than she, had confided that she was on her way to meet her intended husband, and that each day seemed like an endless agony of waiting. Mary didn't know what agony was, Marianne thought wistfully, silently hoping the vivacious woman never would.

She attempted to console her friend. They were, in fact, making record time. Until now the only stops had been scheduled ones. All in all, it had been an uneventful trip. Certainly, they would still make Tacoma tonight.

For all her appearance of calm, inside, Marianne's emotions were in a horrid tangle. As long as the train was moving, at least she'd felt she was making progress, though to what end, she didn't know. With the train motionless, her frustration grew, the cutting edge of panic threatening to slash through her sanity. But too much was at stake to let herself fall apart. She'd made it this far; she *wouldn't* quit now.

"This is just awful, stopping when we're so close. I'll be a nervous wreck by the time we reach Tacoma!"

Mary's continued wails interrupted Marianne's thoughts, and she couldn't help but laugh as she patted her companion's hand sympathetically. "You've had a case of nerves since we boarded in Chicago, and probably all the way from Philadelphia before that. Now don't fret. Your man will be there when we arrive."

"That's right," Mary agreed, cheering immediately. "My man. You know, it's strange saying that about someone I haven't met. And even though I've never been to Tacoma, already I think of it as home. I wish you'd reconsider staying, too. Nothing better than a new home and old friends."

Marianne sighed, shaking her head helplessly. As much as she longed for companionship, she couldn't allow herself the luxury. She'd never risk spoiling Mary's happiness, and so was forced to gently refuse her offer. "We only met a week ago, Mary. That hardly constitutes an *old* friendship. Besides, there are more jobs available in Seattle, and if I can't find one, it'll be easier to sail to San Francisco from there."

"But I'm sure there'll be something in Tacoma,"

Mary insisted. "I told you, the lawyer said Nicholas Fortune is rich. He can find your employment. Better yet, maybe he has a wealthy friend for *you* to marry."

If only it were so easy, Marianne thought, lapsing into silence. Why was it that lately everyone seemed to think marriage was the answer to all her problems? Shuddering, she tried not to think about the one proposal she'd already received, but the memory refused to stay tucked away.

"To be perfectly honest," Mary Cooper continued, "I don't know why a girl as pretty as you isn't married already."

Marianne shrugged helplessly before lapsing into silence. If Mary only knew how close she had come to agreeing to Adam Pemberton's passionless proposal!

Even now, she couldn't quite understand why she had not. For years, or at least as long as she'd let herself dwell on such things, Marianne had carried an image of her future husband around with her like a secret locket hidden close to her heart. His description was vague, his demeanor uncertain, but he represented all the things she felt necessary to her own happiness . . . tolerance, security, the comfort of knowing that her life would be free of the kind of upheavals she'd already known. Adam Pemberton could have met those requirements—at least she'd thought so before witnessing his cold-blooded deed. Now she could not erase the scene of the murder from her mind.

"Is there anything I can do to help you ladies? You seem to be quite distressed."

Snapping her head up, she replied quickly, "No. We're fine."

The intrusion of a soothing male voice had startled Marianne back to the present. Gone were the richly panelled walls and elegant furnishings of her uncle's study; her home now was the poorly lit railroad car, the wooden bench her only comfort until she'd put enough distance between herself and Adam Pemberton.

"Thank you for asking, Mr. Hartley." Mary Cooper purred at the man who leaned toward them, while casting Marianne a puzzled frown. "It's just this confounded delay," she added, turning to peer anxiously out the now darkened window.

Rhys Hartley suppressed a smile and settled back into his seat across the aisle. That was just the reaction he'd expected from each of them. For years now he'd prided himself on his ability to predict people's behavior, a skill made keen by many hours of vigilance. This trip he was finding his talent tested to the limit, but he finally had the two young women figured.

Ever since he'd watched them board together in Chicago he'd been fascinated by the study in contrasts. Indeed, any resemblance between them ended with the similarity of their names.

Mary—as he'd come to think of her after days of eavesdropping—seemed as unpretentious as a child, yet was, in fact, remarkably shrewd in the ways of the world. He supposed that was a trait common to many young widows, and the reason why widows were much sought after as brides to the pioneers of the West. She was not uncomely, though her looks could be more aptly described as handsome. Her figure was rather robust, but she wore plain, tasteful clothing that complemented her well. Her waiting bridegroom would no doubt get exactly what he expected—a hardworking, agreeable young woman who would be a suitable wife.

It was Marianne, however, who claimed Rhys's attention, and his avid gaze sought her now. Though she was utterly beautiful, it was her natural warmth that attracted him, and in spite of his long-kept resolve never to become involved with his quarry, he found his emotions stirred.

She looked so vulnerable, so pure, that he had a hard time remembering who she was. Silky hair, the color of golden honey, was smoothed back into a thick bun that looked far too heavy for her delicately arched neck. Wispy curls framed a face as fine and clear as exotic porcelain. Her eyes were an entrancing shade of blue, vibrant and glowing when she allowed her guarded expression to relax, as she had done with the talkative Mary.

It was her smile, however, that captivated him.

Whether she knew it or not, it radiated with her quiet spirit. He likened it to a rare jewel lying deep within the dark confines of the earth that, once revealed, catches the light and magnifies it with some kind of inner magic, transforming the beholder.

Mentally shaking himself, Rhys Hartley summoned a wry thought. Despite her appearance, the newspaper headline hidden in his bag said she was a murderess. It claimed she'd killed her own uncle, then absconded with a number of bonds and other important papers. The police had found the murder weapon hidden in her room, and a servant had reluctantly come forward, swearing he'd seen her stab her guardian to death.

Rhys had enough experience with women to know that sometimes the most innocent-looking females were capable of heinous deeds. There was no question in his mind that Marianne Blakemore was running from something, and that beneath her attempt at composure, she was as terrified as a child. What *did* confuse him was that she was using her real name. That wasn't the sort of mistake a calculating criminal would make.

At that moment the conductor entered the car, his appearance causing such a cacophony of sound in the crowded enclosure that Rhys's attention was diverted toward the man.

Marianne, too, turned from the window to listen. Though the car was immediately filled with angry shouts, the stout conductor remained unflustered, patiently raising one hand until the furor had died down to a muttering undertone.

"Tracks washed out up ahead," he stated tersely. "Tried to wire for a crew, but the telegraph is out, too. We're only an hour's ride from Tacoma. They'll send men as soon as we don't show up on time, or by morning at latest."

"Morning!"

Resentful voices clamored forward from the rear of the car, all aimed at the hapless railroad employee. Since she and Mary were seated near the front of the car, Marianne could clearly see the tension that worked up and down in the conductor's jaw. She immediately felt sorry for him; there were two passenger cars ahead of them that he'd already faced, and two more to be braved behind theirs. Surely this was a part of his job he didn't relish.

"Yes, morning," he repeated loudly, undaunted by the complaints. "Even if enough men arrived earlier, it's too dark now to see. These delays can't be helped."

"I don't believe this," Mary cried exasperatedly, wringing her hands as the conductor moved past them toward the rear. "I can't stand the thought of another night on this train!"

Secretly, Marianne was glad for the chance for one more day before she had to face reality, but she couldn't bear the note of anguish in her friend's voice. "Then think about tomorrow night," she suggested. "Try to picture your Mr. Fortune."

With a tiny frown, Mary contemplated the possibility. "You know something?" she quipped. "That's the one thing I can't do. The lawyer, Mr. Jacoby, said—and I quote—'he's a well-turned-out fellow.' That can mean just about anything."

"It could mean he's devastatingly handsome . . ."

"Or it could mean he's a little better looking than a grizzly bear. It seems to me that any man as wealthy and influential as Nicholas Fortune shouldn't have much trouble finding a wife. I know there's a shortage of women in the territory, but doesn't it seem odd that he'd have his attorney pick a bride for him all the way across the country?"

"That's really not so unusual," Marianne commented reassuringly. She gestured toward Mary's silk-tasseled reticule, which lay on the seat between them. "Men have been marrying mail-order brides for years. At least your Mr. Fortune has been kind enough to write you several letters, so that you know what to expect."

"But that's just it!" Mary wrinkled her nose. "He tells all about Tacoma, the prettiest little city in the territory, and all about his mountain, and his lumber, and his house. Everything but himself! The man never once mentions what *he's* like. I've come to the conclusion that he's not as fine as Mr. Jacoby implied. My

Mr. Fortune is probably short and fat . . ." she paused, pursing her lips dramatically, ". . . and very likely bald!"

Of its own volition, a grin widened Marianne's mouth; not at the thought of the maligned Mr. Fortune, but at the comical way in which Mary Cooper rolled her eyes, and at her uncanny ability to thrust dreariness away like an unwelcome suitor. Quite suddenly, Marianne was overcome with fondness for her new friend. "Oh, Mary!" she exclaimed. "Whatever am I going to do without you?"

"Why, go right on living, I suppose," Mary responded, slightly abashed by the emotion shining in the depths of her young companion's blue eyes. "Besides, we can always write to each other, seeing as how you're set on going to Seattle. But remember, you can come to visit me anytime you want."

"And what will your Mr. Fortune think of you taking in every stray creature in need of a job?" Marianne teased.

Her head tilting mischievously, Mary arched her brows. "Don't you worry about that. I expect I'll have him eating out of my hand in no time at all. Of course, there's no telling *how* long that'll be if this darned train doesn't move soon! Do you think the conductor might know if anyone lives close by? Maybe that nice Mr. Hartley *can* help us."

Shaking her head with a smile, Marianne marveled at the way the other woman could shift the direction of a conversation in the blink of an eye. "Please don't ask him," she begged. "He's pestered us enough."

Mary cocked her head, truly astonished. "Why, he's only trying to be nice. And he's *very* attractive."

Marianne couldn't help darting a glance across the aisle. To her dismay, a pair of glittering emerald eyes met hers. Quickly lowering her gaze to Mary's inquisitive smile, she muttered, "Too attractive for his own good."

"But nice, you have to admit."

"Mary, he's a professional gambler!" she protested.

"He told us he's an unscrupulous poker player. How can you think of cozying up to him?"

"Not me! It's you he's sweet on," Mary claimed with a strident whisper that earned her a shushing, which she ignored completely. "And I'll bet my Sunday bonnet he's rich."

"But a *gambler*, Mary! He even looks the way I imagined a slick cardsharp would, with fancy clothes and shiny boots."

"Looks don't tell everything. I'll wager he's just trying to make an impression, though God knows all he has to do is turn on that smile and every female between eight and eighty'll be pining for him. Good Lord! Have you ever seen such eyes? And that copper-colored hair!"

Marianne shrugged, trying to remain calm. Let Mary think what she wanted. What really bothered her about Rhys Hartley were the endless questions he'd asked the few times Mary had invited him to sit in the empty seat facing them. He'd looked at her, all right, but not in the way of a man trying to make time. He'd eyed her as if he knew most of her secrets, and wouldn't be satisfied until he knew them all.

Probably, she reasoned silently, she was getting upset over nothing. After all, Rhys Hartley was just a man who happened to be on the same train. There was no sense in turning skittish. What were the chances Adam would find her now?

The chances were good! a voice inside her clamored. Too good! Adam Pemberton was a man who got what he wanted. Of all people, she should know.

But what he doesn't have yet, she told herself bravely, *is me . . . or Uncle Matt's books*. She thought of the two brown leather ledgers hidden in the old carpetbag she'd "borrowed" from one of the servants the night she fled. At the time, Marianne had believed she could take the account books to the authorities and demand Adam's arrest. Not knowing a lot about business, she'd only hoped they would reveal enough about Pemberton's shaky dealings to earn her a hearing, at least. But by daybreak, both Boston and Marianne

had been aghast at the early morning headlines. Once
again, indecision had proved to be her enemy. She'd
waited too long—long enough for Adam to discover
she was missing. Somehow, he had managed to dis-
credit her before she had a chance to point an accusing
finger at him. She'd remembered then, Adam's one-
time boast . . . that half of New York was "in his
pocket."

That was when she'd truly panicked, Marianne silently admitted. Her only wish had been for a chance
to be heard, and she'd known she wouldn't get it while
in the same city with Adam Pemberton. She'd been
lucky to get out of New York without being arrested.

That's not quite true, she amended. *She'd been lucky
to get out alive.*

Now her revolving thoughts centered on her Uncle
Matthew, and the mixed emotions brought by memories of her only relative. She'd always been unsure of
her feelings toward him. Perhaps it was because she'd
been unprepared for Matthew Blakemore to come
storming into her life, whisking her away from the
Boston Asylum for Orphans just after she'd turned
fifteen. He was her father's brother—estranged, yes,
he'd explained—but perfectly willing to shoulder his
responsibility to his flesh-and-blood niece. Without a
backward glance, he'd fetched her to his New York
mansion, showering her with every gift imaginable.

At first, Marianne had been so awed by the daily
splendor of his extravagant life-style, she hadn't time
to wonder about him. But as the weeks and months
passed, it'd become easy to see that her uncle's generosity stemmed not from his heart, but from some
deep-seated sense of guilt. Every now and then he
would drop his very proper facade, and she would get
a glimpse of the pain beneath the surface of his
amiability.

There was no doubt in her mind that he tried to
make up for the years while he'd been in Europe,
unaware of his brother's death or of the disposition of
his infant niece. But despite Matthew's efforts—efforts
that included all the material goods she could imagine—

he was never able to give Marianne what she truly craved . . . love and independence.

Not that she'd have been capable of living on her own. No, at fifteen she'd been as unworldly as a lamb, and nearly as docile. And by making every decision for her, from choosing her wardrobe to selecting her friends, Uncle Matt kept her that way.

Only now did she realize that Adam Pemberton had been behind her uncle's actions.

Biting down hard on her lower lip, Marianne fought the tears that burned behind her eyelids. How could she let herself mourn the man who'd meant to betray her trust in the vilest manner possible? She mustn't forget it was partly Uncle Matt's fault she was now running for her life!

A touch on her hand jerked her mind to the present.

"I'm going to find him," Mary announced. When Marianne gave her a confused look, she paused to explain. "The conductor. I want to ask him if there's any other way off this mountain."

"Please stay here," Marianne pleaded softly. "He'll be back soon."

Mary peered around at the interior of the car impatiently. "I heard someone say the private car at the end of the train is outfitted for a real party. He could be back there for hours. With my luck, the conductor'll settle down for the night with a bottle of Kentucky's finest."

"Surely not while on duty—"

"I'm not waiting to find out!"

Marianne watched helplessly as her friend set her chin at a stubborn angle and patted down a lock of hair that was the unfortunate color of wet straw. Straightening her shirtwaist in an attempt to adjust the bustle that was slightly smashed from days of sitting on it, Mary Cooper stood up.

"Do you want me to go with you?"

"No, you stay here and guard my bags." With a quick motion, Mary indicated her reticule lying on the broad seat. "I'll have my say and be right back," she declared breezily, then sailed down the aisle without waiting for a response.

Once she was out of sight, Marianne turned back to the window, her fingers idly twisting the purse's silky thongs. If anyone needed good fortune, it was she. This trip had been a reprieve, made more pleasant by her new and unexpected friendship, but only a temporary escape from her problems nevertheless. There would be decisions to make tomorrow, and tomorrow she'd be alone again. But then, hadn't she been alone all her life?

"Good luck," she breathed wishfully, unsure whether it was a blessing or a prayer that escaped into the darkness.

Out on the track, Charlie Raymond concentrated on lifting one foot after the other as he trudged up the steep grade that skirted the canyon's wall. At one point he nearly halted for a much-needed rest, but the engineer's words still echoed through his head like the clang of his shovel against the giant boiler.

"Don't stop for nothin', Charlie-boy," he'd said. "It's important!"

Important! Just thinking about the word was enough to make Charlie straighten his broad shoulders and pick up his pace a mite. If only his ma could see him, he thought, a proud grin spreading across his beefy face. She hadn't wanted him to try for a job with the railroad, had wanted instead to keep him on the farm where he'd be safe, she'd said. Charlie knew he was stupid, but even with his limited intelligence he could tell she just didn't think he could do it.

"Look at me now, Ma," he boasted out loud to no one in particular. For just a moment, he was startled by the echo of his booming voice as it cavorted overhead, but then he resumed his lumbering gait with an air of confidence that delighted him because it was so rare.

He'd been called Dumb-Charlie for so long that sometimes his ma had to remind him it wasn't his real name. In the little farming town in Minnesota where they lived, he was often pressed upon to help his neighbors, especially when the task at hand was a nasty one. With his size and great strength, he could hold a half-grown bullock single-handedly, or load a wagon full of hundred-pound sacks of grain in minutes.

And after the work was done, he was just Dumb-Charlie again.

But then an amazing thing had happened. Overnight, he watched his town turn from an isolated farming community to a bustling hub. The railroad had arrived.

For Charlie, the greatest change had been in himself. His fascination with the giant, smoking engines drove him to try harder to read. What was once a chore, forced by impatient teachers, now became a labor of love. Night after night he studied handbills gathered from the station floor and timetables snitched from the board at the ticket office. He would mouth the words over and over, sounding out each syllable until it made sense. His mother was puzzled, but pleased, as she watched her son accomplish more each day. Even the weekly newspaper became a part of his reading material, if it had an article about the expanding railroad.

Before long, Charlie had committed to memory a vast amount of information, and word of his hobby spread. Now people in town would stop him in the street, asking him all sorts of questions. He knew that some were only humoring him, and others were secretly making fun of his obsession, but he didn't care. As long as there was such a thing as trains in his life, Charlie Raymond was a happy young man.

By the time he was nineteen, he was no longer satisfied just watching and reading about the railroad. He applied for a job at the yard, and—joy of joys— was accepted. As assistant fireman, his main duty was to shovel coal into the engine's boiler as fast as he possibly could. Confined to a small compartment with sparks flying and temperatures soaring, some would describe the job as the closest thing to Hell on earth. To Charlie, riding the rails every day of his life was sheer heaven, even if it was a backbreaking, thankless task.

And every once in a while, if he was lucky, he got to do something different—like tonight.

By the time Charlie reached the point where the steep incline leveled off, exhaustion dragged at his every step. His legs felt as if they were weighed down by iron manacles. The lantern he carried cast eerie shadows across the canyon, causing an uncontrollable shiver to rack his huge body.

"Just rest a minute . . . just a minute," he muttered, setting the lantern down. Despite his fear of the mountainous blackness that surrounded him, within moments he was asleep . . .

A long while later, Charlie looked around himself with a dazed expression. He had no way of knowing whether it had been hours or mere minutes since he'd closed his eyes, he only knew that it had been too long.

As high above, the moon reached its summit . . . and far away, a night bird cried out as it swooped up its quarry . . . and somewhere far behind him, Mary Cooper marched to find the conductor . . . Charlie Raymond was rising heavily, peering into the darkness ahead of him.

He struggled to focus his thoughts. Woody, the engineer, had told him to keep walking until he came to the deserted telegraph post on the other end of Devil's Half-Moon, a treacherous stretch of roadbed that hugged the mountain. On the other side of the track was a deep canyon. Since the telegraph lines must have been wiped out by the same storm that had caused the halt of the *Tacoma Flyer*, it was Charlie's job to post the warning lamp where it could be seen by oncoming trains. The reason Woody had told him to keep moving, he remembered now, was because a freight out of Spokane was due to follow the *Flyer* around the mountain.

"Better hurry," he prodded himself, stooping to pick up the lantern. As he bent over, Charlie nearly lost his balance. At first he thought it was his imagination that made the rails shake that way, but when he placed one hand against the cold steel he could feel the tremors that reverberated like a distant hummingbird taking wing. Driven by a force he could barely understand, Charlie snatched the lantern up and began running along the curved track, urgency making him forget the dangerous drop-off just a few feet to his right.

Never in his life had he pushed his large frame to such speed; never had his mind functioned so well. With sickening clarity, Charlie understood the enormity of his situation.

If he beat the freight to the other end of Devil's Half-Moon, the oncoming train would spot his lantern and slow down on the straightaway. But as long as he was on the curve, there was no way the engineer could see him in time. The huge machine would roar down the mountainside, unaware of the washed-out track and the stalled train just ahead.

The steady rumbling grew louder now, drowning the sound of Charlie's gasping breath. Beneath his feet, the rails began to whine and shudder. Vaguely, he wondered where he stood the better chance, pressed against the solid rock wall of the mountain, or falling down into the canyon below.

Or, he thought, fighting the horror that spilled around in his gut like scalding acid, *he could stand very still.*

As if he'd been struck by lightning, Charlie knew what he had to do. Ever since he was a child, his size and strength had been his only worthwhile traits. Maybe—just maybe—he could use his bulk to one last advantage. He couldn't stop the train, but if he could cause such an impact that the engineer would slow down to check . . . ?

With an odd sense of calm, he stopped, placing the lantern at his feet and folding his arms across his broad chest defiantly. Noise like thunder bellowed through the mountains. A warning whistle pierced the air with its petulant shriek. Still, Charlie did not move.

"Gotta stop the train, Ma," he wept. "Gotta stop it—"

His words were cut off as the tremendous engine bore down on him with such force that he sadly realized, even at the moment of death, that his efforts had been in vain.

Charlie Raymond, in trying to carry out this final, heroic deed, had failed once more.

Chapter 2

Nick Fortune had seen the results of several ship-wrecks, countless logging accidents, and even one brutal Indian attack, but never in his twenty-nine years had he witnessed such human destruction as the wreck of the *Tacoma Flyer*. His eyes swept over the bleak scene like a hawk's as it searches for prey from the air, missing nothing, even what he'd wished not to see.

Especially what he'd wished not to see.

Already a group of men was trying to sort through the wreckage, while off to one side, several injured passengers huddled around a small campfire, their painful moans sounding hollow and unreal. A few rescuers knelt near what appeared to be bundles of cloth. It was a moment before Nick realized the men were covering the bodies of victims for whom there was no help. Swallowing bile, he swung from his saddle, dropping to the ash-covered ground.

The cold morning air was acrid with a hovering residue of smoke, stinging his eyes and choking him with the odor of charred wood and the sickening smell of burned flesh. Whipping a handkerchief from his coat pocket, Nick fastened the blue square in a knot behind his head, covering his nose and mouth as most of the other men who surveyed the wreckage had done.

"Fortune! Over here!"

Spotting Marcus Knowles at the far end of the twisted heap of metal, Nick strode toward his boyhood companion, a thousand questions already forming in his head.

"What in hell—?"

"Don't ask!" Marcus growled warningly, at the same time clasping his friend in a rough handshake. He'd never been so glad as when he'd seen Nick's dark head approaching above the others. "How'd you get here so fast?"

"I was up at the Puyallup mill waiting for the *North Star* to come in when I heard. I figured you could use an extra hand."

"Good God, I almost forgot! You don't think there's any chance she was aboard the *Flyer* instead, do you?" Marcus saw a flicker of apprehension pass through Nick's gray eyes like storm clouds that gather suddenly, only to be blown apart by a breath of wind. He was aware, like almost everyone in town, of Nick's harebrained idea to marry a woman he'd never met. Unlike the others, Marcus thought he knew the reason behind such an act.

"She would have written if the plans had changed," Nick answered dismissively, unwilling to dwell on the possibility that Marcus was correct. Changing the subject, he asked, "What happened here? Wasn't there a signal placed behind the *Flyer*?"

"I haven't had a chance to investigate," Marcus explained, adding in a low voice, "Don't even speculate out loud, Nick. You know as well as I that rumors can do irreparable damage to the railroad. Let's just see what we can do about getting these folks out of here."

"Lead the way."

Following the shorter man to the nearest pile of rubble, Nick felt his respect for his friend grow. As an employee of the Northern Pacific Railroad, Marcus threw himself into his work heart and soul, constantly fighting for modern improvements and updated equipment. In the five years since the line had opened up the territory Marcus had invested nearly all his hard-earned dollars in the company, and yet his first thoughts were for the victims of the same crash that might well ruin him.

"Are there many dead?" Nick asked gruffly, knowing his friend was likely to take any casualties in a hard way. Marcus's father had been a railroad man, too, killed when one of his engine's giant pistons snapped, driving its way through the cab and crushing him against the boiler. Now the son stared woodenly at the tangled mess that was once a private car, reliving a hell that had never quite left him.

"At least fifty," Marcus replied. He made a wild gesture over his shoulder. "Survivors are over there. Most of them were in the front of the train. When the *General* rammed her, the last three cars telescoped; they just shoved right through one another. A few of the passengers at the very front of the middle car made it, but the rest . . . we can't even get them out!"

Nick felt his chest muscles tighten at the anguish in Marcus's voice. Grasping his friend by the arm, he steered him away from the smoldering ruins. "Why don't you see what you can do for those folks, then. They'll need your help a damned sight sooner than anyone still inside. I'll get a crew started here."

With a vague nod, Marcus turned and stumbled toward the knot of survivors. Nick watched him for a moment, then began to direct some men toward the hulking wreck.

During the next few hours he learned the destruction was more complete than he'd imagined. When the freight train slammed into the rear of the *Tacoma Flyer*, its boiler burst, sending a cascade of sparks over the mostly wooden cars of the passenger train. In the hours between the accident and the arrival of the first rescuers, flames had engulfed the last two cars, or at least what was left of them. The men working at tearing into the wreck found that most of the crushed and broken bodies there were also burned beyond recognition.

Stepping back from the train to catch his breath, Nick swiped at his brow with a sleeve nearly as black as his soot-covered face. It was now mid-afternoon, and they'd hauled at least forty dead bodies from the worst of the burned cars; now only the middle car remained. At least, he thought cynically, this one hadn't caught fire.

A wall of indifference had settled around his heart, protection against the revulsion that pounded within him like a trapped mountain lion. He knew if he looked too closely at what passed through his hands, listened too carefully to the soft cries of the injured, thought too much about the loved ones who would mourn this day, that he wouldn't be able to take any more. It was easier, he told himself, to keep moving, to drive himself to complete this task.

There would be time enough later for sorrow.

His attention focusing again, he studied the car that lay on its side in front of him, its exposed underbelly reminding him of a giant carcass. The easiest way to get in, he decided, would be through the shattered windows, which now faced the sky, since the doors at the ends were blocked by the cars on either side. A few passengers had crawled out that way shortly after he'd arrived. It'd been silent for a long while. Not much chance that any survivors remained inside.

Pushing forward, Nick placed one booted foot upon the main cross-timber, then heaved himself up onto the wood panel. The sun was now high enough to cast its light into the car's interior. On hands and knees, he peered through a broken window until a movement at his side drew his gaze from the ghastly scene below. Marcus had rejoined him, and now stared into the overturned car.

"Oh, dear God," Marcus whispered hoarsely. His gaze was locked with that of a young woman, whose sightless eyes stared back at him, an expression of vague surprise frozen on her face.

Steeling himself, Nick began to pull the remaining shards of glass from the window, taking care not to let them fall onto the unmoving bodies below. When he'd cleared a space wide enough, he swung his legs over the frame, nodded grimly to Marcus, then lowered himself gingerly until he could drop inside.

He couldn't help but think it was like falling into Hell.

In some dim corner of her mind, Marianne heard the muffled curse and the sounds of someone moving around the compartment, but when she opened her mouth to call out, nothing emerged but a whimper. Her fear and frustration mounting, she tried again, but again her voice failed her. She was caught in an endless nightmare, peopled with faceless pursuers and nameless threats, made worse because it was real.

Like a protective blanket, Marianne felt a thick fog of sleepiness overtake her. She'd been drifting in and out from the first moment she'd awakened after the crash, knowing instinctively that it was shock that clouded her thoughts and senses, blocking reality from her mind. But now she fought off unconsciousness. Whoever was moving around above her was close.

"Damn!" Nick muttered, inching his way toward the front of the car. Behind him, Marcus groped along, poking among the piles of lumber that were all that remained of the passengers' seats. In the past hour they'd lifted several bodies up to the men atop the car; now it seemed their grisly task was done.

"I think that's all, Nick. Let's go back—"

"What was that?"

Marcus watched his friend stiffen, then purposefully move toward a jumbled mess of planks lying against the front wall of the car.

"Nick, there can't be—"

"I heard something. Help me lift this."

Accustomed to obeying his friend's terse commands, Marcus moved to his side, grabbing hold of a heavy beam that weighed down the rest of the boards. Exerting all his strength, he joined Nick in pulling at the large timber.

"It won't budge. We'll have to get more men."

"Shhh!" Again, Nick's face grew intent. From beneath the broken boards came a low moan that was something between a whine and a whisper. It was barely audible, and yet the sound made his gut clench as if he'd been rammed with a fist. Someone was trapped.

With renewed strength, Nick lowered his shoulder into the huge beam. Marcus watched with amazement as his friend strained against the weight, the muscles beneath his shirt bulging, his face growing taut. At first there was no movement. Then, little by little, the timber began to shift.

Stepping forward, Marcus added his assistance to Nick's considerable strength. When the beam was lifted free of the rest of the wood, they guided it a few inches backward, then allowed it to drop, its great weight rocking the entire car as it crashed down.

In her cramped position, Marianne felt the walls around her shudder. Even that small movement sent waves of agony pounding through her shoulder and arm. Dust that had long since settled now rose to fill her nose and mouth. She tried to cover her face, but couldn't raise either hand. Her left was pinned between her hip and the overturned seat that rested atop her; her right arm was numb with pain.

"H-help me," she choked, trying not to cough. "Help me!"

The scraping, thumping noises above her ceased, and suddenly the tiny space around her seemed to grow into a huge black void, engulfing her as panic broke her composure. A lump formed in her throat, strangling her as it rose higher and higher, bursting forth in a raw scream that filled the dark air. "Don't stop! Oh, please, God, don't stop! Help me! Don't stop!"

As if in answer to her terrified litany, the sounds resumed immediately, accompanied by muffled shouts that rose and fell in tempo with her cries.

"Hold on, we're coming! Just hold on!"

It was the first human voice Marianne had heard since the shrieks of the other victims had died out around her, and she let her own screams fade into sobbing whispers.

"That's it, lady. We'll have you out soon." The

screams had stopped, but Nick still worked with feverish urgency until he came to the last obstacle between
himself and the trapped woman. It was another of the
wide benches that had served as a seat on the passenger car.

He paused, studying how best to pull the demol-
ished seat off her without causing more damage. Rocking another board loose, he carefully drew it away,
revealing a slender leg clad in a torn stocking and
high-topped shoe.

"There she is," Marcus said, moving around to grab
the other end of the broad-backed seat. "Easy now."

Grunting in response, Nick pushed a lock of dark
hair from his forehead, then took a firm grip on the
wood frame. To his surprise, it wasn't as difficult to
move as he'd anticipated. Within seconds they had
jockeyed the seat away from the wall, letting it slide
back into a broken heap.

A stab of pain raced through Marianne's leg as soon
as the weight was lifted from it, but she ignored it as
sunlight bathed her face with its warm, life-giving rays.
Blinking slowly, she struggled to rise.

"Lie still. Don't move yet."

The words were spoken sharply, the voice harsh and
grating, as if the owner had spent a lifetime giving
commands that were seldom disobeyed, and yet they
cut through her fear like a sharp sword through feathers. Slowly, she turned her head.

A man knelt at her side, his dark features obscured
by dirt and by her own blurred vision. Light poured
through the windows above him, lining his broad shoulders and black hair with a halo of gold. For a second,
Marianne wondered if she were dreaming this miracle,
then the voice of another man broke the spell.

"I'll get a stretcher," Marcus offered before scram-
bling back to the opening they'd climbed through.

Nick stared at the woman lying before him, watching as tears filled her eyes. She looked so frail, all
huddled into the corner, her face and hair covered
with dust. Never in his life had he felt so helpless. At
least while she'd been buried beneath the wreckage,

there'd been something for him to do. Now the words
stuck in his throat, as he struggled to think of something comforting to say.

"It's all right," he muttered, touching the cool flesh
of her hand. "You'll be fine now."

Again, the sound of his voice vibrated through Marianne, only this time, instead of her fears, it washed
away her last shred of composure. Sobs racked her
body as she turned her hand palm upward, threading
her fingers between his.

Oh Lord! Nick thought, his chest pounding. He
didn't know what else to do, so he edged closer,
taking care not to jostle her as he did. Her grip on his
hand tightened, causing a ripple of unexplained emotion to spread through him.

He was no stranger to having people dependent on
him, but for some reason this was different. He thought
he understood her need for human contact, thought he
knew why she clung to his fingers as if he were a
lifeline. What he couldn't explain was his own feeling
of protectiveness. She was a stranger, and yet he felt
inexplicably bound to her. Maybe it was because of all
the broken bodies he'd touched today, hers was the
only one that was still alive.

"Please," she urged her throat dry and cracking.
"Please get me out of here!"

"My friend is bringing a stretcher. It won't be long."
Nick sensed the panic that glittered wildly in her eyes,
and he automatically tightened his fingers around hers.
It was no use though, for she struggled to rise anyway.

"I have to get out! Take me out now!" All her worst
nightmares were descending, suffocating her, and Mari-
ianne fought to combat them. Her jerking motions
sent explosions of pain rocketing through her upper
body, but she could no more lie still now than she
could have returned to face her pursuer. Either would
be too much like welcoming death.

"You shouldn't move—"

"Help me, please!"

Nick hesitated a moment, torn between following
common sense and heeding her heartrending plea.

"All right," he yielded, bending over her. "Can you put your arms around my neck?"

Biting her lip against the wrenching pain, Marianne released his hand and slid her left arm around his broad shoulder. Her other arm refused to respond. It was all she could do to hold it close to her body as he lifted her.

Almost as an afterthought, Nick reached for the small purse at her side, placing it on her lap before standing. Picking his way carefully through the debris, he moved toward the open window. He stumbled once, causing her to gasp out loud.

"Sorry," he muttered, gazing down worriedly. Beneath the dirt and dust, she was extremely pale, her eyes closed and her full lips parted softly. She'd fainted.

"Damnation!" For all he knew, she'd suffered other internal injuries besides whatever was wrong with her arm. She might even be dying, and here he was, recklessly carting her around. Cursing himself for his foolishness, Nick stopped beneath the opening in the side of the car.

"Marcus! Swede! Somebody lend a hand!"

It was a good thing she'd been unconscious, Nick thought a few minutes later, after he'd placed her in the wagon bed that would serve as an ambulance. Lifting her through the broken window hadn't been easy, and he was sure the pain would have been excruciating.

Leaning wearily against the wagon's side, he stared thoughtfully at her still features, somehow reluctant to leave her in someone else's care. One of the women helping out had wiped the grime from her face, revealing a delicate beauty that left him breathless.

"She's the last one all right," Marcus confirmed, looking down at her from Nick's side. "Sure hope she's gonna make it."

"She will."

Raising a quizzical eye to his friend, Marcus asked softly, "Did she tell you her name before she passed out? I have to start making up a casualty list."

"There's her bag," Nick replied. Out of the corner

of his eye he saw Marcus begin searching through the soiled reticule. Oddly enough, he didn't want to know what his friend found. If she had a name, then somewhere she had family, friends who were waiting for her. For now, he didn't want to know who she was, or who she belonged to.

"Nick."

"Huh?"

"Nick!"

Startled out of his thoughts, he looked up. Marcus clutched a handful of papers in his hand, a queer smile pasted on his lips. "It's her."

A tight knot formed in Nick's gut, one that was a mixture of dread and expectation. He'd been trying not to think of the possibility, hadn't dared to hope. . . . "What the deuce are you talking about?" he rasped, knowing the answer before his friend said the words.

Holding out his hand, Marcus displayed the familiar scrawl on the outside of one envelope. "These letters are from you, Nick. I think this woman is your bride."

Even as she moved through the darkened corridors of her dream, Marianne knew that eventually she would come to the place where it had all begun. Voices called to her, soothing voices that stroked her mind with feathery touches, easing her past the pain and into a world of vague softness. Then the voices changed into screams, indistinguishable from her own as she cried out a warning to Mary. But of course, her cries were never heard; she watched helplessly as her friend retreated into the distance.

Then the nightmare returned. . . .

It always began with a sense of suppression, of suffocation, that she associated with the airless dormitory room at the orphanage. It was, she realized, brought on by more than the tightly closed windows and low, aged ceilings. The general atmosphere there had been one of restriction, one of confinement. Happiness was a frivolity, joy an excess, and Marianne had learned at a young age to quell her tendency toward exuberance; to do otherwise was to invite reprimand.

And so she'd lived with repression, not surprised when it carried over into her dreams, and not surprised that the choking nightmare had not disappeared even after the orphanage was no more than a distant part of her past.

In her dream, memories of the orphanage had mingled with images of Uncle Matt, smiling sadly as he crushed her in an embrace that left her breathless and struggling to be released. But this time the nightmare continued from there, and Matthew's jowly face turned lean and angry, his pale eyes becoming dark orbs as he challenged her with a vicious sneer.

"You belong to me," Adam Pemberton claimed, his fingers growing into sharp talons, his features distorted into those of a strange, unknown beast as he choked the life from her. "You'll never escape now."

And that was when she started to scream. . . .

The echoing cries of her nightmare were in reality little more than a drawn-out moan, yet they woke Nick with a start, causing the sweat to form instantly on his brow as he looked over at the slim, thrashing body on the bed.

Oh God! he thought. *Not the fever!*

Doc Waterson had already seen to the girl, forcing her dislocated shoulder back into place while she was still blessedly unconscious and treating the various cuts and scratches that had been dark with dried blood. "Watch her carefully for any sign of fever," he'd warned before leaving. "No telling what aftereffects she'll suffer. It was damned cold up on that mountain last night, fire or no fire."

The girl—Nick found it hard to think of her as his intended bride—had remained restfully still, until now, when her wild, jerking movements and pitiful sounds had awakened him.

In two swift strides, he was out of the chair and leaning over the bed, reaching a hand toward her damp brow.

As soon as he touched her, Marianne's eyes snapped open, and she realized she'd been dreaming at the same instant that Nick knew it was not a fever that left her borrowed night rail soaked with perspiration. For a long, timeless moment, they stared at each other without moving; then Marianne's lips parted, emitting a mournful cry that rocked his soul.

"Shhh, it's all right now. Everything's all right."

Nick held her then, awkwardly patting her back and smoothing her hair as the girl sobbed against his chest, great, racking heaves shuddering through her body. He tightened his arms to ward off the terror and misery that poured from her.

What was it about her that made him feel this way? For the first time in nearly twenty-four hours, he let himself wonder why he hadn't been able to get her out of his mind. It wasn't that they might soon be married; he'd felt wildly protective even before Marcus told him her name. He didn't think it was the way she looked, either, though God knew she had the kind of beauty that could drive a man crazy. He'd known many women, some beautiful and some not, but the one thing he'd learned, by God, was that the face of an angel could hide Satan's soul.

Which was exactly the reason she was here, he admitted to himself. He was tired of the clinging, simpering women who wanted marriage only as a vehicle to satisfying their own greed. He'd been married to one once, and those few months had been about as pleasant as a canoe ride down the Columbia River without a paddle.

That was six years ago, however. He needed a wife now, and despite the protests of his family and friends, he'd written to an attorney back East to find a suitable young woman.

What he'd wanted was someone to support his dreams and bear him a son. Love, he'd declared, didn't have to play a role in it. But for the first time since he'd made that decision, Nick Fortune wondered if he'd been wrong. She felt so damned good!

As her tears slowed to a trickle and her sobs faded to hiccoughs, Marianne, too, began to wonder at the solace she drew from his gentle embrace. She'd recognized him immediately; he was the same gallant knight who'd carried her from the train. She had surrendered herself to the haven of his arms then—it seemed only right to do so again.

Nick felt the tension ease from her muscles as he caressed her slim back with a circling motion. Beneath his hand, the soft fabric gave way to even softer skin, and his fingers burned with the warm, electric touch of her. The smell of her hair filled his nostrils, blending with the sharp odors of iodine and soap, and a sweet, womanly fragrance that had no name.

"Better now?" he rasped.

Reminded of the comfort she'd found in his gravelly voice, Marianne peered at him through wet lashes and attempted a smile. She recognized him, but mostly she remembered the safe haven of his arms as he'd lifted her from the train. "You . . . you saved my life."

"Not really. It was luck, or fate . . . or maybe even God who saved you. You were protected from the worst of the crash by the seat when it turned over on you. I was just the first one to get through."

"And the others on the train . . . ?" Marianne gazed at him hopefully, knowing in her heart the answer she would hear.

"There were a few survivors from your compartment, a couple of men who were up near the front where you were."

Leaning weakly against him, oblivious to the impropriety of such a gesture, she pressed her cheek into the warm flannel of his shirt. "No women?" she whispered, unable to stop the tears that resumed their course down her face.

Nick shook his head sadly, his voice low and hoarse as he cradled her slender form. "Only you, darlin'. Only you."

The next time Marianne woke, it was to sunlight streaming through a lace-edged window beside her bed. The bright rays danced upon the gleaming, hardwood floor in gay patterns, reflecting a spirit of lightness and hope that made her catch her breath. Quickly —or as quickly as she dared turn her aching head—she scanned the room. The eyes that met hers, however, were not the ones she sought.

"Awake now, are ye? That's good . . . very good."

A woman rose from the rocker in the corner, approaching the bed with youthful, spritelike steps. At first Marianne thought she was a child, until closer inspection showed hundreds of tiny laugh lines radiating from dark, twinkling eyes, and broad streaks of gray highlighting black hair.

"Poor wee thing. You've had quite a fright. But there's nothing to fret over now. You're here."

Pulling herself upright despite the dull pain in her shoulder and arm, Marianne looked around, dazed. Her initial thought was to wonder how sunlight could so fill the room, then she realized it was decorated all in yellow, from the striped wallpaper to the embroidered counterpane and pillows scattered upon a delicate settee. A woman's room; and no man was here.

Marianne's throat tightened. "Where is he?"

"Where's who?"

"The man who brought me here," she insisted, and then, realizing how foolish she sounded, lowered her eyes in embarrassment. "I . . . I wanted to thank him."

With her gaze intent on the delicate lace that trimmed the sleeve of her nightgown, Marianne didn't notice her visitor's satisfied grin. She forced her attention to the small details that surrounded her, the ones it would be easy for her tired mind to comprehend. "Is this yours?" she asked meekly, touching the satin ribbon that brushed the tops of her full breasts. It hadn't occurred to her at the time, but this was what she'd been wearing when she'd awakened before, and the thought of the man seeing her like this sent a wash of heat to her face.

"The nightdress is my daughter's, but you're welcome to it, though it is a bit tight on you."

Marianne looked up slowly, feeling the woman's smile wash over her with kindness. "Thank you," she murmured shyly. "Thank you very much."

"Oh, fiddlesticks!" The woman swiped at the air

with an impatient gesture. "No thanks are necessary. Out here there're few enough people, and even fewer women, so we have to look out for each other. Sure, and we'd be a sorry lot if we didn't."

This time, Marianne summoned her own smile. For some reason, she immediately liked and trusted this woman, with her elfin features and a voice that sang like an Irish melody. "Well, I thank you, anyway," she insisted weakly. "I haven't anyone else to turn to, right now."

"Sure, and I know that. Except us, that is. Just take it easy and let us pamper you for a while. You have a family now."

"But . . ." For a split second she wondered if the older woman were just a bit daft. It was one thing to help an injured stranger, quite another to adopt one. Marianne's protest died as her hostess hurried to the door and opened it, speaking rapidly to someone just on the other side. Footsteps scurried away as she turned around to face the bed.

"Our good doctor has assured us that you'll be fine in no time, Mary. I've sent Sue Kim down for a meal; once you've eaten, you'll feel much better."

Pressing her fingers to her temples, Marianne gave her head a little shake. "You . . . you called me Mary?"

The woman's lips twitched gleefully, but there was true contrition in her voice as she danced toward the bed. "Oh, my dear, I'm so sorry. I can imagine how confused you are. We knew your name because of the papers in your bag."

"You knew . . . you know who I am?" Blood pounded through Marianne's head. She felt unable to cope with anything; not this woman, not this conversation. All she wanted was to sink back into oblivion, as she had when she'd cried herself to sleep in the arms of the tall stranger.

"Mary," the woman said soothingly, "I should have introduced myself right away. My name is Claire Fortune. I'm to be your new mother-in-law."

"I don't understand!"

"Please don't be upset, dear," Claire urged. "It's

very simple. When you were taken from the train, Marcus searched your reticule for some kind of identifying papers. Thank goodness you kept the letters my son sent to you. It's all rather miraculous. Your injuries are relatively minor, and you were delivered, practically from the hand of death, into the arms of your intended. Mary Cooper, you're a lucky young lady."

Suddenly, the terrible irony of it all overwhelmed her, forcing a cry of deep sorrow from Marianne. This woman thought she was Mary! Dear Mary! The man said there were no other survivors in her car, so that meant her friend was dead.

"Are you feeling ill again, dear? Would you like to rest?"

Focusing her blurred vision on Claire Fortune, Marianne lifted her hand, then let it fall limply on the quilted coverlet. "I'm so tired," she replied, helpless tears flooding her eyes, ". . . so tired."

Nodding sympathetically, Claire squeezed her pale hand. "I'll bring your tray later. You just lie here and don't try to figure it out. Sure, and the saints have been with you these past two days."

As Claire gazed down upon the young woman's fragile features, a surge of emotion spilled from her heart. It'd been a long time since she'd seen her son worked up over a woman, even if she was a skinny thing, and too weak to squeak back at a mouse. She'd had her doubts about how this would all work out, but it was grand to see that spark in his eye again.

"I'm so glad . . ." Claire whispered, ". . . so glad Nick brought you home."

Chapter 3

By the time she'd reached the foot of the wide, curving stairway, Marianne thoroughly regretted leaving the comfort of the soft featherbed. She clutched the mahogany banister with her good left hand and hunched over as pain throbbed through her side and shoulder. The slightest motion made every muscle in her body scream out in defiance, for the sling fashioned from a silk scarf wasn't tight enough to completely immobilize her arm. If she hadn't been so eager to clear up the mistake of her identity, she would have gladly stayed in bed for another day. Gasping, she paused on the bottom step to catch her breath.

Her gaze swept the large foyer, noting at once the elegant furnishings. On ornate side tables around the room, decorative lamps added their soft glow to the traces of afternoon sun hovering still, making the gold-tasseled draperies that lined the room shimmer in the pale light. Muted shades of blue and gold graced an Oriental carpet of magnificent proportions, reminding Marianne that her benefactors were wealthy indeed.

Not that she needed another reminder, she thought ruefully. Her most recent visitor had made it abundantly clear.

When she'd awakened for the third time, Marianne had been startled by the sight of a figure staring at her from over the foot of the bed. It had taken her a moment to remember where she was, and to realize it was not Claire Fortune, but most surely her daughter standing watch.

"You're awake," the young woman said at last, a puzzled frown marring her delicate features.

Marianne had twisted slightly so that she could raise herself on one elbow. At closer study, the girl appeared to be fourteen or fifteen years old and bore the promise of great beauty, even though her figure was still as slender as a child's. A mass of black hair was pulled away from her face by a coral ribbon, emphasizing her flawless skin and brilliant green eyes. They were Claire's eyes, Marianne thought, except that where the mother's had been merry and warm, the daughter's eyes were full of guarded curiosity.

"I thought you were going to die," she stated. "You could have. At least, that's what I heard Nick tell Marcus. He said he can't believe you're alive."

Stunned by the girl's bluntness, Marianne shook her head slowly. "I find it rather hard to believe myself."

The girl shrugged as if the entire incident didn't matter to her in the least. "Mother sent me to give you this. It's mine, but you're to have it since your own clothes were ruined." There was no mistaking the resentment that accompanied her words as she flung a blue cotton dress on the bed, along with various petticoats and underthings. "It probably won't fit, but I daresay Nick will buy you plenty of others soon enough."

Thinking that perhaps the child was angry over the dress, Marianne summoned a hesitant smile. "It's very pretty, and I shall take great care not to let it get soiled. Thank you."

Again, the girl shrugged. "You can tear it up, for all I care. Do you think *I* can't have new dresses whenever I wish? My brother is practically the richest man in the territory. You knew that, of course."

Marianne hadn't the faintest idea what the child was getting at, and she was far too weary to argue. "There's been a mistake—," she began, but was cut off before she could finish.

"I'm not supposed to be bothering you," the girl blurted, "but I wanted to see what you were like for myself. You're not at all what I expected. Before

Marianne could respond, the girl approached the side of the bed, her eyes wide and inquisitive. "I can't even imagine what Nick sees in you. He probably just wanted someone else to boss around." Then she turned and fled.

Sighing now as she leaned against the banister, Marianne decided it was just as well she wasn't planning to stay. This whole family was just so confusing! Claire had been friendly and helpful, but there was no telling why the daughter had offered such a bizarre welcome. It also sounded as if this Nicholas Fortune—bald or not—was the domineering sort, and she'd had enough experience with men of that ilk. She shuddered, thinking of Adam Pemberton.

All in all, Marianne thought, moving carefully away from the stairs, she was too much of a coward to stand up to such a mixed lot. Mary Cooper, on the other hand, would have had them well in hand within minutes.

A rush of tears filled her eyes at the thought of her friend. That was another thing she'd have to see to, after she told these people who she really was. Mary's body had probably remained unidentified, and it was up to this Nicholas Fortune fellow to claim it and see that she got a decent burial. That was the very least he could do.

Drawing strength from this new resolve, Marianne paused in the center of the foyer. With her left hand, she smoothed the fabric of the borrowed dress over her hips and adjusted the sling. It *was* too small, as the girl had predicted. Though just a tiny bit snug in the waist, the tight bodice pressed her breasts upward. At least the sling provided a little cover. Unable to put up her hair alone, she'd contented herself with brushing out the tangles until her aching muscles had forced her to stop. Now golden waves curled softly around her shoulders without adornment, but, Marianne thought, her plain appearance would just have to do.

From where she stood, she could hear voices coming from two directions. Through a silk-draped archway across the hall, several men carried on a muted discussion. Behind another door, female giggles rose amid the clatter of dishware and cutlery. Since the only options were to interrupt the gentlemen or to meekly ask the servants for directions, there was really no choice at all—Marianne headed for the kitchen.

Before she'd taken two steps, however, the men's voices fell silent, the gold drapery sweeping back as a tall figure strode through the arched entrance.

A sense of giddy excitement, and something very much like relief, swept through her. She'd begun to wonder if her rescuer had been a figment of her imagination, much like the obscure lover of her fantasies, and yet here was the man, gazing at her with an expression that looked distinctly like pleasure.

"There you are. I was just about to send for you."

His rough tones were even more familiar than the strong features of his face. A gasp of surprise burst from her. "You!"

"So you *do* remember. Mother said you were disoriented when you woke up."

He appeared even taller now, or perhaps it was the way he held his head high, his eyes narrowed to look down at her in amusement. Either way, Marianne felt herself trembling as he came nearer.

She had just assumed that the man who'd rescued her—this man—had carried her from the site of the wreck and then had given her over to the proper authorities, who in turn had identified her incorrectly. Now all the pieces began to fall in place: his being there to comfort her during her nightmare, Claire's exuberant welcome, even the way his sister's stubborn chin had seemed oddly familiar. "You're Nicholas Fortune?" she blurted, instantly knowing the answer.

"I am. And I apologize for not introducing myself the first time we met. It wasn't exactly the reception I had planned."

Unsure whether he was being sarcastic, Marianne glanced upward, swallowing the lump of unease in her throat as his face relaxed into a grin. He was ruggedly handsome, with strong features that seemed as perfectly suited to him as the jagged scars that slashed across the mountains, offering harsh contrast to the untamed life that flourished around them. Slate gray eyes peered at her with a wild, animal-like vitality that sent the blood rushing to her toes. She swayed just a tiny bit.

"Here now, are you all right?" Immediately, concern creased his brow as he stepped forward, clasping her around the waist with a gentle hold.

The clean, familiar scent of him filled her head as she raised her eyes just enough for her gaze to rest on the large dimple in the center of his chin. "I'm perfectly fine, Mr. Fortune," she said breathlessly.

Not surprisingly, he found her more beautiful now than yesterday, and yesterday he thought he'd never seen anything so lovely. It'd be harder than he thought to keep from losing himself in her eyes. "Under the circumstances, don't you think you should call me Nick?" he asked without loosening his hold.

Shaken by the husky warmth in his voice, Marianne was barely able to stammer an answer. "Y-yes. I mean . . . no, there's something I have to tell you."

Once again, he raised his brow quizzically, but then nodded as if he'd come to some decision. "It can wait," he said firmly, pulling her hand through the crook of his arm. "There's someone here to see you."

Before she could protest, he led Marianne through the arched doorway and into a cozy parlor, where Claire was seated in a broad-backed chair, her daughter crouched on a stool at her side. Two men jumped to their feet at her entrance.

"You've met my mother," Nick said, "and this is my sister, Elizabeth."

After exchanging warm greetings with Claire, Marianne turned toward the girl. She saw at once that Elizabeth chewed her lower lip nervously, darting a quick glance in her direction but refusing to meet her eye.

"We've already met," Marianne said softly. "Elizabeth was kind enough to lend me some clothing." The quick look of relief on the child's face was so apparent Marianne felt sure someone would see, but Nick turned and gestured toward the waiting men.

"This is my friend, Marcus Knowles . . ."

Marianne smiled at the stout young man who looked vaguely familiar.

". . . and Horace Squiggs, the territorial marshal. Horace wants to ask you a few questions."

Looking like anything but a lawman, Horace Squiggs sprang forward, his wiry frame reminding Marianne of a puppet show she'd once seen, where all the puppets danced with jerking motions while someone behind a curtain pulled on the strings.

"Pleased to meet ya, Miz Cooper. Sorry ta hear ya been feelin' poorly, but there's some things I gotta know. Yup, gotta ask a few questions, like Nick says."

In less than a moment, the room seemed to lose its protective atmosphere, turning instead into an airless cell. Apprehension clutched at Marianne's throat. She knew they all thought she was Mary, but hearing the marshal say it made her feel like a thief. Should she keep quiet until she knew why he was here? Had news of her uncle's death already followed her? She dredged up a weak smile.

Noticing her sudden pallor, Nick ushered her toward an empty chair. "Just remember to keep it short, Horace," he warned, smiling down into her wide blue eyes. He was rewarded with an expression so achingly grateful that his heart thudded against the walls of his chest like a hammer. God! she was beautiful.

A surge of heat pulsed through Marianne as she gazed back at him. She watched him cross the room as fluidly as a mountain cat, folding his muscular forearms over his chest as he leaned against the opposite doorjamb. Remembering the strength in those arms, Marianne felt herself relax slightly. Why did he make her feel so safe?

Keeping her voice low to hide the tremors, she turned to the marshal. "How can I help you?"

Nick couldn't help grinning as Squiggs hopped from one foot to the other. To anyone who didn't know the man, he might have looked like an addlepated old fool. But not to those who'd seen him in action before. Nick often wondered if the restlessness was a clever ruse to throw off his quarry, or whether Horace Squiggs merely used the trait to his advantage. The lawman had been known to go up to five days without sleep when he was hot on the trail of some outlaw. Whatever the case, he was often underestimated, but almost never outwitted.

Behind that tremendous amount of nervous energy, Nick realized, was a brain as keenly discerning as a hawk's eye.

"First off," Horace began, tossing his Stetson hat from one hand to the other, "this here's an in-formal inquiry. I want ya ta know ya needn't say a God-blessed—'scuse me ma'am—word."

Oddly calmed by a strange sense of inevitability, Marianne replied quietly. "I'll answer your questions."

Horace cocked his head to one side in an attitude of polite attention. "Good. The problem here is this. It seems there was a lady on board the *Flyer* who's wanted for murder back East. I got a wire tellin' me ta hold her when she got in town. Trouble is, this here Blakemore woman's dead now, and ye're the last person seen talkin' to her."

Marianne's heart pulsed once in her throat, and she struggled to conceal her panic. If the shadow of her uncle's death had followed her this far, she was in worse trouble than she thought. And yet, as long as they still believed she was Mary Cooper, perhaps she could think of some way to clear her name. Unfortunately, she'd never been a very good liar, and she knew it was too late to start now.

Staring down at her hand, she slowly unclenched her fist. "I only met my traveling companion in Chicago a week ago," she answered truthfully, "when we boarded the train for Tacoma, so I don't know what else I can tell you."

"I 'spect the law in New York just wants to make sure it was really her. She told you who she was?"

Marianne lifted her head to meet the marshal's gaze. "She told me her name, and where she was from. That's about all."

Horace Squiggs nodded thoughtfully, then glanced

at the square of paper in his hand, clearing his throat as he shuffled from one foot to the other. "It says here light hair, blue eyes, medium sized, and wearin' a gray travelin' dress."

At the instant his eyes met hers, Marianne feared that this man saw right through her, but she was helpless to do anything but continue. Raising her chin, she stammered, "Th-that sounds accurate, but it also describes half the other ladies on board, including me. Perhaps there was some mistake."

"Ya mean, the dead woman we got down at the depot ain't Marianne Blakemore?"

"No!" Taking a deep breath to calm herself as much as possible, Marianne explained, "I mean there might have been a misunderstanding about her. Despite what you've heard, I won't believe she was a murderess. She was my friend."

"Folks ain't always what they seem," Horace remarked quietly.

Silence hung over the room like a storm cloud, ready to burst. Marianne could feel everyone watching her as she kept her eyes fixed on the marshal. *Please*, she prayed silently. *Let this end quickly*.

"Would anyone care for tea? Horace?" Claire asked, her interruption easing the tension immediately. With graceful aplomb, she began passing around cups and saucers, stopping at Marianne's side long enough to give her hand a reassuring pat.

While Elizabeth carried a plate of tiny cakes from one chair to the next, pausing to chat with Marcus, Marianne risked a glance at Nick, only to find him watching her with a look that was strangely contemplative. What was he thinking? she wondered. Who would he believe if the marshal suddenly chose to expose her? Would she be able to face those silver-gray eyes if they ever peered at her with blame and reproach?

But did it have to come to that? In less time than it took for the thought to form in her head, Marianne knew exactly what she had to do. This man had saved her life. His family had cared for her. She would not bring shame to their home.

Once the decision was clear in her mind, Marianne felt hope spring buoyantly from within her. Right or wrong, it was good to be making up her own mind about something. First, she'd stand her ground with the marshal. She'd figure out the rest once he was gone. It was obvious that he didn't plan to arrest her; he would have done so already if that was his intention. Maybe he just wasn't sure, or maybe he had too much respect for the Fortunes, as she did, to just haul her out of here on the end of a rope. Either way, Marianne knew she must buy herself some time.

"Beggin' yer pardon, ma'am," Horace Squiggs said to Claire, who was taking an inordinate amount of time to rearrange the tea tray. "But I'm in a bit of a hurry, so if ya don't mind . . ."

"Certainly, Horace," Claire responded in a firm voice. "But please remember that our guest has suffered a tremendous shock, and has not yet fully recovered from her own injuries. I don't want her becoming overly fatigued."

The marshal squirmed visibly beneath Claire's authority. "Yes, ma'am," he nodded, before turning to face Marianne again. "Just one more question. Did Miss Blakemore ever tell ya where she might have hidden some papers she stole? Did ya see any? Was she carryin' any?"

Startled, Marianne placed her cup on a nearby table, hoping no one would see how badly her hand was trembling. She hadn't thought Adam Pemberton would dare mention the missing papers, but then, she hadn't expected to be framed for murder either. At least she could answer the question honestly.

"No," she replied softly, shaking her head in earnest. "There were never any papers mentioned."

At last, to her great relief, Horace Squiggs appeared satisfied. Marcus rose and joined Nick in speaking with the marshal. He was on his way out the door when Marianne called to him, feeling suddenly guilty for having cheated Mary Cooper of her rightful place. "Will she be treated properly?"

The marshal stopped, turning on his heel to peer thoughtfully in her direction. "I beg yer pardon, ma'am?"

"Will she have a decent burial?"

Lifting his hat to scratch behind his ear, Horace nodded glumly. "There'll be a parson there, if that's what ya mean. But she'll have ta go ta potter's field. Ain't nobody gonna hold no fancy wake for a criminal, female or not."

"P-potter's field?"

Claire saw at once the color draining from Marianne's face, but before she had a chance to speak up, Nick had already stepped forward.

"Bury her in the churchyard, Horace, with the rest of the crash victims."

This time, the marshal didn't try to hide his impatience. "Now, Nick . . ." he began.

"I'll pay for it."

"The railroad's already done that," Marcus interjected. "*Everybody* killed on that train is included."

"It's not the money, Nick. If folks were ta find out—"

"They won't."

Marianne held her breath, her gratitude toward Nick nearly overwhelming her. She only prayed he'd never learn how misguided his trust had been. Her gaze darted to the marshal, who glared at his own boots while he chewed on his lips.

His mind churning, Horace Squiggs sifted through the facts, trying to figure what it was that bothered him most about this case. It was a lot of little things, he reckoned, but then, little things usually had a way of adding up. Like how the steward had insisted, before he died, that Miss Blakemore was the better looking of the two ladies. It was true that the one unidentified dead woman's face had been burned beyond recognition, but it was hard to imagine anyone being any prettier than the one sitting here. And if this

Mary Cooper had nothing to hide, why was she acting so nervous?

"Okay, Nick. Have it yer way." Horace shrugged his narrow shoulders reluctantly. "It don't matter much ta me."

As if by mute signal, Marcus rose to leave as soon as the marshal was out the door, and Claire announced that she would check on dinner in the kitchen. Elizabeth disappeared as well, slipping out the door behind Marcus, so that Marianne and Nick were suddenly alone.

"Thank you," she said, her voice quivering with emotion. Knowing that her future might depend on the next few minutes, she closed her eyes and tried to compose herself.

When she opened them again, Nick had moved to one of the large windows that looked out over the grounds. With his strong profile outlined by the waning light, Marianne could see more clearly than ever the sloping line of his brow, his patrician nose. The angle of his jaw looked as if it were made for stubbornness, and she couldn't help but wonder what it would be like to stroke his cheek, wondered if the rigid muscles there would move beneath her hand if he smiled at her.

The thought made Marianne's heart race uncomfortably, and she jerked herself upward with a start. The movement drew Nick's gaze toward her, and in that same moment she saw the uncertainty in his gray eyes, the pulse that leapt at his throat. He was as nervous as she, and the knowledge left her breathless.

"I'm sorry Horace was so insistent," Nick said. "If I'd known you'd be upset, I never would have let him in."

His voice was a husky baritone that reminded her of a rough stone encased in velvet. It held all the power she remembered feeling when he'd wrapped her in his arms, yet there was a note of vulnerability underlying his words. It only made what she had to say harder. "I don't think I should stay."

"What?"

"I said," Marianne whispered, "I shouldn't stay here. It's not right."

Disbelief washed through Nick, but with a quick shake of his head he thrust it away, forcing himself not to lose his composure. "I know these past few days have been pretty bad," he drawled, studying her face intently. "You just need some time to get over the shock. By tomorrow or the next day, you'll change your mind."

Tearing her gaze from his face, Marianne stared at the teacup which was now perched precariously on her lap. "I have to leave," she repeated, her voice low and urgent. "I'm afraid this is all a big mistake."

Whatever reaction she expected, it wasn't the anger she saw etched across his face when she risked a look at him. His gray eyes had darkened like thunderclouds; one corner of his mouth was drawn up in a frozen smile.

Marianne felt her face grow cold and pale beneath his stare. "It's not your fault," she explained quickly. "It's just all been too much. I'm afraid I'd be a disappointment to you. Please understand."

Nick took a step toward her and then turned away abruptly. God, her eyes were enough to melt a man without half trying! For just a second, his anger slipped away, letting the disappointment burn in his gut like a festering wound.

It *was* his own fault. He'd been dazzled by her beauty, by her sweet softness, so much so that he'd nearly forgotten why he had to pick a woman half a world away in the first place. Without meaning to, he let bitterness creep into his voice. "Then run away," he said curtly. "Forget you ever came."

At that moment, Marianne felt something snap inside her. Maybe it was holding back her emotions for weeks, or maybe she'd just been running too long. Though the reproach in his granite eyes didn't come close to what she'd felt toward herself, it was suddenly more than she could bear. Tears filled her eyes as she lashed at him, "I'm *not* running away. Don't say that!"

"Then why do you want to go?"

There was pain in his voice. Pain so sharp and acrid that it couldn't be disguised, even by sarcasm. Instinctively. Marianne knew that he'd been hurt before, and that she was hurting him now; not because *she* wanted to leave, but because somewhere there was someone else who had already gone. She wished he would turn around so she could see his face.

"Nick . . . ?"

He flinched as if he'd been knifed. It was the first time she'd called him by his name, and the sound rolled off her tongue like a caress, pulling at him with velvet claws. He turned then, his expression hard as he peered at her through narrowed eyes.

A lump caught in Marianne's throat, forcing her to swallow hard before she could speak. "It'll be better this way. I'm not what you want . . . not what you expected. I'm a stranger to you. You'd be taking an awful chance; I realize that now."

Nick managed to shrug offhandedly. "Which was exactly the purpose of our agreement."

"O-our agreement?"

"The one the lawyer drew up. The one you signed."

For the first time, Marianne wished she'd stopped to read the letters in Mary Cooper's bag, as she'd almost done earlier in the afternoon. She had no idea what he was talking about, but it was too late to stop now. She'd have to bluff her way through it somehow.

"Is it really so important?" she asked meekly.

"You found it important enough at the time. After all, you suggested it. And if I remember correctly, I was perfectly willing to give you three months. *You* wanted to make it one."

"One month . . . ?"

"To get to know one another. Before the wedding."

Her quick intake of breath was the only sound in the room as Nick stared at her. She certainly did a creditable job of acting surprised. Her heavy lashes fluttered closed, resting on her cheeks where two spots of color were rising. Was it possible that with the shock of the accident she'd forgotten?

No wonder he's angry, Marianne thought achingly.

What man wouldn't be? He thought he was getting a woman willing to start a new life, to build a future, not one who's held down by her past. The right thing to do would be to tell him the truth, here and now, but the thought of Horace Squiggs made her tremble inside. She had no choice but to keep silent.

But she also knew that if she continued to insist on leaving and aroused suspicion, she may as well tie a rope around her own neck and march straight to the marshal. The only possible way to prevent that, and to keep from hurting anyone else, was to continue pretending she was Mary, at least for as long as it took to decide what to do next.

One month, he'd said. Could she hold on until then? Wondering dismally how close a friend Horace Squiggs actually *was* to the Fortunes, Marianne sighed and opened her eyes. "I'll stay . . . if you want me to."

Nick moved to speak, faltered, then began again, his gaze fixed on her anxious blue eyes. "You don't have to," he said gruffly. "I won't hold you if you want to go."

Which was probably for the best, he told himself. He had admired her determination and resilience after the wreck, but now she seemed confused and helpless. Perhaps he was wrong to want to prolong the ending that was inevitable.

Pacing forward until he towered over her, he rasped, "You're not who I thought you were."

Startled, Marianne's mouth flew open, then snapped shut with an audible click. "What?"

"In your letters you sounded like you knew what you wanted out of life, knew where you were going. But you don't, do you?"

At first, Marianne thought he was calling her bluff, yet even when she realized he was speaking figuratively, the sharp disappointment in his voice sliced through her.

"I don't suppose I do," she whispered.

She thought he would walk away then, but he reached down instead to grasp her hand, pulling her to her feet. For a moment he looked at her and it felt as if the entire universe had stopped, leaving them spinning alone. The sensation of his warm fingers pressed against her palm was her only link to the world, and all of a sudden, breaking it was the last thing she wanted to do. It reminded her too vividly of the moments she'd spent in his arms, long before she knew his name, long before the perfection of her dream had been intruded upon by reality.

This man, Marianne knew, was real. His anger was real; so was his bitterness. She withdrew her hand slowly, not wanting him to think she was pulling away, but too overwhelmed by a feeling of inexplicable loss to endure his touch any longer.

She could only shake her head sadly and whisper, "You're not who I thought you were, either."

Chapter 4

"There you are, dear. Is it still too tight?" Claire took a step backward, her head cocked jauntily as she examined the gown's fit. With a slight frown, she circled around, tugging at a sleeve here or smoothing out a wrinkle there.

Marianne stood perfectly still, afraid to exhale lest she burst a seam. This was the third dress she'd tried on this morning, and it was even worse than the others.

"I can see we'll have to get you to Millie Knowles soon," Claire said, hands on her hips. "She's Marcus's mother, you know, and the best dressmaker in Tacoma. I'd hoped you could rest a few days more, but my gowns are far too short, and other than the one you've been wearing, Elizabeth's frocks won't do!"

Turning to face the cheval glass in the corner of the room, Marianne could see exactly what the other woman meant. Though the pale green morning dress was just a little snug at her waist, above its wide, jonquil-colored sash it was practically indecent. Her breasts strained against the delicate fabric, threatening to spill over the softly rounded neckline. She'd worn low-cut gowns on many social occasions in New York, but this one wasn't intended to entice, and therefore made her feel all the more exposed. "I don't mind wearing the blue dress, Mrs. Fortune," she said, fingering the handworked lace that trimmed her bodice. "I hate to have you going to all this trouble on my account."

"It's no bother. And I wish you'd call me Claire,"

the tiny woman insisted over her shoulder as she riffled through the multicolored pile of dresses covering the bed. "After all, lass, soon there'll be two Mrs. Fortunes. Let's not get things more confused than they need to be."

Marianne gave a brief nod of assent, then stepped aside as Claire flitted breathlessly across the room with an armful of various garments. Things could hardly be more confusing, Marianne thought distractedly, unconsciously flexing her sore shoulder. In the two days since the marshal's visit, she'd realized how lucky she was to be alive. The full impact of the crash had rained down upon her when Nick's friend Marcus, during one of his visits, informed the family that there'd been sixty-three fatalities and more than twenty serious injuries.

She'd also learned that neither her valise, nor Mary Cooper's, had been found in the wreckage. It was assumed that they'd been either burned or stolen by the looters who had inevitably swarmed upon the scene.

But having no wardrobe of her own was the least of Marianne's worries. Since the loss of Uncle Matt's ledgers meant it'd be more difficult than ever to prove her own innocence, she was glad, now, for the reprieve her mistaken identity offered her.

"Here now," Claire remarked, stopping to peer worriedly at Marianne as the young woman continued to massage her arm. "D'ye still have much pain? I can send for Doctor Waterson if you think you need more laudanum."

Shaking her head, Marianne smiled warmly. "My shoulder's not so bad, really. Just stiff and sore. It'll work itself out in a few days." She saw Claire's emerald gaze sweep over her fondly, and felt a sudden twinge of regret. Despite her own doubts about this whole charade, Claire Fortune had a knack for making her feel wanted, a true gift for putting her at ease. Even while Marianne basked in the motherly attention Claire rained upon her, she felt guilty knowing that her eventual departure might cause this kind woman some grief. To make matters worse, Marianne had seen many signs in the past few days that Claire was not well. The last thing she wished was for her own actions to aggravate the older woman's illness.

A sharp rap at the door broke through her thoughts.

"One minute," Claire called, pausing only long enough to glance swiftly at Marianne's bosom. Satisfied that her charge was at least somewhat covered, she grasped the brass doorknob firmly, beginning to speak even before the door was opened wide. "Nick! I'm glad you're back. We've decided these gowns won't do at all. Can Mary ride in to town with you this afternoon? You can drop her at Millie's."

Marianne barely had a chance to wonder at the way her blood thrummed in her ears at the sound of his name, when Nick stepped into the room, halting just inside the door. His long fingers played with the edge of a wide-brimmed hat as he spoke to Claire, ignoring Marianne completely.

"Sorry to interrupt, Mother. That deed is ready to be signed, and there're one or two other things I need to show you. Can you come down?" Nick felt the tension knot up inside him from standing less than five feet away from someone and pretending she wasn't there. What made it harder to avoid looking at her was that he wanted to do just that.

Claire pursed her lips, her tiny frame straightening as she faced her strapping son. He might be acting as if he was blind, but she sure as the saints wasn't going to be a party to his stubbornness. "You haven't answered my question, Nick. Mary needs new clothing immediately."

Marianne felt her blood plunge to her toes when he first turned a blank gaze in her direction. It came rushing back, however, the heat suffusing her face as his eyes widened slightly, dropping to the tops of her breasts. "P-please," she stammered, forcing herself to keep her arms at her sides. "You needn't bother . . . I mean I can't accept—"

"I'll take her."

Halted in mid-sentence by Nick's emotionless words, Marianne saw the warning glitter like sharp steel in his eyes. She'd nearly forgotten about his puzzling request, made just after the marshal left the other day. Though he clearly understood she was only staying because of the agreement, he'd asked her to keep her plans to herself, and to go along with his mother's arrangements for their so-called "engagement." She guessed by the expression on his face that meant accepting a few new dresses in the bargain. She'd almost rather he continued to give her the cold shoulder.

"Good!" Claire turned then, appearing preoccupied with straightening the ruffles on a muslin petticoat. "You've been neglecting your fiancée, Nick. The long ride to town'll give you both a chance to get better acquainted. I'll be down to sign those papers in a minute."

Marianne couldn't help the sigh of relief that escaped her just as soon as the door clicked shut behind him, then wished she'd exerted more control when she saw Claire's expression of concern at the sound.

"Perhaps you'll think me a busybody," the older woman began hesitantly, still fussing with the clothing on the bed, "but as my da used to say, 'I got eyes in me head, and a feelin' in me heart.' All's not as it should be between you and Nick, and knowing my son, it'll take a world of patience to get past that mule-headed streak o' his."

Facing the mirror once more, Marianne struggled to keep her words light. "It takes time for two people to get to know one another," she apologized. "It's nothing to worry about."

Claire might have agreed, but she saw the tremor in the younger woman's fingers as she fumbled with the buttons on her dress. Stepping forward, she laid a gentle hand on the girl's arm. "It's a brave thing you've done, coming all this way to start a new life. I expect you've been sorely disappointed so far, what with the accident and losing your friend. The last thing you needed was to find your man unwilling. Maybe I shouldn't be saying anything, but if Nick takes awhile to warm up to you, he has his reasons."

"It's all right. Truly it is," Marianne soothed, trying

to ease the anxiety from her voice. She wondered what those reasons were. She was no closer to knowing what to do about her situation than she had been three days ago. Nick hadn't helped much, either, for he'd spent so little time in her presence she could have sworn he was avoiding her. It was as if he wanted to pretend she'd never come at all.

"Maybe he's changed his mind about getting married," Marianne offered, trying hard not to sound hopeful.

Claire shook her head, biting her lower lip thoughtfully. "I don't think so," she reflected. "You know, Nick's never had much of a way with women. Not that he isn't manly, mind you, but he spent most of his growing-up years in the company of men. His father died when he was fourteen, and I'm afraid I let him spend too much time up on the mountain with the timber crews. I think he feels more comfortable swinging an ax than he does making sweet talk to a lass. That's the reason he sent for you. He figured on it not bein' necessary to do any courting."

"But I don't expect him to," Marianne protested.

"It's more than that, though. He can be as gentle as any man, when he's a mind to. He just thinks if he never falls in love again, he won't ever get hurt. Even though he tried to hide it, he was devastated when his first wife left him."

Shock spilled through Marianne, washing away all traces of her carefully bred manners. "His first wife?" she blurted. "I didn't know!"

Claire tried to look consoling, though she wasn't sorry to get it out in the open. "I'm surprised Nick didn't mention it. He's usually very matter-of-fact about the whole thing. After all, it's been nearly six years. I suppose that's another sign that he's not over it yet."

With a shudder, Marianne whispered, "That explains so much!" Her mind reeled with the implications. Nick had been married once before, and had been jilted by the woman he loved. Now she thought she could understand the pain behind his angry reaction toward her. She'd guessed at the reason; Claire had confirmed her fears.

"Mary, dear. I'm not trying to justify my son's behavior. He's been incredibly rude to you. But as his mother, I think I know him better than anyone. Nick doesn't take things in half measures. Not his work, not his fun, and not his feelings. I'd be worried if he didn't show any emotion toward you at all. The fact that he can't tear his eyes off you—even if it's only when he knows you're not looking—shows there's hope for him yet. Give him time, child. Please give him time."

Time. What was time? Marianne mused, carefully refolding the letters she'd read over and over again. Only weeks had passed since she'd fled New York, but they seemed like years spiralling back in her memory. She had a month to decide what to do next, but now the days threatened to race by, hurtling her toward her fate as surely as the train had sped toward catastrophe. There was time that froze into eternity, and time that moved inexorably forward. Too much time, and too little.

She paused to study the handwriting on the envelopes before slipping them back into Mary Cooper's purse. Dark, bold slashes demanded her attention, a reflection of the man who'd once sat with pen in hand to summon a woman to his side. She'd taken little note of Nick's handwriting on the train, when he was known to her only as Mary's undisclosed suitor. Now she gazed intently at the black strokes of ink, wishing they would reveal a clue to her future, some hint about the man behind them.

She'd pored over the letters, trying to glean any hidden information from between the scrawled lines. Mary had once told her how little Nick revealed of himself in these messages, and she'd been right. Other than the brief mention of a contract, which was nowhere to be found in the handbag, his letters were descriptive and friendly, but emotionally detached. It was as if his intentions toward Mary Cooper had been purely business.

Now that Claire had explained about his first wife, Marianne wondered if Nick had planned to keep his relationship with his mail-order bride forever distant. And was Claire correct in implying that part of his odd behavior stemmed from the fact that he couldn't remain completely detached toward her?

Dismally, Marianne thrust the letters into the purse and dropped it into the open drawer of her nightstand. She couldn't hurt him more! From what he'd written, she believed the contract gave each of them the right to refuse marriage, with no obligation. If she left now, she would certainly arouse Marshal Squigg's suspicions immediately, but if she stayed and then called off the wedding, she'd never forgive herself for repaying Claire's kindness—and Nick's—with pain.

There was only one other choice. Somehow, she would have to provoke such intense dislike toward herself that Nick would be the one to send her away! Perversely, her heart shrank at the thought, as if it'd been doused with ice water. After the way he'd been snubbing her, that didn't seem at all impossible.

That resolved, Marianne was troubled that she didn't feel more relieved. It was the perfect solution, she argued with herself. Even after she'd gone, she could continue to use Mary Cooper's name for as long as necessary. Nick would probably even help her find the employment she'd anticipated from the beginning. She could wait for the furor to die down over her uncle's death, and then approach the New York authorities cautiously—in her own good time—and with the cover of a new identity. She'd be safe. Utterly, infinitely safe.

Then why, she wondered bleakly, unable to hold back a sigh, did her chest ache with hollowness at the thought of leaving?

Because, her mind warned, even though she'd only been here a few days, it felt more like a home to her than any she'd ever had before. Her heart told her there was a place here for her, if only she dared to make it.

Washington Territory was a treasure trove of resources covering more than 65,000 square miles of land, but nowhere was that claim more evident than in the bustling community of Tacoma. Copper ore and lumber vied with loads of grain and produce, all crowding the docks as they waited shipment to ports far away. Tall masted barks, graceful clippers, and even one squat, ugly steam vessel perched on the edge of Commencement Bay, silently calling their promise of the sea to restless hearts ashore. But in most cases, they called in vain. Anyone who saw Tacoma fell in love with her; instantly, irrevocably, wholly in love.

Sitting alongside Nick on the buggy's cushioned seat, Marianne gazed around in awe. They had not yet reached the center of town, but approached it from the east, riding easily down the sloping green hillsides toward the plateau on which Tacoma thrived. Evergreen trees—fir, pine, and hemlock—hugged the town like a living, protective shield; tall centurions that nearly blocked the view of the majestic mountain range behind them. In the distance, like a benevolent giant guarding its domain, Mt. Rainier thrust its head toward heaven.

"It's so beautiful," Marianne whispered, her spirits lifting as her eyes followed the soaring tree line. There was a stark aura of strength about this wild land that filled her soul with a sense of freedom—and hope.

Beside her, Nick nodded and chucked the reins. "That's Tacoma— "

"—prettiest little town in the territory," she finished without thinking, her voice in unison with his. Startled, she looked up. After a quick flash of astonishment, Nick's face relaxed into a half-smile.

"I see you didn't forget *everything* I wrote," he said dryly.

Inside, he felt the band of tension ease from his chest as her laughing eyes met his. He'd almost convinced himself this morning that she was the money-hungry female he'd partly expected; that she was using his mother's generosity to ensure for herself the niceties his position afforded. But as he was harnessing the horse to the open buggy after lunch, she'd come out of the house alone, softly imploring him to go without her.

He would have, too. He'd have gladly bid her stay
home if his mother hadn't been watching from the
window. But disappointing Claire was something he'd
done once too often, and since she'd taken such a
liking to Mary, he'd do well to remember his manners
and act civil toward her—at least until she made up
her mind to go.

Now, however, he was almost glad of her company.
He loved Tacoma, and enjoyed seeing it afresh through
her joyful eyes. Each time she exclaimed over the
beauty of the land or pointed out some new sight, a
rush of pride filled him, renewing his own enthusiasm
in the process.

They traveled on in silence for a few more minutes,
until a friendly shout drifted toward them through the
warm summer air. Tugging on the reins, Nick slowed
the buggy to a stop and turned to look over his shoulder.

"Hey there!" Marcus called, urging his bay gelding
alongside them. With a huge grin, he tipped his hat
toward Marianne. "So you've finally decided to share
her with the rest of the world," he teased Nick, wink-
ing broadly as he did. "We thought you were hoarding
all that beauty for yourself."

"Not a chance," Nick scoffed. "You know Claire.
She's already making plans for an engagement party,
and we're on our way to your mother's shop now."

"In that case," Marcus chimed, "I think I'll join
you." Swinging from the saddle, he quickly tied his
mount to the rear of the buggy and hoisted himself up
beside them. "Mother can hardly wait to meet Mary.
And Claire must've mentioned the party to her already, because she was carrying on last night like it'll
be the social event of the season."

With an unintentional jostling motion, he nudged
Marianne across the red leather seat. From shoulder
to thigh, she was pressed against Nick's rigid form, the
heat from his body seeping through layers of cloth to
singe her flesh. His forearms were sprinkled with crisp,
dark hair, which brushed her skin as he slapped the
reins sharply over the horse's rump, grunting in response to Marcus's comment.

Undaunted, his friend proceeded to explain. "Everyone in town is curious to see how you've done for yourself, and I assure you," he added mischievously, "no one will be disappointed. Unfortunately, the crash has added a certain drama to the event. I daresay Claire'll have a full house."

Marianne glanced up at Nick, almost hoping her ears had deceived her. She hadn't been told anything about a party.

Catching her puzzled expression, Nick explained tersely. "Mother wants to introduce you to her friends."

The next moments hung suspended in time as she absorbed his words. His meaning couldn't have been clearer if he'd spelled it out. *Claire* wanted to introduce her to *her* crowd; *he* did not.

No slap in the face could have hurt so much. For an instant, Marianne was tempted to blurt out the entire truth in defense against his callous treatment, but then she recalled what Claire had said about the end of his first marriage. It reminded her that Nick was still feeling the sting of *her* rejection, and would continue to until she made him glad to be rid of her. Unsure how to go about that yet, she merely dropped her gaze to her hands, which trembled in her lap.

"Do you like parties, Mary?" Marcus leaned toward her slightly, his tone almost apologetic.

A shock of hair the color of sun-ripened straw fell across his forehead, and that, added to one slightly chipped front tooth, gave Marcus a certain boyish appeal that made Marianne feel immediately comfortable. Her troubled heart soothed by his charm, she replied softly, smiling at him, "Yes, most of the time I do. Especially when there's lots of music and dancing."

"I, myself, prefer to eat," he boasted. "Give me a table spread with platters of rich foods, half a dozen pies for dessert, and I'm a happy man. Unless, of course, there's a beautiful waltz partner distracting me from my meal. Will you dance with me, sweet Mary? You won't mind, will ya, Nick?"

Ordinarily, Marcus's friendly banter would have amused him. Nick knew better than anyone that his friend was still madly in love with his pretty wife of five years, and that this mild flirtation was put on mainly for his benefit. He was too disturbed, however, by the soft press of womanly flesh at his side to remember that. Why in hell did Marcus have to ride along, anyway? Couldn't he see this buggy was made for only two? "It's not up to me," he growled in answer. "Mary makes her own decisions."

"Good girl!" Marcus crowed. "Laid down the law already, have you? So what'll it be? Do I get that dance?"

She drew a quick breath. The chill in Nick's voice was almost palpable. For whatever reason, he didn't like the idea of his friend paying her attention, so therefore he would probably dislike their dancing together even more. And yet, if she agreed to dance with Marcus now, Nick might take that as further proof of her disfavor.

"Surely there must be some other young lady who claims your affections," she declared lightly. "You're far too gallant to need to steal a dance from one who belongs to another."

With a burst of laughter, Marcus nodded his head. "That's the slickest refusal I've ever heard. You're right, though. There *is* someone who, as you put it, 'claims my affections.' I'll bring Kathleen around sometime next week. I know you two'll like each other. Here we are now," he announced, waving his hand toward the white painted door of his mother's dressmaking establishment.

Swallowing her relief, Marianne turned her attention to the bustling little road lined with houses and storefronts. She noticed at once how different this all looked from eastern cities. Instead of stately brick and gingerbread-trimmed mansions, the buildings of Tacoma were mostly made of wood. Though a few were whitewashed to sparkling brilliance, many boasted a plain exterior of weathered board, with a smattering of log houses to remind her that civilization was as new to this tree-covered territory as independence was to her. The thought made her feel a thrill of kinship with her new home, temporary though it may be.

The buggy slowed as it approached a building with a small sign hung from the verandah by a pair of wooden shears. Marcus leaped from the rig, reaching up to assist Marianne before Nick had finished tying off the reins. Unprotesting, she allowed herself to slip down into his waiting grasp, suddenly eager to face this next, less intimidating challenge. Taking hold of Marcus's proffered arm, she lifted her chin and smiled broadly.

"I'd watch out if I were you, Nick," Marcus warned cheerfully over his shoulder as his sulking friend followed them onto the porch. "Not every fellow in town will accept a refusal as gallantly as I. This one's worth holding on to."

Rhys Hartley stopped short—if stopping short was what you could call it when one hobbled and swayed on a makeshift crutch—and stared across the wide street. For a second there, he'd have sworn he'd seen a ghost. At least, he thought skeptically, someone he'd figured for a ghost by now. Shaking his head as if to clear it, he swung around awkwardly to face the white clapboard building where the apparition had disappeared. A dressmaker's shop, the sign indicated.

"Need a hand there, fella?"

His ruminations interrupted, Rhys twisted his head until he could see a spindly-legged old man peering at him with a quizzical expression on his wizened face. He looked to be at least seventy, and couldn't have weighed much more than his age.

"I'm all right, thank you," Rhys replied. "Just stopped for a breather."

"Uh-huh." Spitting once into the street, the old man squinted skeptically. "Ya had a kinda lost look in yer eye. Thought mebbe ya was one o' them train victims."

Turning slowly, Rhys faced his inquisitor. If there was anything he'd learned in the past few days, it was that folks around here had an intense fascination with the details of the crash, so he might as well face up to a few questions right away. Maybe he could learn something in the bargain. "I was on the *Flyer*," he affirmed. "Broke my leg and two fingers, and knocked my head a bit. Lucky for me it's as hard as redwood."

The skinny man let out a high-pitched chortle, reminding Rhys of the hissing sound made by a steam engine wheezing to a stop. "Ah could tell, ya know. Not many strangers walkin' around town with sticks under their arms. From the way ya was starin' at Miz Knowles's place, I thought ya had that-there am-nee-zhe-ah."

He pronounced it with four syllables, and Rhys had to stifle a laugh at the hopeful expression on the wrinkled old face. He almost hated to spoil the man's expectations. "No, I'm fortunate to have escaped amnesia," Rhys admitted with a rueful smile. "Once these bones heal, I'll be good as new."

"Glad ta hear it, young fella. Glad ta hear it. Name's Josiah Barnes. If'n I can help ya out in any way, I'd be happy ta do it. Need a job? Ask me! There ain't no one or nothing about Tacoma I don't know."

With an inward grunt of satisfaction, Rhys nodded to the old man. Though he hadn't anticipated it being so easy, this was exactly what he wanted to hear. There was more than one way to track down a varmint, and sometimes a smart hunter could find clues in unexpected places.

"Much obliged, Mr. Barnes." He stretched his hand forward, leaning his weight into the crutch beneath his arm. "I'm Rhys Hartley. If it's not too much of an imposition, can I trouble you for some information?"

Weathered eyes widening with delight, Josiah Barnes's mouth split into a broad grin. "Not 'tall, young man. Not 'tall."

"In that case . . ." Rhys responded, ". . . perhaps you'd like to join me for a drink." He glanced over at the restaurant just a few yards down the walk, noting that the large, plate glass window in front afforded an unimpeded view of the buildings across the street. With a wag of his head, he said, "This looks like the perfect spot."

Luckily, Josiah Barnes was of no mind to disagree.

"Ornery! That's what you are, Nicholas Fortune. Just plain ornery!"

Marianne couldn't resist a peek through the curtain at the sound of Millie Knowles's strident voice turned against Nick. Not sure what to expect, she was nevertheless surprised to see amusement dancing in his sooty eyes as he looked down at his accuser. He stood, appearing far taller and broader in the tiny shop, with his hands placed jauntily on his narrow hips. Without a hat, his ebony hair had a rumpled look, as if no amount of combing would ever slick those thick waves into a tamed and refined coiffure. For the first time since the night of her dream, she saw the lines of tension erased from his jaw and forehead. It was amazing, she thought, how a grin transformed his face from harsh to handsome.

"Now Millie," he drawled, placing one large hand on her bony shoulder. "Can I help it if you don't come visit anymore? I couldn't bring Mary before she felt well enough."

"Hmmph. You're darn lucky, 'cause that's the only excuse I'll listen to. Poor thing's been wearing Lizzie's dress for days now, and no one says a word to me about it. Surprised you didn't see for yourself it was too small."

Marianne smiled at the resemblance between this woman and her son, not just in their thickset stature, but in the way they both excelled in showering Nick with affectionate banter. Marcus had taken his leave shortly after escorting her inside and greeting his mother, but not without a few additional teasing remarks directed toward his friend. And now Millie Knowles seemed bound to carry on the privilege.

Nick mumbled something unintelligible, but Marianne could only hear Millie's laughing response.

"So you *did* notice, huh? Well, Marcus told me you was right took with her. I shouldn't be surprised. Prettiest little thing I ever sewed a seam for, exceptin' maybe Lizzie."

Looking over her shoulder, Nick's gaze locked with
the one staring at him from the rear of the shop. Eyes
the color of a cloudless sky met his, smiling from a
face that flushed as pink as a spring apple before she
ducked back behind the drape. He'd noticed the dress,
all right. Just like he'd noticed everything about her,
from the way she walked so smoothly, it seemed as if
her feet never touched the ground, to the way her full
breasts rose and fell with each breath she took, turning all rosy every time she blushed . . . like now.
Feeling the heat rise on his own neck, he turned his
attention back to Millie.

"Now that you mention her, do you think you'll
have time to fix up something special for Elizabeth
before the party? She's been feeling a little neglected
lately." He hadn't missed the sullen pout on his sister's pretty lips that morning, and he thought he knew
both reasons why. The fact that he was indirectly the
cause of her resentment made him feel a trifle guilty,
though that didn't change his mind any.

"Do I have time!" Millie exclaimed, indignant that
he thought she'd forget her favorite godchild. "I've
already got the pattern picked. I was waitin' for you to
say somethin'."

In the cluttered corner that had been curtained off
as a dressing room, Marianne smiled absently. This
wasn't at all the bossy brother Elizabeth had described
on that first day. Nick treated his younger sister with
teasing affection, and his concern for her was endearing. How then, Marianne wondered, could he turn
into such a different person whenever she was around?
He was polite, distant, and completely aloof. And
don't forget contradictory, she reminded herself. For
all his show of not wanting to bring her to town, she'd
heard him whisper to Millie not to let her leave without at least three frocks, and an order for several
more.

Tugging on the tight sleeves of a blue serge riding
habit, Marianne wondered gravely how long it would
take to pay him back on the salary she'd likely make
as a lady's companion or governess, for pay him back

was exactly what she intended to do. Whatever else he might think of her when this was over, he'd never be able to claim that she didn't honor her debts. At least, she thought wryly, the ones you could name a price to.

"Ready yet?" Millie poked her head into the corner, sizing her up with a practiced eye. In a loud whisper, she added, "Best to hurry. Men get mighty tired of waitin', and there's still the ball gowns to try."

Nodding, Marianne stepped quickly from behind the drape, moving toward the large, double mirrors that lined the opposite wall of the shop. She was immediately aware of Nick's intense gaze burning its mark into her shoulder blades. Holding her breath, she waited for a sign of approval.

"There now," Millie gloated. "Didn't I tell you it'd be perfect? Half an inch at the hem'll do it." She circled Marianne, appraising her own work. "Lucky for you that Missy Kingston was such a foolish twit. Her mama was set to show her off real fine with a debutante season and two trunkfuls of clothes, but the silly little thing ran off with a lumberjack from up Seattle way. The girl hadn't a brain in her pretty head, but leastways she's the same size as you."

The woman's cheerful prattle brought a smile to Marianne's lips. As she raised her head so that Millie could make an adjustment to the collar, her glance met Nick's. He, too, was grinning broadly, his gaze warm with gentle humor. An odd thrill made her heart skip a beat before she lowered her head.

"Won't take more than a whistle to fix this one up. That'll make four you can take today, and the rest'll be done by day after tomorrow. Now off with it. Put on the rose silk next."

Nick's smile disappeared the instant Marianne emerged after changing. *This* dress was covered with intricate patterns of lace and seed pearl, and far too many tiny bows of pink ribbon. The variety of trims ornamenting the gown made it difficult to distinguish the shape of the woman inside, much less the color of the material supporting them. Of all the garments displayed so far, it was the most hideous concoction he'd laid eyes on.

He was about to state his rather decided opinion when he was cut off by a soft, melodious voice.

"It's lovely, Mrs. Knowles. But I'm not certain it suits me." Marianne touched one of the frilly bows near the neckline and smiled apologetically, hoping her dislike of the dress wouldn't cause offense.

Millie pursed her lips as if giving the matter great consideration. "Missy was plum tickled with it," she frowned.

"And with good reason. It's a beautiful gown." Biting the inside of her cheek, Marianne racked her brain for a kindly defense. "But my color is all wrong," she finally pleaded. "This shade of rose makes my skin look sallow."

Silently, he disagreed, but Nick couldn't help admiring her for the care she'd shown toward Millie's feelings. As a matter of fact, she'd been remarkably discriminating all afternoon, unobtrusively selecting for herself several attractive, yet tasteful gowns, even while flattering Millie with praise for her more extravagant efforts. On the whole, she'd made the entire expedition amazingly painless for them all. Not at all what he'd expected.

A few minutes later, Nick decided he was well pleased with her tactics. Marianne had exchanged the too-small, borrowed dress for a simple frock of deep green that complemented the rosy hue of her cheeks. The skirt, drawn back to a small bustle, emphasized the slender, yet womanly, curve of her hips, belying a modest—almost prim—neckline. The sight of her, flushed and ready, made him stand stock-still in the doorway, his arms loaded with the boxes Millie had piled high.

"Thank you, Mrs. Knowles," Marianne murmured sincerely. "I don't think I've ever had such beautiful clothes, or had so much fun choosing them."

" 'Twas a pleasure . . . a pure pleasure, dear. Wasn't it, Nick?"

Startled by Millie's unexpected question, he jerked

his gaze away from the two women and out toward the waiting buggy. "Sure," he answered abruptly. "Thanks, Millie. Be seeing you."

Marianne followed him quietly outside. Nick continued to confuse her. Though he hadn't seemed to mind spending hours watching her choose a new wardrobe, now he appeared agitated and eager to leave. The muscles beneath his blue chambray shirt bunched and stretched as he placed the dress boxes into the buggy, then unhitched the team with quick, efficient motions. She nearly jumped when he touched her arm, then blushed hotly, realizing he only meant to help her up onto the high seat.

Tilting her head, she looked up at him questioningly. The afternoon sun, slanting through the trees with bright fingers, threw cascades of light across his face, turning his eyes into clouded mirrors. Even so, his expression was completely unreadable. For a moment, Marianne wondered if she'd ever come to know what he thought, *how* he thought, before she remembered she'd not be here long enough for it to matter.

Curving his fingers beneath her arm, Nick met her gaze with a steady one of his own. His gravelled voice cut through the silence like the sound of a whipsaw rasping through a hushed forest. "It's late," he grumbled. "We'd best be getting home."

Green eyes glittered knowingly from behind the plate glass window of the Bay Restaurant. Despite having seen and heard nearly everything a man could fathom in his thirty-two years, Rhys Hartley couldn't hold back a muttered "I'll be damned!"

Ignoring the puzzled expression of the old man seated next to him, he stared across the street at the departing rig. How in hell had she done it? Not only had she managed to pull through the train wreck relatively unscathed, she was now living free and easy as the fiancée of one of the finest men—so said the garrulous Mr. Barnes—in the territory. The trouble was, he thought discontentedly, she'd nearly gotten away with it. If it hadn't been for luck, he mightn't have survived

the crash himself, and it was clearly *his* good fortune
—he smiled wryly at the pun—to have seen her at all.
A couple of hours ago he'd planned to leave this town,
posthaste. Now he would stay.

Raising his tankard for one last sip of fine beer,
Rhys pondered over the situation. A dull wash of pain
rose from his lower leg, reminding him that even had
he wanted to approach the lovely and elusive Marianne Blakemore today, he'd not have been able. She'd
get away with her ploy for at least a few more weeks,
because he had no intention of causing her to bolt
until he was fully prepared to take up the chase. He
couldn't help wondering just how far she'd carry her
scheme in that time.

If it was a scheme at all.

Now what in the world had got into him? he chided
himself. *Of course* it was a clever ruse. If she was
innocent, as he'd been wont to believe on the long trip
west, then why had she stolen a dead woman's name,
not to mention her man? It just didn't figure.

Rhys recalled the look that had passed between
Marianne and the favored—if you cared to see him
that way—Nicholas Fortune. Even from this distance
he'd felt the electricity crackling. Telling himself that
he wouldn't have given much to have her gaze at him
with those same doelike eyes, he swilled the last of his
drink and slammed the pewter mug on the table, with
just a little more force than was necessary from a
supposedly impartial observer.

He'd get to the bottom of it, he vowed silently as he
massaged his thigh above the splint. The weeks it
would take for his leg to heal should give him ample
time in which to formulate a plan. It might seem long
to him now, but would be very short compared to the
years Marianne Blakemore would spend in prison.

Time, after all, was relative.

Chapter 5

The trip home began in awkward silence, broken only by an occasional greeting from one of the many townsfolk who peered curiously from their shops, hoping for a glimpse of Nick Fortune's latest acquisition. At least, that was how Marianne was beginning to feel by the time they reached the edge of the business section. Nick could afford to send for a woman much as he would a piece of equipment, and even though she had no intention of filling the role as his mail-order bride, his arrogant treatment rankled.

Straightening her spine just a little, she took care not to let her elbow bump his as the buggy left the smooth, bricklined streets of Tacoma and bounced onto the corduroy track that led to his home.

Though she'd moved less than a fraction of an inch, Nick felt her withdrawal as surely as if she'd thrown up a wall around her. His gut tightened at the idea that she couldn't even stand to touch him, but was quickly replaced by a sense of guilt. It was not, he admitted wryly, as if he'd given her much chance to feel otherwise. He almost wished Marcus were still with them, if only to bridge the vast silence with his indomitable charm, and yet Nick realized he should take advantage of the time alone. While they were in Millie's shop, he'd come to a few conclusions.

As they drew up alongside a clearing beside the road, he pulled back hard on the reins, ignoring her puzzled glance.

"Why . . . why are we stopping?"

"So we can talk." With no more explanation than that, Nick set the brake and looped the reins over it, jumping over the side of the buggy in one graceful motion. "Come on," he said.

Startled by this sudden turn, Marianne's mouth went dry. It wasn't that she was afraid of him, she told herself, struggling to quell the rapid pounding of her heart. It was simply that she wasn't sure what he had in mind. "Can't we talk up here?"

His answer was to step around to her side of the buggy. He clasped her firmly around the waist, not even hesitating when she flinched at his touch, though once her feet hit the ground he let go of her quickly, his fingers automatically curling into fists as if to prevent his hands from lingering on the sloping curves of her hips. "There're some things you should know. I don't want anyone to hear us, and the trip home isn't long enough for what I have to say."

With that he turned away, striding toward the row of trees that edged the clearing. His lean frame slid easily to the ground, one long leg stretched in front of him, the other knee propped high. Marianne stared at him with a mixture of amazement and anger, then marched closer when he lifted his gaze to challenge hers.

"Sit down," he drawled as she came near.

She eyed the grassy spot next to him skeptically, then opted for a sawed-off stump that stuck out of the earth a couple of feet to his right. Gathering her skirt primly in one hand, she lowered herself.

"Don't sit there!"

A swift hand clasped her wrist, jerking her away from her seat. She swayed precariously, then landed in an ignoble heap in the exact place she'd meant to avoid—on the ground, and far too close to Nick.

"Sorry," he apologized hastily. "That stump's covered with pitch. You'd've ruined that dress before it's even paid for."

"Oh!" She felt the blood rush to her face, turning her cheeks into uncomfortable pinpoints of flame. "I didn't . . . I didn't notice."

Nick wished he could somehow lessen her embarrassment, but the fact that the incident had occurred at all only emphasized his need to clear some things between them. His voice low and rumbling, he said, "I want you to tell me the truth about why you're here."

It was a struggle, but somehow Marianne managed not to stare at him, openmouthed. "What . . . what exactly do you mean?"

Nick flicked his hand, his gesture indicating her dress. He remembered Millie's claim that this gown was too plain, yet to his eyes, it was perfection. The fine fabric molded itself to softly rounded breasts, narrowed about her slender waist, then flared gently over a small bustle. Yes sir, he agreed silently. It was perfect. "What made you pick a dress like that?"

Confused, Marianne glanced down at the green frock. "Is something wrong with it?"

"Nothing, except that it's not something I'd expect the wife of a poor farmer to choose. It's not very . . ." He paused groping for the right word.

"Practical?" Marianne caught her lower lip between her teeth when he nodded. "It wasn't my intention to spend your money frivolously. But Mrs. Knowles seemed to understand what you wanted ordered, and when you didn't say anything . . . I'll pay you back." Her hand fluttered as she spoke, then fell to her lap dejectedly as her voice trailed off.

Ill at ease, Nick shifted his weight a little. "That's not what I meant," he growled. "I don't begrudge you the dress. It's just that it doesn't fit in with what you told me about your life before you came here. Neither does the way you act, or the way you talk. Damn it, you're too much of an Easterner!"

"But I can't help *that*!" The words were out before she could stop them, though they had the desired effect. Nick's expression changed from total bewilderment to wry amusement in a flash, his face relaxing into a disarming grin. Relief swept over her. He hadn't been referring to her *real* secret.

"All I wanted to know," he explained roughly, his

smile growing dim, "is why you made out as if you'd lived a hard life, when anyone can tell you've never done a lick of real labor."

"Did you think you were buying a workhorse, Mr. Fortune? And how can you be so sure what I'm capable of, since you haven't even examined my teeth yet?" Surprised by her own audacity, Marianne thrust her jaw a little higher.

Her spunk caught him off guard, but only for a moment. Nick reached for her hand, pulling it toward him at the same time he turned her palm upward. With the tip of his index finger, he traced a line across the soft inside of her hand.

"I don't need to see your teeth," he said.

His touch set off a reaction that shocked her. Nick's charcoal eyes sought hers, sending a little shiver of anticipation racing up and down her spine. Warm tendrils shot up her arm from where his hand still held hers lightly, gently, and deep in her abdomen something fluttered, as if some wild, unknown creature was just awakening within.

She jerked her hand away. "Then what *is* it that you want?"

Tearing his gaze away, he muttered, "I'm not sure I know anymore."

Her lungs burning as she held her breath, Marianne watched him struggle with the doubts that must have carried the shadow of his past. She wondered if it would be easier if she just came right out and told him she knew about his first wife, but before her words were more than a sigh upon her lips he spoke.

"I was married before," he said quietly. "Her name was Alicia, and she's dead now. I thought someone—a widow like you—would understand better."

She could see the rigid control that kept his taut muscles from betraying any emotion, but that in itself was a betrayal of sorts. *He must have loved her a great deal,* she said to herself, unsure why it should make her heart feel like lead.

"I do understand," she whispered softly.

His gaze returned to hers. "I don't think so, but that's why I wanted us to talk. I need a woman who's strong and sure of herself. I don't have time for flowers and I don't know any pretty courting words. My mother and father never knew each other before their wedding, and things worked out fine between them. Respect, satisfying work, a son; that's all I want from marriage now. I have no use for a woman who needs pampering, and even less for one with notions of romance and true love."

Marianne drew herself up, indignation making her forget that only that morning she had *wanted* him to feel this way about her. "Well, for your information, I've never been pampered in my life." That wasn't a lie, she told herself. She'd never really adjusted to the luxury of Uncle Matt's house. "If I seem too educated for a backwoods barbarian like you, then blame it on the teachers at the orphanage where I grew up. I learned manners in between scrubbing floors, and deportment from being punished any time I spoke out of turn. I've been alone nearly all my life, Nicholas Fortune, and I don't *need* anyone. Especially you!" She pushed herself up onto her knees, struggling with the petticoats that tangled around her legs.

Now it was Nick's turn to stare at her with frank amazement, but he woke himself to action just in time to keep her from getting all the way up. "Hold on there," he said, hiding another smile as he clasped her wrist gently. "I didn't mean to get you all riled. You never mentioned anything about an orphanage in your letters."

Marianne realized at once just how close she'd come to destroying her own cover by losing her temper, and the thought was a sobering one. Willing her heartbeat to slow, she settled back to the ground, her gaze pinned on her tightly clasped hands. "I'm sorry I got so angry," she said, closing her eyes as she sighed heavily. "I guess I didn't mention my childhood because it's not worth remembering."

She waited with bated breath for Nick's response,

and the one that finally came allowed her to release her aching lungs gratefully.

"Come to think of it," Nick said, his voice thoughtful, "you didn't say much about your past except that you had no kin after your husband died. I just assumed . . . I'm sorry, Mary."

His use of that name caused a stab of guilt to pierce her heart, but Marianne was still uncertain how far she could trust him. "It's all right. Let's not talk about the past anymore."

"Good." Nick agreed readily, eager to get on with what he'd wanted to tell her in the first place. "There's another reason I was in such a hurry to get a woman out here, and that's what we have to talk about. My mother is not well."

Marianne glanced up at him sideways, then nodded as genuine concern replaced her anger. "I did notice that she's short of breath quite often. Is it her heart?"

Nick paused, as if admitting it was so was too difficult, but after a few seconds he spoke. "It is. Doc Waterson thinks she'll be okay for a while yet, if she takes it easy. But getting Mother to sit still is like holding on to a salmon with your bare hands. She won't go back to the house in town until I'm 'settled,' as she puts it, and I hoped that would be soon."

"And instead of me taking care of her, it's been the other way around," Marianne said quietly.

"You couldn't help that, but now she's got to talking about this party. She never mentioned it before, so I thought maybe you put the idea into her head."

"I never heard of it until today," Marianne replied. No wonder he'd reacted so angrily when Marcus had brought up the subject. Not because of her, but because of the extra strain it would put on his mother.

Nick hesitated again, clearly uncomfortable as he spoke in a gravelly voice. "I was wrong when I asked you to keep your plans to yourself. I realized that today. It'd be better to come right out and tell her you're leaving soon. Or . . ."

Marianne grimaced at the thought of trying to explain to Claire just *why* she didn't want to marry her son.

"Or we get married right away," Nick continued. "We forget about waiting the whole month."

Marianne felt herself grow hot beneath his scrutiny. She knew he was watching her carefully for her reaction, and despite the irritation she'd felt toward him earlier, she couldn't let herself hurt him the way she knew he'd been hurt before. It still seemed best to let him be the one who made the final decision. "Or I could . . . I could talk to your mother," she stammered. "I could tell her I'd feel uncomfortable with a party, seeing as how so many people died in the train crash and how I'm only recently widowed—"

"Two years ago," Nick reminded.

"Well, that isn't so very long for some people. I think I can convince her that a reception isn't appropriate."

Now the silence around them clung like a web, fragile as glass but as unavoidable as the dark of night.

"You still don't want to stay, do you?" Nick asked thickly, his gaze focused on the blue and gold wildflowers that grew in clumps beneath the trees.

Marianne heard the apprehension in his voice; not pain this time, but something more like resignation. Pausing, she stared at his strong, work-worn hands, remembering how they managed the reins with confident ease. Did he do everything, tackle every problem, with the same equanimity? On Adam Pemberton, that brand of self-assurance had manifested itself in cruel arrogance. Nick wore it like a second skin; so right, so perfectly fitting that one merely accepted authority and fearlessness as an undefinable, inseparable part of him. She might even have trusted him with the truth now, if the sudden recollection of Pemberton hadn't reminded her of how frightened she'd been just a few days ago.

"I can't," she insisted gently, "and I'm not sure I can explain to you all the reasons why."

"Try."

Inhaling shakily, Marianne wondered how it'd come

back to this. She understood a little better why he had such a cynical approach to marriage, and it added up to yet another reason why they were ill-suited to one another. He'd once had a deep and wondrous love, and felt no need for any more; she had never experienced love of any kind, and wasn't sure she would know what to do with it if she ever found it.

But that, she knew instinctively, she could never explain to him, and an explanation was exactly what he wanted now.

Marianne glanced upward at his profile, starkly outlined in the warm afternoon light. "I didn't realize until I was already on the train how wrong it was of me to come. Perhaps not wrong, exactly, but definitely not right. There were problems back East I should have dealt with, and it didn't occur to me until it was too late that running away wasn't the proper choice."

She watched for his reaction. Nick's head nodded once, his jaw remaining firmly set, as if he were digesting her words with great care. When he finally turned his penetrating gaze toward her and spoke, she was dizzy from holding her breath.

"Running usually isn't," he agreed. "What kind of problems?"

"Mostly money," she admitted softly. Here was where it could get tricky, Marianne thought. She had to make her story sound believable, and yet she knew herself to be a poor liar. Nick, she was sure, would see right through her if she strayed too far from the truth. "There was also a man," she whispered.

"Hmmph." Not allowing himself to respond with any more than that single, noncommittal sound, Nick kept as careful check on his emotions as he had on the buggy's reins. A man! Despite the wild thumping of his pulse, he wasn't surprised.

"He . . . he wanted to marry me," Marianne continued. "I refused, but he was very insistent. It just seemed easier to go away than to put up with him any longer."

"The idea of marriage to a stranger was preferable?" Nick's eyebrows flew up as he twisted his neck to peer at her.

Put that way, it *did* sound ludicrous, but then, anything was better than what Adam Pemberton had planned for her. Marianne met his gaze directly. "Yes," she said. "It was."

Though his face was deceptively casual, she could almost see the tension snapping in the air around him. Bleakly, she realized she'd done it again. She'd made him feel that she'd once been prepared to accept his proposal, but that meeting him had changed her mind.

Nick watched as sorrow clouded her azure eyes, but he felt none of the remorse she attributed to him, only an incredible surge of anger toward the man who'd driven her to such dire straits. He must have been a monster. Obviously, it wasn't marriage itself that she'd shied away from, or she wouldn't be here. She was a widow, too, though her sweet youthfulness often made him forget. So there was something more, something to do with this man that made him too awful for her to even consider.

He wondered . . .

"So you see," Marianne continued, "I didn't come here with any fanciful illusions, but I'm still not sure I can adjust to your way of life, either."

Nick rose without answering, pulling her easily by the hands until she stood beside him, fussing with her skirt. He smiled at the sight of her twisting her head over her shoulder as she brushed one hand lightly over her bustle while she daintily shook out the fabric she had pinched in the other. She was the proper little lady in some ways, he thought, though she didn't seem to realize how far sheer determination could take her. Hidden beneath a layer of gentleness was a measure of steel.

"Why don't you give it a try, then?" he suggested, keeping his tone noncommittal. "If you'll lend a hand at keeping Mother from taxing her strength, I'll do my best to show you that we're not all backwoods barbarians out here."

It was like a tiny flame lit up inside her when she

smiled like that, Nick thought. And behind each smile was a little part of herself, something genuine and true. No matter what she thought herself lacking, at least she wasn't one who gave smiles away like cheap favors in return for blind adoration.

Give it a try, he'd said. Something inside Marianne wished it were so simple. Her thoughts raced around in her head as they returned to the buggy and resumed the journey home. He still didn't seem to take her request to return to New York seriously, she mused, so she was faced with the task of convincing Nick that she was completely wrong for him. She was sure of it; why wasn't he?

The road rose slightly, enough to provide a view of the house as they broke through the shelter of trees that had lined their way. Marianne studied the white frame structure, relieved to have something to occupy her mind, relieved that she could flee, soon, from Nick's presence.

The house topped a small knoll, marked by the absence of the tall trees that seemed to dominate everywhere else. Here, the austere beauty of dazzling white against a backdrop of evergreen-clad mountains claimed one's eye, accentuating the startling contrast between wilderness and civilization that was one of the contradictions of this land.

Six Doric columns, two stories high, stretched upward from the wide porch to the sloping roof, their slender grace ornamenting the otherwise plainly decorated building. At the sides, two wings spread from the main structure. Wisps of black smoke drifting from the chimney above one indicated the kitchens; behind the other, she remembered, riotous colors and fragrant scents fought one another for attention in the garden.

Though the house had existed less than ten years, Marianne knew it rivaled anything of its kind, from the stately old homes of New York to which she was accustomed, to the gracefully weathered plantations of the south. It was elegant, yet built to withstand the wind and the rain and the sun. Inside the heavy redwood door—brought, Claire said, from the California forests that dwarfed even these woods—was a haven of safety.

Nick guided the team expertly through an open, wrought-iron gate, stopping in front of the outbuilding that housed the stables and various storage rooms. When he tossed the reins to Jan, the young man in charge of the home stock, Marianne threw him a puzzled glance. "Aren't you going back to town today?"

"Nope. It's too late to get anything done now." Stepping down from the side of the buggy, Nick turned to her. He ignored the dainty hand she held out, reaching for her slender waist with both palms and lifting her easily to the ground.

His fingers nearly circled her, the strength of his hands sending tremors through her flesh, as if every nerve in her body was tuned to his touch. She should have walked away then—*would* have—except that he didn't release her from his gentle hold. "I-I'm sorry," she stammered.

"For what?"

"For taking up so much of your time today. I'm sure you would've rather been working."

"Mary . . ."

Marianne felt herself grow hot when he said the name—or maybe it was the way the muscles in his upper arms bunched beneath her hands like dock ropes. She forced herself to meet his gaze, so close to hers she could see her reflection mirrored in his gray eyes.

"There's nothing to apologize for," he said huskily. "You might have rushed two thousand miles away from home without examining the consequences, but I've spent months thinking about what I want from this marriage. If it means spending a few days away from the mill getting to know you, then that's exactly what I intend to do. And if it means convincing you to stay . . . well, then, I guess I'll do that, too. What I won't do is watch you tear yourself apart feeling guilty because you're not sure. There's no crime in that."

"I know, but it's more than just uncertainty." Marianne's voice was a whispered plea, weakened by the

subtle yearning that was growing stronger in her heart.
"There are problems I have to take care of, to
resolve—"

"That's just another thing I mean to teach you,
Mary Cooper." His mouth had turned up slightly,
forming a half-smile that made her pulse flutter. "Not
that I expected a passel of trouble when I sent for a
wife, but now that you're here, I reckon there's not
much I can't take care of."

He began to move his hands, slowly at first, barely
caressing the smooth fabric that covered her trim waist.
She wasn't wearing a corset—he'd known that from the
moment he'd touched her—and he couldn't resist massaging the warm softness that fit so perfectly into his
grasp. It was the softness of her eyes, though, that
finally proved irresistible, eyes an incredible shade of
blue that could look as calm as the sky or as tempestu-
ous as the sea.

Marianne felt her heart stop, but what she first
mistook as fear that he might kiss her, she soon realized was breathless anticipation. His eyes, heavy-lidded
and still, blazed with a feral intensity that mesmerized
her, even while it made her ache to feel his mouth on
hers.

"Nick, I-I thought you wanted our relationship to
be . . . well . . . platonic."

His eyes narrowed with grim amusement. "I'm quite
sure I never said that," he chuckled deeply. "Don't
you want to know if we're truly compatible?"

"Not like this!"

"I can't . . ." he said quietly as his head dipped low,
". . . think of a better way."

The satiny heat of his lips surprised her, stilling her
objections. She hadn't known that a kiss could be so
warm, so undemanding . . . so deliciously simple. There
was nothing in it to frighten her, nothing to force her
will. There was only the gentle invitation of his lingering mouth, brushing hers as lightly as an ocean mist
resting upon the shore. Her breath sighed out in wordless surrender.

Nick deepened the kiss, slanting his mouth across

hers in a way that opened her parted lips further. She made a startled sound when he touched the tip of his tongue to hers; her eyes widened quickly, then her lashes swooped heavily toward her petal-soft cheeks. He knew in that instant that, though she may have been a widow, she wasn't an experienced lover. The realization sent pleasure bursting through his veins. Some men never bothered to learn that where loving was concerned, giving was receiving. In that, at least, he would be first.

Melting against the solid comfort of him, Marianne let herself accept his tender exploration. She was filled with wonder at the smoothness, the newness, the sheer beauty of his touch. A distant part of her mind shouted a warning, too late, that here was not the way, that this would only complicate matters, but an instinct stronger than reason forced her mind to cease making futile threats. Something deep inside her, some inborn, womanly knowledge that had remained hidden until now, surfaced all at once, claiming every fiber of her as its own.

After a long, aching moment, Nick lifted his mouth away. "I've wanted to do that for days," he whispered. "Beautiful Mary . . ."

With dizzying speed, reality struck her a shocking blow. Marianne jerked away from him, awkwardly bumping into the buggy's lower step with the back of her legs. Nick's powerful hold on her waist was the only thing that kept her from falling.

He watched her eyes change from limpid pools of light and darkness to glittering spheres, ringed with fright. Beneath his hands, a tremor worked its way through her slender body like a young tree whose branches have been touched by the first cold autumn wind. And then, as if bracing for winter's fury, she grew stiff and unyielding within his gentle grip.

Nick let his hands drop slowly to his sides.

Marianne forced her eyes downward. She'd seen it all in his hungry gaze: the passion tempered with patience, the uncertainty hovering behind boldness. It made her weak with wanting, even while her sorrow and confusion grew to nearly unbearable proportions. "It can't be this way, Nick," she cried softly.

A thousand emotions played across his face in the instant before he smiled. His eyes seemed to take on a new dimension, deepening so that she was nearly lost in their cloudy warmth. His mouth, lips still full and aching with the taste of her, curved ruefully. "It already is, my dear. It already is."

Chapter 6

Adam Pemberton stared across the desk at the man seated opposite him, his large hands steepled in a thoughtful pose. *Worthless piece of dog shit!* was what went through his mind, even while he smiled and leaned forward ingratiatingly.

"You see my position, Senator Collins, do you not?" he asked, taking care to add a note of respect to his voice. "Until this matter is resolved, my hands are completely tied. Naturally, I will continue to support your campaign, but, as I have told you, the search for poor Matthew's murderer demands a great deal of my time, not to mention the enormous expense involved."

"I understand your concerns, Pemberton," Senator George Collins said, pursing his lips. "You have not, however, answered my question. Two of the bonds you say she stole have been cashed, one yesterday in Albany, one four days ago in Charleston. Both transactions are untraceable so far as identifying the payee, but we've been unable to match the numbers on the bonds to the list you gave the police. How do you explain this discrepancy?"

Pemberton cringed inwardly, yet forced himself to remain completely calm, even managing to summon an expression of true conciliation. "I'm afraid Matthew's records are in an abysmal state," he explained. "I have bookkeepers reviewing them now, and I have no doubt that their search will result in an additional list of numbers. When it is found, I will see that your people get them immediately."

The senator looked doubtful, but eventually he nodded. "I had no wish to be appointed to this investigation committee, Pemberton. But since I am, I fully intend to do the job. For your sake, I hope your assumption is correct."

George Collins waved aside the offer to be escorted to the door. He had never cared for Adam Pemberton, and cared for him even less since Blakemore's death. He was weary from the strain of playing politician for the past hour, when what he had really wanted to do was give the bastard a bash right between his sanctimonious eyes. Poor Matthew, indeed! He slammed the door behind him.

The good senator would have been pleased to know that his visit was more unsettling to Adam Pemberton than his host had let on. Alone in his office, Pemberton massaged his throbbing temples and cursed aloud.

"Damn him," he muttered, his mind already searching for a way to get around this considerable obstacle. Reaching for an old-fashioned rope pull behind his head, Pemberton yanked hard, then began shuffling through the papers on his desk. He didn't bother to raise his head when the door opened and closed quietly. "What do we have on Collins?" he asked.

Shuffling forward, Barney Clawson squeezed his scrawny hands together nervously. "I don't know, boss. What did you have in mind?"

Pemberton looked up impatiently. "Anything. The usual. Women? Kickbacks? Family skeletons?"

"Nothing like that, boss. Collins is as pure as a newborn babe. You know that."

Damn! Stabbing at his desk with a letter opener, Adam furrowed his brow. Why, just when he'd begun to make some real strides in his life, had everything fallen apart now? People just didn't seem to appreciate the difficulties he'd overcome to get where he was today. He once thought Matthew Blakemore had, but the damn fool showed his true colors in the end. And Marianne!

Pemberton felt his blood grow hot as fury pounded through him. That ungrateful little bitch! He had *paid* for her, and still she'd run away. Did she think it had been easy for him to keep her and Matthew satisfied? Didn't she know there was more to wealth than simply going out and earning it?

Just like Mother. The thought sprang, unbidden, into his brain, and Adam shuddered, inwardly denying the comparison. That would mean that he had failed the way his father had, and he would never admit to that.

He had been thirteen years old when his mother left them, old enough to feel the sting of her rejection, but too young to understand all the reasons why. His father, a complacent man who had always been content with his job on the docks, could not comprehend his wife's departure, even though she left him a long letter, detailing all his shortcomings. Love, Allen Pemberton reasoned, should have been enough.

As the years slipped by, and hope for her return became a distant dream, Adam watched his father wither away as if his wife had cut a vein and slowly drained him of life. Adam hated her then, as only the young can hate, with every fiber and sinew of his strapping young body. And when his father died, poor and broken, he hated him, too. Hated him because he wasn't the man that could make her stay, and despised him for giving up once she was gone.

That hatred became the driving force in his life, for he vowed never to let complacency rule when ambition would serve. Enough would never suffice, when more was better. And when he found the woman he wanted, he'd sworn, he would have the power to keep her within his reach, and the wealth to ensure that she never wanted to leave it.

He had been very near to reaching that point when Matthew Blakemore introduced him to his young niece. Still little more than a child, Marianne had possessed, nevertheless, all the attributes Adam found necessary to suit his needs. She had known only poverty, and so would appreciate the niceties of finer living. She was inexperienced and unworldly, and therefore could be molded as he saw fit, willing to accept his domination.

Best of all, she was utterly beautiful, yet completely unaware of her effect on men. Before she had even turned sixteen, Adam had decided he wanted her, and he set out to accomplish his goal with his usual determination and efficiency.

First, he allowed Matthew, who, up until that time, had been a minority partner in only a few of his business endeavors, to assume a larger portion of responsibility, both financially and otherwise. Then, through careful planning, he arranged to have some of those businesses fail after skimming the profits into his private accounts. When Matthew asked for more funds, he gave them cheerfully. When Matthew complained that his gambling debts were mounting, Adam commiserated, offering countless loans.

Within a year he owned Matthew Blakemore. That was when Adam made his move.

To his great surprise, Matthew hadn't been as reluctant to sign the betrothal agreement as Pemberton had anticipated. "After all," Blakemore had rationalized, relief apparent in his rheumy eyes as he signed the document, "it's not as if she'll ever get a better offer. It's damned decent of you to wait until she's older, too."

That had been his least favorite stipulation, but Adam Pemberton realized that a man with his political aspirations would do well to tread carefully. No use exposing himself to accusations of "robbing the cradle." Besides, most of the time he found a perverse enjoyment in knowing that he now possessed what he wanted. Physical ownership was far less important to him.

Until recently.

Adam clenched his teeth as his thoughts traversed the years, settling on the more recent past.

Unbelievably, Marianne had grown more and more lovely, and Adam's heretofore benevolent manner toward her had changed, as well. It was time, he reasoned, to make her aware of him as a man, in order to lessen her surprise when he revealed himself as her future husband. Subtly, at first, and then with increasing authority, he began to let her know that he desired her. So absolute was his resolve, he didn't even worry when she resisted his initial advances. He looked upon it as a challenge; a game really, for she was already his, willing or not.

What he hadn't expected was that when his patience with the game finally wore thin, Matthew Blakemore would surprise him with a rare display of defiance. Adam quelled it, of course, by reminding his partner that there were certain branches of the law that would show keen interest in knowing *why* he'd spent several years abroad.

And that tactic had worked, for a time. It wasn't until Blakemore threatened to take him down with him that Adam Pemberton found it necessary to commit murder.

As he'd done on many previous occasions, Adam recalled that particular crime without the slightest twinge of conscience. Nothing done in the course of pursuing his goals was wrong, only expedient. He'd felt no rage toward Matthew Blakemore, merely sadness that his friend was too foolish to see what he'd brought upon himself.

The rage had come only when he realized that, despite all he had done for her, Marianne had run away from him anyway.

Adam lifted his head, suddenly remembering that Barney Clawson still waited for instructions. They'd been talking about Senator Collins and his damned committee.

"What do you think, Barney?" Adam watched the man's startled expression change immediately to one of wariness.

"You want to know what I think?"

"That's what I said, isn't it?"

Barney Clawson studied on it a second. What he really thought was that his boss was drowning in a shithole of his own making, but that opinion was one better kept to himself. Nobody believed Marianne Blakemore had killed her own uncle, just like nobody believed that Pemberton was unaware of the discrepancies in Blakemore's books. The only reason Pemberton hadn't been arrested yet was because he had the money and the connections to buy his way out of trouble. But not everyone could be bought, and Barney had a feeling that Senator Collins was one of those people. He just wasn't sure how to say it without raining shit on his own head.

"If I were you . . ." Barney began, glad for the first time in over ten years of employment that he wasn't, ". . . I'd stop cashing in those bonds. There's too much heat on them right now. Besides, it won't take long for the police to wonder how Marianne Blakemore can be passing hot paper when she's supposed to be dead, way out West somewhere."

Adam frowned. He was afraid to touch any of his private accounts, aware that he was being watched too closely. He didn't want the authorities swooping down on his money, yet he needed the funds the bonds could bring in. Clawson was absolutely correct, however. "All right," he conceded. "What else?"

Barney shuffled his feet. He could feel the sweat beading on his forehead, but he didn't dare wipe his face. "The ledgers," he said, swallowing tightly. "Nothing's really safe until you get them back, or at least make sure they're actually gone. If Collins ever got hold of them—"

His speculation was cut short by the violent glare Pemberton shot in his direction. "You don't have to tell me what I already know. I don't *pay* you to repeat stale phrases and quote old news. Get out of here, and don't come back until you think of something original to say."

Barney Clawson scurried to the door. He'd have gladly *never* come back, but he knew his life wouldn't be worth a nickel if he left Pemberton's employ. Instead, he would pray that his boss's ire cooled before the next time he was summoned.

Adam watched the door close, clenching his jaw against the wave of blackness that threatened again. It was all her fault, his mind repeated over and over again. All her fault.

He yanked the letter opener from the desk, clutching it so tight in his fist that the sharp edges bit into his palm. With one swift movement, he flung his arm backward, then threw the opener with all his might at the solid oak door. It stuck there, quivering, much the way a person would while in the final throes of an agonizing death.

Adam Pemberton smiled.

Chapter 7

That kiss seemed to hover in the air between them like a magnetic force, unwanted, but as unbreakable as light or space. All through dinner, Marianne was aware of its power drawing her gaze to Nick as he attacked his food with a vigor that barely hid his tension. He had changed before dinner into a shirt of fine white lawn, yet he wore it open at the throat in keeping with the casual manner he obviously preferred. She could hardly keep her eyes off him, and she'd barely touched her own food. The only thing to be thankful for, Marianne thought disconcertedly, was that Claire was too preoccupied to notice. They were now more than halfway through the main course, and Elizabeth had not yet appeared.

"Where did she say she was going?" Nick asked between mouthfuls, avoiding Marianne's cautious glance.

Claire laid her fork down carefully. "She told me she would be riding with Colleen, but I already sent Sue Kim to check at the Delaneys'. Colleen has been in bed with a cold for three days. Elizabeth was never there."

A frown creased Nick's forehead and Marianne could sense the worry that rode heavy in the air. Claire, who usually presided over meals with cheerful precision, had been oddly silent. Caught up in her own tumultuous thoughts, Marianne hadn't detected the older woman's concern until now. "Perhaps she met up with another of her friends," she offered.

Nick rose abruptly, scraping his chair back and throwing his napkin to the table. There was something close to accusation in his stormy eyes as he glared at her. "You're closer than you know!" he grunted.

She looked on in stunned surprise as Claire's hand shot out, clutching her son's arm with gentle restraint. The look that passed between them was unfathomable, but Marianne sensed there was much more to Elizabeth's strange absence than she knew.

"It's not," Claire said quietly, "the time for jumping to conclusions. Let me handle it."

The muscles in Nick's arm were taut beneath Claire's tiny hand, but after a long moment he relaxed enough to nod and take his seat again. Marianne shifted her puzzled gaze from one to the other.

Something was definitely wrong! She'd learned in the past two days that Elizabeth was allowed a great deal more freedom than most proper young ladies in the East could hope to be afforded. Claire had told her carefree tales of picnics and socials, fairs and frolics, all designed to provide entertainment for the young people of Tacoma. And Elizabeth had attended many of those; that much Marianne knew for sure.

Then why, she pondered, was it such a crime to be late for dinner? Unless Nick's sister made a habit of disappearing, she didn't see why they were so disturbed now.

Only the tinkling sound of cutlery broke the ominous silence. She should have been relieved that no one expected her to make polite conversation, but Marianne felt as though something had to be done to relieve the tension. "Mrs. Knowles mentioned the Fourth of July celebration coming up," she addressed Claire. "Is there anything I can do to help?"

Nick turned to her then, his lips curved in a wry smile. He recognized what she was trying to do, and he couldn't help feeling grateful. "If the saw blade comes in on time, we'll celebrate the new mill opening on the same day. We'll all be busy enough then."

Claire sighed, her attention aroused once more. "I

suppose you were right about the party, Mary. It *will* be a hectic few weeks. Sure, and I just wanted to give ye a nice welcome."

"Oh, but you have!" Marianne reached over to squeeze Claire's hand.

The woman shrugged, her eye regaining its impish twinkle. "At least I'll have Elizabeth's wedding to plan someday."

"Hmmph. Let's hope not for a long while yet," Nick said, looking at Marianne quizzically. "In the meantime, let's get past this one."

Before Marianne could respond to this unusual statement, a loud slam reverberated through the house and the sound of hurried footsteps echoed across the parquet floor of the front hall. Flushed and dishevelled, Elizabeth burst through the dining room doorway with a dramatic entrance that would have made an actress sigh with envy.

Another look passed from Claire to her son, clearly warning him to keep silent. With a grunt, Nick took another bite of food, but his angry stare never left his sister's overheated cheeks. Marianne watched with growing curiosity, not a little thankful that all attention was diverted away from herself.

"Where have you been?" Claire's softly spoken question bore just the slightest hint of apprehension, but Elizabeth seemed not to notice at all. She was either completely insensitive to the anxiety she'd caused, Marianne thought, or the girl was an expert at dissembling.

Lifting her chin proudly, she met Nick's glare eye for eye. "I was out riding with Billy Turner."

Portentous silence filled the room, then was broken by the sound of Nick's heavy fist as it hit the table with a clattering thump. "I told you to stay away from him!" he growled.

Again Elizabeth's chin lifted a notch, but Marianne thought she could see a glimmer of fear beneath her bold stare. Despite the fact that the girl hadn't spoken more than a few words to her in two days, she couldn't help admiring her show of courage. *She'd* be trembling in her skin if Nick ever shouted at her like that.

"You did," Elizabeth confirmed brazenly. "But I don't happen to agree with your opinion. Billy *likes* me! I'll see him if I want."

"We'll talk about this later."

"No! You always say that, but we never do! You just hand down orders like you're the king here. Well, you're not!"

"That's enough," he warned.

Elizabeth glanced from Nick's angry expression to Marianne, and her voice took on an unmistakably petulant note. "*You* get to choose whomever you want, no matter what the rest of us think. I'm old enough to make my own choices, too!"

Marianne watched Elizabeth carefully. Though the challenge she'd thrown her brother was a childish one, her slender young body shuddered with emotions that appeared all too genuine. Nick, however, seemed to dismiss them as just so much theatrics.

"All the pouting in the world won't change my mind, Elizabeth. If you want to be treated like an adult, then act like one. Because if you don't, I'll handle Billy myself."

As if this last condemnation finally pierced through her bravado, Elizabeth's eyes filled with tears. It probably wasn't that he'd called her a child, Marianne thought compassionately, it was the disparaging tone Nick had used. At least now she was clear on what the conflict was. Elizabeth had a young beau who did not meet with her brother's approval. That still didn't explain the girl's reticence toward her, but she could sympathize with her, nevertheless.

"You just don't understand!" Elizabeth cried, then spun around and fled from the room with a muffled sob.

Smiling apologetically, Claire rose to follow her daughter, leaving Nick standing at the table, glowering after them.

As if their absence removed a barrier of restraint

from the room, Marianne felt her gaze drawn irresistibly toward him, and it was with a start that she met his steel gray glare. With his fists clenched against his narrow hips, he looked like a statue, immobile but for the livid fire in his eyes.

"Go ahead and say it!" he demanded abruptly, an odd tone of despair edging his voice. "I can tell by the look on your face you think I was too hard on her."

Marianne ached for him. She could only imagine the mixture of anger and sorrow that came from hurting someone you love, and yet she couldn't deny that he was right about her thoughts. "You *were* hard on her," she agreed softly. "But only because you care. I'm sure she realizes that."

Nick forced his tensed muscles to relax slightly, then shook his head with a rueful smile. "Right now she can't see beyond a pair of ogling blue eyes."

"Maybe it's not that serious," Marianne offered hesitantly. "Perhaps the best thing to do is let it die out naturally."

As soon as she spoke she could tell her suggestion would get nowhere with him. His jaw stiffened stubbornly as he placed both hands on the table, leaning over to peer at her. "Naturally? Letting things proceed naturally will only lead to trouble! Elizabeth is hardly out of pinafores. I won't have her mooning over the first handsome face to come along."

Something about his pronouncement struck a chord in Marianne's memory. She vaguely remembered Uncle Matthew making a similar claim shortly after she had gone to live with him. Of course, she now knew the reason behind his protective attitude. It was because he dared not risk having her fall in love with anyone other than Adam Pemberton. They had tried to manipulate her, and the thought rankled her beyond belief.

"But what is it you're shielding Elizabeth from?" she asked bluntly. "Do you think you're doing her a favor keeping her from making her own decisions?"

"She's too young to decide anything!" Nick growled.

Beneath his weight the table shuddered, and Marianne reached for the still-full wine decanter that swayed and nearly spilled. "I know you think so," she insisted, surprised at her own obstinacy. In a way, it felt good to rebel against him over something that had nothing to do with herself. Squaring her shoulders, she met his harsh gaze steadily. "Would you be so concerned if Elizabeth were a boy?"

Nick stood up. "You're missing the point completely."

"A young girl must learn to think for herself, too," Marianne insisted. "What if, God forbid, she had to survive on her own? Hiding her from life isn't helping her one bit."

"Is that what happened to you?" Nick heard the plaintive tone that laced Marianne's words, and he immediately regretted the sarcasm with which he had phrased the question. He watched as her face grew pale, her blue eyes widening slightly as she bit her lower lip.

Fighting down the urge to fling an angry retort, Marianne paused long enough to form an answer that wouldn't reveal too much. "To a certain extent, it is," she said quietly. "I wish now that things had been different."

"There's no comparison," Nick responded. "You're older than Elizabeth—"

"Not by much . . ."

"And stronger."

This, Marianne seriously doubted, but she let the statement pass without comment. She could see that Nick's anger was not lessening, despite her attempt to assuage his temper. She made one last effort, smiling consolingly. "Forbidding her to see him will only make her want him more. I remember that much about young girls."

"You don't, however, know a damned thing about men!" Nick straightened abruptly, thrusting his fists against his hips once more. "You think men here in the territory are like the dandified Easterners you're used to? They're not. Boys grow up into hard men because they have to, and most don't have the luxury of womenfolk to soften their meanness and curb their greed. Billy Turner is a good example."

"But if Elizabeth loves him . . . ?" The question died in her throat as soon as she saw the fierce blaze that turned his eyes to hot steel. He shoved away from the table, his harsh gaze never leaving her.

"Stay out of things you know nothing about," he rasped. "Love doesn't have anything to do with it!"

A stone's throw from the waterfront, yet easily accessible by land, Dock Street was proof that anyone with a liquor license and an out-of-tune piano could thrive in a land of free enterprise. Bawdy houses threw their doors open wide so that the sounds of raucous laughter and jangling music could be heard blocks away, enticing eager young men to a night of pleasure, while dark, smoking dens catered to the souls whose only wish was for strong liquor—and a great deal of it.

The Golden Lady Saloon, like many similar establishments, stood in a row of buildings all bent on providing the working men of Tacoma with the means to dispose quickly of their hard-earned pay.

But unlike her neighbors, the Golden Lady bore a regal air, bringing a touch of elegance to an otherwise tawdry environ. A small part of this was due to her appearance. The three-storied Victorian mansion stood apart from the clapboard saloons that surrounded her. Soft yellow light played through lace curtains at every window, offering a welcome that seemed almost homey. Most of the Golden Lady's success, however, was because she reflected the personality of her owner: cheerful, but still alluring: down-to-earth, yet hinting at paradise.

The real golden lady, as every male citizen of Tacoma knew, was Katey Muldoon.

Katey's had not always been a respectable career. She'd never intended to become a prostitute—what woman did?—but once she'd found herself in a predicament that made such a profession necessary, she'd made up her mind to be the best. And after twenty successful years, she was able to retire to an easier life.

The Golden Lady was Katey's gift to herself. It represented not only financial security, but a certain status in a world ruled by men. Since liquor was the only commodity sold beneath her roof, Katey found the business end delightfully simple compared to her past endeavors. She was able to pass many hours in the pleasant company of her guests, and before long, hers was the most popular saloon on Dock Street.

Katey vocally credited her accomplishment to a natural head for business, but secretly she knew that she possessed a talent far greater. That this talent had been nurtured in red-velvet parlors and darkened rooms did not lessen its value. Katey still liked men, but she had learned to assess more than the size of their wallets. She admired their strengths, sympathized with their weaknesses, cajoled the boastful ones, and respected those who were honest. And never, since one single, catastrophic mistake so many years ago, had Katey Muldoon misjudged a man.

Which was why, when she descended the wide staircase and saw Nicholas Fortune seated alone at a table below, she knew unquestionably that her favorite customer was in love, just as she knew he did not yet realize it himself.

With a pleased smile, Katey sauntered toward Nick, cheerfully acknowledging the greetings of her other guests, but always keeping an eye trained on him. He was dressed all in black from the toes of his shiny boots to his silk shirt, which was opened at the neck in deference to the hot night. The effect was one of total masculinity, and Katey couldn't help wondering why he was here at all. When she was halfway across the room he looked up, his smoky eyes narrowing as he grinned at her. She had a hard time keeping herself from grinning back.

"You . . ." she pointed gaily when she reached his side, ". . . look like the cat that swallowed the canary."

As she placed a friendly hand on his shoulder, Nick chuckled. "It's no wonder. This whiskey is so raw it makes my throat feel like I swallowed a damned ostrich. Where d'ye get this stuff, Katey?"

Sliding into the seat opposite him, Katey picked the glass tumbler from his strong fingers and took a delicate sip. "I'll have you know, Nick Fortune, that this is the best scotch whiskey to be had. You timberjacks are just so used to home-brewed rotgut, you wouldn't recognize a decent drink if it grabbed you on the behind. But that," she said pointedly, "doesn't explain the gleam in those gorgeous eyes of yours."

His grin widening, Nick signalled to the barkeep for another glass and leaned forward conspiratorially. "I never could keep a secret from you, Katey."

"Well then, are you planning to make me stew in my juices all night? What's she like?"

It took only a second for him to decide there was no use pretending with the buxom, redheaded woman. She was as honest as a judge, and as wise as Solomon. And he knew, in the way that one friend knows of another, that she would understand what he was feeling no matter how awkward and insufficient the words. "She'll do, Katey. I think she'll do."

"That's it? Isn't she pretty?"

Nick grinned wider. "I imagine she's about the prettiest woman around." He had calmed down considerably on the ride into town, and somehow the confrontation with Elizabeth had receded to the back of his mind as he envisioned, over and over, the fire in Mary's eyes as she stood her ground with him, both during the ride home and at the dinner table. For the first time in days, he had seen a glimpse of the same woman he'd pulled from the train. It was no wonder he couldn't hide his feelings from Katey. He felt hope sending up flames from deep in his soul.

Expelling a long breath, Katey finally let a broad grin surface. "Well, that just about sums it up, doesn't it? No need tellin' me her name, or the color of her hair. I'll just watch out for the prettiest woman in Tacoma and I expect I'll know who she is right off!"

"I wouldn't be surprised," Nick drawled. "Though it'd be a sight easier if you'd just come calling sometime."

"You know I can't do that." Katey dismissed his words with the wave of a jeweled hand, but her black Irish eyes sparkled moistly. "But thanks just the same. When's the wedding?"

"Don't know for sure," Nick admitted. "I want to give Mary some time, you know, to get used to the idea."

"You've been writing to her for two months now. Seems to me that's time enough."

As usual, Katey was peering at him knowingly. Shrugging, Nick continued. "She's more shy than I thought. She was in that wreck—"

"Marcus told me."

"Figures he would. Anyway, she's just now getting over that, so I didn't see any point in rushing her."

"But that's not the only reason, is it?" The soft tinkling of piano music drifted over to them, filling the momentary silence. Standing up, Katey moved around behind him, again placing her hand on his broad shoulder. "New fella just came in, darlin', so I gotta go. I'll talk to you later."

Nick watched her as she swayed toward the door in a gold satin gown that would have done a queen proud, and he lifted his glass in salute. "You're a smart woman, Katey Muldoon. A mighty smart woman."

Six miles away, Marianne stood in the room that was not hers, wearing a dress she did not own, staring out the window at a land that was as strange to her as the moon, and wondered how she could ever have been so foolish.

A weary sigh escaped the lips that still burned with his kiss, and she remembered the way Nick had silently watched her all through dinner, as if that same kiss had a compelling energy that drew their gazes together, blue eyes to gray. But that was before the argument had begun.

Why on earth did I let him kiss me? she cried silently. A tendril of heat wound itself around her insides, beginning low in her abdomen and ending somewhere in the vicinity of her heart. Though she struggled to quell it, to smite the flame within until nothing remained but a cold memory, she couldn't forget the feel of his mouth teasing at her lips, his hard, lean body close to hers, the touch of his tongue . . . *Oh, God!*

Swallowing convulsively, Marianne leaned closer to the window, pressing her burning cheeks against the cool pane. The smooth glass reminded her of another time when she'd gazed into the night, searching for a clue to her future. From the train she hadn't been able to see further than the next day. Now the promise of many days stretched before her, and she desperately wished for blessed ignorance again.

"This never should have happened," she whispered. "What can I do now?"

"Did you say something?"

Whipping her head around, Marianne gulped once to hide her surprise from Elizabeth. Nick's sister stood in the doorway, blissfully unashamed at having entered without knocking. The girl was dressed in a dark skirt and bodice over a starched white blouse. The effect was one of childish innocence, though Marianne wondered.

"Can I come in?" Elizabeth asked hesitantly.

Suppressing a smile because she was clearly *in* already, Marianne nodded.

"I came to apologize," the girl explained, running one hand along the foot of the shining brass bedstead. "I've been terribly rude to you, and I wanted to tell you that I'm sorry."

Now it was Marianne's turn to be curious. Elizabeth had avoided her for days, casting long questioning glances that seemed to be tinged with resentment.

Was the girl simply more shy than she appeared?
Marianne gestured toward the bench at the foot of the
bed. To her surprise, Elizabeth quickly seated herself,
her green eyes turning bright with anticipation.

"I know I haven't been very nice to you at all,"
the girl babbled nervously, "and I want to make it
up."

"I *did* wonder if you were angry with me," Marianne agreed. "I don't understand why, so perhaps it *is*
time we had a talk."

Elizabeth nodded eagerly, her black hair spilling
over her shoulders as she did. "Believe it or not, it's
Nick I was mad at, not you. You saw at dinner tonight
how dominating he is."

Marianne *had* seen it, and the memory still stabbed
at her like a hot brand against her side. He was right
when he said she should stay out of things she knew
nothing about, but he had no idea how complex her
life already was.

Elizabeth continued, taking her silence as affirma-
tion, "I suppose you'll get used to it, but then, that's
why I came in. I thought maybe we could help each
other—you know—like sisters?"

"What do you mean?"

"I mean, there are things I can tell you about Nick
that might make him like you better. I heard you
arguing before you went to town today, and then
again after dinner. I know you were trying to defend
me, and it made me feel sorry that you don't know
enough about what he wants."

Wondering what a child such as Elizabeth could
possibly know about a man's likes and dislikes, Marianne was nevertheless intrigued by the idea. "But how
do you want me to help you?" she asked suspiciously.

"You can give me advice. You know, like a con . . .
a con—"

"A confidante?" Marianne supplied.

"Yes, that's it!"

The expression on Elizabeth's face was so earnest,
Marianne felt herself softening toward the girl. De-

spite her doubts, she didn't wish to break the tenuous friendship offered now. "That would be very nice," she confessed. "I'd like to have someone to talk to."

"Good!" Elizabeth cried exultantly, jumping up from the bench. "Let's go for a ride first thing in the morning. I have so much to tell you."

Before Marianne could protest, the girl was halfway out the door, but she turned and poked her head inside one last time. "This will be so much fun!"

Marianne smiled as the door slammed shut. For a brief moment she wondered if she hadn't seen just a little bit of friendship in Elizabeth's eyes.

Chapter 8

Nick glanced once more at the pair of red queens in his hand and released a slow breath. Usually a bold gambler, he warned himself against betting recklessly tonight, since luck seemed to have deserted him.

"I'll see your five," he said, "and raise you ten."

"I'm out," Lou Spencer growled, slapping his cards face down on the table.

Horace Squiggs deliberated just a little longer, but eventually he folded his hand as well. "Me too."

Which left only the fourth man, who smiled pleasantly from across the table. "Give me one," he said, sliding a single card to the dealer. His eyes never left Nick's as he placed the new card in his hand, seemingly without a glance.

With a silent nod, Nick discarded a four of spades and a two of clubs, trying not to smile at Spencer, whose baleful expression clearly conveyed his disgust at the way this game was proceeding. Several neat stacks of coins rose before the stranger, while the three local men were rapidly nearing the bottoms of their respective coffers.

"What'll it be, son?" Horace asked the new man.

Long, aristocratic fingers toyed with a mound of silver, then moved surely toward his smaller pile of gold. "There's your ten, and fifty more."

A collective murmur rose around the table, since the intensity of the game had begun to draw an audience. Nick ignored the curious glances of his friends, concentrating instead on the two cards just dealt to him. Another queen and a nine to match the one already in his hand. A full house.

The silence had grown so thick, Nick could barely detect the sound of clinking glassware from behind the bar. Silas, he knew, would take advantage of the sudden lull at the rail to ready another round for the inevitable surge of thirsty celebrants at play's end. Out of the corner of his eye, he could see Katey watching. A hot game of poker was good for business, especially when one of the regulars came up a winner. For that, Nick was glad he'd come here tonight. Not that Katey needed the help, but if she benefited from him beating the likable stranger at his own game, then more the better.

"Call," he said, matching the wager with five ten-dollar gold pieces of his own.

"Jacks and fives," was the response. The murmur rose to a dull roar as necks craned to view the displayed cards. Two pair was a tough hand to beat.

When the sound had died down once again to breath-holding anticipation, Nick finally let himself smile, laying out his hand for all to see.

"Full house!" Lou Spencer cried gleefully, slapping his hand against his thigh. "By gawd, it's a full house!"

The saloon's patrons broke into a clamor, everyone shouting congratulations to Nick at one time. Horace Squiggs chuckled at the ruckus, while Lou Spencer continued to expound his joy by alternately slapping the table and Nick's back. Amid the noise, the loser managed to make himself heard.

"Hell of a game," he exclaimed amiably, reaching his arm over the heap of glittering coins. "Where'd you learn to play?"

Nick took the man's proffered hand, surprised at the strength of his grip. "I grew up hanging on the shirttails of one of the best timberjacks in the north. Besides knowing how to handle a crew of rowdies, sixteen oxen, and a snot-nosed kid, he was as sharp a cardplayer as you'd ever want to meet. How about you? You got a mighty easy style."

The stranger answered with a slow grin. "Got my

start in a little place in Louisiana not too different from this." He waved a hand to indicate the Golden Lady's elegant decor. "Worked on up to riverboats and gaming halls. Even spent a little time in London. But I've rarely enjoyed matching wits as much as I have this evening. I'm indebted to you, sir."

A professional gambler thanking him for a lesson? Had it truly been luck that helped him win this last hand? Nick couldn't help the twinge of suspicion that worked its way into his head. The man was a smooth operator, all right, but it was hard not to like a fellow who lost so gracefully. "Buy you a drink?" he offered.

"I'm much obliged for your hospitality, but I'm afraid I must decline. I've an early appointment, and not much of a head for strong spirits. Perhaps you'll favor me with another friendly game soon? I'll be in Tacoma several weeks more."

"It'd be a pleasure," Nick agreed. Excusing himself, he rose and headed toward Katey, who eyed him happily from the other side of the bar.

"This must be your lucky day!" she exclaimed, as he reached for the glass in her hand. "And with a handful of ladies, too."

Grinning, he lifted the glass to her before draining it with several quick swallows. "Lucky at cards, lucky at love," he quipped.

Katey's gaze softened as she patted his cheek fondly. "No one deserves it more than you," she murmured as she moved away to serve her other guests. "It's high time."

Was it? Nick pondered as he stood at the bar, one foot lifted to the brass rail that skirted the counter six inches off the floor. He'd never been one to dwell much on the complexities of fate. Life dealt you a hand, you played it out, took another one, played it, too, and so on, until the game was over. He remembered the days when it was a struggle to make ends meet too well to fall into the complacent trap of thinking good things were *owed* to him. A man who started thinking that way was bound to be disappointed.

And he knew what it was to be disappointed.

Despite his promise to forget the past, Nick found himself recalling the frustration of those days. He'd been god-awful young—only twenty-two—and the hankering for a woman to call his own had been singeing hot through his blood. Maybe it was just that Alicia was there at the right time, or maybe there was something about her haughty air that had challenged his vanity.

Nick had first seen her at the party her father had thrown upon the launching of his West Coast line. A prominent New England shipbuilder, Lawrence McFarland had expansion on his mind, and no compunction over using his daughter as a tool to further his own aims. Due in part to a jest, he believed Nicholas Fortune to be far wealthier than he actually was. Marcus and some of Nick's other friends had set Nick up when they learned of his fascination with the beautiful Alicia. None of them anticipated the disastrous outcome of their prank.

For a while, Nick admitted silently as he tipped his glass for another drink, things had been fine. Alicia had been as attracted to him as he had been to her—or at least she had given a good imitation. When her father had initially resisted the match, her tears of frustration had seemed genuine, as had her satisfaction when McFarland relented after reading the false financial report concocted by Nick's imaginative companions.

It was on the day he had taken Alicia to his cabin that the first hint of her discontent had appeared.

"You don't expect me to live here!" she had exclaimed petulantly. If he tried hard, Nick could remember the pout that turned her delicate features into a hard mask.

"Only until I build us a house," he had promised. And then, with the extravagance of youth, he had described the mansion that would one day be hers. That seemed to satisfy Alicia, for she had let him make love to her then, responding with a passion that had left him aching for the day they would marry.

He couldn't have known how rare her ardor was, or

that she would become an expert at the game of withholding her favors until she got what she wanted.

And when she learned, as soon as they were married, that what she had gotten wasn't *nearly* what she—or her father—had planned, Nick had been on the receiving end of a tirade the likes of which Tacoma would never see again!

The most surprising part of the entire ordeal was that Lawrence McFarland had then taken Nick's side in the argument, even to the point of refusing to give his daughter the money necessary to build their dream house immediately. He had come to respect young Fortune in the short weeks of their engagement, and admitted that he'd known for some time his true status in the town. It was, he'd declared, the kind of foundation from which he had begun his own empire. McFarland knew it would take a strong hand to curb Alicia's willfulness, and he hoped that Nick would be the man to do it. With little more than his good wishes, he left the young couple and returned to Massachusetts.

Unfortunately, Alicia had no intention of letting *anyone* curb her desires—and they proved to be many.

Gowns, jewels, parties, delicacies . . . her appetite for what she called the finer things in life seemed to be insatiable. She had insisted that they live with Claire in the small house she owned in town, refusing to move into the cabin where Nick had hoped to woo his bride in privacy. Alicia nearly drove them mad with her unpredictable changes of mood. One minute she would attempt to sweep them all into plans for her next extravagant ball; the next she would be weeping despondently for her father, her maid, her lost youth—anything she knew was impossible for Nick to provide her.

All things considered, he thought ruefully, he shouldn't have been surprised when he eventually learned she had found another lover.

By that time, of course, his own feelings had taken a sharp turn from the blind adoration he had first felt. Alicia never once let him forget that he had married her under false pretenses, though she knew he had been innocently unaware of that at the time. That particular thrust to his pride had festered like a savage wound. The only benefit was that the pain finally opened his eyes to the truth.

His gorgeous, angelic-looking wife was a bitch.

Setting down his empty glass, Nick wagged his head at the barkeep when the man went to pour a refill. Enough was enough, he reasoned. Too much whiskey led to too much reminiscing, and either one left a sour taste in his mouth.

After six years, there wasn't much left of his memories of Alicia but a vague sense of anger at his own failure. His friends and family had tried to console him by casting all the blame on his errant wife. He *had* made a bad choice, that was true, but he couldn't help feeling there might have been something he could have done differently, something that would have made her want to stay.

He might not have been any happier if she'd stayed, he acknowledged, but he might have gained something far more precious.

As usual when his thoughts turned in that direction, bitterness crept up from deep within to burn at his mind. With a silent cry of disgust, Nick shoved himself away from the bar and turned to scan the room. He'd come in here to relax, and to savor the pleasure of Mary's kiss out from under Claire's watchful eye, not to get maudlin. There was nothing about his present situation to remind him of the past, was there?

But there was, and he knew it. Looking around at the other men who frequented the Golden Lady, Nick wondered how many of them would have guessed at his dilemma. He rarely lacked for female company when he desired it, and he had more than his share of ambitious mothers thrusting their daughters in his direction, but did his companions know that when it came to a woman *he* wanted, he knew less what to do than . . . than Lou Spencer knew about poker!

"Is that a smile, or are you in pain?" Katey's husky voice interrupted his thoughts. Like a contented feline, she arched her back and covered a yawn with a fluttering hand. "I'm getting too old to be on my feet all day," she complained brightly. "Why don't you buy me a drink?"

As he followed her to an empty table, Nick grinned at Katey's obvious ruse. If she was tired, then he was a one-eared grizzly. He didn't know anyone with more energy—or more curiosity—than Katey.

"So tell me," she began as soon as they had settled into a pair of gilt-edged chairs, "you've always been a popular fellow, but why is it that everyone in Tacoma is talking about you lately? Could it be," she ventured without pause, "that folks are excited about the new mill opening? Or is it simply that romance stirs up the blood in even the most ornery timberjack?"

Nick shifted in his seat so that he could see nearly everyone in the room. Except for a couple of ship's officers at a corner table and a few unfamiliar lumbermen holding up the bar, he knew every face in the place. Had he been the topic of conversation, or was this just Katey's way of getting him to spill his guts? "Don't ask me, darlin'," he shrugged. "You know how men like to talk after a few drinks."

"*Some* men," she laughed exasperatedly. She studied Nick fondly, from the dark lock of hair that fell across his forehead in an unruly fashion, to the black, springy hairs on the backs of his wrists. If she were only a few years younger . . . but no. She smiled resignedly. Nick Fortune was one of those rare men who expected nothing from her but honesty and friendship. No sense spoiling that by wanting more.

"The reason I asked," she relented, "is because an uncommon number of souls have been bringing up your name tonight. Horace Squiggs mentioned that he met your young lady, but he had a danged peculiar expression on his face when he said it. And that other fellow, the one you were playing poker with . . .?"

Nick nodded. "I never did catch his name. He said he'll be around for a while."

"Well, he asked me to point you out near as soon as

he walked in the door. He said he might know a friend of yours from back East."

"He didn't mention it to me." Nick frowned. Now why would someone purposely look him up, and then not introduce himself properly? "What do you think he's up to?"

"He's a good-lookin' man, sure enough. A gentleman, too, by the way he's dressed. But it seems to me," Katey mused, "that he wants somethin' you got and he's takin' his time studyin' on how to get it."

Nick silently concurred with Katey's assessment, but he was in no mood to worry over something beyond his control. He had problems of his own to contend with.

He could admit it now. Sitting here with Katey had a way of forcing him to look the truth square in the eye. When he'd held Mary in his arms—soft and giving and oh, so sweet—it was as if nothing in the world could stand in the way of what he wanted. But thoughts of Alicia had brought him crashing back to Earth like one of his giant trees.

There were still too many unanswered questions between them. He had been less than honest with Mary about Alicia, and totally unfair when she had simply tried to make him see Elizabeth's side regarding Billy Turner. It was no wonder she had doubts about marrying him. Would those doubts lead to the same result as six years ago?

Not when she was so different, he reasoned. Surely he was a better judge of character by now. The way she received his kiss, had opened herself to him in the kind of helpless innocence that made him want to bury himself in her . . .

But wasn't that the way he had once felt about Alicia?

The thought was sobering, and despite the whiskey and the memories and the smoky room, he saw one thing as clearly now as he had ever seen anything in his life. The words he had spoken to Mary in anger had somehow rung true, and they left him feeling indescribably empty.

Love didn't have anything to do with it.

The following morning, Marianne awakened with the same agitation that had plagued her all night. Her precarious position made her uneasy, Elizabeth's startling request left her dubious, and thoughts of Nick threw her into a state of sheer, unadulterated panic.

But this, she rationalized, was better than facing a prison sentence. Wasn't it?

Despite her trepidations, Marianne was surprised at how eager she was for the day to begin. She hadn't realized how much fear had ruled her actions these past weeks until now, when she was temporarily released from its suffocating hold. Telling herself it was only curiosity that spurred her on, and the fresh mountain air that made her feel wide awake and full of energy, she sprang from bed, ignoring the staccato rhythm of her heart. She dressed hurriedly, donning the new riding skirt she had tried on in Millie's shop. The light jacket she discarded after a glance out the window showed the morning fairly bursting with sunlight. The lace curtains fluttered softly, stirred by a warm breeze that promised warmer temperatures as the day went on.

Sitting on the edge of the bed, Marianne tugged a pair of dark leather boots over her calves, another donation from Elizabeth's wardrobe. The sound of voices downstairs was the first sign that the rest of the household was awake. The one other time she'd risen this early, Nick had already been gone for over an hour.

So at least there was the chance that she wouldn't run into him this morning, she prayed, giving her reflection a quick perusal. If she and Elizabeth stayed away long enough, they might miss him when he came home from the mill at noontime. Then she wouldn't have to face him again until dinner.

But when she rounded the corner at the top of the stairs and looked down, Nick's upturned face met hers. His gaze raked her from head to toe, and she felt the panic rise again, and then evaporate beneath his

blatant stare. In its place welled an incredible gladness
that overrode all the questions and fears that fought
for attention in her mind. How could they matter,
when there was this between them?

Nick stopped short, one foot raised to the first step,
and let his eyes feast on her as if he were seeing her
for the first time. The thin white blouse she wore
couldn't hide the unsteady rise and fall of her breasts,
and Nick felt the dull ache of wanting spread through
his belly like a belt of hard liquor. He waited for her
there, and the waiting seemed like forever until she
began to take the stairs one at a time, until her eyes
were even with his as she stood on the next-to-the-last
step.

"It's a fine morning," he offered in greeting, searching her eyes for an answer to the questions that ham-
mered at him relentlessly.

"Yes," she replied, her voice dry and cracking with
the strain of trying to sound normal, when nothing
would ever be normal again.

"The mountain's out." When she only peered at
him uncomprehendingly, he drew her elbow against
his side and spun her around to face the open door.
"There," he indicated, his mouth just inches behind
her ear. "You can tell it'll be a clear day when the
clouds break away from Mt. Rainier. The Indians
called it Tacoma long before any white man laid eyes
on the mountain, but it's still the best weather gauge
around."

At any other time, she was sure, she would have
given proper respect to the snow-capped summit, but
just now it was the way Nick's breath sent little rivu-
lets of warm air cascading down the side of her neck
that made her knees feel weak. While her mind was
busy wishing he wouldn't stand so close, her body was
protesting the space that remained between them, longing to feel more than just the pressure of his strong
fingers as they gently wrapped her elbow.

She had pulled her hair back into a tight knot that
morning for the dual purpose of keeping it out of her
way for riding and in the hope that the severe style

would make her appear older and more composed. What she didn't know was that her neck was now lined with feathery wisps that curled above her nape, and that it took all the control Nick could muster to keep from brushing his lips along that delicate stretch of skin.

He wasn't sure which was worse, the urge to embrace her protectively from behind, or the desire to see passion flare in her eyes again like it had yesterday. But since neither action was appropriate for a man who was supposed to be keeping control of his senses, he forced his gaze back to the mountain. "I thought we might take a picnic up there today, but something's come up at the mill and I can't leave. Maybe tomorrow."

Marianne ignored the stabbing sense of disappointment, reminding herself that she really didn't want to be alone with him again. "That's all right," she replied, stepping down and out of his grasp before turning to face him. "Elizabeth asked me to ride with her this morning, and then I promised your mother I'd help her deliver some things to town later today. Don't worry about me."

Nick detected the false brightness in her voice. Should he be glad she was uneasy near him, or perturbed that she was still denying the attraction? He just didn't know.

"I want to apologize for the way I acted last night. I had no business shouting at you that way."

His husky voice shot right through Marianne, so that she had to force back a gulp in order to answer. "I shouldn't have interfered."

"But you were right. It's better not to push Elizabeth so hard that she does something foolish. Anyway, I'm glad she's decided to be civil to you."

Marianne placed a hand on his arm. A muscle jumped beneath her fingers, and she saw his throat move convulsively as he swallowed hard. "I think it's going to be all right, Nick. I can feel it."

It wasn't until after he had gone that she realized he didn't know it was his sister she was talking about.

Chapter 9

Bouncing up and down on top of a creature ten times her weight had never been Marianne's idea of fun, but when Elizabeth suggested a morning ride, Marianne had pictured the sedate mounts she had often seen crossing Central Park with their riders relaxed and in complete control. If either of them had control, Marianne thought, gritting her teeth against the jarring gait, it was this monstrous piece of horseflesh beneath her. King George, Elizabeth had told her with a winsome smile, was as gentle as could be, but Marianne had her doubts as to whether she'd been accurately apprised of the gelding's true nature. It was all she could do to grip her knees and hold on to the reins whenever the horse decided to break into a trot.

To be quite honest, Marianne admitted silently after several miles of bone-shaking travel, King George was a very responsive animal. If only he would respond to *her* commands, instead of following Elizabeth's mount pace for pace. Her mind churned over the possibility that her young companion had known—and had taken shameless advantage of—the fact that Marianne was not an experienced rider. If that was the case, she vowed, squeezing her eyes shut as both horses bounded easily over a narrow stream, she would be the *last* person to let Elizabeth know.

"Are you all right?" Elizabeth shouted over her shoulder after a particularly harrowing climb up the side of a steep hill. The smile on her pert lips had just the right degree of concern to keep Marianne guessing, but the playful gleam in her eyes could not be mistaken.

"I'm fine," Marianne panted, waving to the girl to continue. "Lead the way."

Elizabeth faced forward in her saddle, breathing rapidly with pleasure. She hadn't really believed it when she said last night they would have fun. She'd only been trying to keep Mary from changing her mind, the way Alicia had always done.

A measure of guilt stabbed through Elizabeth at the disloyal thought. Maybe she shouldn't have tried to make friends with Nick's new lady. After all, she had loved Alicia.

A memory came to Elizabeth unbidden: Alicia, clothed in a splendid dressing gown of velvet and lace, brushing her hair before the fire. She remembered peeking into the room, hoping for a glimpse of Alicia in her finery before guests arrived, but instead she had witnessed an ugly confrontation between her brother and his wife.

"I don't see why I'm expected to attend your silly little barbecue," Alicia had pouted.

From where she had hidden behind the door, Elizabeth could see only Nick's back, but his words, low and menacing, had stayed in her mind all these years.

"You're going because you're my wife, at least in a legal sense. I won't have people saying otherwise."

"Who cares what they say, anyway?" Alicia retorted. "We're talking about your damned lumber crew and their dumpy wives, not people who count. I don't belong with them, and I never did."

With deliberate slowness, Nick stepped behind her, placing both hands on her shoulders, as if to hold her down. "Do you think I don't know why you wish to hide in your room tonight? I have eyes and ears, Alicia. I know what's been going on."

"Rumors," she said, her laugh sounding high pitched and false even to Elizabeth. "Will you believe the lies of a bunch of jealous fishwives?"

"Lies, no. But the truth? I know the truth when I hear it." Nick inched his hands up along the curve of her neck, stopping just beneath her chin. With his thumbs pressed against her nape and his fingers laced around her throat, he leaned forward so she could see his face in the mirror. His eyes blazed with pure, unadulterated loathing and his lips were twisted into a mocking smile. Alicia glared back at him, but her already white skin grew a shade paler. This was the reflection Elizabeth saw as she watched, terror-stricken.

"You will go with me tonight," Nick demanded, "and you will behave as graciously and courteously as you can, even if you must fake every ounce of kindness. My people deserve that much. And if you're worried about a confrontation, you needn't. I sent Jake Walters and his wife up to the mountain camp. You won't have him to toy with any longer."

"I should have known," Alicia replied acidly, "that you'd show more concern for one of your men than you would for me. You act as if he weren't guilty of seducing me."

"I think I know just who seduced whom. But trust me, my dear . . ." He tightened his fingers until she gasped with alarm, ". . . it won't happen again."

That was the moment when Elizabeth fled from the door.

Looking back on the incident now, she wondered why she hadn't feared for Alicia more than she had, for the only thought in her mind at the time had been slipping away before she was caught eavesdropping. Perhaps, she reasoned now with the benefit of several years more wisdom, it was because she'd known Nick would never hurt Alicia with Mother just down the hall getting ready for the party. Neither had she understood what the word *seduce* meant, but she certainly did now. A man had made advances to Alicia, and Nick had blamed her. It was no wonder she left him shortly afterward!

Elizabeth didn't question why she had clung to the belief all these years that Nick had been at fault. It was easier to accept that it was love, however jealous and obsessive, that had driven Nick and Alicia apart, than it was to admit there had been no love at all.

People had to love each other in order to get married, didn't they? That's what she'd always thought, but Elizabeth knew she would find out for sure in just a few minutes. Anxiously, she spurred her horse to go faster.

They had been climbing steadily, weaving through a maze of forest trails that reminded Marianne of a story she had once heard of Greeks and bulls and balls of string. She had no string in her pocket, she thought ruefully, so there was little she could do but follow her young guide—and pray that Elizabeth was not bringing her this way to play a childish prank.

After a time, Marianne noticed the ground had levelled, and that the giant firs had thinned enough so that she could see ahead several hundred yards. There was little undergrowth here, only a thick loam produced by years of evergreen needles falling to the ground. From the amount of sunshine making its way down through the branches spread like enormous umbrellas far overhead, Marianne guessed they were coming to a clearing.

She guessed correctly, for just minutes later they broke out from under the dense shade into a secluded opening, bordered on one side by a sheer wall of rock and by the forest all around. The reason for the clearing, Marianne could see, was the stony ground upon which no living plants could grow. Once there had probably been a rockslide here; now it was simply a natural hollow cut out of the forest. This would be one of the white scars she had seen slashing across the side of the mountain when she'd looked up from far below.

"This is it," Elizabeth exclaimed, dismounting quickly and tying her horse's reins around a pointy boulder.

Without hesitation Marianne did the same, thankful to be on solid ground again. She gave King George a desultory pat on the neck before hastening toward a large, flat rock ideal for resting her wobbly legs. "Do you come here often?" she asked, taking note of the ring of stones that marked a burned-out campfire. A couple of discarded tins littered the area around the enclosure, and the ground beside the horses was soft with traces of old manure.

Elizabeth flopped down upon another large boulder, spreading her arms wide and leaning back against the sun-warmed rock. "As often as I can," she answered, watching Marianne slyly from the corner of her eye. "Are you shocked?"

Facing the girl, Marianne replied evenly, "Should I be?"

Elizabeth shrugged. "You probably would if you knew that I usually don't come here alone."

Marianne's first impulse was to laugh at the obvious attempt to startle her, but instead she merely smiled. "So that's one of the secrets you wanted to share with me."

Elizabeth snapped her head around, but a grin quickly surfaced on her delicate face. "One of them," she agreed. "I thought you'd lecture me about why it isn't proper for young girls to go off on their own."

"But," Marianne pointed out, "you just told me you don't usually come here by yourself. You're not alone now, and I don't see any breach of propriety yet."

With a puzzled frown, Elizabeth shook her head. "But that's not what I meant."

"I know," Marianne said softly.

The sun beat down harshly through the thin mountain air, adding to the heat that already wafted from the white boulders and bare ground. Elizabeth jumped up suddenly, facing Marianne with her hands on her hips and a jaunty expression on her face. The girl had worn a pair of breeches cut to just below her knees and tucked into her boots, and a chambray shirt similar to the ones her brother wore to the mill. With her hair pulled back and shoved up under a broad-rimmed hat, she looked more like a lad than a blossoming young woman, but Marianne was too recently at that age herself not to see the vulnerability in Elizabeth's flashing green eyes.

"I may as well come right out and tell you. I have a

beau. His name is Billy Turner. He's seventeen and Nick hates him."

From the way she stated it, Marianne wasn't sure which boast was the strongest. There was more than a small note of defiance in Elizabeth's tone, so it must have been her brother's disapproval that was part of the attraction. "Perhaps Nick just needs to get to know your friend," Marianne replied tactfully.

Elizabeth wagged her head. "He won't let Billy come to the house. He says I'm too young to have gentlemen callers." She cocked her brow. "Do you think I'm old enough?"

"I think," Marianne replied carefully, "that friendships should never be discouraged, so long as no one involved is being hurt. All Nick wants is that Billy doesn't hurt you."

"He won't," Elizabeth announced, but was unable to hide the uncertainty in her eyes. She tugged a strand of dark hair from beneath her hat and coiled it around one finger, casting her gaze to the ground. "Nick means well, I suppose. But how do I . . . I mean, how can someone be *sure* if she's in love?"

Good question, Marianne thought wryly. She was hardly an expert on the subject, but Elizabeth seemed so genuinely in need of reassurance there was no avoiding the issue. "It's something . . . it's something that grows in you over time," Marianne began haltingly, "until one day you're so sure, so positive it's true love, that all your doubts disappear."

"That's what I used to think," Elizabeth responded with a puzzled expression. "But you're going to marry Nick without even knowing him. How can you love him so soon?"

Was this what was bothering the child? Marianne wondered which would do the most damage to the girl's fragile grasp of matters of the heart: implying that she loved Nick, or admitting that people sometimes wed for other reasons. "Your brother and I *are* getting to know one another. If it comes to love, then, and only then, will we be married. And as for you and Billy, remember that you've all the time in the world to make up your mind. I don't think you can hurry these things."

The expression of relief on Elizabeth's face told Marianne that her answer had been the right one. Elizabeth sat down on the rock again and scooted closer to Marianne, then buried her face against her knees before she spoke in a confiding whisper.

"Sometimes I *do* feel like Billy's rushing me. He makes me feel so . . . so strange. Like I'm not even me."

Recalling the similar emotions that had plagued her since the previous afternoon, Marianne smiled. "That," she spoke with surety, "is perfectly normal."

"And sometimes . . ." Elizabeth admitted sheepishly, "I don't like Billy very much at all."

Marianne smiled again. So she'd been right to think that part of the attraction had been a play for independence. A poignant ache seeped into her heart. How she wished she'd been able to experience the natural pain of growing up that Elizabeth now felt. She laid her hand on the girl's shoulder. "You know, I'm enjoying this talk more than you realize. I can use a good friend, too."

Elizabeth's grin grew impish as she lifted her head, tossing off the hat so that her thick mane of hair cascaded over her shoulders. "Then *I'll* help *you*," she declared. "I'm going to tell you about Alicia!"

Marianne struggled to conceal her surprise and growing curiosity. A tiny stab pinched up beneath her ribs, though she refused to acknowledge that the mere mention of Nick's first wife made her jealous. To admit that would be to admit feelings she wouldn't allow herself to have. "Go on," she prodded.

"We were all surprised when Nick decided to marry you," Elizabeth began, attempting an adult tone. "He and Alicia were so much in love, no one thought he'd ever get married again. *I* knew he would, because he wants a son to inherit the business, but I still thought he would pick someone more like Alicia."

Marianne's heart gave a lopsided thud. "How am I different?"

After a long appraisal, Elizabeth heaved a dramatic sigh. "In just about every way . . . but don't worry. After I tell you how she acted and why he loved her so much, maybe you can be the same way and he'll start liking you better."

Her opinion was so incredibly naive, Marianne could scarcely believe Elizabeth was only a few years younger than herself. Had *she* ever looked at love so innocently? She thought not. The orphanage was not a place that fostered romantic notions, and she had seen several of the friends Uncle Matthew had allowed her make complete fools of themselves trying to lure young men into noticing them.

No, Marianne decided. As inexperienced as she was with romantic entanglements, she knew instinctively that you couldn't *make* a person love another. It either happened, or it didn't. If not, then you waited for the right person, but if it did . . . A vision flashed before her: Nick's eyes narrowing to fiery slits as he bent his head low to kiss her.

Stop that! she commanded silently, looking quickly to see if Elizabeth had noticed her flight of fancy. The girl did have an inquisitive expression on her face, but it was just as likely she was waiting for a reaction to her own suggestion.

"What do you think I should know?" Marianne managed to ask.

"Everything, I suppose. How she looked and dressed, what she liked to do. She was beautiful, you know. Her skin was so white and her hair so shiny and black she looked like a fairy princess. She used to let me brush it sometimes, if I was careful not to pull on it too hard."

Her wistful tone reminded Marianne that Elizabeth would have been only about eight years old when she knew Alicia, so her memories were those of an impressionable child, and were now being interpreted by a troubled adolescent. Even so, Marianne's interest was piqued. It was possible that Elizabeth could reveal much about the relationship. Wasn't it true that children often saw and heard more than adults credited to them?

"She had the most gorgeous gowns," Elizabeth continued. "I remember standing in her closet once and closing my eyes to see if I could tell the color of her dresses just by feeling them. The velvet ones were all red and the silks were mostly bright blue. There was even one satin ball gown that was dark purple. She told me every time she wore that one, no one could take their eyes off her.

"That's why Nick was so jealous. He thought she was the perfect wife, and he didn't want her to have any friends because everyone else was less than perfect. She never rode, because she said riding made her dirty and smelly like a horse. She asked once to go to the mill, but he forbade her to step foot in the place. He must have thought that was beneath her, too."

All this sounded so different from her impression of Nick that Marianne found it difficult to believe. But then, didn't people behave oddly when they were in love? Claire had told her Nick was devastated when Alicia left him, and his own reaction to the subject suggested that the memory of his wife was still painful. Didn't that prove how much he had cared for her?

Then why, Marianne puzzled, had Alicia gone away?

Before she could voice the question, Elizabeth answered it after hesitating slightly. "I guess," she said in a soft voice, "he shouldn't have been so strict with her. One day she simply disappeared. Nick went absolutely crazy. He spent weeks trying to track her down, and when he couldn't find her he hired men to look in cities all over. Six months later he got word that she was in San Francisco. He went after her right away, but when he came home he said she had died."

Elizabeth wiped a tear from her cheek, and Marianne knew that no matter how distorted the girl's memory, her emotions were genuine. Elizabeth had obviously admired her sister-in-law, and had not taken her death lightly.

"You must miss her terribly," Marianne said gently, laying her hand on Elizabeth's thin shoulder. Beneath her fingers, the slender form trembled, but only a second passed before the girl jerked away.

"Of course I do," she retorted. "So does Nick, though you'll never hear him admit it." Suddenly realizing to whom she was speaking, Elizabeth's expression grew contrite. "I—I'm sorry. I didn't mean to hurt you by telling you that."

"It's all right," Marianne replied quickly. It wasn't as if she hadn't known as much, she told herself, but that didn't explain the aching throb at hearing the words spoken out loud. Besides, given her situation, how could it matter?

Despite the warmth of the sun, Marianne felt a chill shadow creep over her. In a strictly physical sense, she was safe for a time. She had been given food, shelter, a place to recover from the accident, and—strangest of all—a new name to protect her. Yet all that wouldn't help her with the most difficult struggle of all—how to clear her name and make Adam Pemberton pay for murdering Matthew Blakemore!

"I'm glad we talked, aren't you?"

Startled out of her thoughts, Marianne returned her gaze to Elizabeth, who had risen and was brushing the dust from her pants with both hands. Her long dark hair was again tucked beneath the brim of her hat.

"Yes, I am," Marianne agreed.

On the return trip, Marianne was relieved to find that Elizabeth didn't push them quite as hard. King George behaved nicely, and though she still considered him a bit much for her to handle, at least she was able to let her thoughts wander without having to concentrate solely on staying in the saddle.

And though she would have liked to deny it, her thoughts kept coming back to Nick. And Alicia. And everything Elizabeth had said about their marriage.

To add to the wealth of impressions swimming around in Marianne's confused mind, Elizabeth continued to regale her with scenarios from the days of Nick's seemingly blissful marriage. The girl didn't realize it, but she was revealing more about Alicia's personality than she probably intended, and not all of it positive. Marianne had formed an image of refined elegance, but now she added to that a picture of a woman whose selfishness had no bounds. Nick might have loved her, but it certainly sounded as if Alicia had made him pay dearly for that love.

Again, a twinge of jealousy had her silently chastising herself. Why should she care that Nick loved his wife? Wasn't it only natural?

Angrily, she forced herself to reassess her own situation. What she *should* be concentrating on was how to get away from here without causing any suspicion. Perhaps, Marianne considered, she needn't have discarded her plan to make Nick ask her to leave. Now that Elizabeth had told her what her brother wanted in a wife—at least what he had wanted years ago— Marianne knew what *not* to do.

But could it work?

Apprehension, and a giddy sense of hope, rose in her chest. Could she pull it off? Everything that Alicia had been—raven-haired and elegant, sophisticated and stunningly beautiful—all were things Marianne was not. So, in order to convince Nick that she wasn't the kind of woman he wanted, all Marianne had to do was be herself!

It sounded so easy, and yet Marianne knew deep in her heart that it could very well be one of the most difficult things she had ever had to do in her life. How could she think it easy to purposely drive away the person she most wanted to be close to?

And that silent admission left her reeling. Was that what she wanted, to be closer to Nick? How could she even consider such a thing, when her very life could be at stake?

The more she tried to deny the truth, the more it persisted. The thought came to her, unbidden, that she could let things stand as they were. That was yet another alternative to her dilemma, but she thrust it away immediately, shocked that she even dared consider such a deceitful act.

Spurred by her own cowardly thoughts, Marianne vowed to carry through with her original plan no matter how hard it might be. The sight of Elizabeth riding ahead of her on the narrow trail, her slender form ramrod straight, made Marianne ashamed of her own weakness. Elizabeth might be immature, but she possessed, nevertheless, qualities that Marianne felt herself sadly lacking. She could take a few lessons in determination and backbone from the girl.

In the next few weeks, she would need all she could get.

As the morning had only hinted, the day unfolded gloriously, the vibrant blue sky clear and distant, broken only by wispy banners of clouds that flirted with the mountaintops. Marianne breathed deeply of the tangy air, redolent of pine needles and wildflowers with just a hint of sea spray to tease the senses. Next to her in the open buggy, Claire glanced at her sideways, her emerald eyes sparkling gaily.

"You're beginning to like it here, aren't you?" she asked pertly, clucking the reins with a firm, but delicate hand. "Sure, and you've brightened up some in the last few days."

Marianne was startled by the older woman's observation, but the response that came to her lips was undeniably the truth. "I *do* like it here," she admitted, as if it hadn't occurred to her until this very moment. "Everything is so fresh and clean, and . . . and wild!"

Claire chuckled agreeably. "I expect there're some folks here would deny that last by all the saints in Ireland, but I know just what you mean. Civilization has come hard here, and despite the politics and money and fancy houses, there's something raw about this territory that statehood won't be able to take away. I knew it when I set foot in Seattle with my Joshua thirty years ago, and my breath still wants to catch in my throat every time I look up at the mountain. There's some things, my dear, that man wasn't meant to change.

"And some folks . . ." Claire continued pointedly, ". . . might even be surprised that an Eastern girl would see it the way you do."

In the distance a pair of gulls wheeled gracefully,

pirouetting on a dance floor made of wind and air and light. Beneath the birds a single tall tree swayed, its pointed top counting cadence in the breeze. Marianne felt a stab of envy—and a burning desire that made her forget for a moment that her life now was bound by secrets.

"I was eleven years old before I ever saw a real tree," she confessed. "There was one scraggly old thing that leaned over into our play yard, but the fence was so high I could never see more than the very highest branches. I thought that was how it grew—one mass of leaves from the ground up, like a giant bush. Then one day Mrs. Kendall took me with her to buy the weekly provisions, because her daughter Kristen was sick. When I saw that the trees had leaves only on the top, and the rest was an ugly bare trunk, I felt cheated. I remember I cried, and Mrs. Kendall said I was silly, and that it should be a lesson to me. She said if I always expected things to be only half as good as I wanted, then I wouldn't be so disappointed by life. 'Remember the trees,' she said. 'Most of them are rough and hard, and them pretty leaves don't last long.' "

Claire continued to drive along in silence, her heart too full to trust herself to speak. She couldn't fathom teaching a child not to dream—not to hope. That was almost as bad as keeping a child locked away from the sunlight. For the first time, she considered the life that Mary had left behind and realized the vast amount of uncertainty she must feel.

Marianne, too, was contemplating her past, but not in the way Claire might have expected. She was *glad* Mrs. Kendall had forced her to look at life realistically. During the years following the experience with the trees, she had called upon those words of advice on many occasions, and nearly always they had been true. She hadn't forgotten them until long after Matthew Blakemore had rescued her from the orphanage, and then only because she had allowed the relative comforts he offered to lull her into a sense of security.

That had been a huge mistake, she knew, but it was one she would never make again.

"It's good of you to help me today," Claire finally said. "I never considered that working at the orphanage here might bring back unpleasant memories. If you'd rather not stay, I'll understand."

Marianne was touched by the older woman's concern for her feelings, but in truth, she was eager to reach the converted mansion that Claire had told her housed the town's orphans. The fact that her reasons weren't entirely altruistic, however, made her a trifle guilty. "I *want* to help," she insisted. "Please tell me more about what we'll be doing."

"I'd best start by telling you a wee bit o' history," Claire said, her voice slipping into a singsonging brogue as she began the story. "It happens that some twenty years ago there was a fire on the mountain. Joshua and I were living in Seattle then, for he was still captain of his own ship and had not yet caught the lumber fever. Nicky was a lad, but if you ask him, he'll tell you he still remembers hearing tales of that fire.

"It swept down from the top of the mountain so fierce there was no turning it back, and no time to flee. Some say it was a lightning bolt that started it, but there are those who'll swear it was the hand of God, riding on the wind and smiting down the very forest He created."

Claire paused here, whether for effect, or to catch her breath, Marianne wasn't sure.

"There was a little lumber town called Jackson just a mite north of Tacoma then. Mostly it was men who lived in the bunkhouse, but there were some thirty families, too, living in cabins built up all around the camp. Ruth Lyons answered their advertisement for a teacher, never knowing that the job would turn into a lifelong commitment.

"Folks around here say it was a miracle that saved those children on the day of the fire, but if you ask me," Claire said decidedly, "the miracle started the day Ruth Lyons stepped off the boat in Seattle. She was one of the girls Asa Mercer brought around the cape from New York to be wives to the lonely men of Seattle, but Ruth never did take much to the idea of clinging to a man just for the sake of bein' married. She found a job right away as a schoolteacher, and stayed there until she trained a younger woman to take her place. Then she moved deeper into the woods to where another school was needed, and so on. About the time Jackson started looking for a teacher, Ruth was finishing up in Olympia. She never even asked what the pay was.

"On the last day of the school year, Ruth decided to take her students on a picnic. She hired a man with an old, rickety sloop to take them all to Bear Island out in the bay. It got its name because some drunken sailor once said he saw a grizzly on it, but as far as I know it's always been deserted except for a few wild pigs and about a million gulls. Anyway, the name didn't stop the children from looking forward to their trip.

"They'd been planning it for weeks, so most of the children brought what they could from home. Bread, baskets of apples, cheese; more food than they could eat in a day. It was the Lord's own blessing that they did, though. The fire swept through Jackson while they were out there.

"Well, it was three days before the boat returned, and by then there was no use trying to pretend to the children there was nothing wrong. Hungry and cold, they huddled into the hold of the sloop while Ruth sang to them to hush their tears. There was no point in stopping in Jackson, because there was nothing left. They came straight to Tacoma.

"Now, things are a little different out here than they are in the East," Claire cautioned. "Usually, when a poor child is all alone, someone takes him in. But twenty-three orphans? No, that was just too many for the good folk of Tacoma to absorb. A few people offered to adopt one or two children, but everyone quickly realized that wouldn't solve the problem. The townfolk set to finding a place for the young ones, and

Ruth stayed on to see it run right. I think it was her intention to stay only as long as it took to find good homes for all her pupils, but when word spread that Tacoma had an orphanage, towns from miles around started sending children. Eventually, the original twenty-three orphans moved on, but the home is still here. Ruth Lyons never left."

These words were spoken just as Claire pulled the rig up in front of a huge, three-storied Victorian mansion. They paused for a moment, and Marianne's eyes scanned the front of the house, taking in every elaborate detail from the high, gabled roof to the gingerbread that trimmed every protruding edge. Before either woman could say a word, the front door swung open, smacking hard against the aged wood shingles covering the outside walls.

"Claire Fortune!" A loud voice preceded its owner through the doorway, imperious in its tone, yet exuding goodwill by its very clamor. One got the impression that no veiled meanings hid behind words so brazenly spoken. "Where in blazes have you been? We've been waiting two weeks for those books!"

Ruth Lyons barreled out onto the wraparound porch, her tall, robust figure halting just on the edge of the top step, swaying a little as she waved her arms wildly. Marianne's first thought was that she was slightly touched, but then she saw the wide, welcoming grin on the woman's face and changed her mind.

"You brought her!" Ruth exclaimed happily, moving down the four steps so quickly she nearly fell forward into the open carriage. "Hello, Mary Cooper. I'm glad to meet you, at last!"

"It's a pleasure to meet *you*, Miss Lyons." Marianne knew she shouldn't be surprised any longer at how the people of Tacoma knew all about her, but she couldn't help feeling overwhelmed by the effusive greeting. After hearing Claire's story she'd been prepared to like this woman, but meeting her was like being awakened from a deep sleep by a splash of cold water.

"Claire told me you were coming and I heard from Millie Knowles that you were up and about, but I didn't expect to see you here so soon after the accident. Come on in."

There was more than a smidgen of respect in Ruth's tone, but she didn't stand still long enough for Marianne to dwell upon it. Claire had stepped down from the carriage and was loading packages into Ruth's beefy arms, so Marianne joined them in carrying the boxes of books and used clothing into the house. The sound of laughter echoed from the rooms overhead, and through a pair of paneled doors to the right of the foyer she could hear the painstaking notes of a simple melody as someone practiced at the piano. Muffled giggles from the top of the stairs made her look up, and two heads peeked through the banisters, then disappeared when she smiled.

"That's Gracie and Leigh," Claire explained, setting another box down on the floor of the large entranceway. "They're the youngest here. Too small for the schoolroom," she pointed toward the ceiling, through which laughter could still be heard, "and too big for cradles. They just roam the house, collecting hugs from everyone they see. When they're not pretending they're shy, that is. It won't be more than a minute before they're down here, mark my words."

Claire's prediction proved to be correct, for by the time Marianne returned from the buggy with another armful of clothing, the two girls were sitting on the third step up, surveying the unloading with wide eyes. "Who are you?" the biggest one asked, her thin arm hung protectively over the smaller girl's shoulder.

Marianne could tell at once they were sisters, and that their ages could have been no more than four and three. "I'm Mari—Mary," she said, catching herself just in time. "I came for a visit."

"With Aunty Claire?"

"Yes," she acknowledged.

Gracie, the oldest, turned toward her sister with a superior air. "Mary is the new teacher," she announced. "She's going to teach me to read, and if you're very good, next year you can learn, too."

"Gracie, dear," Ruth interrupted before Marianne

could utter a single, surprised word. "It's not polite to repeat things you overhear, especially when I haven't even asked Miss Cooper yet."

Marianne was stunned, not just by the child's assumption, but by Ruth's tone of conspiracy. A quick glance at Claire confirmed that something was definitely going on. She hesitated. "Ask me what?"

"I told Ruth you were a teacher in Philadelphia, before you married Mr. Cooper. Forgive me for not mentioning it earlier, but we hoped you would consider taking a position here. It would be only a few hours each day. Some of the women from the town volunteer an afternoon now and then to give Ruth a break, but there's a real need for another qualified teacher to help out."

"You want me to teach?" She prayed her voice didn't sound as panicked as she felt, but Marianne could tell by Claire's puzzled expression, this wasn't the reaction they had expected. If Mary Cooper had been a teacher, then she must pretend she was, as well.

"Of course, we didn't expect you to make a decision immediately," Ruth said, reaching one arm to tousle Gracie's blonde curls. "I wanted to show you around first, so you could see how things are run. You're not obliged in any way."

Marianne chewed thoughtfully on her bottom lip as she looked down at the two little girls. She wondered if Nick knew of his mother's plans for her. Would he object? From what Elizabeth said, he might, and from what she knew of Claire, it was likely the woman had not consulted her son. Maybe, she pondered, this was her chance to put her theory into action.

But what about the children? Her mind parried. How fair would it be to them if she took on a task for which she was not equipped? And how long would she get by Ruth? Surely the woman would know the minute she entered the schoolroom that she was not a teacher.

It's impossible!
So was surviving that train wreck, but you did it.

I can't do this!
You can carry it off for a few weeks.
But I can't teach!
It's the only way.

And that, Marianne knew, was the final argument. No amount of shilly-shallying would change that single, irrefutable fact. And yet, a part of her still balked at committing yet another act of deceit. "I'm just not sure . . ."

Her voice trailed off as she looked from Claire, to Ruth, and then back down to the children. Four round, questioning eyes peered at her, and Marianne felt her heart—and her resistance—melt completely. "I'm not sure I remember everything," she sighed. "It's been a long time, but I'll do the best I can."

After all, she reasoned silently, wasn't that what she'd been doing all along?

Chapter 10

By the time Marianne came down to dinner that night, she'd forgotten why she had ever resisted the idea of working at the orphanage in the first place. Her hand sliding down the smooth banister reminded her of the bat she'd swung while playing ball with the children, and the clattering of serving dishes from the kitchen made her think of the noisy, joyous lunch she'd shared with thirty-four youngsters and a deliriously happy Ruth Lyons.

She was still smiling to herself when she entered the dining room, where Elizabeth and Claire were already seated at the table. Nick stood, looking splendid in dark, tight-fitting trousers and a shirt of white linen that was so stiff with starch it crackled when he moved toward her.

"You look lovely tonight, Mary," he said, cupping her elbow in his palm. His warm fingers on her bare skin sent a tingling sensation up her arm, and she could tell by the barely suppressed ardor in his eyes that this brief touching did the very same to him.

"T-thank you," she murmured softly as he led her around to her place. He pulled her chair out from the table, standing so close behind her as he did that she could feel the whisper of his breath caress the back of her neck. She turned her head as if to say something, but found his face bent so close to hers she could only blink in dismay. Surely he wasn't going to kiss her again? Not here . . .

"Mary?"

His gentle, husky voice wrapped around her like a summer breeze, making her want to tremble all over. . . ."Yes . . ." she whispered tentatively.

"Would you like to sit down?"

With a start, she realized Claire had spoken, and at the same moment Nick released her arm and took a step back, moving her chair forward smoothly until it pressed behind her knees. Embarrassment swept over her, replacing the stark longing that tightened her every muscle to screaming knots.

After she was seated, Nick moved around the table, taking the seat opposite her. Marianne could barely lift her eyes from her plate, so careful was she not to let him see how his nearness affected her.

She needn't have bothered, because Nick had no intention of letting this meal turn into a mawkish exchange of meaningful glances. During the day he'd had plenty of time to think about how to handle her without investing too much of himself. He would *not*, he was determined, turn his life around for any woman.

He had told her he would do what he could to make her feel more comfortable about marrying him, but that had been before he felt her inviting lips part beneath his. He had told her he wanted a wife to share his vision of the future, but now she was invading his dreams. Did he like her? Yes. Did he desire her? Certainly. But would he let himself fall in love again?

The answer to that was a resounding, fist-slamming no.

And it would be a lot easier to hold with that, Nick thought wryly, if she didn't always look at him as if she wanted the answer to be yes.

While all this was going through Nick's mind, Marianne was busy pushing the food on her plate around in little circles. *How can I let myself feel this way*, she wailed silently, *when I'll be gone in a few weeks?* Until now, her main consideration had been to protect Nick from suffering another rejection. She never would have believed that her own heart might need protecting instead, that she'd end up *wanting* to stay.

But there it was.

Now that her heart had made the admission, Marianne was left to mediate as it wrangled with common sense.

There was nothing left for her in New York, therefore she might as well make a new life for herself.

For herself, or for Mary Cooper?

She was *needed* here. She could continue working at the orphanage, and gladly.

There were orphanages everywhere, including the one she'd left, not so many years ago.

She'd always wanted a family, and she was just starting to feel like she belonged to this one.

But did she? Or was that just her own wish?

And if she did stay, would she tell Nick the truth?

That thought made all the others wither away like flowers wilting in the heat, because she knew, deep in her soul where the truth can't be denied or rationalized, that if she did tell him, he wouldn't want her to stay anyway. And if Nick didn't want her, there was no place for her here, after all.

The sigh that escaped her was less than a tiny fluttering of air, but it didn't escape Claire's notice. Her eyebrows puckered together as she watched first Nick, stabbing at his food as if it would run off his plate if he wasn't careful, then Mary, swallowing bits so puny it'd take her hours to eat enough to satisfy a rabbit.

What was wrong with those two, anyway? Claire wondered. She thought they'd worked everything out yesterday on the way back from Millie's—at least, that was how it looked from the way they kissed—she'd seen that much through the parlor window. And then, at lunch today, everything seemed fine. They didn't talk much, of course, but there was none of this avoiding one another until the tension was so thick you could feel it wallowing around your head like smoke. She wondered if Nick knew about the teaching job at the orphanage yet.

Before she had a chance to ask, however, Elizabeth did.

"Did you meet Ruth today?" With one eye on Nick to gauge his reaction, Elizabeth lifted her fork and smiled winsomely.

"Yes, I did," Marianne replied softly. "She's a delightful person. I'm going to enjoy working with her."

Caught off guard, Nick stared hard at her, trying to figure out what the deuce she meant by that.

Oblivious to his penetrating gaze, Marianne directed her next comment to Claire. "Everything you told me about Ruth is true. I can't help admiring her for her courage and fortitude, and yet, she's one of the gentlest souls I've ever met. And the children—well, they're just adorable."

"I knew you would think so," Elizabeth exclaimed.

Laying down his fork with great control, Nick leaned back in his chair and eyed the three females, one by one. Normally, he would have paid little attention to feminine chatter, but something about this conversation didn't ring true. His mother was casting wary glances in his direction, which was so very unlike her usual forthright manner that he was immediately suspicious. His sister's cheeks were abnormally flushed, and he knew that to be a sign that she was nervous. And Mary was looking at him with the same defiant expression she'd worn yesterday when she challenged him to check her teeth. Her small, pointed chin jutted forward, though her eyes faltered when he returned her gaze with a questioning one of his own.

"Would someone," he asked dryly, "please tell me what you're talking about?"

As if suddenly aware that he was in the room, all three women stopped talking at once. Claire was the first to speak. "Ruth Lyons has asked Mary to teach at the orphanage. I took her over today."

Nick lifted one brow. "I had the distinct impression," he replied drolly, "that you were merely delivering the books you ordered, and that I paid for. I had no idea you had grander schemes in mind."

Misinterpreting his grave amusement for displeasure, Marianne lifted her head a little higher and returned her gaze to his, determined not to back away from a confrontation. It was important to stand her ground against him when she had two allies, because by herself she was powerless to resist him. "I offered to help," she declared, and then wavered only slightly. "I mean . . . I'd like to."

And then, to everyone but Claire's surprise, Nick nodded thoughtfully. "I should think you'll enjoy it very much. You're absolutely right about Ruth—she's a true angel—and I'm glad you'll have something to occupy your time. You did say, though, in one of your letters, that you'd grown tired of teaching. What made you change your mind?"

Marianne heard the skepticism in his voice and stiffened slightly. Lord, how she wished she knew everything Mary Cooper had written! How many more times would she be caught like this? "I . . . It was the children, I suppose," she replied truthfully, recalling the adoration that filled Gracie's and Leigh's eyes when she promised to return tomorrow. "They were so sweet and loving."

"No enforced labor?"

Nick's tone was gently teasing, irresistibly pulling a smile from Marianne. "None that I could see. I don't think Ruth would ever resort to that."

"You're absolutely right," Claire interjected. "Ruth rules with a firm, but loving, hand."

Claire continued to tell them about some of the events she'd witnessed over the years of helping out at the orphanage, and her light, melodic voice served to ease Marianne's tension. She found herself laughing out loud over a vivid description of Gracie's antics, and the joyous smile was still bright on her face when she caught Nick's eye as he studied her thoughtfully.

Despite his earlier resolve to keep her at a distance, Nick couldn't tear his eyes from her now. She had a smile that lit up her face like a hundred candles burning at once, and he realized, suddenly, that this was the first time he had heard her laugh since she arrived. The sound rose from deep in her throat like frothy bubbles, bursting into musical notes that floated through the air and tugged at his heart.

Why wasn't she always like this? Except on a few rare occasions, when she looked at him her eyes grew shuttered and her expression guarded. She was gentle and thoughtful in his presence, but would he ever see the joy in her eyes directed at him? And if he did, would it release him from his self-imposed bondage, or would it only make it more difficult to be a decent husband to her?

From her place at the table, Elizabeth watched and listened to the others, careful to contribute to the conversation occasionally, but otherwise offering little. Why wasn't Nick angry about Mary teaching? she wondered with genuine puzzlement. She'd thought for sure he would forbid it, but instead he seemed almost pleased about the whole thing.

For the first time in six years, Elizabeth paused to wonder if she hadn't been just a little bit wrong about her brother. Alicia *had* been difficult to get along with, she admitted silently. Was it possible that Nick's anger toward his wife had been justified? Elizabeth just wasn't sure. It was so confusing, and it had all happened so long ago. But there was one thing for certain, she thought as she gazed at Mary Cooper with grudging admiration, things sure were going to be interesting around here from now on.

Marianne laughed as little Gracie Johnston shoved a bedraggled bunch of daisies under her nose and attempted a curtsy that abruptly set her on her small bottom. Leigh, seated cozily beside Marianne beneath a sprawling apple tree, let out a high-pitched squeal when she saw her sister fall. Gracie rose unharmed, however, flopping down next to them on the tattered quilt spread in the shade. Leigh immediately stretched a hand forward for her sister to clasp, taking care not to move too far from beneath the protective arm that cuddled her close.

As she had been on several occasions in the past four days, Marianne was touched by the bond between the two little girls. Though in all other ways they appeared happy and healthy, they both showed signs of a dependency upon one another that bordered on obsessive. Ruth had voiced her concern over their clinging behavior, but Marianne found it difficult to blame them. How many times had she longed for something, or someone, to latch on to and call her own? -

"*Now* will you teach me to read, Miss Mary?" Gracie begged, her brown eyes imploring. "You said you would soon."

"I meant soon, as in a few weeks," Marianne replied gently, trying not to let the disappointment in the child's expression bother her. *All* children were impatient, she reminded herself. On the subject of reading, however, Gracie was more than adamant. "Remember, you must learn all the alphabet first," she told the girl. "You must know how to write each letter, and also learn what sound it makes. *Then* you'll be ready to put them all together into words."

"But I already know them!"

"Most of them," Marianne nodded, acknowledging Gracie's rapid absorption of the past few day's lessons. "But wouldn't you rather study only in the mornings? It's such a pretty day to be cooped up inside."

The girl's fair brow knit fiercely as she struggled through this dilemma. Apparently, her growing affection for Marianne won out, for she released a resigned sigh. "All right," she consented. "But do you promise we'll learn tomorrow?"

"We'll learn more letters tomorrow."

"And you'll teach me to read in a few weeks?"

"I will, or Ruth," Marianne replied carefully. Sometimes, she thought dismally, she got so caught up in the children's needs that she forgot her days here were limited. She'd begun her work at the orphanage the very morning after Ruth and Claire had presented the challenge, and so far it was one she had managed to meet without qualms. She enjoyed having something to do, and she also liked the growing feeling of independence that came with having a job, paying or not.

It even, she was loathe to admit, helped fill the hours since Nick had departed for the monthly inspection of his logging camps. The house had seemed desperately quiet without his presence, though Marianne forced herself to ignore the part of her heart that

listened each night for the sound of an approaching
wagon.

All things considered, she was glad she had said yes
to Ruth's plea. She only hoped she was doing the right
thing by taking on this responsibility, knowing that
soon she would have to abandon the children.

Nonsense, she warned herself. She wouldn't be aban-
doning anybody, not with Ruth here. Ruth was the
one they loved and depended on, the one who loved
them day and night in return. Marianne spent only a
few short hours each day giving lessons to the younger
children. They would hardly miss her when she left.

But she would miss them.

Unconsciously, Marianne's arm tightened around
Leigh's frail little shoulders, and she bent her head to
inhale the warm, soapy scent of her golden hair. Maybe
this wasn't such a good idea, spending extra time with
the two little ones. Perhaps she should restrict herself
to seeing them during classroom hours.

She recalled, however, that first day, when Gracie
had struggled over her slate tearfully, unable to block
out the sound of Leigh's loud sobs from the room
where Ruth tried valiantly to console the younger girl.
In the end, they'd been forced to allow Leigh to ac-
company her sister to her lessons, and it had worked
out well enough. Leigh was happy and quiet, so long
as she was seated within arm's reach of Gracie, and
Gracie thrived at her lessons with her baby sister at
her side.

That fiasco had probably been at the bottom of
Ruth's suggestion that she take the girls on a picnic
today. The other children, Ruth had explained, were
involved in preparations for the annual bazaar the
town sponsored for the benefit of the orphanage, and
Mary would do them all a service by keeping the two
young ones occupied. Ruth had also hinted that perhaps she could figure out a way to ease the sisters
apart gradually.

But how could she teach them to stop clinging to
one another, Marianne wondered, when in their troubled little minds they thought they had no one else but

each other? And what would happen if she managed to earn their trust, and then, with no explanation they could possibly understand, she left Tacoma?

She was still worrying over that question when Gracie began to sing softly, and slightly off-key. Within a few moments, Leigh joined in, lisping over the sounds. *"A-b-c-d-e-f-geee."*

Marianne picked up the familiar tune, adding her clear voice to the melody, *"H-i-j-k . . ."*

"Elepano me." Leigh grinned up at Marianne as Gracie burst into wild giggles over her sister's mixed-up rendition.

"Q-r-s and t-u-veee," they continued. *"W-x and y and zeee. Now I know my ABC's, tell me what you think of me."*

"Again!" Leigh cried clapping her small hands together.

After singing the "Alphabet Song" four times through, they began an earnest game of "Ring Around the Rosie," which quickly led to "Blind Man's Bluff." They let Leigh go first, and made it easy for her to catch them by staying in one spot and singing so she could follow their voices. When Gracie took a turn, Marianne darted around silently, letting the child catch her only after a few minutes of eager searching. Marianne then wrapped the scarf they used as a blindfold around her own head and let Gracie twirl her in a circle.

"Where *aaare* you?" she chanted, groping for the youngsters.

"Here I am." Leigh darted forward, wrapping her thin arms around Marianne's legs. It took a little longer to tag Gracie, who skillfully stayed just beyond her fingertips, but for some reason the girl stopped moving suddenly, and Marianne nearly tripped when she reached her.

"I've got you, Gracie. Now it's Leigh's turn again."

Unexpected silence took her by surprise, and she reached behind her head for the knot in the blindfold when a husky voice chided, "Not yet. You've got one more to go."

Marianne froze with her hands high and her elbows pointed forward, remembering, too late, that she had hitched her skirt up nearly to her knees by tucking a handful of the blue flowered fabric into the belt at her waist. Even without the use of her eyes, she could picture Nick standing about three feet from her, an arm's length away.

"Come on," he teased. "Can't give up yet."

With a slow smile, Marianne lowered her arms, settling her fists on her hips. "Not fair, Nick Fortune. Latecomers have to be it."

A deep, rich chuckle crossed the gap between them, making her heart jump up into her throat. "I'd rather take a forfeit. *After* you catch me."

Springing forward, Marianne swung her arm wide, hoping to snag him before he was ready, but Nick proved too agile. Even though he kept up a constant spate of taunts and jests to lead her in the right direction, she never more than brushed the ends of her fingertips on his shirt.

"I'll tag you yet," she threatened.

"Only if I let you," he cajoled.

And apparently, that wasn't going to be for a long while, she thought disparagingly as she lunged forward, missing again. He laughed at her then, which only made her more determined. So intent had she become on their game, she didn't notice that theirs was the only laughter filling the small meadow.

It wasn't until she took a step toward Nick and slammed into his chest that she realized something was wrong. His fingers circled her upper arms. His voice was grave. "Game's over."

"Nick . . .?"

The question died on her lips as he raised a hand to her head, fumbling in back with the scarf. A strand of her hair was caught in the knot, and she winced as he tugged the cloth free.

"Over there," he said, murmuring low.

Following his gaze, Marianne turned to look at the two figures huddling beneath the tree. Gracie and Leigh clung together, arms wrapped around each other so tightly they looked like one small, forlorn body with two heads. It was their frightened expressions, however, that stunned her completely. Fear, stark and vivid, made their eyes appear like four black pennies staring from faces as white as bleached muslin.

"Gracie . . . Leigh? Oh, my dears," Marianne flew to them, falling to her knees on the worn quilt and gathering them close to her. "What is it, darlings? What's wrong?"

From where he stood, Nick watched her embrace the children gently, but from over her shoulders two pairs of eyes, dilated with terror, stared back at him. In any other circumstance, he would have let her tender affection toward the girls warm him, but he didn't have time to wonder about it before the realization hit him with a shuddering jolt.

It was him they were afraid of.

Purposely keeping his voice low and unthreatening, Nick said, "I better wait for you in the buggy. Can you manage?"

Marianne gave him a quick glance and nodded. "All right. Tell Ruth we'll be along shortly."

She heard the stones crunch beneath his boots as he turned and strode away, and she couldn't help but send a part of her heart with him. There'd been too many times already that she'd heard him use that stiff, unemotional tone to cover bewilderment—and stinging rejection.

Torn between the urge to run after him and the need to find out why Gracie and Leigh were so frightened, Marianne swallowed the hard knot of indecision that clotted her throat, closing her eyes tightly. Within her arms, the two trembling forms began to relax and wilt against her, soaking her bodice with hot tears. Achingly, she turned her attention to the children.

They were the ones who needed her now.

The afternoon heat had just settled in for the long spell that would break only after sunset trailed fire across the bay, but Nick was more concerned with the doings inside than he was with the sweat trickling down between his shoulder blades underneath his shirt. Unmoving, he sat hunched over the reins with his elbows planted on his thighs, contemplating the tail-swishing rump of the carriage horse as it took hapless aim at the insects buzzing all around.

He consulted his watch, snapped the gold case closed, and rammed it back in his pocket.

Forty minutes.

With the slightest of movements, he lifted his eyes enough to peer out from under the brim of his hat at the sky, as if to confirm the timepiece's accuracy by a more ancient method.

Was it taking this long to calm the children? Or was Mary playing at keeping him waiting, the way he'd been doing for three days now?

His reasons for the unexpected trip had been legitimate, he argued inwardly, but the length of his stay had not. From boyhood, he'd sought the high timber country whenever the city and its confusion pressed too hard at him. This was the first time, he frowned ruefully, that he'd let a woman chase him away.

Only she hadn't been chasing, and that was part of what had been eating at him all this time.

He wanted her, but he didn't want to want her any more than she wanted him. He would marry her, but only if she showed an unquestionable willingness to be his bride. He thought he should share with her a little more about his goals, his expectations, but he longed for her to do the same with him.

And that was why he came back.

He still had every intention of keeping his feelings in perspective, but he'd been unprepared for the shaft of desire that pierced him when he first heard her laughter ripple across the grass like a sweet summer wind. Her singing carried a wistful note of childhood along with the mature clarity of a rich, fine wine, and her eyes had shone with love for two orphaned children who needed her care.

He could picture the way she'd looked when he first came up the hill, her hair flowing loose over her shoulders, tangled by the scarf and by the exertion of

scampering after the girls. The hiked-up skirt displayed
flashes of trim ankles hugged by elastic-sided kid boots,
and thin cotton stockings over shapely calves. Her
breasts had strained against the thin fabric of her dress
when she'd lifted her arms, and he remembered the
fluttering pulsebeat at the base of her bare throat
when he had entered the game.

God, he wanted her!

The horse stirred in the traces, jolting Nick out of
his reverie and back to his place in front of the mansion. Should he go in and check on them? he wondered. Curiosity over why the two children reacted to
his presence so violently was nearly as strong as his
desire to have Mary beside him on the buggy seat for
the long ride home, but he stifled the urge to knock at
the front door. He didn't want to frighten anyone else.

His patience was rewarded shortly, when the broad
mahogany door opened part way and Marianne slipped
through. Pausing for a second at the top of the steps,
she ran a hand through her disheveled hair, then hurried down to the buggy. She clasped Nick's proffered
hand and let him haul her onto the wide seat.

"All set?"

She nodded quickly, staring straight ahead as the
horse ambled forward. Nick kept throwing her questioning glances, but Marianne hardly noticed. She
couldn't think of anything except what she'd just
learned!

It was a full ten minutes before Nick dared to break
the silence that wound around them like a taut wire.
He knew from the second she'd come out the door
that she was upset, but there was no telling whether
she was mad as spit or getting ready to cry.

As it turned out, she was both.

"Tell me about it?" he asked solemnly.

Through clenched teeth, Marianne shook her head,
staving off the tears that scalded her eyes like acid.

"It might help."

The husky tones drove through her resistance like tiny
arrows into her heart. "It's so awful," she said in a choked
whisper. "Oh, Nick, how can people be so cruel?"

The tears fell then, spilling down onto her flushed cheeks. He felt each one as if they burned into his own chest, instead of landing on her rapidly heaving bosom, adding to the dark splotches of moisture that already marked her dress.

"What happened back there?" A vague idea had already formed in his head, but he wasn't sure until she hesitated, embarrassment—or maybe anger—making her face grow the color of ripe apples.

"I n-never s-saw anyone as scared as those p-poor little things," Marianne stammered.

Nick had, but he wisely decided that now was not the time to remind her.

"I c-couldn't f-figure out what they were afraid of." She took a deep breath to calm herself, but now her mournful tone was replaced by anger. "They told us— Ruth and me—about a man who used to do awful things to them. Ruth guesses it was the man their mother lived with before she left them for good. I couldn't understand everything they said, the poor dears were almost incoherent, but there were things . . . things that don't even bear thought. I just can't believe a mother would allow anyone to . . .! How can a person . . . ?"

Nick had already stopped the buggy, and now he wrapped his arms around Marianne and pulled her closer. "I don't know, either," he spoke into her hair. "But people do. People do."

She let the fresh spate of tears run its course, so terribly glad just to allow some of the confusion and grief and rage to spend itself against his warm, man-smelling shirt. She was aware of his hand pushing through her hair, tenderly massaging her scalp and then wandering to the nape of her neck and back again. Words were spoken, too, but what they were was unimportant compared to what they felt like, falling on her ears as softly as the wind-tossed leaves that floated down upon the ground in autumn. They were a balm to her sadness and they soothed her anger.

But they didn't relieve her confusion.

"They never told anyone before today," Marianne

puzzled, sniffling as she lifted her head. "I'm not sure that they would have, if Ruth hadn't encouraged them—nearly *forced* it out of them. She seemed to know that it was seeing you that terrified them. . . ." Her voice trailed off.

"I suppose they would have reacted that way toward any unfamiliar man." Nick wasn't sure which touched him the most, the hesitation in her wide, blue eyes when she thought she might have hurt his feelings without meaning to, or the fact that she found it impossible to believe that the children were frightened of him. But it was this, more than the temptation of her swollen lips or the inviting feel of her breasts pressed hard against him, that made him realize that he already loved her a little, and might some day love her a lot.

If she would let him.

The thought was a bullet ricocheting through his chest, wounding him with its unyielding bluntness. In a way, this was what he had asked for. He had wanted a woman who would make no emotional demands on him, who would be content to have every part of him but his heart. If she had come to him expecting protestations of undying love, he probably would have looked at her with displeasure. Instead, she asked for nothing, and in her gentle, unobtrusive way, she was capturing his heart anyway.

"You really do care about them, don't you?" he asked softly.

Marianne nodded. "How could I not? They need so badly to be loved."

"But don't all the children?"

"Yes, but not in the same way." She raised her gaze to his warm gray eyes, wanting him to understand. "Most of the other children knew parents who loved and nurtured them, and even though they may miss them now, they still have the memory of that love to comfort them. I know that's how I felt when I was alone. With Gracie and Leigh, it's different. They need to be convinced that their mother's neglect wasn't their fault, that they can be themselves and still be loved!" Marianne stopped, suddenly embarrassed by her impassioned speech, not just because she'd been clutching Nick's sleeve, but also because she recognized how very revealing her words had been. "I-I just want to help them," she finished lamely, drawing her hand away.

"I know." Nick silently allowed her retreat to the other side of the buggy seat, wisely sensing that he would learn more about her like this, letting her show him bits and pieces of her past, than if he pressed her into an unwilling confession. He urged the horse to a smooth trot once again. "I'm sure Ruth is glad for your assistance. Mother used to help out more, but now it tires her too much, though she'd be the last to admit it. Not many others have the time or inclination."

Marianne looked sideways at him, relieved that he'd returned the conversation to a more normal tone. "Ruth also mentioned the donations she receives regularly from you." She watched for his reaction, wondering what his answer would be if she asked him about the only other patron of the orphanage who matched his generosity. Katey Muldoon was an old friend of Nick's, Ruth had let slip, before quickly changing the subject. An old friend, Marianne frowned, or a current paramour? She knew Nick spent many an evening at the Golden Lady, but it wasn't until Ruth's revelation that she gave it a second thought.

And why should you care! an inner voice scolded. *You won't be here in another three weeks.* With an anxious sigh, Marianne squirmed a little in her seat, casting her gaze out over the distant foothills.

Nick noticed the movement, misinterpreting its meaning. "You're still upset. Would you rather talk about something else?"

"Yes . . . anything!"

"Okay, you start."

Glancing up at him to see if he was teasing her, Marianne studied his profile. The brim of his hat sloped down to a point just over his line of vision, shading his eyes from her perusal, but only the trace of a smile creased the hard plane of his face. Deciding that he was merely being polite, she allowed her thoughts to revolve slowly. What *did* she want to talk about?

She remembered part of her conversation with Elizabeth, and choosing that tack, she swallowed back the hesitation that clogged her throat. "Tell me more about your mills."

"My mills?"

Marianne nodded.

"What do you want to know about them?"

"Everything."

Nick dropped his gaze to hers once, then turned his attention to the afternoon sun as it arched lower in the sky. "The best way to understand is to see one up close. If you're not too worn out from working all morning, we could make it down to the new building and back before supper. Most of the equipment's in place. It's not open yet, but then I can explain things to you without having to shout over the saws. We can go back next week when she's up and running."

Marianne had to hide her surprise over the eagerness in his voice. She'd been fully prepared to meet with his disapproval, even censure, over questions about his business. Elizabeth had said . . .

Never mind what Elizabeth said, a tiny voice told her. She *had* wanted something to take her mind off Gracie and Leigh. Here was the opportunity.

Grabbing the side of the buggy with one hand to steady herself as Nick directed the horse in a tight turn, Marianne ignored the fluttering anticipation that cavorted through her stomach. She would go with him to the mill, and perhaps once there he would see just how unsuited she was to this life. She wouldn't even have to pretend ignorance about the workings of his livelihood, she thought with a wry smile.

He'd know it soon enough.

Chapter 11

"Okay now, watch this!"

Leaning out over the smooth rail that was all that prevented her from plunging to the floor twenty feet below, Marianne searched warily for Nick. From the sound of his voice, he was somewhere under the observation platform she was standing on, but even stretched as far out into the open space as she dared, she still couldn't see him.

On the ground floor of his newest mill, Nick surveyed the rows of machinery and gleaming saw blades that stood ready to turn raw timber into sturdy beams and smooth planks. With his hand on the start-up lever, he felt nearly the same sense of awe and power that came when he dropped his first tree some fifteen years ago. Not quite, but almost the same.

"Here goes." Thrusting the lever upward with both hands, he watched as the largest of the circular blades spun slowly to life, seeming to consume the broad, flat belt that moved toward it, only the belt dropped safely away just inches in front of those deadly teeth.

Marianne heard the roar begin just a moment before she saw Nick step out almost directly beneath her feet. He glanced upward once in her direction, and she caught a glimpse of his flashing grin as he moved toward the source of all the noise.

"This would be nothing," she remembered his telling her a few minutes earlier, "compared to the din when a log actually moved beneath the wheel." Quickly stuffing two bits of cotton into her ears, she watched as he did the same.

Now Marianne could see Nick clearly, even without bending over the pine railing, but she was so entranced that she forgot to step back. From the moment they had entered the mill, she had been fascinated with the long building and all its trappings. Maybe it was partly Nick's enthusiasm that infused her with such a feeling, but she found herself enthralled by the power and noise and wonder of it all.

Unlike his two other mills, located farther upriver, this newest was right in town, close enough to the docks to make shipping easy and inexpensive. Nick had explained how the cut logs made the trip from the timber camps, first traveling down skids and then floated downriver as far as the city. A nearby stream had been dammed up, forming a mill pond that was already full of swollen tree trunks just waiting to be turned into marketable lumber.

The mill itself was a huge, open-sided building surrounded by mounds of uncut logs. When Nick and Marianne first arrived, a crew of several men had been busy lining up and fastening a single enormous blade to an overhead pulley. It was, Marianne had noted, only one of four similar blades.

After guiding her to this spot high above the bustle and clamor, Nick had ordered the men to start up the steam engines that powered the central saw in order to give her this impromptu demonstration. She watched, mesmerized by the precision with which the men worked together. Nick had removed his shirt to assist in wrestling the huge log onto the carriage, and now he stood with his fists planted on his hips as the raw timber moved toward the spinning blade. Legs spread, muscles bunched beneath the glistening surface of his back, he reminded her of a primitive god standing guard over his domain.

Nick glanced up at her, his cheerfulness fading, turning into something far more intensely pleasurable when he saw her leaning over the railing, a transfixed expression of rapture on her face. She gave a start when the log hit the saw blade and sent an earsplitting wail careening through the air, but it was not fear that made her flinch; it was excitement, it was awe. He turned back to the machinery, stunned by the feelings that poured through him.

Now that he had resolved to win her over, impatience gnawed at him like a hungry beast. He could no longer deny that he wanted her desperately, but even so he told himself that this longing would dissolve once their marriage was established, consummated. Only then would he be able to erase her haunting golden beauty from his mind. It would, he hoped, be soon.

Marianne backed away from the railing when the log completed its journey past the razor-sharp blade. She saw the slab of bark that dropped to the ground before a couple of men carried it away, then the giant log was shifted on the carriage for a return trip. As Nick had instructed her, she stepped into the small, enclosed office behind her.

It was different, looking out over the mill from behind the huge, plate glass window. She could see nearly everything she had from the balcony, but the noise and vibrations were far less intruding. Glancing around at the solid-looking desk and shelf-lined walls, she supposed it *would* be easier to work without listening to that constant racket, yet she almost had the urge to return to the narrow platform, to let the sound of the saw screech through her bones and the fine wood shavings dust her clothing. It was no wonder Nick had wanted his office up here where he could see everything. She imagined he would spend a good deal of his time standing just where she'd been, his strong hands clutching the railing where she had.

The descending whine of the saw as it rotated slowly to a halt broke into Marianne's fanciful thoughts, and she quickly brushed the back of her hand across her cheek, removing flecks of sawdust from her skin. Below her, Nick stooped low to pick something off the ground beneath the blade and stood up again, running a loving hand over the silent belt as he strode toward the stairway. His footsteps clumped upward rapidly, and Marianne spun to face the door just as it opened.

"Well?" he asked, a grin splitting his dust-covered face from ear to ear.

"It's wonderful! I've never seen anything like it."

"With this mill running at full capacity, it'll just about double production. That's still not enough to meet the demand back East, but the logging crews'll be hard put to cut fast enough to keep this mill up to speed."

"Can't you hire more loggers?"

Nick bent at the waist, swishing both hands briskly through his hair to clear out the dust. With a cursory swipe at his shoulders first, he slipped his arms through the sleeves of his shirt and smiled as he attacked the buttons good-naturedly. "I could," he explained. "But I'd rather not strip the mountain too fast. I'd like to leave a *few* trees for my son to fell."

Marianne smiled stiffly. This was not the first time he'd implied that he wanted only one child. It reminded her there were still things she didn't know about him, and probably never would. "And what if you have daughters instead?" she asked.

Nick paused. "Male babies run in the family." At her puzzled look, he explained. "My father had four brothers, and I had two brothers who died shortly after birth." He hesitated then, unsure whether to go on. When he spoke his voice was low and emotionless. "Also, Alicia was pregnant when she died. It was a boy."

"Oh, Nick," Marianne gasped. "I *am* sorry."

He shrugged. "It was a long time ago. At times even I forget."

She doubted that, but followed his clue to change the subject. Swallowing back the sorrow for him that swelled in her throat, she turned and gazed back out over the now-silent blades. "Are your other mills as large as this one?"

Nick studied her thoughtfully, aware of how deeply affected she'd been by his admission. Somehow, instead of making him regret telling her, it made him glad. He watched her pick a fleck of sawdust from her sleeve. "No, they're not."

"Can I see them sometime?"

"If you wish."

Something in his tone caught her attention, and she raised her chin defensively as she faced him once more. "I do."

Nick let a rueful smile surface. He'd seen that look before, and things were beginning to make sense to him now. Folding his arms across his chest, he leaned against his desk, hiking one leg up over the corner. "I'm *glad* you're taking an interest in my work," he said evenly, gauging her reaction. As he expected, her blue eyes registered confusion.

"You are?"

"Yes. Surprised?"

His eyes looked as warm as smoldering ashes, studying her with a calm that was at complete odds with the state of her own nerves. She opened her mouth once to speak, but since words seemed pointless, she let it close again in surrender. Marianne nodded weakly.

"The way you were surprised when I wasn't angry about your job?"

"I thought you didn't want a wife with outside interests," she said slowly.

"And how," he asked dryly, "did you arrive at that conclusion?"

She took a hesitant breath. "Elizabeth told me about Alicia."

Nick stared at her so hard she thought her knees would give out, and she waited, almost wishing for the moment when she would sink right into the floor. His face was an unreadable mask, but a half smile was frozen on his thinned mouth.

"Alicia," he said evenly, "did exactly as she pleased."

"Oh." Marianne popped her mouth shut over the inane syllable.

"And it appears you do, too."

She gazed back at him mutinously, but Nick's expression had softened to one that was tenderly quizzical. She couldn't tell whether he expected an explanation, or whether the question lurking behind his eyes was a different one altogether.

"I . . . I only thought you should know how I felt, too."

"Then tell me yourself. Don't ask Elizabeth, or my mother, or anyone else about me, either. I'll fill you in on whatever you want to know."

Confronted by such utter reason, there was nothing left for her to do but agree, despite the part of her that wondered how she could ever hope to break away from a man who was trying so hard to make her want to stay.

"I don't mind your working with Ruth," he clarified, a wry smile raising one corner of his mouth. "In fact, I'm glad you'll be setting an example for Elizabeth. Not that I expect her to work away her summer, but I don't want her to grow up thinking she needn't do something useful just because she's not forced to work for her living. She's going through a difficult stage right now, and I was hoping that having you here would help."

"She thinks she's in love," Marianne said feeling more than a little guilty for getting the girl involved.

"And she thinks," Nick continued, "that I don't know what that means, I suppose."

Almost, Marianne silently agreed, but not quite. Elizabeth had clearly remembered the passion between Alicia and Nick, and it was doubtful that she would have misunderstood that, even if there were other, more subtle aspects of the relationship that had been beyond her youthful comprehension. Besides, there were too many other circumstances that confirmed it: the closed, painful look on Nick's face whenever Alicia was mentioned, the fact that he had no desire to love another woman, except in the strictest, physical sense; and the way, after all this time, that he defended his wife's actions, even though they hadn't always been what he might have preferred.

Nick moved closer to her, so close that Marianne could smell the mixed odors of perspiration and sawdust clinging to him. His rueful smile had softened somewhat, but there were still lines of worry marking his brow.

"I don't want you to think you have to compete against my past, Mary. If I'd wanted the same thing as before, I never would have sent for you in the first place. Understand?"

Marianne's chest tightened. She understood all too well. No one would ever mean to him what Alicia had, and he wanted to make that perfectly clear. Nevertheless, something indefinable was thrumming between them, something that made her skin prickle and her heart beat higher and higher in her throat. For a minute, she thought he was going to kiss her—was *sure* he was going to kiss her—but then he dropped his hand to his side again and leaned away slightly. She was afraid the disappointment would show in her eyes, so she let her gaze fall to the safety of his shirtfront.

As they left the mill, Marianne found herself shaking so hard she could barely negotiate the narrow stairway that led outside from the office, and her legs trembled as Nick helped her board the buggy. Though she tried to tell herself it was because her plan to escape from Tacoma would now have to be changed, there was a part of her that would not be lied to.

You're falling in love with him, it admonished.

It's nothing! It's only when he touches me like that!

Exactly. And if not love, then what would you call it?

Need, desire, lust? I don't know! The same thing he feels for me! Not love!

Not love. Of that much, she could be sure. Love was what a man felt when he tried to keep his family from harm. Love was what made a person feel safe and happy and at peace. Love was what made memories last for years. Six years, to be exact.

"There's one more thing I want to show you."

Nick's voice interrupted her thoughts, and she looked around in time to see that he had turned the buggy off the main road and onto a narrow path through the trees. Before long, the branches overhead became too thick and the trunks of the huge firs crowded closer together. Without a word, Nick halted the buggy and hopped down, coming around quickly to her side.

"Through there," he indicated with a nod of his head. He lifted his hands to her waist and swung her to the ground.

"What is it?" Marianne asked, her curiosity piqued. They were too far from the mill for it to be another building Nick wanted to show her. Besides, the stillness of the great forest filled her with a sense of awe and wonder that pervaded her senses, making them come alive to every sight and smell.

Nick didn't answer, but looked back at her once, just long enough to take her hand and decide that he dared not look at her again when she wore that particular expression, or they would never reach their destination.

Content to follow, Marianne held tightly to his strong hand, allowing him to guide her over fallen logs and dipping below the branches that he held aside for her. At one point, a giant tree trunk lay across their path, and Nick had to lift her onto the top, then hoist himself up beside her.

"I didn't know this one had gone down," he said, pointing toward the spiked foliage that now spread across the forest floor. Marianne's gaze followed the direction of his finger. All along the length of the downed giant, smaller trees and bushes lay in tangled heaps, victims to its humbling fall. It was a sight that sent an unexpected shiver up her spine.

"I chopped my first tree right over there," Nick said, nodding his head in the opposite direction. "I was twelve, and had decided on this one, but Pa told me never to start with the biggest tree in the stand, or else you'll take down too many smaller ones with it. He was right, of course. These giants have been here longer than any of us. It doesn't seem right to fell them indiscriminately." He gazed up at the canopy of green that hid the sun, then back at the dark trunk that stretched along the ground until it was swallowed up by the rest of the forest. "Sometimes, though, they go on their own."

Marianne looked at Nick and tried to imagine the boy who had been thrust unwillingly into manhood, who had stepped into his father's place at an age when most boys were content to hold off responsibility with both hands. Claire had eased his way, she was sure; now even his mother was a source of concern for him.

And sooner or later, Marianne realized, she would have to tell him the truth about herself. Would his shoulders bear yet another burden, she wondered achingly, or would he cast her away like an unwanted encumbrance when he learned of her deception?

"Come on," Nick said abruptly, breaking her pensive mood by sliding down the other side of the tree trunk. He reached up for her, drawing her into his arms so quickly she hardly had time to react.

Startled by the sudden movement, Marianne clutched his shoulders tightly as he swung her around, lowering her only until her eyes were on a level with his, her feet remaining stretched a few inches above the ground.

His strong hands gripped her just above her waist, his thumbs hooked forward, one beneath each breast. She could feel the heat radiate outward from his palms, as if the layers of cloth that separated their flesh didn't exist. Her fingers automatically crept over the firm muscles of his shoulders, splaying his back possessively.

"It's only a little farther."

Nick lowered her gently as he spoke, keeping hold of her until her feet touched the forest floor. It was an effort to tear her eyes from his, but she was afraid he would see too much if she continued to let his hypnotic gaze penetrate her soul.

Clasping her small, trembling hand in his once more, it was all Nick could do to continue walking in a casual manner. What he wanted to do was sweep her into his arms and rush deeper into the wooded protection of the forest, where he could make love to her among the towering trees. Only the brief flare of panic in her wide, blue eyes had prevented him from taking her already, and patience, he realized, had never been his long suit.

"This land is part of my pa's original grant," he

said, struggling to make conversation. "Except for a
few trees like the one we saw, the rest of this forest
isn't mature enough to cut yet. It'll be another ten–
twenty years before it's ready."

Marianne recognized the instructional tone he had
used when telling her about the mill's operation, but
she wasn't immune to the unusual huskiness in his
voice, sensing immediately that he had been as affected by their nearness as she had been. An unbidden
thrill raced all the way down to her toes, even while
she was thankful for his attempt to keep the mood
light.

"They look awfully big to me," she responded in
kind, tilting her head upward to view the ceiling of
greenery high above. It seemed as if the branches held
up the sky.

Nick followed her gaze with a smile of amusement.
"Wait till you see some of the stands higher up on the
mountain. They make these look like matchsticks."

But would she ever see them? For a moment, Marianne was torn between laughter and bitter tears, but
she forced herself not to dwell on her questionable
future now. This day had evolved into one of unexpected joy and indescribable pleasure, and she wanted
to forget everything but the forest that surrounded her
and the man who walked beside her.

Because of the uneven landscape, Marianne soon
lost track of how far they had come. The sun, though
still bright enough to send thin streamers of light through
the occasional break in the foliage, was hidden so well
that she couldn't begin to guess at the time. It hardly
mattered. She savored the sense of unreality, of inevitability, that had enveloped her from the moment they
left the buggy. The dark solitude of the trees, instead
of making her feel uneasy, only reinforced the illusion.

She heard sounds at the same split second that Nick
stopped. At first she wondered where the musical
tune came from; it took a moment for her to recognize
the tinkling tones of water rushing through a creek
bed.

"Hear it?" Nick asked, watching her face for the

fleeting expression of delight he had begun to anticipate. He was not disappointed as he led her into the clearing.

"It's . . . why, it's a house!"

Not ten feet from the opposite bank of the stream, nearly hidden by the forest's shadow, sat a small, snug cabin of unpeeled logs. A stone chimney scaled the wall to their right, and was flanked by a pair of shuttered windows. Another, larger window faced the creek, and beside it was a door, fastened closed by a crosspiece that appeared to be nailed to the frame.

As Marianne studied the cabin, she was acutely aware of Nick observing her with a careful gaze. His gray eyes rested questioningly upon hers, telling her more than words.

"This is yours?" she asked, not needing to hear the answer. She turned to face him once again, suppressing a smile.

Nick slowly released his breath, unaware until that moment of the pressure that had been building within him. "It's mine."

"Is there a way over?"

Enchantment lit her face like a flame from deep within, lighting a spark in his own chest that burned like a hot, unquenchable blaze. It was all he could do to answer her.

"The bridge washed out a few years back. Most months the stream is low, like now, and you can walk across. I come by three or four times a year to make sure no one's broken in."

Marianne eyed the rushing water skeptically. It was impossible to tell exactly how deep it was, and she guessed that, like most of the waterways nearby, this one originated high in the mountains where the snow was just melting. A few rocks jutted above the fast-moving swell, but she could tell at a glance that they were too slick to provide firm footing.

Before she could open her mouth to ask how, Nick sat down on the low bank and began removing his boots. "Let's go," he said. When she hesitated he grinned at her. "It's not too bad if you keep moving. Don't you want to see the cabin?"

"Yes, but . . . but I can't swim!"

Nick's laughter rang through the clearing like a deeper echo of the stream's sparkling sound. "We're going to wade," he said, "not swim. Now take off your shoes and stockings."

Marianne stared at him. He had rolled his denim pants up, and the sight of his long, bare feet, strong ankles, and muscular calves covered with crisp, dark hair made her feel as if she were seeing him naked. Never had she seen a man thus exposed. And never had *she* exposed her legs to a man.

"I-I can't," she croaked, aware that her cheeks were burning and were most likely as red as a sunset.

"Why not?" Nick shrugged, his grin widening as he watched her expression change from shock, to wistfulness, to chagrin as she struggled to make up her mind. He stuck his big toe in the water, testing, then swung his leg sideways, tossing a spray of icy droplets in her direction. "Haven't you ever waded through a creek before?"

Marianne grimaced as the cold water splashed over her. "Hardly," she said ruefully. "Children in orphanages are taught to be sober, productive citizens. Fun isn't in the curriculum."

"Then I bet you've never gone swimming, either." She shook her head. "Or sledded down a hill in winter? Run outside in the rain? Sneaked out after dark in your nightie?"

Unsure whether he was teasing her, or was truly dismayed at her prim upbringing, Marianne could only shrug. "I never did any of those things."

"Well, at least you know how to play Blind Man's Bluff. It's not too late to learn the rest. Unless," Nick grinned, "you want me to carry you over?"

Left with that alternative, Marianne shook her head quickly and sat down on the bank. As if he sensed her shyness, Nick took a step back and looked away while she slipped off her shoes and rolled her thin cotton stockings over her knees, down her calves and ankles, and off the tip of her toes.

"I'm ready," she said meekly.

"Okay, hold on." Nick moved to her side again, reaching for her hand and eyeing her clothing. "You'll have to hold your skirt up—no use being shy now—or it'll drag you. Put it like it was earlier today."

Marianne had hoped he had forgotten that, but she followed his order nevertheless, glad that he seemed to be studying the rushing current instead of her goose-bumped flesh. She clasped his hand tightly when he stepped into the stream, then plunged in behind him.

"Oh! It's freezing!" Her feet felt as if she'd just stepped into a snowbank, and the swirling water wrapped around her ankles with icy fingers. The force of the channel was stronger than she had anticipated, and it was all she could do to keep her already-numb feet planted where they were. To lift one forward, only to sink it further into the water, was the last thing she wanted to do.

"Come on," Nick shouted over the sound of the rushing creek. He tugged gently on her hand. "What's wrong?"

"It's too cold!"

"All the more reason to hurry. Think how good you'll feel once we're out."

Marianne couldn't help laughing at his distorted logic, and after watching his feet carefully so that she could place hers in exactly the same spots, she soon found that they were nearing the bank in front of the cabin. Nick bounded out, hauling her up behind him as he stamped his feet in what looked like some kind of primitive dance. Again, she followed his lead.

"You were right," she laughingly exclaimed. "It feels *wonderful* out here. But now I don't want to go back!"

For just a split second, the expression on Nick's face altered, and she thought she saw the hint of a question buried beneath the yearning in his eyes. Just as fast, however, his grin returned, and the fleeting moment was gone, swept away like a wisp of cloud on a windy sky.

"You will soon enough," he said teasingly. "The only food in there is a three-year-old stock of canned beans."

Marianne watched as he moved to the door, easily prying the cross-board loose with a stick of firewood from the pile under the window. Hinges creaked as he shoved the door open, and dust particles sparkled in the waning sunlight like tiny stars.

"It's not much," Nick apologized, suddenly wondering why he'd brought her here. There was nothing to see, nothing to do except dredge up old memories that hid in the corners like cobwebs. Or maybe, he thought, the cobwebs and the memories had seen their final day.

As if she had read his mind, he watched Marianne enter the cabin ahead of him, her eyes wide with curiosity, her lips perched on the edge of a smile.

"It's lovely!" she cried, as soon as her eyes adjusted to the dim light inside. Despite the dust and musty scent of disuse, the main room was neat and orderly. Blue stoneware dishes were displayed prettily on a shelf, and curtains that had once matched, but were now bleached nearly white by time, hung at the shuttered windows. A sturdy table and four chairs occupied the center of the plank floor, and various shelves and cabinets of carved wood adorned every wall except the one filled by the stone fireplace. A closed door on the opposite side beckoned to her.

"Two rooms?" she asked, stepping forward eagerly to throw the door wide. A large, four-poster bed nearly filled the smaller room, but it wasn't until Marianne went all the way in that she saw that there was one more piece of furniture squeezed into the corner. A rosewood vanity table, with a mirror hung over it, hugged one wall. Sitting before it was a small tufted stool, covered with dust and looking somewhat forlorn.

"Who . . . ?" Marianne spun around, only to find that Nick had not followed her into the bedroom. Feeling slightly sheepish, as if she'd been caught eavesdropping, or worse, she slipped back out into the main room. Nick was prying the nails out of the shutters and opening the windows.

"This is what I wanted you to see," he explained, dropping the nails into an empty mug as he turned around.

Moving to the window, Marianne gasped out loud when she saw what he meant. The view, even in a land where stunning vistas were an everyday occurrence, was breathtaking. She could see now that behind the cabin the ground sloped down abruptly, and a natural break in the tree line afforded an unimpeded perspective of the valley below. In the distance, Puget Sound sparkled a deep, turquoise blue, and behind it the snow-capped Olympic Mountains blended with the sky.

Nick smiled as she crossed her arms and leaned against the chest-high windowsill. Stepping right behind her, he placed his hands against the frame on either side of her head. His cheek brushed against her hair, but she was too entranced by the scene below to pay any attention. He, however, had looked out this particular window hundreds of times, and so it was difficult to keep his attention on the valley when she stood so close within his arms. To make matters worse, the fresh air from outside mixed with the scent of her to swirl through his brain, and it was a long moment before he could speak again. "Beautiful," he managed to murmur.

"Oh, it is, Nick. It is!" Not quite as oblivious to his nearness as she appeared, Marianne struggled to keep her voice from quivering. "I've never seen anything so beautiful. The water is so pretty, and look!" She pointed a little to the left, leaning over so Nick could bend forward to see. "There's a ship. You can just make out the sails!"

Under normal circumstances, he would have enjoyed her exuberance, but just now it was making his chest ache to stand so close without touching her. Would she be frightened, he wondered, if he spun her around now to slake his thirst with her tempting lips?

Marianne felt his breath hot against her temple, and

though she wanted, more than anything else, to turn into his embrace, she knew there could be no good end to it. "This cabin was yours?" she asked softly. "How could you bear to leave it?"

Nick did draw back from her then, but only enough to suck a mouthful of air into his lungs. Hadn't this been what he wanted to hear? Wasn't this the purpose behind bringing her to this place? To compare?

Then why, now that he knew what was in her heart, was he so reluctant to reveal his?

"I built this shortly after I took over the mill," he said slowly. "I wanted a place to get away from the rest of the crew once in a while, and this was faster than going back to town every night. You're right about it being hard to leave. At one time I thought I could live here forever." He didn't mention the bitterness associated with his memory of this place, because he had once been foolish enough to believe Alicia would be happy with him in this cabin.

Marianne detected the odd note in his voice, and incorrectly attributed it to sadness. Of course the dressing table in the bedroom had not been his, she realized now. This cabin had once been his home, and now that the wife with whom he'd shared it was gone, returning here was painful. Her shoulders sagged just a little, and she turned to face him.

"It must be hard for you," she offered hesitantly. "To remember those times, I mean."

Shrugging, Nick touched her face with one finger, tracing the pattern of light that silhouetted her smooth cheek. "That was all a long time ago. I never think about it."

Her breath caught in her throat as he continued to run his forefinger up and down the side of her face, from her hairline to the tender skin under her chin. Trapped by his lean form, with only the tiny window behind her, she could not move away from him. *As if she wanted to!*

The traitorous thought made her heartbeat quicken, and with it came a sense of wonder that she should feel so. The excitement she had once justified to herself as a healthy reaction to an obviously attractive man had blown into something far more compelling—and dangerous.

Nick watched the doubt flicker through her eyes, but he was beyond heeding all the reasons why he should not press her. He let his hand fall to the base of her neck, his thumb resting against the hollow of her throat. For some reason, the feel of her pulse beating crazily beneath his fingers nearly drove him wild. "Mary," he whispered, his voice hoarse with wanting. "You're far too lovely for such an ordinary name."

For one dizzy moment, Marianne wondered if he actually knew how little she *deserved* even that name, but there was no question or accusation in his darkening eyes—only passion. "What . . . what would you call me?" she stammered inanely, simply to keep from embarrassing herself by kissing him before he kissed her.

My love was the first thing that came to Nick's mind, but he let it slip away before mouthing the words. "Beautiful," he said instead. "The most beautiful thing I've ever seen."

He lowered his head, tasting her lips as if they were a delicate nectar, meant to be savored and enjoyed for a very long time. Beneath his hands, he could feel the vibrations as she trembled, and yet moved subtly toward him.

So gentle. His touch was so very gentle that she couldn't help a little inward sigh of pleasure. She wound her hands upward over him, letting her fingertips absorb the sensations: his coarsely woven shirt, the body heat seeping through it, the sleek hotness of the skin on his chest. And then, when the sweet pressure on her mouth was no longer enough, there were the parted lips, the warmth and moistness of his tongue, and the joining with hers that changed the kiss altogether.

Nick felt the change too, felt how it carried them both from a tentative beginning through a passage of sorts, and beyond to where neither had the desire, or the will, to resist. He deepened the kiss to something fierce and demanding and hard; she wrapped her arms around his neck, moaning low in her throat.

He couldn't hold her tight enough. There was a mindlessness to her response, one that frightened her nearly as much as it made her want it never to end. She let her head fall back as he moved his lips down over her throat, and for just an instant she wondered if this was what it would be like to touch heaven. Then his hand closed over her breast, gently, more firmly, and she knew this wasn't even close.

A thousand sensations pounded within her, each one desperate to be set free, to be thrilled to. A hundred emotions demanded to be released. But in the end, the one that won out was the one that had dominated her so well lately—uncertainty. Adam Pemberton had seen to that.

"Nick, I . . . Nick, please stop."

It wasn't so much the words that penetrated the fog of his desire as the way her body stiffened against him, as though she found his touch bearable only if she turned into wood.

In a sense, that was true, for it took all of her resolve to force her limbs not to mold themselves back to his warmth. She pressed her eyelids together tightly, willing herself to stop trembling, willing him to stop making her tremble. And when, at last, he did release her, she nearly sobbed with relief.

Nick was stunned by the way his own hands were shaking, and by the way his frustration turned, not to anger, but to tenderness when he saw her eyes squeezed shut like a child's who is afraid of the night. He raised his hands to within a hairsbreadth of her shoulders, for the first time in his life unsure whether or not a woman needed touching. Usually, he could tell, but this time was different. *She* was different.

"It's . . . it's all right," he finally said, his voice scratchy and dry. "I didn't mean to scare you."

Marianne's eyes flew open. Her heart wrenched at the sound of his apology, an apology both unnecessary and unasked for. "Oh, Nick," she whispered achingly. "I'm not afraid of you."

There was nothing in his face but growing confusion. "Then what?" He dropped his hands to his sides.

"I'm afraid . . . afraid of the way you make me feel. I never felt this way before. No one ever told me about . . ."

Her voice had dropped to a whisper, seductive in its innocence. Once before he'd wondered at her inexperience, despite a marriage that had lasted over a year. Now he doubted she had the vaguest idea what marriage was. "Mary," he began gently, curling his fingers beneath her chin to tip her head upward. "In one of your letters you told me you had conceived a child, and that you had miscarried. Is that true?"

Marianne chewed on her lower lip, torn between telling him the truth and perpetuating the lie. She chose a course somewhere in between.

Shaking her head slightly, she lowered her eyes. "N-no. Not . . . not everything in those letters is true about me."

"Then your marriage was in name only?" Nick didn't wait for an answer before drawing her into his arms and pressing her head against his chest. "No wonder you were reluctant to marry me," he chuckled. "And here I was, planning to ask you to forgo the one-month stipulation, and you haven't had time to get used to the idea of marriage, let alone me. But don't worry, my darling," he said, brushing his lips against her temple. "I'll give you all the time you need."

"You mean . . . you mean you want to marry me, anyway?" Marianne didn't know which surprised her more, his reaction to what must have been a disappointing revelation, or hers to the idea that what was in Mary Cooper's letters might not be as important to him as what had passed between them now.

"That's exactly what I mean," Nick said, turning her face so that he could see full into her eyes. "I knew from the minute you got here that you weren't what you claimed."

"I'm sorry, Nick."

"Don't be. I should have known better. What I wanted was a woman who knew just what to expect, and wouldn't expect too much. After Alicia . . ." He paused, frowning. "After Alicia, I wanted a woman who had always had to fend for herself, so she would know the value of hard work. I wanted one who would be content to be my partner, my help-mate, but who would never threaten my heart, a woman who judged her own worth by more than the wealth of her husband, so I would never feel that she was dependent on me alone to survive, and therefore I would never be dependent upon her. Do you understand what I'm saying?"

Marianne nodded hesitantly.

"You're not that woman, lovely Mary."

Regret stabbed at her with a sharp thrust, but she managed to smile crookedly. "No, I'm not."

His lips touched hers with an infinite sweetness that brought tears to her eyes. Lifting his head a fraction of an inch, he murmured, "You're not that woman, but you *are* the one I want."

Chapter 12

The frame of the thin metal bed rattled ominously, but neither of its occupants were of a mind to notice that it was on the verge of collapse. The woman was glad for the rhythmic squeaks and groans that came from the over-stressed structure; they were the only sounds that reminded her she was not alone in the room overlooking New York Harbor. The man never heard them at all, for his concentration was centered on pounding all his considerable frustration into the willing body beneath him.

Velma, though she preferred to be called Violet because she had once been told the name conjured images of sweet-smelling flowers, lifted her legs higher, hoping to hurry her visitor along, but the action only caused him to grunt angrily. Velma sighed indifferently. It would take even longer now.

After several minutes, as usually happened when her body was subjected to such relentless, yet totally unstimulating use, her mind began to roam in other directions.

She wondered, for example, how much money he was carrying with him tonight, and how much of it would find its way to her when he was finished. She also wondered, as indifferently as she did everything, if tonight's activities would include a beating. She thought about the possibility. On one hand, he was known among the other girls for his brutal proclivities, and Velma had experienced true terror beneath his cruel fists on other occasions. On the other hand, she'd always gotten over the fear, the cuts and bruises had healed eventually, and right now she could really use the extra money. It didn't, she decided matter-of-factly, make much difference to her.

By now, the man's breathing had turned harsh, his face contorted into an expression bordering on pain. Velma knew he didn't like her to look at him—didn't want her, in fact, to make her presence known in any way—but she couldn't resist watching the way his lips twisted into a demonic grin at the moment of his release.

And then, as he always did just an instant before withdrawal, his unfocused gaze rested on the cracked wall behind the bed and he whispered, "Goddamn you, Julia."

Velma didn't know who this Julia was, but it didn't matter. She'd been called many names by many men, and at least Julia had a pretty ring to it. Kind of classy, she thought, already testing the sound of it on her dry lips. Maybe it'd be better than Violet, even.

"Julia," she said out loud, forgetting for a moment that he was there yet, though his inert form still weighed heavy upon her body. She sucked in a breath, hoping he hadn't heard, or was at least too spent to care. She felt his muscles tense, however, and realized at once that luck would not be with her this night.

"What did you say?" His voice had the effect of an ax-head slicing through the air.

Velma laughed uneasily. "I didn't say nothin'. Jest talkin' to myself. Don't pay me no mind."

"Perhaps that's exactly what I should do. If I don't *pay* you, maybe you'll learn to keep your mouth shut."

There were many forms of abuse that, over the years, Velma had forced herself to take. She'd been pistol-whipped, tied up, and even endured having her flesh burned with the hot end of a cigar, but always, *always*, she had been paid for her time. "Oh no, you don't," she sputtered, heedless of the warning glitter in his eyes. She wriggled sideways, slipping out from under him and levering herself up on one elbow. "You gotta lay your money out, jest like every other fella.

You can't start makin' up rules afterward. You got what you want—"

Her indignation grew limp as she glanced over at his face. Something was there, or maybe it was something that was lacking. Velma didn't know. She only knew that the fear was coming on strong in her gut, and she didn't like the way he was staring at her like . . . like she was something he scraped off his shoe.

"Aw, come on," she cajoled, trying to keep the anxiety from making her throat tighten up. "It ain't worth gettin' worked up about. How's 'bout I do ya once more. On the house." Her hand crept over his thigh, closing on him. She might not understand the minds of men, and this one, to be sure, was even harder than most, but there was one part of a man Velma understood very well.

"There, now," she said soothingly, trying to hide her surprise when he surged in her hand. Since it usually took him nearly an hour to reach his climax, and sometimes never, she was amazed, now, that what she was doing to him instigated such a complete recovery. "You like that?" she said, her face relaxing into a smile as he leaned back against the bed frame.

His eyes narrowed to pale slits, causing her image, bent intently over her task, to blur and change shape. No longer was the woman above him redheaded and hard-looking. Instead, her hair was a glistening spun-gold, her features delicate, refined, and maddeningly aloof. He groaned, the desire to wipe that expression of disdain from her eyes swelling inside him like a force from Hell, unspeakable, and utterly unstoppable. In a distant portion of his brain, he knew that what he was about to do was wrong, would get him into deeper trouble, but there was no way now to turn back the tide of hatred that drove him onward.

Velma had not noticed when his hands left his sides to creep slowly over her breasts, but now that they rested on her shoulders, his fingers tickling the back of her neck and his thumbs pressing lightly against her collarbone, she risked a glance at his face. What she saw there made her freeze.

"Don't stop," he ordered hoarsely. "Don't stop, Julia."

Automatically, Velma obeyed, but her fright had turned to sheer panic, and her mind, normally slow, lighted on the truth with sickening speed.

His fingers grew tighter, his thumbs having moved to the center of her throat. Velma began to resist, her flabby muscles straining uselessly to escape his grasp. Ironically, the more she struggled, the more her hands continued to work at him, clutching, pulling, squeezing, bringing him to the edge at the same moment that consciousness started slipping away from her.

"Good-bye, Julia," he whispered.

Velma's eyes flew open one last time, and her final thought was to wonder how someone so rich and handsome could be so insane.

Chapter *13*

"I want to leave tomorrow." Marianne tilted up her chin, appearing for all the world as if she knew where she might go. Two days had passed since the incident at the cabin—she refused to look at it any way other than clinically—and she'd had plenty of time to let the cold voice of reason snuff out any lingering flames of passion. "I thought it only fair that I tell you now, before this goes any further."

If only . . . She sighed disconsolately, frowning at her reflection. If only she could maintain the same degree of determination when she repeated the words to Nick. The woman who peered back at her from the mirror *looked* as if she meant what she said. She stood with her shoulders thrown back and her spine straight as a pine log, her head lifted high. Even the healthy color in her cheeks and sparkling clear eyes seemed to command more respect than her counterpart of a few weeks ago. That pale, sickly creature was gone now, and in her place was a woman of strength and courage . . . she wished.

Why did I ever think it would work? Marianne thought miserably, remembering her embarrassment and the way Nick had looked at the mill when he first realized she'd been testing him, amused and detached, yet unable to hide the puzzlement. It was a wonder he hadn't been livid, but then, that was the one thing she had learned about Nicholas Fortune. He got angry only over things that were important to him, not over what he saw as feminine foolishness, and certainly not over her.

So she would leave. No more depending on Elizabeth's advice, no more pretending that they were *his* feelings she was trying to protect. Tonight, after dinner, she would tell him of her decision. When he protested, she would cite the agreement he'd made with Mary Cooper, the one allowing either of them to call off the engagement. She would ask him only for a job reference, taking with her nothing but the clothes she wore, and even for those she would reimburse him out of her first wages.

And if he was disappointed, she reminded herself, it would only be because of the delay involved in finding another suitable bride. He might think of her as a callow, unfeeling girl to whisk away for no apparent reason, but better that than have him learn the truth; that she'd fallen in love with him, so utterly, completely in love with him that she'd nearly forgotten that happiness was something she could never have.

At least not as Nick Fortune's lady.

She steeled herself, not only against his inevitable resistance, which she anticipated, but also against the dull ache of loss that already throbbed deep in her chest, threatening to crumble her into a thousand tiny slivers if she didn't get out of here—out of this house and out of this town—as soon as possible.

With a resolute nod to the stranger in the mirror, Marianne sighed and went downstairs.

As it turned out, the opportunity to confront Nick did not come that night, or even the next. The mill opening was scheduled for that week, and Nick was spending many hours each day supervising the extra crews hired to ready the mill for its debut. Once in a while he appeared for an occasional meal, looking exhausted and happy, but Claire and Elizabeth were present at those times, preventing Marianne from speaking.

On the morning of the big day, Marianne spent an inordinate amount of time choosing an outfit, settling

finally on a dress of washed rose. It fit her as perfectly
as all the others, shaping her silhouette from her full
breasts to the curve of her hips, though its high, ruf-
fled neck and leg-o'-mutton sleeves were modest
enough. The back of the skirt was gathered into a
stylish bustle, falling into a cascade of flounces that
swayed saucily behind her as she practiced walking in
front of the mirror. She wasn't used to wearing the
newer, tighter skirts, for the seamstress Uncle Matthew had commissioned always steered her toward a
more youthful, less enticing style, and Marianne had
never found reason to protest. Now, however, she was
glad for the aura of maturity the latest fashion provided. Her hair was gathered into an intricate knot at
the back of her head, providing the ideal resting place
for the straw bonnet Millie Knowles had fussed over,
insisting that its rose silk flowers made it perfect for
this dress. Studying her reflection critically, Marianne
was forced to agree. The hat *did* provide a final,
dignified touch. Today, of all days, she didn't want to
appear young and frivolous.

Marianne joined Claire and Elizabeth in the drawing room, where they waited for Marcus, who had
offered to escort them to the festivities. Nick had been
at the mill since daybreak, having taken a change of
clothing with him.

"Here he is now," Elizabeth exclaimed from the
window where she watched for Marcus's carriage, unable to keep the sound of childish excitement from her
voice, though she had obviously taken great pains to
dress like a proper young lady. She wore a dress of
buttercup yellow, trimmed with white lawn ruffles that
matched her white gloves. Her hair was pulled back
from her forehead, and only a few wild curls escaped
to fly around her face. "Oh, good," she clapped,
"Kathleen's with him."

Marianne found Marcus's wife completely charming
and Marcus, too, was as cheerful as always, though
Marianne noted with a smile that he'd dropped his
flirtatious manner toward *her* in Kathleen's presence—

and Nick's absence—settling instead for a more general gallantry.

"And Nick thinks *he's* on top of the world today," Marcus gloated as he headed the crowded open carriage toward town. "I'll wager no one'll look twice at that mill of his after I pull up with this bevy of beauties. Ladies, what d'ya say we just ride on all the way to 'Frisco? I've always had the urge to be the envy of the West Coast."

"Get on with you, lad," Claire responded gaily. "Isn't is enough that you're already the envy of Tacoma with your beautiful wife? Sure, and you're as bad as Nick, what with always wantin' more than ye've got."

The remainder of the trip passed in much the same way, though for all her attempt at cheeriness, Claire's words seemed to echo over and over in Marianne's mind. Even his own mother recognized that Nick would never be satisfied with anything but the best, and Marianne knew herself to be a poor substitute for Alicia. To make matters worse, not only was she not Alicia, she wasn't the kind of woman he would have chosen as a second wife!

His words came back to her, the remembered sound of them sending her blood skittering through her veins. *You're the woman I want*, he'd said. But did that mean he wanted her love?

Marianne blinked hard, turning her head away from the other occupants of the carriage so no one would notice the tears pooling in her eyes. It would be easiest, she realized, to believe that. In the weeks to come—*years*, she corrected silently—when the pain of leaving was at its most fierce, she could console herself with the knowledge that she wouldn't have been completely happy with Nick anyway, knowing that he could never love her as thoroughly as she loved him. And he, in the end, wouldn't be happy with her, once he learned that her feelings for him went far beyond the limits he had set on his own emotions.

With that idea firmly entrenched in her thoughts, Marianne allowed herself to speculate on the notion she had forbidden herself to consider before. How long, she wondered, could she continue to use Mary Cooper's identity as her own? Every so often, in the days since the train wreck, an unbidden thought would slip into her mind, trilling beneath the surface of her consciousness with a seductive whisper. *Who would know?* it had taunted her. But each time she had thrust it away, unwilling to acknowledge how much she wished she could let herself heed its siren call.

She had believed the reason was because she couldn't bear to continue lying to Nick, because she hated to take advantage of Claire, but now, when her own decision had ruled out those possibilities, she found she was no more inclined to continue the charade than she had been before. She felt like a thief, except that most thieves stole only material possessions, which were easily replaced. How could one ever recover a lost name? Would she run the risk that one day she might stop thinking of herself as Marianne Blakemore, that the person she had once been would cease to exist?

Her thoughts turned back to when—was it only last week?—she had told Nick how important it was that the orphaned children have something to call their own. For Marianne, it had always been the fact that she knew who she was; that and the vague memories of her parents that remained with her throughout the years. How could she allow her own name to be defiled by the likes of Adam Pemberton? How could she stand still for his taking the one legacy that remained of the people she loved?

But, an inner voice echoed hollowly, *how can you stop him*?

The town of Tacoma had turned out in full regalia for the celebration of Nicholas Fortune's latest venture, and it was apparent from the start that most folks held to the belief that as long as there were trees on the mountains, there was always room for one more sawmill.

Marianne was slightly overwhelmed by the boisterous crowds, but since goodwill was the general feeling, she soon found she was actually enjoying herself. Now she knew why Nick had worked so hard to open the mill on this particular day. She wasn't sure which the people were more excited about, celebrating the Fourth of July in their annual festivities, or christening Tacoma's newest business, but since it didn't seem to matter to most folks, Marianne refused to spend any time wondering.

Besides, it was hard to think about much of anything once she saw Nick.

Despite the condition of the roads—blessedly dry, for once, but teeming with people on their way to the mill—Marcus managed to negotiate the carriage right up to the same office steps where Marianne had first wrestled with the enormity of Nick's accomplishment. Even filled with jubilant townsfolk, the lumberyard looked no less impressive, the huge buildings, no less noble. Pride for Nick filled her chest with a sweet ache.

"My, he certainly looks happy today," Kathleen said.

He was standing on the wooden platform at the base of the stairs, his eyes scanning the crowd narrowly even as he laughed and joked with the men who surrounded him. He looked splendid in a suit of charcoal gray, exquisitely tailored so that it emphasized his broad shoulders without adding bulk, tapering over his narrow hips in an elegant line. Marianne could hardly tear her eyes from him long enough to answer Kathleen with an incoherent murmur.

When Nick spotted the carriage—not a difficult thing with Elizabeth waving wildly and Marcus hallooing loud enough to carry over the buzz of the crowd—his intense gaze ignored the members of his family, searching instead for a pair of eyes blue enough to rival the ocean waves. And when they looked up to meet his, he felt one more link from the past fall away from the chains that bound his heart.

"She's a beaut, Nick. Never saw nothin' like her."

At his side, Lou Spencer's voice was uncommonly

hushed and filled with awe. Nick's eyes never moved as he acknowledged his friend's statement. "Me neither, Lou."

It took only a second for Spencer to realize they weren't talking about the same thing. His eyes rolled once in mock disparity, then he cackled out loud, slapping Nick soundly between the shoulder blades. "I *meant* the mill."

By the time Nick woke up to the fact that he'd completely missed the point of this conversation, Lou Spencer was already ambling away, his shoulders shaking with suppressed mirth as he hiked his beltless trousers higher up over his skinny frame. Nick was treated to one final glimpse of Spencer's grinning face as the man turned once, shaking his head before disappearing into the gathering crowd. A sheepish grin of his own tugged at Nick's mouth as he made his way toward Marcus's carriage.

"Have we missed anything?" Elizabeth asked, her glance darting around anxiously as Nick helped her down first.

"Not yet." Nick lifted Claire from the carriage. "The two representatives from the governor's office haven't arrived. Horace is waiting for them at the station. We won't be starting up for another hour at least."

"Then may I look for Colleen, Mother? She said they'd be here early. Her cousin Lawrence is visiting from Portland."

Claire paused for a moment, considering. "All right. But stay with the Delaneys so we know where to find you when it's time to leave."

Marianne saw Nick's mouth turn up at the corners, but he refrained from commenting as Elizabeth turned on her heel. Her yellow dress was like a bright splash of color threading among the more sedate hues around her, but it was soon swallowed up as she made her way through the flood of people.

They watched her go, Nick shaking his head. "Lawrence?"

"Now if you young folks'll excuse me," Claire spoke

up, "I think I'll just make sure that Sue Kim got those pies down here in one piece this morning. I'll meet you back here in an hour."

Marcus, having tied the horses to the railing, lifted Kathleen from the carriage and winked broadly. "I've a mind to check out those pies, myself. I have a feeling," he chucked Kathleen under her chin, "that there's an apple-cinnamon pie with my name on it. See you two later."

"We can walk around a bit, too," Nick offered softly, his hands lingering at Marianne's waist after he'd set her lightly on the ground. "There's not much left to do here for a while."

"But . . . but I told Ruth I'd help her with the children," she stammered, her nerves screaming wildly at the thought of spending the next few hours at his side.

Nick, however, had already drawn her hand through the crook of his arm, holding it there with a steady pressure from his strong fingers. "I know. But she's not expecting you to meet up with them until after the ceremony. We have plenty of time."

She didn't even think to ask how he knew, only wondered at the way her heart flip-flopped at the thought that he'd made it a point to find out. Now, walking beside him, she realized how much she'd missed him in the past few days, and not just because she'd been anxious to tell him of her plans to leave. She was inordinately aware of him, her breasts tingling each time his arm brushed against her side. Her fingers ached to smooth down the sleeve of his jacket, to inch past the crisp whiteness of his starched cuff, to spread along the back of his hand, seeking out the spaces between his own fingers and clasp them tight. She could smell the scent of his soap, mixed with the faint tang of sawdust, and could see the weathered texture of his face when he leaned closer to her as they walked.

Dozens of booths lined the street, selling a wide variety of trinkets and goodies. Every civic organization, every church, every sewing circle in town had something to offer, but Marianne was oblivious to them all.

Nick, too, could hardly keep himself from stopping in mid-pace to kiss her thoroughly, as he'd been wanting to do ever since that day in the cabin. His mouth nearly touched her ear each time he bent to speak, and it was all he could do not to flick the shell-like perfection with the tip of his tongue, to press his face against the sweet softness of her hair. His hands itched to frame her face; he wanted to feel her satin cheeks beneath his fingertips, to push the pins from her hair as he cupped her head gently. He wanted to see her lips tremble with anticipation, waiting for the touch and the taste that would make her longing match his.

Instead, Nick pointed out with pretended interest, in a voice that was oddly pitched, a nondescript building owned by a man he did not know.

Marianne barely heard what he was saying. She didn't really care *what* he was saying.

She only knew that she loved him, and that she would never, *ever*, love this way again.

Less than twenty paces behind them, Rhys Hartley followed, alternately cursing and blessing the crowd that made it difficult for him to maneuver, yet wrapped him in its protective cloak more thoroughly than even darkness could. Much had happened in two weeks; unfortunately, the complete healing of his leg was not one of them. He hobbled about on a single crutch, thankfully without pain, but without much speed, either.

Looking up just in time to see Nicholas Fortune and his beautiful companion stop in front of another booth, Rhys halted in mid-step, teetering awkwardly before he regained his balance. Damn! he muttered beneath his breath. One of these times he was going to fall flat on his ass, and then so much for remaining unobtrusive. He eyed his prey with a speculative glare, then moved surreptitiously to a spot behind them, close enough to see what they were doing.

He was almost surprised—at least as much as he'd

ever been surprised in this business—by the change in Marianne Blakemore. And it wasn't just the clothes, he thought, though his admiring scrutiny swept her from head to toe. She'd gained a few pounds over the weeks since he'd seen her on the train, and her face was now soft with radiant health, no longer the gaunt, frightened mask she had worn then.

At Fortune's direction, Marianne began to move toward a booth laden with handmade quilts. For a moment, Rhys was torn between following her or remaining hidden, but it turned out he needn't have worried over the choice. As soon as the girl stepped away, Nick Fortune pointed to an object on the vendor's table. Money changed hands rapidly, though whatever it was he had purchased, Fortune obviously was not taking it with him now. Rhys was soon treated to a view of his quarry's back once again.

An hour later, Rhys was more than ready to admit that he was exhausted. It was not without a sense of relief that he realized Nick Fortune had circled the area of the festivities, and was now making his way back toward the mill. Edging his way through the crowd, Rhys found himself a spot on one of the many benches that had been set up along the waterfront and stretched his aching leg in front of him. From here, he could spy on them easily, with plenty of opportunity to consider his next move.

In truth, that shouldn't have been one of his concerns. Normally, his instructions were fairly clear, with little room for variation. This time, by his own choice, he was on his own. The first thing he had done, once he was up and around after the crash, was to wire his employer with news of the untimely death of Marianne Blakemore. Two factors had made him decide not to correct his mistake after spotting her outside Millie Knowles's Dress Shop. One was the knowledge that, as far as his employer was concerned, the papers she'd stolen were far more valuable than the woman. The other was fear that he would be removed from the case if he revealed the extent of his error.

Rhys Hartley had never once failed in the undertak-

ing of any job, and he was damned if he would start
now.

The pitch of the crowd had begun to rise, signalling
the start of the formal opening. Several people gathered at the bottom of the stairs near Nicholas Fortune.
Rhys recognized a few of them. Horace Squiggs, the
territorial marshal, was shaking hands with a short,
balding man in a dark suit and vest. *Ira James*, Rhys
recalled. *Banker.*

For a short while, Marianne was the only female
among the gathering of men, but she was soon joined
by an older woman who Rhys correctly placed as
Fortune's mother. Even from this distance, the com-
radeship between the two women was apparent as
they spoke quietly to one another. They, like everyone else, waited expectantly for Nicholas Fortune to
call for silence.

It hadn't taken her long, Rhys thought dryly, to fit
right in. But then, she'd been raised to wealth and
prestige that surpassed anything this backwoods logging town could even imagine. He almost sneered at
the look that passed between her and Nicholas Fortune before the man stepped to the rail. For just a
second, Rhys was tempted to jump up right then and
there, tempted to give these folks a jolt they'd be
talking about for the next twenty years.

But he didn't.

Experience won out, and despite the gnawing in his
gut that could only be described as a combination of
frustration and jealousy, Rhys remained seated, his
jaw clenched in silence.

The ledgers came first, he reminded himself. And
just now, Marianne Blakemore was sittin' too pretty
to give them up easily. Somehow, he'd have to bring
her down, but not so fast that she'd spook and run.

It would be a delicate thing, Rhys Hartley cautioned
himself. But it was one part of this job he would
thoroughly enjoy.

The sun had almost reached the end of its slow
descent behind the Olympic Mountains, but the town

of Tacoma was still wide-awake. Gaily colored paper lanterns kept the impending darkness at bay; laughter and loud music rose and fell, a bright contrast to the sound of the wind soughing through the treetops. By day, the townspeople had teemed with excitement. By night, that excitement had evolved into a feverish giddiness that swept everyone into its swirling wake.

Balanced precariously upon a hitching rail with her feet braced against the lower rung, Marianne clapped in time with the others, completely caught up in the festive spirit. A reel was in progress, with Nick and Elizabeth leading the long row of dancers as they skipped from one end of the town square to the other. She had a hard time following their progress, for they all ducked and swayed and twirled so fast they were soon little more than a blur of flashing petticoats and checkered shirts.

Though she had pleaded for a rest just a few minutes before, Marianne watched the dancers enviously, eager to rejoin them for another lesson. She couldn't remember when she'd had such fun. The dances she'd attended back East had been *nothing* like this!

Lessons with New York's finest ballroom instructor couldn't have prepared her for the apparent chaos of a square dance. It had taken all Nick's teasing persuasion, plus a rather firm grip on her elbow, to get her to join in, but once she finished that first, breathless round, she found that all her initial doubts had disappeared. Nick guided her expertly through the steps, and the dance didn't seem nearly as disorganized, once she became familiar with a few of the basic calls.

Not that anyone would have cared if she had skipped backward and stepped on each and every toe in the town.

After the reel had come to a rollicking finish, the musicians paused for a moment, then started up again with the lilting strains of a waltz. Marianne was surprised but pleased with the restful change, though it proved to be a signal to most of the dancers to break for refreshments. Only a few couples continued to sway to the romantic melody.

"May I have this dance?"

She lifted her gaze to Nick's, shivering lightly as he laid his hand over hers where it rested upon a wooden post. His strong fingers curved around her wrist, lifting it until her palm fit snugly within his. Even now, she could feel her treacherous emotions swell as his gray eyes twinkled warmly, his crooked smile driving straight to her heart.

Marianne swallowed hard. "You mean, waltz?"

"Don't you think I know how?"

Nick's voice was gently teasing, but she wondered if there wasn't just a trace of impatience hiding behind the humor. "I didn't mean—"

He tugged at her hand, urging her to her feet. "We're not *all* barbarians, you know. Some of us even understand what a civilized pastime dancing can be."

But when he stood so close to her, his hand wrapped around the curve of her waist, the other hand lightly cupping her own, Marianne's heart pounded in anything but a civilized manner. The only other time she'd been this close to him, he'd been kissing her until she was dizzy and oblivious to all but his lips. Now she was aware of every nuance of sensation: the rough texture of his jaw, now lightly shadowed with whiskers, the strength of his muscled shoulder beneath her arm, the warmth of his fingers as they tightened around hers. He danced with an easy grace that belied his power, yet she knew the tiny flutter in her stomach to be one of apprehension.

She forced herself to relax, to let her troubled thoughts float through the night air like the musical notes that circled and dipped and then spun away. Wasn't that what she'd vowed to do anyway? To enjoy one last day, and now this final night? Surrendering herself to the magic she felt only when in his arms, Marianne let her mind drift over the events of the day.

The mill opening had been a complete success. She'd expected to be uncomfortable so near the center of attention, and yet it had seemed natural to take her place at Nick's side, sharing his pride when he threw the switch that brought the giant saw roaring to life.

They'd laughed, along with everyone else, when the sawdust flew high, baptizing them all with a shower of fine, yellow dust.

Later, when Nick was occupied with demonstrating to the other men some of his more innovative additions to the mill, she had searched for Ruth Lyons, finding the woman attempting to spirit her charges away from the booth selling homemade taffy. Willingly, Marianne had helped out with the group of youngsters, watching them enjoy the rare opportunity to explore the town. She remembered all too well that sense of freedom, for it had truly come to her only since she'd left New York.

So why, she chided herself, *do you want to risk that freedom by going back?*

It was a question that had no answer, other than the belief that she would never be completely satisfied until the truth was known, and that she would never feel utterly safe until Adam Pemberton was behind bars. Only then could she return to where her heart would remain, always.

But could she? Searching Nick's face as he gazed down at her with a tender expression, Marianne felt suddenly desolate. If she left him now, he would never welcome her back. Not as Mary Cooper, not as Marianne Blakemore. She might tell him the truth before she went, for she trusted him enough now to realize he would never turn her over to the law, but could she stand to see the doubt, the suspicion, the *betrayal* that would turn his eyes to shards of steel?

Tears stung, forcing her to lower her head, and she concentrated her gaze on the strong column of his throat, bared now that the formalities were over. *No*, she moaned inwardly, longing to lay her cheek against the warm flesh, *I can't tell him yet.*

She could only cherish the rare moments she had now, to press them into the pages of her memory like flowers, hoping that in the uncertain times to come she could draw strength from their sweet fragrance.

Nick's hand at her waist tightened imperceptibly, and she raised her eyes once again, compelled by the dark hunger that burned deep in his. It called to her, and she felt herself answer with a part of her soul that had never been touched, but now longed to be awakened before it was too late.

Tonight she would not allow the past or the future to cast their shadows on the present. There was magic here, and whether it was a magic born of desperation, or a magic born of love, she didn't intend to let it slip away.

Tomorrow would come soon enough.

Chapter 14

Overhead, the tops of the trees were dancing to the wind's incessant tune, their branches outlined in silver from the moon's pale glow. The breeze had picked up slightly, bringing with it the smell and feel of the sea, or maybe it was just that this was the only time he stopped long enough to savor the tangy air.

This was Nick's favorite time, after the sun was gone and the work done, the household quiet. He leaned back and stretched his legs, adjusting their position high on the back porch railing. Each night, long after his mother had retired for the evening, he claimed Claire's rocker and sat in this spot, contemplating life as he smoked his one and only cigar of the day. It was a habit that had its beginnings during his marriage, on the nights when Alicia barred him from her room, and had continued into the years when his after-hours were spent in town, many times at Katey Muldoon's, and he'd needed the fresh air to clear his head before lying down to sleep. Now it was simply routine, to stop here for a while each night before turning in, to let the day's events run through his mind.

Anyone watching him would have expected to see a satisfied man, for the mill opening had been as successful as he could have hoped, and yet, Nick felt nothing of the peace which should have been his. Instead, a restlessness stirred deep inside of him, making him feel like a wild animal trapped within a snare that had no wires, no nets. What made it worse, he admitted to himself ruefully, was that he was caught in a snare of his own making.

High above, the moon laughed down at him.

Marianne stopped just inside the French doors that led to the garden, hesitating only a moment before slipping out into the night. She didn't notice the silent figure on the porch, or the watchful eyes that followed her as she crossed the lawn. Her own gaze was trained on the awesome sight that had first drawn her from her room for a closer look.

The breeze had cleared the sky of every cloud, so that the mountain glowed with reflected moonlight. In the surrounding darkness, Mt. Rainier shone with an ethereal light that seemed to magnify it to even larger proportions. It looked, at once, as if it were nearer than ever, and yet was as unattainable as the moon itself. Each snowcapped glacier, each dark hollow, was outlined in sharp relief by the seductive light, and Marianne didn't doubt for a minute why the Indians believed it was the home of mighty spirits.

At first, when he saw the wisp of white floating along the garden path, Nick wondered if he weren't seeing one of those very ghosts. Her silent footsteps had barely disturbed the night sounds he was accustomed to hearing, and it wasn't until she stopped to gaze once more at the mountain that he guessed what brought her out. Rising slowly from the rocker, so as not to make any noise, he watched her disappear into a small stand of trees a short distance from the house.

Nick didn't stop to think about why he was following her, only that it would have been impossible not to.

He found her in the high field behind the house, and wondered how she had known it was there, until he remembered that she'd probably ridden past this spot when she'd gone out with Elizabeth that day nearly two weeks ago. Now she was leaning forward against the upper rungs of a split-rail fence, her slim form silhouetted by the moon and the mountain. Her hair blew long and loose, swirling around her head like a light, gossamer cloud, and whatever it was she was wearing—her nightgown?—fluttered wildly behind her like the sails of a sleek cutter.

She turned her head slightly to gaze across the tree-tops to the left and he could see her profile: the sweep of her brow, the delicate line of her nose, the fragile curve of her jaw sliding down to meet the arch of her long, slender neck. Her lips were parted and her breathing quick, as if she were overcome by some unnamed emotion, and Nick found his own breath growing labored. He shuddered with a longing so violent it reached deep into his soul.

The slight movement behind her caught Marianne's eye, and she spun around, a scream edging up into her throat.

"It's me," he said quickly, stepping further out into the moonlit meadow.

"Nick . . . oh, thank God."

He suppressed a smile. "I'm glad you're so happy to see me. You didn't look like you were expecting company."

"I wasn't . . . I mean, I didn't think . . . You're laughing at me again!" Marianne dropped her raised hands to her hips, letting the momentary fear slide away. It was true she hadn't thought about being followed, but she couldn't deny the pleasure—and the anticipation—that had raced through her when she recognized Nick.

"Not laughing at you, my sweet," he chuckled. "Laughing at myself for daring you to try something new. Last week it was the stream, and tonight it's the nightgown." He looked to the sky. "Now, if only it would rain . . ."

Embarrassment flooded over Marianne, and she felt her entire body grow hot beneath his blatant stare. Once wet, her nightgown would be nearly transparent, and she was fairly certain he *knew* that, too.

"I didn't come here because you *dared* me to," she said, mortified. "I wasn't even thinking about what you said that day."

"There's nothing to be ashamed of," he soothed. "I told you before, everyone needs to cut loose once in a while. However, I'll let you in on a secret that'll flatter your sense of propriety. I heard Elizabeth asking Mother if she could have a riding skirt like the one Millie made for you. Not that I have any objections to comfort, but it'll be good to see her wearing something besides dungarees."

Though under different circumstances she might have been pleased to learn that the gap between Nick and his sister was narrowing, Marianne found it difficult to appreciate the fact now. "I-I think I'd better go back," she mumbled.

Before she could dart away, Nick blocked her escape with one arm. "Not yet," he said huskily. "Stay and look at the mountain with me."

His voice proved to be more compelling than even the moon-dressed peak, his silver-gray eyes more of a lure than the glittering snow behind her. Try as she would, Marianne could not turn away from him.

He had placed his hands on her waist, fighting the urge to run them up and down the swelling curves of her body. Instead, he contented himself with drawing her into a gentle embrace. "You know, even when I was telling myself I didn't want this, I think you were in my dreams anyway. Whenever I close my eyes, you're there, and every time I hold you in my arms, I know I never want to let you go. Today . . . today was very special, because I finally know you feel the same way."

"No . . ." Marianne tried to shake her head, but he had already cupped her chin with one hand to hold it firm. His tongue traced her lips, leaving no room for protest.

And she wanted to protest! She wanted to cry out against the way her body flamed beneath his hands, wanted to fight the growing need to forget New York, Pemberton, and dear Mary—all the things that kept her from drowning in a passion unlike anything she'd ever known. She wanted to shout for him to stop, but when she opened her mouth to speak, just one word formed on her lips. "Nick . . ."

Her breathless moan only drove him to wilder heights. After learning the afternoon in the cabin that she was still a virgin, he had vowed to draw out her passionate nature slowly, so that she would never have reason to look at him with fearful eyes again. But her response to him was anything but hesitant. He could feel the tremor that reverberated through them both like the growing rumble of thunder, making his control slip away.

This time, when his tongue stroked hers, she joined him willingly, savoring the tastes and textures of his mouth. Her mind had ceased to function, except in the most primitive way, absorbing each new sensation. The kiss grew in intensity until it brought them, not only profound pleasure, but a kind of bittersweet pain because it was no longer enough—would never again be enough.

Nick threaded his fingers through Marianne's thick, silky hair, emitting a low groan as he lifted his open mouth from hers, sliding it across her cheek and down along the curve of her neck. He left a trail of kisses, hot and wet, that ended only when he reached her quaking breasts. Dropping to his knees, he pulled her down against him so that her weight was balanced in his arms. Her legs straddled one of his until she was resting on his lap, her nightgown riding high up on her thighs.

Marianne gasped as his mouth hungrily captured her breast, and she marveled at the exquisite pain that shot through her as he drew her taut nipple into his mouth. And yet, it was nothing compared to when he pushed her nightdress over her shoulders, exposing her to the cool air and moonlight.

"God, you are so beautiful," he murmured hoarsely, his hands caressing her reverently, cupping her full- ness between work-roughened palms.

Her breasts tightened still more when his attention turned to first one, then the other, lips and teeth and

tongue contriving to drive her to the brink of madness.
A knot formed deep in her abdomen, spinning slowly,
pulling every nerve in her body into one huge, shuddering coil. With both hands she clutched his head as
if to hold him to her forever, her fingers furrowing
through the shaggy softness of his hair. She covered
his brow and temples with tiny, fluttering kisses, pausing between each just long enough to draw ragged
breaths.

When his mouth returned to hers, it was a rejoining
of their hearts, hot and eager and wild with frenzy.
Nick's fingers slid possessively down the satiny con-
tours of her back, pushing away the filmy material that
kept his hands from knowing her fully. Past her slender waist and over the swell of her hips, he stopped
only when he reached her buttocks, his palms fitting
perfectly around the firm, soft flesh. With her arms
still wrapped around his neck, he leaned forward carefully, easing her to the ground beneath him.

The cool, prickly feel of the grass brought her back
to her senses momentarily, and she made a startled
sound, her eyes flying open wide. "Nick . . ." she
moaned. "We mustn't . . ."

"Yes," he contradicted, his voice low and shaking,
"yes, we must. You know that, don't you?" His eyes,
heavy-lidded with passion, pleaded with her.

She wasn't even sure she'd given him an answer, but
something in her expression must have, for she saw
the flash of joyful triumph in his eyes as he bent to
capture her lips again. This kiss was more tender, and
as she felt her resistance swirl away like leaves against
the wind, she realized, in one blazing instant of recognition, that there was only one answer in her heart.

His hips were moving over hers, the leg she had
once straddled now pressing against her most intimate
parts, inciting her to a feverish excitement. Her blood
pounded, filling her veins to the bursting point, and
yet somehow leaving an emptiness that ached to be
filled. And only Nick could fill it.

At the first touch of his hand, Marianne gasped and

tried to squeeze her legs together, but his hard, muscular thigh was already wedged between them. "Hush, sweetheart," Nick crooned against her lips. "It's all right." Easing his weight from his elbows, he stretched alongside her, rolling her toward him so they faced each other. He swept what remained of her nightgown down the length of her legs.

Marianne hardly even noticed that she lay naked in his arms, and only marked the brief moments that he released her in order to remove his own clothing by the number of heartbeats before he returned to her. His hands, circling and caressing, soothing and igniting, filled her with a kind of shivering pleasure that fulfilled and promised all at once.

The second time his fingertips dipped near her secret fire, she only shuddered, letting him part her thighs gently. She stifled a cry of sheer pleasure when his hand pressed against her core, and nearly wept with joy when he began to move slowly, and she realized that this was just the beginning.

"Relax, my darling," Nick urged, barely able to restrain his own burning need long enough to make the way easier for her. Once again he knelt over her, bathing her face and neck and breasts with soft kisses, while his fingers parted her flesh, delving into her inner moistness.

White heat drove through her, building to a raging crescendo that threatened to destroy her, and still it was not enough. She didn't know what it was, knew only that it began and ended with Nick, and that Nick would show her.

Through his own passion he saw her eyes widen, saw the questioning innocence that passed over her face at the moment he lowered himself over her. He felt the cool smoothness of her belly against his heat, and yet, where he expected to see an expression of shock, he saw only incredible wonder. The image sent a burst of desperate longing through him, but he knew she was not yet ready, and he wanted—more, even, than he wanted to feel her closed around him—he wanted to see the wonder in her eyes turn to a need that matched his.

"Touch me," he whispered, his voice rasping through her like a familiar ache, startling her with its rawness. "Touch me."

Hesitantly at first, but gaining confidence with every moment, Marianne spread her palms over his shoulders, her hands gliding across his glistening skin. Her fingertips circled forward around his neck, joining together at the juncture of his throat, then separating again, flattening against his chest. "Like this?" she asked. She smoothed her hands down over his male nipples, returning again when he groaned softly and pressed a hard, bruising kiss to her mouth. Continuing past his narrow hips, she felt his muscles grow taut beneath her light touch, and he lifted himself from her just enough for her to slip her hand between them.

"Ah, God" he cried against her lips. Her warmth bathed him, not only the heat of her fingers closing around him, but the hot sweetness that rippled over his own hand, buried deep within her hidden flesh.

It was with iron control that he let her go on, knowing that she needed to familiarize herself with him as he had done with her, that she must know that the completion of their love was merely the final moment of an intimacy begun long before. Already, he could feel her body quivering inside and out, begging for release, but he held it from her until her moans became frantic and her breath short.

Then he covered her with a fierce, powerful movement, his strength sliding into her, filling her with his heat. She knew it would hurt, bit her lip in anticipation, but the hurting was nothing compared to the glory of fulfillment, the wondrous knowledge of what they shared.

"Ah, love . . ."

Her hips moved instinctively, drawing him deeper and faster and harder, blindly seeking release from the web of tension he had built around and through her. Something inside her flowered open, like delicate petals that spread to the sun's life-giving rays.

His hands ceased their wild caress, pressing her hips against him so that he felt ecstasy shimmer through her at the same moment it burst from him. She uttered a single sound, unformed and frantic, but it was lost against his mouth as he kissed her to the final peak of pleasure.

A long while later, it seemed, Marianne heard his voice murmuring words that fell like sweet raindrops upon her ears, and she followed them back to where the moon and the trees and the earth became reality once more. He cradled her gently, his weight pressed comfortingly against her body, his hands lingering, trailing shivers along her flesh.

Nick wanted nothing more than to lie this way forever, her slim form melded into his, joined in an intimacy that would transcend all else. Instead, he felt her skin grow rough with gooseflesh as a cool breeze wafted over them. He tightened his embrace. "Are you cold?"

"N-no." She pushed lightly against his chest, his arms giving way at the slight pressure, though she could see his puzzled expression by the moon's bright light. Turning her back to him, she searched the ground for her nightgown.

Nick reached out, touching her shoulder with his fingertips, surprised when she started like a skittish colt. "Mary . . . ?"

Her voice was a plaintive whisper, the words not intended for him. "Oh, God . . . what have I done?"

Her cry tore through him like the cutting edge of a sword, impaling him with the sharpness of her despair. Nick almost groaned with disgust at himself, but quelled the impulse to walk away. He sat up. What kind of man was he? Just because he'd made her body respond didn't mean she'd been emotionally prepared to accept his lovemaking. She didn't love him—was, despite her brave denial, still scared to death of marriage and all it implied—so what she was feeling now was probably closer to shame than anything. He watched her fumble with her torn nightgown, struggling to turn it right side out. Hunching behind her, he reached over her shoulder and took it from her gently.

"I'm sorry," he rasped.

Mortified to be sitting before him, helpless in her nakedness, helpless even to move away from him, Marianne only stared straight ahead at the mountain. She knew Nick thought she was ashamed because she'd let him make love to her, and the knowledge added another dart of regret to a heart that already felt as if the life were being bled from it. She *was* ashamed, but not in the way he feared.

"Here." From behind her, he settled the nightgown over her head, having somehow untwisted the knots. She raised her arms automatically, slipping her hands into each sleeve as he held them up for her. The ribbon that had once fastened the neckline together was now torn, so she had to clutch the fabric above her breasts to hold the gown on.

Nick wanted only to wrap his arms around her, to cradle her shivering form into his warmth and comfort her, but when he laid a hand on her shoulder she flinched visibly. Wretched, he dropped his hand. "Mary—"

"Don't call me—" She stopped short. She'd been about to tell him not to call her by that name, but had caught herself just in time. It was bad enough to have him thinking she regretted what happened tonight; it would be far worse to hear his voice harden with anger and blame if she told him the truth now. "Please," she begged instead, "don't tell me you're sorry."

Nick was stunned, frustration and remorse welling up in him. She didn't even want to hear his apology! He was determined, though, to give it anyway. "But, I am," he insisted, his voice rough with emotion. "I'm sorry I rushed you into this. I wanted . . . I wanted so much more for you."

More? Marianne shook her head in awe. How much more could he have given her? Before tonight, she'd never imagined . . . never dreamed it could be so beautiful. And he wanted to give her more?

He watched her lower her head, seeing denial there, and a shudder rippled through her, making her shoulders quiver convulsively. "I won't touch you again. Not until after . . ." He sighed heavily, evidence of how difficult this promise would be to keep. "Not until you're ready. You'll feel differently once we're married."

Marianne choked back an hysterical laugh. "Marriage doesn't solve everything! Why does everyone always think it does?"

Puzzled by this strange exclamation, Nick gathered his clothes and donned them quickly before crouching before her. He was amazed by the expression of wild despair as she lifted her face to him, and though he could have sworn she'd been crying, her cheeks were dry and her eyes clear. "Not everything," he admitted, knowing that was a promise he could *never* make, "but in a few days, when the . . ." he cringed, ". . . when the shock has worn off, you might decide it wasn't so bad."

There was nothing Marianne wanted to do more than to turn to him then, to throw herself back into his arms and cry that making love to him had been wonderful, that she would remember this night for the rest of her life! Instead, she dropped her face into her hands and bit her lower lip until the coppery taste of her own blood brought her back to her senses.

Nick stood then, looking down on her dejected posture with true confusion. He *knew* she had responded to him with pleasure. Had he been so blinded by passion that he hadn't seen her fear, as well? He didn't think so.

He shuffled his feet uncomfortably, and said in a low voice, "It won't hurt so much the next time."

The next *time!* Marianne stood slowly, blinking hard against the threat of tears. There would be no next time, but that was a pain she had brought upon herself. Deep inside, she'd known that before she'd taken one step outside of the house tonight. Maybe it was even the reason she'd come. What she would never forgive herself for was that Nick's eyes were shadowed with remorse. Remorse because he thought *he* had hurt *her*!

There was no way to change what had happened, no amount of wishing would reverse the clock. Only *she* could ease the doubt from his heart, if but for a short time. Taking a step toward him, Marianne laid her hand gently against his chest, letting the strength of his heartbeat flow through her veins. She lifted her gaze to his, hoping that in this, at least, he would remember and believe.

"I know, Nick," she whispered. "I know."

Chapter 15

Horace Squiggs had never intended to be a lawman, and on days like this, when faced with a particularly unpleasant task, he often reminded himself that he could have been content to farm wheat in Nebraska with his brother-in-law, instead of chaffing over how best to go about ruining someone's life. Most times, under similar circumstances, Horace consoled himself with the thought that people made their own trouble. He was merely a pawn in a Bigger Game, whose role it was to hasten unscrupulous players toward their deserved fate. But in this case, he was afraid, Fate had dealt out one mighty rough hand, and it was his unfortunate duty to proceed, not according to what he felt was right, but according to the law of the land.

With an agitated *haarrumph*, Horace reached again for the sheaf of papers that he'd gone over at least twenty-five times since last night, when his deputy had plunked the muddy bag in the middle of his desk.

"This the one?" Phil Owens had asked with a satisfied grin.

Reminding himself that young Owens *would* make a decent marshal someday, that it was only inexperience that made him ask so many dumb questions, Horace refrained from answering and pried open the carpetbag's misshapen clasp. In the two weeks since the crash, they'd searched and identified no less than eighty-three assorted pieces of luggage, and he had no doubt there were many more strewn down the side of the mountain that would never be found. He reckoned the chances of this being the one were slimmer 'n a skinned coyote.

For once, however, Horace Squiggs had reckoned wrong.

Now, the tattered bag lay on its side, limp and harmless when emptied of its volatile contents: one plain, worn dress of faded calico and a lace chemise that was obviously expensive and therefore incongruous when compared to the other garment, a scuffed pair of dancing slippers, and a hand-crocheted shawl wrapped around two hide-bound ledgers.

The latter items were the ones, naturally, that had claimed Horace's attention throughout a long, sleepless night. He had pored over the pages, trying to make sense of the columns of figures and system of initials that marked each entry. To make matters worse, scraps of paper had been jammed between the pages, adding to the confusion. It would probably take an accountant to figure exactly how much money was involved, but on his own, he'd still managed to learn enough.

If these were the books that Adam Pemberton claimed had been stolen by Marianne Blakemore, niece of one Matthew Blakemore, then it was no wonder the man was desperate to get them back. Horace didn't doubt for a minute that the ledgers spelled out a lengthy jail sentence for anyone involved.

And therein lay his dilemma.

Setting aside the clutch of papers, Horace stuck his hand deep into the carpetbag, pulling out the last item inside. A prayer book, small enough to fit snugly in the palm of his hand, fell open at a page that was marked by a photograph about the size of a folded dollar bill. Posed against a background of massive bookshelves and potted plants, a slender girl smiled shyly at her unseen admirers, her blonde hair billowing around a face as innocent as an angel's.

It hardly does her justice, Horace thought grimly.

The sound of the outer door opening and closing gained his attention, and Horace leaned back in his swivel chair, the photograph still nestled in his hand as he placed his feet on the desk, careful not to disrupt the evidence.

"Hey, Horace. You in there?"

Silently wondering where else he would be, Squiggs looked up just as Phil Owens popped his head inside the office doorway, looking disgustingly chipper considering the fact that he'd ridden all the way to Olympia and back in a twenty-four-hour stretch to testify in another case.

"How'd it go?" Horace asked.

"We got the bas——, I mean, the suspect was convicted." Phil stepped inside the office, attempting a more serious demeanor. "If old Judge Ryan runs the state the way he runs a courtroom, he'll be the best danged governor this side of the Mississippi. That's all most anyone could talk about. How long d'ya think it'll take Congress to approve the petition for statehood?"

This was another unanswerable question, but one Horace could forgive, since it was on the minds of every man and woman in Washington Territory. He had his doubts about the judge's chances in politics, but right at this moment the fate of the territory was not uppermost in his thoughts.

"I want you to take a look at this," Horace said, indicating the desktop with an abrupt gesture. He watched as Owens strode forward with barely suppressed eagerness. It was about time he started letting the younger man have a look at some of the thinking that went on behind crime solving, instead of just depending on him for the physical work. Besides, just about now a second opinion would be welcome. *Anyone's* opinion.

While Owens pulled up a chair to study the ledgers, Horace continued to stare at the picture in his hand. She sure was a pretty thing, he pondered. But hadn't he been a mite suspicious all along? Now the suspicion was justified.

The day after he'd questioned Nick Fortune's new lady he'd sent a wire to New York reporting that Marianne Blakemore was, indeed, dead. Despite the finality of his pronouncement, telegrams from New

York had continued to arrive almost daily, pressing him for more details and proof of his claim. He'd decided that someone must have been swinging a mighty big weight over the police chief's head, for him to be so persistent.

A few days later he'd received word from Adam Pemberton himself in the form of a letter. In a cool, efficient manner, Pemberton had requested a detailed description of the accident, of any belongings recovered, and finally, of the body of Marianne Blakemore. He had reiterated the claim that Miss Blakemore had stolen a great deal of money and numerous bearer bonds from her uncle's home. He only wished, he'd written, to see justice done.

But would it? Horace wondered. Who should he believe, one of the most influential men in the state of New York, or the evidence as it lay before him? There hadn't been a single penny in the old carpetbag, let alone stock certificates. Only the disturbing ledgers that appeared to be a list of government officials, from town clerks to state senators, and the amounts they'd been paid by Pemberton and Matthew Blakemore over a ten-year period.

Owens was just closing the second book, his expression a mixture of stunned surprise and determination. "No wonder Pemberton was so all-fired crazy for these books," he said, echoing Horace's earlier thought. "I don't reckon he really wanted them to be found."

"Nope. And remember, he instructed us to contact him immediately if they were."

"You gonna?" Phil's brow shot up.

"Not until after I ship these ledgers to Washington, D.C. I expect there's folks there'll take a mighty keen interest in what's inside. The girl must've known that when she took them."

"But to kill her own uncle . . . ?" Phil shook his head in confusion.

"And what if she didn't?" Horace posed the question quietly, letting the words sift through his mind like sand dunes in the wind, swirling, shifting, finally changing their shape.

"But the New York police said—"

"They told us what they believed, but that doesn't make it true. There's only one other person besides Pemberton that knows the whole story."

Phil Owens nodded. "And she's dead."

Letting his chair creak forward, Horace swung his legs to the floor and leaned toward his deputy. "No," he said, "she's not." He laid the photograph on the desk, pushing it around with one finger so that Owens could see clearly. The younger man's silence was confirmation that he understood the enormity of the situation.

"She's not dead," Horace repeated. "But if we let Adam Pemberton know about this, she may very well wish she was."

"What're you gonna do?"

So intent was Horace on the upside-down image, he didn't even notice that Phil's questions had ceased to irritate him. All he could think of was the decision he'd just now made, and of how much he hoped it was the right one. "You better," he instructed the waiting deputy, "go find Nick Fortune."

If Marianne had looked up at the right moment, she might have seen Phil Owens cross the street in front of the buggy Ruth drove haphazardly through town. She was, however, too intent upon keeping her seat to notice the people scurrying out of their way. By the time they stopped near the corner of Main Street and Tenth, her fingers ached from clutching the side of the carriage so tightly. Flexing them carefully, she glanced sideways at the woman next to her.

"You go on now, before it gets dark," Ruth said, nodding briefly toward the shop where she intended to make her monthly purchases for the orphanage. "I'll get a ride back with Mrs. Delaney, like always." Her wrinkled face splitting into a wide grin, Ruth Lyons slapped the reins into Marianne's hands, startling the horse so that it lurched once before settling back down. "And thanks for letting me drive, honey. It's been a long time since I had so much fun."

Marianne chuckled as she shifted to the center of the seat. "Me, too," she admitted. "That ride wasn't what I expected."

Ruth smiled. "Most things aren't. That's why it's just as important to go through life with a mind as wide open as your eyes. It's one of the traits I've always admired in your Nick."

Marianne suppressed a sigh as she waved good-bye to Ruth and started for home. Nick may have been broad-minded about some things, but when it came to the subject of her leaving he had been as stubborn as a hunk of petrified wood. And now, to her shame and dismay, it would be harder than ever to convince him to let her go.

Since the evening of the mill opening, she'd spent three long days trying to avoid Nick's watchful gaze, overly aware of the extraordinary effort he was making to appear patient for her benefit. It only made it more difficult to deny the feelings that engulfed her, shattering her composure each time she looked up and caught him staring at her through hooded eyes.

And if the days were an agony, the nights were sheer torture, filled with bittersweet reminders of the moments she'd selfishly stolen from him. Every breeze rustling through her open window brought the memory of his touch, lightly caressing her skin until she writhed beneath perspiration-soaked sheets. Night sounds were endearments whispered softly, fleeting words that teased her senses and taunted her heart.

You fool! she chided herself miserably. *You stupid fool!*

She was sure he would never let her leave willingly, and so, short of creeping out in the middle of the night, there was no way she could possibly escape. The only thing left for her to do was to tell him the truth, even if it meant she'd have to turn herself in to Horace Squiggs in order to keep from starving in the streets.

With a determined flick of the reins, Marianne steered the horse toward the place she now thought of as home, even if only for a little while longer.

*   *   *

Rhys Hartley touched the rump of his rented mount lightly with the switch, satisfied by the quick response it evoked. The livery owner had assured him the horse would do well for a man in his condition, but it wasn't until now that he mentally allowed that the animal had passed the test. It took only another tap to increase the pace to a steady trot, which was just the speed he needed in order to keep up with his quarry.

Rhys squinted against the slanting rays of the late afternoon sun, watching as Marianne Blakemore guided her buggy between the two towering firs that marked the shortcut between Tacoma and Nicholas Fortune's home. This was the spot he had chosen to waylay her, and once her shining head had disappeared into the shadows of the wooded lane, he urged his horse forward.

It was with great trepidation that he had decided to approach her now, before he was completely recovered, but after seeing the way she and Fortune had gazed at each other while they danced together a few nights ago, Rhys was more afraid of waiting too long. His conscience wouldn't allow him to let her go through with marrying the man, though he reckoned the fool deserved it.

When the road curved a little he could see her profile clearly. She appeared to be lost in thought, and gave no indication that she knew she was being followed. With grim determination, Rhys waited patiently until she reached the place where the road widened slightly. It would be necessary to time his next maneuver precisely, so with a silent word and a sharp rap for his unfamiliar mount, he broke into a gallop.

Marianne was startled by the sudden motion when she saw a rider flash past her, but then, if she'd been paying attention, she probably would have heard him come up behind. Ever since leaving Ruth in town, she'd been mulling over her decision to tell Nick the whole truth. Now, however, her attention was concentrated on keeping her own horse from bolting. The man who had so recklessly passed her stopped suddenly, turning in his saddle to wait for her. Though the sun was still high enough to throw ample light on the road, his face was shaded ominously by a broad-rimmed hat.

Beads of perspiration broke out on Marianne's forehead as she drew back on the reins with all her strength. She'd grown so used to driving back and forth from the orphanage without incident, it had never occurred to her to be on her guard against an unpleasant encounter. In fact, if she remembered Nick's description correctly, she was on Fortune property now.

Not that it mattered, she quickly realized. The man appeared the sort not to grow overly concerned about trespassing, and she was still too far from the house to be heard should she find it necessary to cry out.

Keeping her voice steady, she called, "Kindly allow me to pass, sir. I'm expected home, and I'm already late."

The horseman gave no response, only turned his mount so that he faced her squarely. She could not make out his features, but she could now see that he was too well dressed for a common outlaw, and that he sat on his horse awkwardly, with his right leg bent at an unusual angle.

A frisson of fear crept up the nape of her neck, but she forced herself to smile and appear to look past him. "In fact," she said loudly, "I'm surprised that my fiancé hasn't come by to look for me already, so if you don't mind . . ."

Her words drifted away as she saw, with not a little consternation, that his shoulders shook with suppressed laughter. She didn't understand what he thought was so funny, but she wasn't about to play at guessing. Glancing over her shoulder, she estimated the distance to the wide spot where she could turn, silently hoping the horse was trained to back up.

"You'll never make it."

Marianne wasn't sure which unsettled her more, the fact that he'd correctly guessed her thoughts, or that his voice was strangely familiar. Was this one of the men she'd met at the mill? She couldn't fathom any of

Nick's friends or employees acting this way, besides, his accent was too cultured, too . . .

Dread settled deep within her then, like a weight which has suddenly become unbearable. Her throat grew unaccountably dry and scratching when she tried to speak. "Who . . . who are you?"

He eased toward her with slow precision, touching his horse lightly with some kind of thin prod. She felt as if time had taken on a new dimension, one which paid no attention to minutes and seconds, but heeded, instead, a bizarre schedule of its own, complete with horrifying flashes from the past and alarming visions of the future. She knew him now, and with recognition came the certainty that his presence here was not by chance, but by the design of someone too evil for words.

"So, we meet again?" Tipping his hat from his head, Rhys Hartley rode closer, stopping only when he had drawn even with her, a mere four feet away. "I must admit, Miss Blakemore, when I heard you had met your untimely demise up on that mountain, my remorse was great. It's a pleasure to find you looking so well and so . . . how might I put it . . . alive?"

"What do you want?" It took every ounce of courage she had in her to keep from screaming, but she somehow managed to convey a sense of dignified hauteur. At least she thought so until he began to chuckle again.

"My, my," he said, shaking his head. "Just a little bit defensive, aren't you? What makes you think you have anything I would want? Unless . . ." He paused as if giving the matter great thought, though it was clear he thoroughly enjoyed mocking her. "Unless you have something to hide?"

Panic rose in Marianne's throat, but she had no choice but to continue the charade. "Of course I don't," she replied, choking down her fear. "It's just that I'm not accustomed to being badgered on my way home—"

"Home?" He nearly shouted with gleeful disdain. "*You* don't have a home. Even the pitiful gravestone that bears your name shelters someone else. And you'll be without a roof over your own head soon enough, once the illustrious Nicholas Fortune learns he's been hoodwinked by an imposter."

"No!" The protest slipped out before she recalled that everything he said was true. Along with the sickening realization that her reprieve had come to an ignoble end, she couldn't help feeling immeasurably guilty. A dull ache of foreboding began to seep through her. "What good would it do you to tell him?" she asked wretchedly. "You have nothing to gain."

"You're right."

Marianne stared at him, the sudden hope that pounded in her chest dying when she saw his calculating smile. Again, she felt her spirits plummet.

"I have given that very factor a great deal of thought," Rhys said cannily. "And it has occurred to me that I'd gain far more by *not* sharing our little secret. It goes without saying," he added after a slight pause, "that *you* will gain as well.

"Soon . . . within weeks I would guess . . . you could well be the wife of a very rich man. That should make you extremely happy, and I have no doubt Mr. Fortune will share in that blissful state—so long as he doesn't make the mistake of naming you beneficiary in his will. We *know* how dangerous a proposition that might be."

Marianne blanched, torn between lashing at him with the ends of the reins she clutched so tightly or succumbing to tears. As if reading her mind, he leaned over quickly, snatching the leather strips from her before she could move to retain them.

"With a doting husband and a fortune at your disposal," he continued smoothly, as if they were sharing pleasant conversation over a cup of tea, "you should find it quite unnecessary to hoard whatever cash you've managed to accumulate through your own efforts. I, on the other hand, would genuinely appreciate such a windfall."

Blackmail? Marianne could scarcely believe her ears, but then, hadn't Rhys Hartley admitted he was a professional gambler? She supposed if one didn't put too fine a line on it, there wasn't much difference between fleecing inexperienced cardplayers and extorting money from fools. What Mr. Hartley didn't realize, she thought with grim satisfaction, was that she had no money of her own, and she wasn't *about* to drag Nick into this.

"I-I need time to think about it," she stammered, studying her hands, which were clasped together in a white-knuckled grip. She needed to stall him, needed time to decide what to do next. When he didn't answer immediately, she risked a glance in his direction to see what was his response. The emerald green eyes she now remembered so well assessed her, analyzing her as if she were a racehorse upon which he was considering placing a large bet. She shivered violently.

Wordlessly, Rhys Hartley leaned forward again, urging her to take back the buggy's reins. "Don't make the mistake of thinking you can get away again," he warned quietly. "You have until tomorrow to bring it to me."

"Tomorrow?" she croaked. "It's not possible—"

"Tomorrow!" His voice was low, but had the impact of a threat shouted across the mountain. "I'm at a boarding house on Main Street. You'll have no trouble finding it. Just remember . . ."

He paused ominously, letting his words pass beyond her swirling, chaotic thoughts, to settle where they would be heeded and feared. She heard them as if through a thick blanket of fog, so that his voice sounded distant and unreal—and more than a little menacing— and she reacted just as he hoped, by trembling so deeply that her limbs grew weak.

"Just remember," he repeated, "that if you don't come to me, I will most certainly find you."

Chapter 16

Katey Muldoon lifted her head as a soft rap sounded at her door. She quickly laid aside the book she'd held in her lap and tightened her dressing gown sash before crossing the room.

"What is it, Silas?" she asked, opening the door to admit the bartender. She saw at once the worried expression that creased his brow beneath his grizzled hair, and wondered what might have gone wrong so early in the evening. The last time she'd peeked downstairs there'd been only one or two seamen at the bar. For most of her customers it was still dinnertime.

"Mistah Fortune's down theh, Ma'am. Ya bettah come down."

"Nick wants to see me now?"

Silas shook his head. "He didn' say, but I 'spects ya mought come anyways. He looks 's if he's fixin' ta drink the house dry."

Katey pondered over Silas's troubling words as she dressed, wondering what Nick was upset about. He was one of her regulars—at least until the past week or so—but even then he was rarely a heavy drinker, content instead to sip leisurely at a glass of whiskey over a game of cards. Therefore, the report of his unusual behavior caused her to hurry as she donned the gown she'd planned to wear this evening, and urgency lent wings to her feet as she sped down the stairs.

"Hello, Katey," Nick grumbled thickly as she slipped into the chair opposite him. "Just keep the spongers away and the bottles coming. I'm in no mood for conversation tonight."

Katey nearly obeyed him, but she caught the note of quiet desperation in his voice. "Tonight?" she quipped lightly. "The sun won't go down for hours. Sure you ain't wantin' company?"

Finishing off the drink in his hand, Nick reached for the bottle sitting in the middle of the table and poured himself another. "I said I didn't want to talk. Can't a man drink in peace?"

Quietly, but with a firmness that had won her many a battle of will, Katey rested her hand on his wrist and held it there until he raised his angry eyes to meet her gaze. "There are plenty of places for that kind of drinkin', and not at Katey Muldoon's. But you knew that before you came in. So talk."

Nick stared at the dark brown eyes, sparkling with concern, then clenched his jaw tight. "You don't want to hear it."

"Try me. You also know by now I'm a pretty fair listener."

Maybe she was right, he thought. If anyone would understand the way he felt, it would be Katey. At least he could depend on her to give him an honest opinion about what to do.

"Seems to me," Nick grunted after taking another swallow, "you'd get tired of hearing how many ways a man can be a fool."

Katey chuckled gravely. "Since you're the least foolish man I know, this should be interesting."

It took Nick a little over two hours to relate the entire story from the day he'd pulled his would-be bride from the wreckage to what Horace Squiggs had told him just that afternoon. He punctuated the tale with short swigs from his bottle, having given up the glass long before. What he really wanted was to drink himself into forgetting the pain of betrayal that stabbed through him, but ironically, the head for liquor he'd developed over the years kept his mind punishingly clear.

". . . and so you're ready to condemn her?" he

heard Katey saying, interrupting his thoughts. He didn't
even stop to think why he wasn't surprised by her
reaction.

"Shouldn't I be? According to the facts Horace so
efficiently collected, she's unquestionably a thief. And
quite an accomplished liar, too, by the way she has
everyone around here, from Ruth Lyons to my own
mother, singing her praises."

"You were too, not so long ago," Katey pointed
out.

"Don't remind me." Nick took another drink. "That's
the part that sticks in my craw. I fell for her tricks so
goddamned fast it's a wonder they haven't heard her
laughing all the way to 'Frisco. Of course," he said
bitterly, "we know already what an adept judge of
character *I* am."

Katey sighed, eyeing the bottle as it made another
trip to his lips, then was slammed back to the table.
"Yes, I *do* know," she insisted. "I know you're not a
man to make the same mistake twice. I also know that
nothing you've told me about your Mary—"

"Marianne!" he said, his voice a low growl. "Her
name's Marianne Blakemore, and she's wanted for killing a man, so you can add murder to her list of sins."

Silence stretched through the room like a saw belt
tensed to near breaking point. Nick felt it, even though
the murmur of voices from the swabbies at the bar
continued to drift over to them. Slowly, almost as if he
didn't wish to, he lifted his eyes to meet Katey's unwa-
vering gaze, knowing in his gut what she would say.

"I don't believe that any more than you do."

Her voice was soft and quiet, but it rang with a
certainty he couldn't have denied, even if he'd wanted
to. He inched his fingers toward the half-empty bottle
again, then stopped just short of it, clenching his hand
into a tight fist. The sound that escaped him then was
part sigh, part groan, echoing with all the frustration
and anger and loss that warred inside him. "No," he
said, rasping. "I don't."

"Then it seems you have some strong thinking to do,"
Katey said decisively. "Has Horace arrested her yet?"

"He gave me a week to let her turn herself in. I'm just supposed to keep an eye on her, so she doesn't go anywhere."

Katey chuckled. "Then he doesn't believe she done murder, either. You know Horace as well as I do, and he's a sight more careful than that. So there's the proof she's not guilty. Silas!" she called over her shoulder. "Bring some hot coffee. Lots of it!"

Nick hadn't given much consideration to the marshal's unusual request, but now it seemed Katey had made a good point. Horace had been sure about the details, and of course, there'd been no getting around the photograph of Marianne, but the lawman had also hinted that there was a lot more to the case than he knew. Phil Owens had appeared damned near apologetic!

"This doesn't change anything," he stated firmly, once Silas had moved away from the table and out of earshot. He watched as Katey poured a cup of steaming liquid into a large clay mug. "She's using my family and friends to her own advantage. I won't stand for it."

Gently shoving the mug across the table, Katey frowned. "Assuming the poor thing *didn't* do anything wrong," Katey asked, "then why is she still running away, and from whom?"

Nick blew on the rim of his cup before sipping the scalding brew, letting the burning sensation chase away the taste of whiskey from his mouth and throat. Hot coffee and cool thinking. It'd been one of his father's favorite expressions, and he wondered, for the first time in years, how Joshua Fortune would have handled the situation.

"I don't know," he admitted, both to Katey, and to himself. "Horace wouldn't go into that, but it's probably safe to guess that whoever *did* kill her uncle, he's the one Mary . . . Marianne is afraid of."

As he uttered the words, he remembered their conversation after that first trip to Millie's shop, and how she'd told him, more or less, that she was running from a man. He also recalled the way she'd insisted that she couldn't stay here, that she had problems too pressing to ignore.

He had been the one, he admitted ruefully, who'd ignored the warnings.

"Poor thing," Katey repeated, shaking her head. "She's a long way from home, and likely scared to death. You said she was awful nervous when Horace interrogated her that first day. If not because she was guilty, then she must be just as frightened of being sent back there."

That was when she'd told him!

He remembered now, remembered the appeal in Marianne's blue eyes as clearly as if it'd been yesterday, and with the memory came a sense of relief that nearly made him dizzy. Right after Horace left that day, she'd tried to tell him that she couldn't stay here, that they would never be happy with each other. Nick felt a sudden twist of shame snake around his heart when he recalled how quickly he'd blamed her for changing her mind, when what she'd really been trying to do was protect him from disappointment.

If you looked at it closely, he thought, hunching over the table with his head cradled in his hands, *she'd never actually lied outright*. But it was just as bad, not telling the truth.

"She should have told me," Nick protested softly, watching Katey's face for acknowledgment.

Instead, she fidgeted on her chair, brushing an imaginary wisp of red-gold hair from her eyes. "That'd be a terrible risk, don't you think? You might've turned her over to Horace, and from what you told me, without that bag of hers he found, he would've shipped her right back to New York on the first train. No . . ." Katey paused, ". . . I think she did the only thing she could."

"Is that what you would've done?" Gazing at her quizzically, Nick wondered how a woman as inherently honest as Katey could condone dishonesty in another.

Katey shrugged. "Who knows? We're all entitled to at least one whopper of a mistake in life. I made mine nearly twenty years ago, and you made one with Alicia. But I don't think you're making one now. Give her a chance to learn that she can trust you."

"And then what?"

"Whatever happens next," Katey said matter-of-factly. "Whether she expected it or not, Marianne needs you more now than ever. Horace'll only wait as long as he has to, and then there'll be some answering to do. Just don't forget the most important thing . . ." Placing her hands on the table in front of her, she leaned forward intently, hoping Nick would heed her words. "She might not be the girl you sent for, but she's the one you fell in love with. Nothing changes that."

Though she'd been waiting hours for Nick to return, Marianne jumped when the front door opened and closed with a muted click. Rising quickly, she ran a nervous hand down the front of the same riding habit she had worn the day Elizabeth took her up into the foothills. Already, that afternoon was as distant as a memory, as vague as a wishful thought. Reality was here, in the darkness, waiting for a dream to end and a nightmare to begin.

Nick whisked a hand through his rain-soaked hair as he paused in front of the drawing room entrance, showering droplets of frigid water across the floor. He hesitated for a moment, considering which would warm him faster, dry clothes or fiery liquor. Neither, he decided, striding toward the kitchen.

When the door swung shut behind him, Marianne stirred from her hiding place, squaring her shoulders resolutely as she lifted a small carpetbag from its place at her feet. She followed Nick's footsteps to the kitchen, pausing only a moment with her palm on the door before entering. Nick stood in front of the stove, a match held between the thumb and forefinger of one hand, a pot of cold coffee in the other. He looked up at her, his face registering surprise before settling into an expressionless mask.

His gaze flicked from her wide eyes to the bag she gripped with knuckles as white as ocean pebbles. "Are you going somewhere?" he asked smoothly, flicking the match away as he lowered the coffee back to the stovetop. With deceptive calm, he turned toward her, propping himself against the stove and crossing his arms over his chest.

Marianne opened her mouth to speak, faltered, then pushed her chin up mightily with what little determination she had left. "I have to leave Tacoma. I was waiting . . . I had hoped you would help me."

"Why?" No shock, no protests. Just a single syllable. Damn, how he wished he could erase her from his heart! Katey had been right about that, Nick admitted as he struggled to keep from hauling Marianne into his arms without a second thought. Emotions crammed up inside his chest, making it impossible to speak without his voice sounding like sandpaper over a raw board. "Perhaps I should rephrase that," Nick said. "What I meant was, why now, Marianne?"

Swallowing the dry lump of despair in her throat as she met his gaze, Marianne fought against tears. How many times had she heard him use that voice, the one so empty of feeling you could hear the hollow echo of his pain? But he was waiting for an answer now. Her head tipped sideways, her brow wrinkled. She'd expected his questions, had expected his anger. Not this detached acceptance, this—

The truth slammed the breath from her. "You . . . you called me Marianne?" Her words were little more than a gasp of air, yet they plunged into the room like a whirlwind, swirling away the restraints between them.

Nick dropped his hands, his fists tightening as he stared over her head. "I know everything Horace Squiggs knows, which isn't a whole hell of a lot. For God's sake, Marianne! Why didn't you tell me before?"

Now she saw that the agony etched in his face came, not from the knowing, but because she hadn't given him her trust. At last there was nothing left to hide, nothing left to hold back. She raised a hand to her mouth, choking on a sob of pain and relief. "Oh Nick, I wanted to! But first I was so afraid of what would happen to me, and then . . ." Marianne's eyes brimmed as she shook her head slowly. ". . . and then I was afraid of what would happen to us."

Now anger surged through him, unaccountable rage at the world for frightening her so thoroughly, and at her for denying him the chance to help. He reached her in two strides, grasping her shoulders roughly. "Us? Has there ever been an 'us', or were you planning to leave all along?"

"Don't you think I didn't *try* not to love you? I didn't want this to happen. It hurts too much, and . . . Oh God, Nick! I never wanted to hurt you . . . I love you so!"

He started to say something, then stopped, crushing her against him as his mouth joined hers hungrily, joyfully, until they were both breathless with passion and a sense of wild release. Marianne kissed him with all the willingness, all the unrestrained longing she'd denied him before, and still it wasn't enough.

"My love," he whispered hoarsely, his lips raining kisses upon her forehead and eyelids. "My sweet love."

She allowed herself to feel the comfort of his strong arms around her, to let the steady rhythm of his heart seep through her, calming, holding. Healing.

Nick rested his chin on the softness of her golden hair, emitting a shaking breath into the night. So much for making her pay, he thought wryly, thinking back over the vow made on the road home from Katey's place. He could no more keep his distance than he could have ripped his own heart from his body. His chest swelled with love, sheltering her, guarding her.

After long moments that were lost in time, Marianne raised her head and placed a loving hand over the place where his heart beat strongest. "I should have trusted you from the beginning," she said. "Will Marshal Squiggs believe me if I tell him I never killed anyone?"

"He already knows that," Nick answered slowly. "So we have plenty of time to—"

"No, we don't!" Marianne's whispered cry was fraught with panic. Quickly, she told him about meeting Rhys Hartley on the train, and then the frightening experience of that afternoon.

Renewed anger swept through Nick, but he schooled

himself to consider the situation rationally. "Hartley won't get a blasted dime from us!" he said through clenched teeth. "If he thinks I'll pay him to keep quiet—"

"But that's not it at all," Marianne pleaded. "I've been thinking about this all day, and I remember now that he talked as if I already had money of my own. Nick, I've checked the local papers everyday since I've been here. There was a brief article mentioning my uncle's death, but it never said anything about me, or the ledgers I took. So how could Rhys Hartley know, unless he followed me from New York?"

"There was no money, was there?"

Marianne shook her head. "Only the ledgers. I'm sure that Adam Pemberton hired Rhys Hartley to get them back. But I don't have them—"

"Horace does. He said the books were incriminating enough to land Pemberton in jail for a long time. Was it Pemberton who killed your uncle?"

Marianne nodded, shivering as she did. "I saw him do it, but after I ran away he must have paid one of the servants to say he'd seen me with the knife."

Nick drew her close again, caressing the sensitive skin on the back of her neck with a comforting motion. "Then we'll ask Horace to find out about this Hartley fellow. If Pemberton did hire him, he'll have some explaining to do."

Closing her eyes, Marianne gratefully leaned against him. Despite her resolve to stand up for herself, it felt wonderful to let Nick shoulder the burden for just a minute. The tension drained from her as he continued his tender massage, and for the first time in weeks, hope sprang from deep within her when he crooned reassuring words.

"Marianne," he whispered huskily, cupping her chin with his free hand and wiping away her tears with his thumb. "Don't worry, sweetheart. It'll be all right."

Chapter 17

Marianne woke with a start. The moon was high in the sky, only a few wispy clouds attempting to block its brightness. Disoriented, she sat bolt upright, still clutching Nick's sleeve where her head had rested just moments before. Then she remembered. After insisting that she return to her room to pack more clothing while he hitched the team, Nick had loaded up quickly. Once they were on their way, Marianne had slipped into exhausted slumber, lulled by the rhythmic rumble of the wagon's wheels.

"Where are we?" she asked groggily, looking around. Nick was drawing the team to a halt, which was probably what had awakened her in the first place.

"About halfway to Olympia," Nick answered, as he tied off the reins. "Thought I'd give the horses a short rest and stretch our legs a bit. Coming down?"

"Olympia?" Marianne gasped. "I thought you were taking me to Marshal Squiggs!" Her shock was tempered a little by the sheepish grin that spread across Nick's face, but then his look changed to one of utter seriousness.

"I had the distinct impression," he said levelly, "that you were in a hurry to get away from Tacoma. Were you not?"

"Yes," Marianne admitted, despite the catch in her throat.

"Well, then, you've got your wish."

He stood beside the wagon, obviously waiting to

help her down, but she was too stunned by what he had said to move toward him. "Why . . . why Olympia?"

Nick shrugged impatiently. "Because I have friends who'll help you there. If you're not getting down, then I'm going to take a short walk into the trees."

Marianne watched him go with a mixture of shock and growing confusion. He wasn't preventing her from leaving; in fact, he was going to help her. Even after she had admitted she loved him, he still did not expect her to stay.

A sickening shame crept over her as she tried to make sense of what was happening. From the moment she'd arrived in Tacoma, she'd fought him, fought her growing feelings for him. And she felt sure, deep in her heart, that his feelings for her had grown as well. Maybe he didn't love her the way he had Alicia, but hadn't he offered her more than she'd ever known before?

And she'd paid him back by trying to leave. No warning. Little explanation. Only good-bye. Was it any wonder that he wanted to pack her off, which was, after all, what she'd been saying she wanted all along?

When Nick returned to the wagon, he found Marianne leaning against the side, staring wistfully across the bay. A feeling of great tenderness seized him, so strong it nearly took his breath away. Quietly, he came up behind her, wrapping his arms around her waist.

"The water is so beautiful when the moon is out," she sighed, leaning back into his warmth, loath to waste one single moment of his presence. "It makes the waves sparkle like a million stars dancing across the sky."

Nick inhaled the sweet scent of her hair, enjoying the feel of her slender body pressed along his. She trembled within his embrace. "Beautiful," he murmured in agreement, hardly looking at the water. After several minutes more of holding her torturously close, he said thickly, "We'd better get going. I want to make Olympia by morning." He felt Marianne's shoulders tense beneath his hands, but then she sighed and nodded.

He chuckled. "We'll come back at night sometime since you like this spot so well, but it's not bad by daylight, either."

"Come back?"

"Of course we will," he said gently. "I travel to Olympia several times a year. You can come with me anytime you'd like."

"But, why . . . ?" Her voice caught in her throat, ". . . why are we going tonight?" She turned in his arms.

Running his thumb over the soft curve of her cheek, Nick peered uneasily into her questioning eyes. "I guess it wasn't very fair of me to whisk you away while you were sleeping, but I didn't . . ." He cleared his throat. ". . . I was afraid you'd change your mind." His voice probed her with gentle insistence. "I don't want to wait any longer to be your husband."

Her eyes widened in disbelief. "You want to marry me?"

He grinned happily.

"After all I've put you through . . . all the trouble yet to come?"

"Marianne . . ." Nick's voice was husky as he drew her closer, one hand still cupping her chin. "Do you believe me when I say there isn't any problem we can't conquer together?"

"Y-y-yes," she answered against his lips.

"Don't you know I'll protect you if it takes every penny I have, every minute of time for the rest of our lives? I told you once before I could handle whatever came up, even if it was more than we bargained for."

Happiness surged through her, tinged with the strange sensation that she was caught up in a crazy, beautiful dream; one too good to be true. "But Nick," she protested weakly. "I don't expect . . . I couldn't ask you to . . ."

"You didn't ask." Pulling her hard against his chest, Nick slanted his mouth over hers in a kiss that was tender and bold, relentless, yet questioning. When he finally lifted his head to draw a breath deep into his lungs, he said quietly, "You didn't ask, I did. And you haven't answered yet."

She knew she should refuse, at least until her name had been cleared, but Marianne was powerless to deny her heart. "Oh, yes, Nick. I do want to marry you."

It was much later before they moved away from each other, and then only enough to walk arm in arm to the wagon. Though Marianne could have happily stayed there forever with him, wrapped in his arms in the middle of nowhere, Nick was anxious to complete their journey. With a stab of guilt, she remembered that *he* had had no sleep at all, and wouldn't until they reached their destination.

"Claire will worry," Marianne mused aloud.

"I left her a note while you were packing, explaining what happened and why we left. I figured you'd be more comfortable away from Tacoma until we get this straightened out."

There was only one way to "straighten it out," Marianne knew, but in the wake of Nick's proposal, even the thought of her imminent journey to New York wasn't nearly so frightening.

Nothing they couldn't conquer together, Nick had said. As the wagon carried them toward an uncertain future, she could only pray he was right.

They rolled into Olympia just as the orange-red glow of the sun rose behind them, their long shadow leading the way into the city that was the heart of the territory. Nick had told her once of Washington's struggle for statehood. The territorial government had petitioned thrice, in 1861, 1867, and again in 1887, and was refused all three times. Just recently, another request had been made, which was still under consideration by Congress. When she saw the waking city with its modern, three-story buildings and prosperous storefront businesses, Marianne felt as though she'd been swept back to civilization.

Nick glanced over at her, assuring himself that she had recovered from the frightening ordeal of the pre-

vious day. Though she was still a bit pale, her eyes
were bright, eagerly taking in the sights, and she held
herself high, her posture projecting anticipation. His
arms ached to reach for her, but he curbed his own
rising excitement.

They drove through the center of town, just waking
to the start of a bustling new day. Shopkeepers, sweeping the boarded walkways in front of their stores or
setting up wares for display, looked up as they passed,
nodding in silent greeting. A couple of seamen staggered toward the waterfront, their bedraggled appearance in sharp contrast to the men in business attire
scurrying to work.

They neared a large hotel on the main street, but
Nick gave no indication of slowing. At Marianne's
puzzled expression he smiled enigmatically. "First things
first," he explained.

Thinking he meant to find a place for the horses,
Marianne continued to look around at the city of
Olympia as he drove. It was when he reined in before
a small office building of dubious architectural style
that it dawned on her what he intended. A sign, painted
white with black script lettering, proclaimed Justice of
the Peace. Wordlessly, she looked at Nick.

"We may be a little early," he said with a slow grin,
"but I didn't want to check into the hotel before it was
official." His expression changed to one of great tenderness and concern. "Do you mind not having a
fancy wedding?"

It struck her then, another reason why she loved
him so, and she felt its force lift her soul a notch
higher. He would have laughed to hear himself called
sensitive, but how else could she describe the way he
reached deep into her, knowing how to touch her
heart in ways that left her weak and trembling with
love? Afraid to trust her voice, Marianne could only
smile in answer, but it was a smile that told him
everything he wanted to know.

As it happened, Nick was wrong about arriving too
early. When he knocked at the door, his impatience
sounding in each hollow thump, they were greeted by

a bespectacled gentleman whose rotund figure belied the quickness of his step as he led them through a short hallway and into his office.

Justice Vernon Hobbs, as the magistrate introduced himself, raised not an eyebrow when Nick made his request. "From Tacoma, are ya?" he asked, filling out the required license. "And you, pretty lady?" His unaccusing gaze fell on Marianne.

For just a second her heart lunged crazily, but then Nick reached to clasp her hand. Lifting her chin, she replied, "Marianne Blakemore, recently of New York. Now, Tacoma."

There was a long, tortured moment when Judge Hobbs hesitated, his fountain pen poised above the paper. Holding her breath, Marianne clutched Nick's strong fingers tightly.

"All right then," the man frowned, "let's just put Tacoma. Makes things simpler."

It was a struggle to keep from expelling an audible sigh of relief, but she somehow managed to let her breath out slowly. It felt good to use her real name for the first time in over a month, she realized, and she was glad their marriage was beginning without the spectre of dishonesty shadowing them. From the way Nick's gray eyes met hers with an approving glow, she knew he understood, too.

"Shall we get on with it?" Judge Hobbs asked, pushing his portly frame away from the desk. He rose and walked to the wall that separated his office from that of the attorney next door, rapping soundly on the plaster as he explained, "Usually someone in by now. They'll come on over soon."

True to his word, within moments his office door was opened by a wiry young man wearing a striped vest, his sleeves held tight by a pair of black elastic garters, and an older woman in a gray bombazine dress that was hopelessly out of style. In one hand, however, she carried a bouquet of half-wilted flowers, probably snatched from a vase on her desk. Smiling shyly, she handed the improbable mixture of daisies and roses to Marianne.

"They're from my own garden, miss," she offered kindly.

Swallowing sudden tears, Marianne thanked her.

Judge Hobbs uttered a loud "Ahem" and they all stepped forward. Eyes twinkling behind his glasses, he motioned to Nick to step around to Marianne's other side. "We want to do this right, now, don't we?" he chuckled. The two witnesses—law clerk and stenographer—took their places behind the couple.

Reverently, Nick placed Marianne's hand in his own, then gave the judge a solemn nod.

Though she tried to retain the magic of these few minutes in her mind, compressing it into a memory she could hold and savor for the rest of her life, she barely heard the words the magistrate was saying. All of her senses were tuned to the man beside her, the man who was pledging to cherish her for better or for worse. When her turn came to repeat the vows, her response was heartfelt and automatic, as if the lovely ceremony, so perfect the words had changed little in hundreds of years, had already been performed in some other dimension of time.

When she looked up at him with melting eyes, Nick felt the warmth of a thousand suns spread through his veins, quickening his pulse with its penetrating heat. Though he would have denied anything had been missing from his life before, this woman had come into his world and filled a void that surprised him with its depth. Now she was entrusting herself to his care with a quiet confidence that thrust away every doubt, every hesitation that ever shadowed his heart.

". . . now pronounce you man and wife."

The words hung suspended, the moment stretched into timelessness as Judge Hobbs playfully paused. He liked to watch the expressions that came to the faces of the young people as they waited in agonizing anticipation for the best part—*his* favorite part of the ceremony, and a line that he would never tire of repeating. Spreading his palms wide and smiling benevolently, he proclaimed, "You may kiss the bride."

He needn't have bothered; it was already too late.

*   *   *

Claire Fortune sat with her hands folded primly upon her lap, fighting the familiar heaviness in her chest that threatened to leave her breathless and weak. She would *not*, she vowed silently, allow those she loved to pay for her frailty. And so, with calm determination, she hushed the warning ache that clamored through her side and smiled at the man seated across from her, as if nothing on earth could be wrong.

"Why, Horace!" she exclaimed in a mildly reproving tone. "You can't expect me to keep a bell around his neck. He's a grown man."

"I know that, Claire. But I've got some important information for him and his young lady, so if you know where they are . . ." Horace hated to press, for he could see the effort it took for Claire to maintain her facade of normalcy. He was too close a friend not to see the way her skin was stretched as thin as parchment across her cheekbones, or that her lips were taut with unspoken pain. It made his heart ache to see her fading, but as always, his job took precedence over sentiment. Even so, he tempered his impatience.

"I don't know where they are, Horace. Have you checked with Nick's friend, Marcus Knowles?"

Marcus, as Claire well knew, had been called to San Francisco on business with the railroad, but Horace didn't blame her for trying that track. He decided he'd been wrong to shield the truth from her; in this case, honesty had to be less painful. "I know about the girl. You'll just have to trust me when I tell you she could be in danger."

"I do, Horace, but I have nothing more to say." It wasn't as much a matter of trust, Claire thought, as it was a question of loyalty. Nick had asked her to keep their whereabouts a secret, and she would do it even if Horace tried to strangle it out of her, which she was sure he would never do.

"Then will you answer me this question?" Horace knew when to accept defeat, at least temporarily, but there were so many intriguing facets to this case, he could afford to let go of one long enough to study another. "Knowin' that she never intended to marry Nick in the first place, how far d'ya think he'll go to keep her out of trouble now? I mean, ya don't think he'll do anything foolish, do ya?"

Beckoning to the servant who waited in the doorway, Claire gave the marshal an enigmatic smile. "What exactly would you consider 'foolish'?"

Sue Kim entered, bowing slightly as she handed Claire a folded piece of paper. Horace paid little attention to it; he was more concerned with finding a tactful way to present his next question. "He wouldn't consider . . . ?" He paused, more flustered than he cared to be. "He isn't goin' ta marry her anyway, is he?"

Claire studied the bold, squared-off letters that spelled out the message in her hand. Just as suddenly as it had begun, the pain in her chest eased, simply floated away like a tiny bubble drifting downstream on a gentle current. She felt a lightness that had long eluded her, and she found herself wanting to laugh like a girl. Instead, she merely cocked her head and dimpled as she handed over the telegram.

Horace couldn't help returning her contagious smile, but his grin turned to one of chagrin when he read the missive in his hand. *Mother*, it read. *Have arrived safely. Stop. Will come home when we can. Stop. Love to you and E. Stop.*

It was signed Mr. and Mrs. Nicholas Fortune.

The sweet scent of honeysuckle wafted through the steamy air, circling around her head like a lazy cloud. Marianne lay back in the tub, luxuriating in the hot bath provided by the hotel, glad that Nick's errands had allowed her some time to herself. The events of the past two days left her bewildered and slightly breathless. She was grateful for the chance to collect her scattered thoughts.

Stretching her head back, she lifted the soft, absorbent sponge to her chin, letting the soothing water trickle gently down the curve of her throat, easing the tension from her limbs.

Married.

Her mind played with the word, turning it over and over, examining it from all sides with a sense of wonder and awe. She knew the meaning—to be joined in legal wedlock, to be made husband and wife—but did she know the reality, the embodiment of that word into a state of being that would forever be a part of her existence? Would she ever?

Sighing, Marianne reminded herself that no one could—especially when a mere four hours had passed since they'd spoken their vows. It was much easier, she decided, to think about something more substantial, more tangible.

Nick. Only one syllable, but the sound of his name filled her mind's eye with a thousand images, each one more beloved than the last. She said it again to herself, and would have left it there, comforted, but she remembered the way he'd looked when he left her, his expression guarded once more, his words awkward. Her eyes knew every angle and plane of his rugged face, her hands ached to learn each hard expanse of his body, but would she ever know his mind, his heart?

Nick. She repeated it in silence, wanting to capture again the reassuring strength of him, his powerful essence, but instead she felt it slipping from her grasp. She closed her eyes.

"Nick," she said aloud, panic wrapping around her as the sound fell lifeless from her lips, nothing more than movement of her tongue, a constriction of her throat.

Marianne struggled upright, splashing water onto the thick Oriental carpet beneath the tub as she reached for a towel. Her mind was spinning rapidly now, trying to recover the substance, the solidness that had slipped impossibly beyond her reach. She dried herself roughly, savagely, forcing her senses to sting with awareness. Flesh tingling, she donned the robe that lay in wait across a large, horsehair sofa, pulling the sash so tight she winced. With hurried steps, she crossed to the window overlooking the street.

Nick. She spotted him almost immediately, though there were more people out and about than there'd been that morning. She recognized his proud stance, the rhythm of his walk, even before she could distinguish his features in the distance. Relief cut through her fears like a diamond through glass, clear and vivid, sharpening her vision and honing her senses until they thrummed with life.

He was coming toward her. Her husband. Nick.

By the time the doorknob rattled at his entrance in the next room, Marianne had calmed down considerably, making herself take several deep, cleansing breaths before discarding her robe for one of the dresses she had hastily packed at Nick's request. She chose a simple shirtwaist, plain except for the twin ruffles that descended from her shoulders to her waist in a wide V. The vibrant, cornflower blue nearly matched the color of her eyes. After a quick glance in the mirror, she opened the connecting door that led to the suite's sitting room.

Nick looked up, his shoulders flexed back in the process of removing his shirt. Surprise registered on his face in the split second before he grinned. "I thought you'd be asleep."

"You forget, I slept most of the way here last night. You're the one who must be tired."

She stepped toward him, her trembling hands reaching for the soiled garment, easing it from his arms. Cool fingertips brushed the crisp, dark hair of his forearms, sliding between the fabric and his skin as they pushed the cuffs over his wrists and hands in a gesture so intimate, so . . . wifely . . . that his chest ached. He watched her fold the shirt lovingly, placing it atop a low bureau before turning to him again.

"Thank you for the bath. It was heavenly." She lowered her eyes demurely. "I can send for more water, if you'd like."

Nick's smile quickened as a blush suffused her face, as red as a twilight sun reflecting its glory upon the ocean's waves. Her lips twitched once, as if she would have spoken again but thought better of it, though he knew it was shyness that kept her silent.

"Only if you promise to scrub my back."

Marianne's gaze flew upward, meeting his laughing eyes for a brief moment before skittering away. Flames licked at her cheeks, not because the thought of performing such a task was repellent to her, but because his request evoked a wave of longing so intense she wondered if he could see her heart pounding in her throat. "I . . . I will if you want me to," she whispered in return, daring to look straight at him. His breath took a tiny catch.

"I do," he rasped.

The next few minutes passed in an agony of waiting as Nick rang for more water, then quickly told Marianne what he'd done since dropping her at the hotel that morning. She smiled when he quoted his telegram to Claire, picturing the way the woman's emerald eyes would sparkle with tears.

Her smile turned to a frown when he mentioned the wire he'd sent to Theodore Jacoby, the New York attorney who had handled the marriage contract with Mary Cooper. "He's discreet," Nick explained, "and as honest as the ocean is wide. I've worked with him ever since I started shipping timber East and needed someone close by to protect my interests. He'll find out exactly what the charges are against you and where we stand, now that Horace found those ledgers."

Marianne's eyes showed her doubt. "There's no way to know for sure whether those papers will do any good," she said, shaking her head. "I *hoped* they would when I took the books, but Adam Pemberton may have found a way to get around whatever is in them."

"Not likely," Nick assured. "Horace thinks he's a sight too anxious to get his hands on them. But you've nothing to worry about now. I'll take care of it."

"But . . ." Marianne let her protest die as the maid knocked, entering the room with two large pails of steaming water. It might have been comforting to let Nick shoulder her burden last night, when she was too frightened and exhausted to think what to do, but now, in the light of day, she was unwilling to force him into that position.

Somehow, she would convince Nick that, married or not, she must carry out her original decision to go back to New York and trust that justice would be served. She sighed as she watched Nick move to the bedroom. If only she weren't such a coward!

Sensing her troubled mood, but thinking it was merely modesty that made her hesitate, Nick reached for her hand, capturing her fingers and drawing them to his lips. "Wait here. I won't be long."

Marianne stared at the door closed between them. Through the walls, she could hear the sound of water being poured, then the sloshing ripples as something heavy settled into the large tub. She smiled when Nick's groan of pleasure reached her ears through the thin walls.

God, how she loved him! Her love was a living, growing thing, pulsating with energy that at once made her weak and gave her strength. Never once had he asked her for an explanation of her actions. Perhaps, to him, that meant little, but to Marianne it was a gift that lifted her out of a darkness of spirit just as surely as he had carried her out of the train's uncertain hell. He repaid her lies with his protection and her distrust with acceptance; she could do no less than to return his passion with her heart.

Nick heard the soft click of the latch as it turned, felt the whisper of chill air touch the back of his shoulders when the door opened and then closed again. Words came to his lips—something gentle and teasing about changing her mind—but they froze there, unspoken, when she touched the nape of his neck where it rested on the tub's curved rim. When her fingertips moved sensuously, delight shuddered through him, and he quickly grasped the brass on either side of him, pulling himself forward so that her hands would have the whole of his back to explore.

And they did.

Tentatively at first, then with growing boldness, Marianne splayed her fingers over him, measuring, searching, absorbing the multitude of sensations playing beneath her hands; rigid shoulder blades hidden by pliant flesh, hard muscle rippling under satiny smooth skin, made warm and musky by the hot water beading like myriad jewels upon his back. Slowly, she bent nearer, brushing her lips against him in a kiss as light as an angel's wings.

Nick shuddered again, but made not a sound as he waited for the next touch, the next word. And when it came, he felt as though his heart would break.

"Thank you," she whispered achingly.

He tensed.

"Thank you for believing me," she continued before he could speak. "No one . . . no one has ever done that before."

"Never?"

"No, never. Once, when I was little, one of the other girls in the orphanage accused me of stealing a piece of ribbon from under her pillow."

"Just a ribbon?"

"A very tiny, ragged one," Marianne acknowledged, "but no less special to her. We had so little of our own, it's not surprising that she treasured that ribbon."

The note of compassion that touched her voice made Nick's heart swell. He wished he had known her as a child, wished more that he could have turned her childhood to one of happiness and light. Her melodic voice drew him back into her remembering.

"The ribbon must have been lost when the bed linens were changed, but Jane said I took it. She was older than me, and so distraught that she must have sounded very convincing to Mrs. Kendall and the other teachers. They made me feel . . ."

He nearly turned around when she paused, but she pressed her cheek against his back and continued, a sigh tremoring from her lips as she did.

"They made me feel so helpless, because I couldn't make them understand that I hadn't taken it. That awful feeling of desperation was far more punishment than the whipping that followed. And it was nothing compared to the past few weeks. I . . . I didn't want to trust anyone, least of all you."

"Why?" Nick's question was softly spoken, and he could no longer keep himself from reaching for her. Swiveling in the water he pulled her toward him, framing her face in his large hands as if it were the most precious, fragile treasure he'd ever seen. The smile on her lips held all the wonder of discovery, plus a measure of regret that knifed through him with a keen thrust.

"When you grow up in an orphanage," she whispered sadly, "you learn very fast that love and trust are illusions, existing only by the degree with which you long for them. I taught myself not to wish for something that could never be, until you showed me how wrong that lesson was. You trusted me even when you had nothing to gain."

"I had *everything* to gain," Nick growled softly. Her eyes were vivid sapphires shimmering in the dim afternoon light, and he found himself drawn into their glittering depths, caught in a whirlpool of emotion.

"I love you, Nick." Marianne saw the passion that flashed in his eyes like quicksilver, growing darker and deeper and more compelling with each moment that passed. She held her breath, waiting for a response that would not come, yet reveling in the one that did.

It would have to be enough.

Chapter *18*

Hungrily, he covered her mouth with a kiss that was more forceful, yet more compelling, than any they had shared, then broke it off abruptly, leaving her dazed and shaking.

"Your dress is getting wet."

Marianne couldn't help smiling at the way his voice rasped, its rough texture revealing the depth of his desire. Through the haze of her own need, she recalled what Claire had told her about Nick's innate shyness where women were concerned, and the memory brought to her a heady sense of confidence she had never before imagined. Sitting back on her heels, she trailed her fingertips over his wet shoulders, sliding them down his muscular arms with a touch that was purposefully light, and unquestionably seductive.

"I wouldn't want that to happen," she murmured, shaking her head with pretended concern. Her gaze met his as she raised her trembling hands to the buttons at her throat.

Nick's lungs contracted sharply, his breath snatched away by the rapturous expression on her face, a combination of innocence and longing and pride that all but shattered his control. And that before he realized what she intended to do.

Slowly, for her fingers fumbled with the buttons as though they were objects alien to her, Marianne unfastened the front of her dress from chin to waist, revealing a tantalizing amount of her chemise. Her breasts ached and she felt the blood rush upward to fan her cheeks with flame, yet she did not falter.

Broken laughter spilled from him. "Shall I come out or will you come in?" Nick asked.

Marianne eyed the tub skeptically. His long legs were folded, knees jutting from the water, his elbows propped on the narrow sides that looked hardly wide enough to bear his broad shoulders. But his chest, the smooth, bare skin beaded with moisture, looked so inviting that she paused, considering what it would feel like to rest against him.

"Come," he murmured, sensing her secret wish. He beckoned to her, knowing that her shy smile meant she had decided. He watched impatiently as one by one, each article of her clothing met ignominiously with the floor. Her blush was the only thing covering her body, yet she moved toward him, reaching a dainty hand to his for support as she stepped into the tub.

Warm water lapped over Marianne as she lowered herself between his knees, facing away from him. At one point she nearly slipped and her hand, reaching for the rim of the tub, instead clutched his knee. She started, the furred texture of his skin so foreign to her experience that she would have jerked her hand away were it not that she would have lost her balance without him. But by the time she had settled into the water she decided she liked touching him there, and she left her small hand lying against his leg.

Marianne would have been shocked to know how the sight of her fetching bottom, temptingly close, had nearly driven him wild, but Nick took care not to frighten her with his need. Since they'd first made love—had it been only a few nights ago?—his head had been filled with her. On that night he had overcome her denials with frenzied desire; now he knew there would be no resistance, that he could coax from her the same urgency that turned his own blood to molten lava.

Gently, he grasped either side of her waist, sliding her backward until her hips fit snugly between his thighs, then raised his hands, his fingertips grazing the sides of her breasts. She shuddered once, then leaned back slightly.

"Sweet," he murmured into her hair, drawing her closer into his embrace. She tensed when her back touched the rigid evidence of his desire, but he tightened his arms, not allowing her to escape. "Relax. Enjoy the warmth of the water. Feel the way it touches your skin."

His voice was deep and persuading, luring her into obedience as if she was no longer in control of her own senses. In a way, she was not, for her mind swirled with a thousand thoughts, a thousand images, each one new and exciting and intimate.

She felt her muscles grow weak and pliant beneath his touch, for he *was* touching her now, his hands beginning a gentle exploration that she hadn't the will to forbid. And then she remembered, joyously, that there was no need to put a stop to this exquisite pleasure, for it was now within her rights.

"Oh, Nick . . ." she sighed, contentment and arousal warring with each other. "Are we truly married?"

His laughter vibrated through her. "We'd better be," he growled playfully. "I paid two dollars for the license and I don't relish the thought of giving you up now. It's taken too damn long to get you here as it is." His voice lowered huskily. "Now, Mrs. Fortune, what do you say we get out of this tub? I find there's not nearly room enough after all."

Marianne picked up his playful note, though her own words were thick with emotion. "As you wish, Mr. Fortune. But like you said, I was just beginning to enjoy the water."

Nick lightly nipped at her shoulder. "I think," he murmured, "that you'll enjoy this much better."

They stood then, Marianne stepping out first, Nick following. Their eyes wandered lovingly over each other, tentatively at first, then with greater boldness as hot desire melted away their hesitation.

Marianne stood still except for the trembling of her legs as Nick toweled her gently from shoulders to toes, lingering at her breasts and thighs. When he finished, he held the damp cloth out to her, his smoldering eyes inviting her to do the same for him.

The heat of his skin burned through the towel, but was no match for the fire that coursed through her own veins as she smoothed away the droplets that clung to him. His muscular arms, his broad chest, the flat plane of his belly; all were favored by her gentle ministrations. She paused, however, before moving any lower.

Nick sensed her shyness, but rather than being disturbed by her timidity, he was overwhelmed with tenderness. With one finger he traced the feathery line of her eyebrow, then cupped her chin until her shimmering gaze met his. "You are my wife," he said. "I want to know every part of you . . . and for you to know every part of me." But when he saw her bite her lower lip to stop it from quivering he smiled and added softly, "In time, my darling. In time."

Remembering that first night together—his gentleness, his patience—Marianne met his gaze unashamedly. "I don't want to wait any longer," she whispered. "Will you . . . will you teach me what to do?"

Nick, too, remembered their night of lovemaking. Every detail was as sharp and refined as crystal in his mind, so perfect that her innocent request surprised him. What he recalled most was the depth of emotion behind her every response, the instinct that was genuine and true. Those were lessons that could not be taught. They were lessons she already knew well, but he did not have the words to tell her so.

Instead, he stooped just enough to catch her legs behind the knees, lifting her into his arms, his eyes locked with hers in silent communication as he crossed into the other room. A moment, a heartbeat, and they were lying together on the bed, flesh to flesh, mouth against mouth, hardness to softness.

As it had before, shyness became a thing long forgotten beneath his fevered touch, and Marianne's hesitation skittered away like a whirlwind, gone so fast she wondered if it had ever been there at all. Her lips parted to accept his searching kiss, her own tongue

quivering with the need to touch and taste, to probe
and savor. His hands brought her to life, his fingers
caressing and lingering over her skin in ways that
teased and tormented and made her ache for more.

But the aching was a sweet thing now, because this
time she knew better how it would end, and the wanting it to end and the wanting it to last was the most
glorious battle of all.

Nick felt the shudder that went clean through her
when he flicked his tongue over the dusky peak of her
breast. Her fingers buried themselves in his hair, gently
holding him there as he suckled and nipped and laved,
then guiding him to its engorged twin when the first
became so hard and sensitive she thought she would
scream.

His hand slid down the satiny curve of her backside,
cupping her rounded bottom possessively, pressing her
against him even more tightly than she was already,
then trailing up across her hip and thigh to nestle in the
soft curls that hid her femininity. With a breathless
sigh of wonder, Marianne let her legs part enough to
admit him.

What followed was little more than a blur of exquisite sensations and unutterable cries that blended together in a blaze of white heat. His touch drove her to
the sky, his entry drove her even higher, and when
Nick tensed and trembled and threw his head back in
a wordless shout, her own blood surged to the boiling
point, then drained away so quickly she felt as if she
were floating clear up to the stars.

It seemed a long, long time before she came down,
but when she did it was to the warmth and safety and
comfort of Nick's arms, and she knew that heaven was
not on some faraway cloud; heaven was here.

Nick watched the smile that touched her lips. "Not
bad for a beginner, Mrs. Fortune."

His voice cracked just a little, so endearing that she
would have cradled his head against her breasts—if
she'd had the strength. "You're an excellent teacher,
Mr. Fortune. Shall we continue with the instructions?"

Nick rolled lazily to one side, propping himself up

on his elbow. He loved the way she looked at him, her expression wondrous, replete. Trailing a languid hand clear up to her breast from where it had rested on her thigh, he watched as anticipation filled her eyes, once heavy-lidded with satisfaction. "Continue . . . or repeat the class?"

She shifted her weight toward him so that they lay face-to-face, boldly allowing her free hand to roam across the broad plane of his chest. The blood was beginning to return to her limbs, and with it came a quickening of her senses. She hadn't known one could feel this way so soon after . . .

Without thinking she glanced down quickly. Up again.

Nick grinned at her startled look, and at the blush spreading all the way from her breasts to the roots of her hair.

"I guess," she murmured, her eyes shining with delight despite her embarrassment, "I've just learned the first lesson: a woman should never underestimate her husband."

Nick sucked in his breath as her hand drifted low over his belly, the gentle, fluttering motion ending only when she found what she had sought. Her fingers traced the length of him, drawing a response that, in spite of his own taunting words, surprised him, too. He growled low in his throat. "In that case," he said, "you may pass to the next class."

Later, after they had risen to eat the wedding supper delivered to their room, Nick broached the subject that had all but slipped from his mind. It returned when he saw Marianne's expression turn thoughtful as she stared vacantly at her plate.

"You're still troubled," he said in a quiet voice.

"I know I shouldn't be," Marianne laughed ruefully. "I should be the happiest woman in the world—and I *am*, truly—but just knowing . . ."

Nick captured her hand in his strong grip. "We should have an answer from Jacoby in a few days. Then we can go from there."

Marianne sighed. "I suppose the more we know, the

better I can defend myself. I just wish I could be sure that I'll get a fair trial when—" Nick clamped down on her hand so hard that she broke off in mid-sentence.

"What are you talking about? There'll be no trial."

Puzzled, Marianne shook her head. "There will be unless Adam Pemberton admits to murdering my uncle, and there's as much chance of that as there is that the moon'll fall out of the sky. We'll just have to hope that the judge will believe my side of the story. Nick, what's wrong?"

He had shoved himself away from the table and stood, towering over her with a thunderous look on his face. "I won't allow you to go back."

"But I must!" Marianne insisted, craning her neck up at him. "You said the marshal already knows who I am, and even if he didn't, Rhys Hartley will send word back to Adam that I'm here."

"I'll handle Hartley myself, and anyone else Pemberton sends after you. And as for Horace, I think I can convince him to keep quiet. He doesn't believe you killed your uncle, either, so there's no reason for you to risk going back."

Swallowing the knot of confusion that had crept into her throat, Marianne frowned. "But surely you can't think that this can go on forever?"

Nick placed his hands on the table and leaned forward, his voice intense and pleading. "Why not? As far as everyone in Tacoma is concerned, you're Mary Cooper . . . now Mary Fortune. There's no need to let on otherwise."

Her stomach took a sickening lurch, realizing at last what he wanted her to do. "But I'm *not* Mary Cooper," she cried. "Please understand. I *want* to end this once and for all."

"It's not worth it—"

"It is to me!"

Seeing that she'd lifted her chin stubbornly, Nick retreated, making a silent vow not to let her take that risk, but not wishing to upset her when nothing was yet decided. He stepped around the small table, placing gentle hands on her shoulders and drawing her up from her chair. "Sweetheart," he said, "at least let me check with some people on this first. If what Horace said is true, the charges may be dropped soon. You were right to take the ledgers; they prove Pemberton is crooked, and maybe more. Please trust me. I only want to protect you."

And how was she to say no to that? Marianne thought ruefully. The man she loved wanted to shield her from harm, and whether or not he was right, she *owed* it to him to let him try his way first. Anything else would be less than grateful.

Sighing, she allowed Nick's arms to warm her shaking limbs. At least they would have more time together this way, she reasoned. She would make the most of the next days.

She knew deep inside, however, that she had already made up her mind to face Adam Pemberton, and delaying the inevitable left a disquieting ache in her heart—though she was damned if she knew why.

At the southernmost tip of Puget Sound, Olympia rested nearly two hundred miles from the Pacific, yet was no less privy to her fits of temper than the coastal cities that balanced on the edge of the continent. The same ocean currents that kept the winters temperate retaliated in the summer by dropping bucket after relentless bucket of rain upon the territory. Washington was known as the evergreen land, but that distinction was not without its price.

Pulling the edge of his collar tighter, Nick shucked a cascade of water from his oilskin slicker as he reached the relative dryness beneath the hotel's covered porch. It'd been raining fit to drown a whale for two days now, but he took the foul weather in stride without even looking back at the two weeks of unusually cloudless skies. Rain, even in July, was the standard for this part of the country.

Slinging his coat over the back of one of the porch chairs so as not to trail water across the lobby floor, Nick ran a hand through his soaked hair and checked to make sure the package he carried had remained dry before entering the hotel.

It was midday and, despite the rain, the lobby was nearly empty. Two elderly men, one in somber black, the other in a red flannel shirt and suspenders, engaged in a somnolent game of chess in the far corner. Nick's mouth curved upward; it looked like they hadn't moved in days. The manager was nowhere in sight, but his appearance was instantaneous when Nick tapped the round bell at the front desk. After settling up with the man so they could get an early start the following morning, Nick nodded his thanks and strode toward the broad stairway, taking the steps two at a time in his eagerness.

Marianne looked up when he opened the door, her blue eyes widening expectantly as she rose from the small desk. His heart careened around the inside of his chest when she opened her arms in welcome, smiling happily, and he couldn't help wondering if she'd be smiling after he told her what he had planned for them.

Tossing the rectangular box on the bed, he folded his arms around her, her scent mingling with the smell of rainwater and wet wool to tease his nostrils. "Hmmm, you feel good," he murmured, pressing her close.

"And you feel . . . wet." Wrinkling her nose, Marianne brushed a few lingering drops from his cheek and laughed. "This constant rain'll take some getting used to. And I thought New York was damp!"

"It's not so bad," Nick teased. "Why, it's only rained twice this week—once for two days and once for three. Besides, you have to admit it's been a good excuse to stay in."

"We don't need an excuse," Marianne reminded him playfully. "Everyone from the cleaning girl to the manager knows we've just been married. Why do you think they wait until nine o'clock to bring up our breakfast every morning?"

"Is that why? I thought they were trying to starve us out of the room."

After dropping a kiss lightly on her upturned lips,

Nick motioned toward the box on the bed. "I brought you a surprise. I wasn't sure about the size, but it was the only one they had that looked right."

Marianne opened the paperboard lid and lifted out a dress of midnight blue taffeta so stiff it rustled when she clasped it to her breast. "Oh, Nick, it's beautiful! Just look at this lace ruching. And these tiny little pleats." She spun around to face him, her smile hesitant. "But I didn't need another dress. I've dozens I haven't worn yet."

"And none of them here," Nick answered, crossing his arms over his chest to watch her fingering the crisp fabric. Even so, he was glad he'd brought her another gift. He liked the way her face lit up like the northern lights whenever he did. "I won't take my wife to dinner with the future governor of the future state of Washington in a riding skirt."

Marianne's eyes flew up to meet his. "Governor?"

"Well, maybe that is speculating a bit too much, since he hasn't decided yet whether to run. But Judge Ryan has a lot of influence in these parts. We're dining at his home tonight."

Nick caught the fleeting expression of fear that swooped over her face like a shadow, then disappeared as quickly. His chest tightened. "He's a friend, sweetheart."

Marianne spread the dress upon the quilted bed-cover, smoothing her fingers over the satiny fabric. The question that had plagued her since their wedding night was now unavoidable. She swallowed hard. "Am I to go as Marianne . . . or Mary?"

Nick sliced his hand through the air impatiently. "Of course we'll tell him who you are. I said he's a friend."

"Well, I just wanted to be sure, you see," Marianne retorted, knowing full well that he was already at the edge of anger, and that his temper would not take much more prodding. She couldn't help herself, though. For three days she'd been mulling over the very possibility of an occasion arising such as this. "I suppose I'll always have to check with you before introducing myself to anyone. On the other hand, we could move away from here and change *both* our names. Then no one would ever guess the truth."

"I'm planning," Nick ground out the words, "to ask Judge Ryan to help you."

"But I should be helping myself!" Marianne's tone turned from irate to pleading. "Oh, Nick, don't you see? I've been running away for more than a month now, and I'm sick to death of it. We should be back in Tacoma, not hiding in a hotel room."

"I had the distinct impression," Nick said archly, "that we were here for more than just hiding."

Choosing to ignore his last remark, Marianne continued. "If you're correct about Marshal Squiggs believing I'm innocent, we should go back and ask him to arrest Rhys Hartley. Then I can return to New York and tell the police there what happened."

Nick could barely restrain the bitter laughter that sprang into his throat. "You think it's that simple? With what crime do you suppose Horace would charge your friend Hartley? Being a 'bad man'? And will the police in New York believe you any more now than they did before you ran away? Or less?"

"I . . . I don't know," Marianne admitted. "I only know I have to try. Besides, have you considered that to do otherwise is against the law?"

"Exactly my point!" Now his bitterness was more than apparent, but Nick no longer cared. He waved one arm in a wild arc. "It's against the law for me to protect my wife, but a murderer is free simply because he knows the right people. The law is not automatic, nor is it infallible. If it were, you wouldn't be here."

Marianne felt the starch leave her all at once, and her head drooped dejectedly as she chewed at her lower lip. "Yes," she said quietly, "there is that."

It was as if the spirit had simply drained out of her like blood, leaving her limp and broken. Just a minute ago he'd been wishing she weren't so all-fired stubborn, but now he ached at the sight of her standing before him, compliant and meek. It wasn't *her* fault, he reminded himself, but he knew with bitter certainty that he'd treated her as if it were.

He raised a hand to her shoulder, then let it fall back to his side helplessly as he forced words past the thickness in his throat. "I can't help the way I feel, Marianne. Let's see what the judge has to say. Maybe he'll know what to do."

Marianne nodded dismally, wanting more than anything else to bury her stinging face in his shirt and feel his arms wrap around her so tight that the rest of the world fell away. But that, she admitted silently, was what she'd been doing for the past three days, and she knew deep in her heart that from now on, it wouldn't be enough.

Chapter 19

Nick left her alone to prepare for dinner, pleading another errand, though Marianne correctly guessed he was making an excuse to put some much-needed distance between them. In truth, she admitted ruefully, it wasn't such a bad idea. For three days she'd wallowed in blissful ignorance of the harsh facts. Now she was grateful for time to consider what was happening.

Foremost, she decided as she toweled herself briskly after her first bath alone in days, was the very obvious evidence that Nick had no intention of helping her get back to New York, now or ever. Why he felt that way she could not begin to fathom. He was a law-abiding citizen, was he not? Then what had caused him to view the system of justice so cynically?

Secondary to that, but just as puzzling, was her own uncharacteristic behavior. Marianne frowned as she snatched clean pantaloons and a chemise from her trunk. Never—or at least not since she'd been seven years old and had called Mrs. Kendall an old poop, earning for herself a mouthful of rancid soap suds—had she stood up to anyone with quite the forcefulness she had summoned today. Was it as she had told Nick? Was she tired of running away, or was it more than that?

She stopped what she was doing, doubled over with one stocking rolled midway up her calf. Three weeks ago she'd been too frightened to admit even to herself how dangerous her situation was, and now she was brimming with more confidence than she'd ever known in her life. And only one thing had changed during that time.

She was in love now, and that made all the difference!

But was it love that made her argue with her husband until he couldn't bear to stay in the same room with her? No, she decided stubbornly. It was love that allowed her to look beyond the here and now, to long for what could truly be.

As she wound her hair into a golden halo on top of her head, Marianne studied her reflection in the mirror. She looked different than she had three weeks ago, she concluded. Not in any way that was readily apparent, but in ways too subtle to describe. It was in the set of her mouth, still shaped the same, but somehow softer, as if closer to a smile. It was in the way her eyes shone bright and clear and free, no longer guarded. It was a look she had recognized in others, but had never seen on herself. Happiness.

And that was just another factor to consider, she thought doggedly. She was happier than any woman had a right to be, and was just selfish enough not to want anything or anybody to intrude on that feeling.

By the time Marianne slipped her arms through the sleeves of the blue dress, her mind was far more at ease than it had been an hour earlier. She felt strong enough to face anything, even Nick's obstinacy. This Judge Ryan, no matter how influential, would never convince her that the lawful way wasn't the right way. On the other hand, if he truly was a good and wise man he might just swing Nick around to her way of thinking.

And she was sure that her beliefs were justified. After all, it had been illegal activity at the root of the problems between Uncle Matt and Adam Pemberton, and that had escalated into crimes far worse. She wouldn't add to the dilemma any more than she already had by fleeing New York. That, she resolved, was the only right way to look at it.

Marianne smiled softly at her own reflection. Now, if Nick would only return to fasten the back of her dress, she could get on with the business of changing her husband's mind.

Marianne found that by the time they reached the Ryans' mansion, some of her nervousness had returned. Perhaps if Nick had continued to rail at her she'd have been fine, but instead he was tenderly solicitous, assuring her again and again that she would *like* the judge and his wife, so much so that she began to wonder why he was concerned.

When her hands clutched his shoulders as he lifted her from the hired buggy, the sudden urge to cling to him swept through her. With a show at brushing a piece of imaginary lint from the lapel of his gray suit, the same he had worn on the Fourth of July, Marianne tried to hide the trembling of her fingers.

"Have I mentioned yet how beautiful you look tonight?" Nick murmured softly as he ushered her through the mansion's doors, his hand splayed across the small of her back.

Marianne returned Nick's smile, but any further answer was halted by the approach of their host.

Judge Ryan was a premier citizen of Olympia, having made his reputation as a lawyer during the days when Washington Territory was but a dark green rectangle on most maps. He'd represented the interests of anyone with a worthy case, rich or poor, and had earned the respect and affection of everyone who ever had the good fortune to cross his path. Nick's first encounter with the illustrious man had been nearly fifteen years earlier, when claim jumpers had threatened Claire's tenacious hold on the land that was now his. Calder Ryan had provided the winning defense, forging a lasting friendship between himself and the Fortune family in the process, even to the extent of assisting Nick through the university in Seattle. Now he and his wife were overjoyed to see their young friend again, and by the warmth of their welcome, were equally prepared to accept his new bride.

"Nick, lad," Calder greeted him effusively. "My congratulations to you."

Judge Ryan was a tall man, as tall as Nick despite the slight stoop to his shoulders. Hair that had once been black was now silver gray, thinning at the top just enough to emphasize his high, sloping forehead. His expression was formidable, and Marianne could imagine the guilty trepidation that would overwhelm any suspect confronted with his hooded stare. Her initial hesitation was soon swept away, however, by the sincerity in his dark eyes as he gazed at her fondly. "My dear," he said, bowing over her hand, "I don't know whether to extend my best wishes for your happiness or to thank you for bringing this rascal to his senses. Please accept both."

Delores Ryan proved to be just as glad to meet Marianne as her husband, though by all appearances she was his exact opposite: short and plump, quick-footed where her husband paced deliberately, talkative while her husband contemplated his thoughts in silence. Before long, Marianne felt completely at ease in her company.

Once, during their sumptuous dinner, Nick threw Marianne a look that seemed to say, "I told you so," but he was obviously pleased that she was enjoying the Ryans as much as he. The conversation was friendly yet fast-paced, forcing Marianne to pay attention so as not to miss anything. Even then, she was startled by the unexpected shift to politics.

"Have you given much thought to running for the state senate, Nick?" As usual, Calder Ryan was blunt.

"Aren't you jumping the gun a bit?" Nick grinned uncomfortably. "I thought you'd given up on that business."

"Not at all. It's never too soon to plan for the future. And just because I've decided against pursuing the governor's seat doesn't mean I don't want the best men at the helm of this state—when Washington is a state. You should consider it."

"You know me, Calder. I'm happier on the mountain than cooped up in an office. I don't know anything about politics."

The judge sipped his brandy slowly, then placed his

glass on the table with a resolute nod. "Exactly why you should run."

Nick smiled humbly in Marianne's direction before addressing Calder Ryan's statement, but she interpreted his gaze as one of resignation. Of course he couldn't enter the political ring now! she thought despondently. Not while his wife was a fugitive from the law! Her heart twisted painfully as she realized the enormity of his sacrifice. She had vowed to be the best wife to him that she could, but would it be enough? Before she had done more than bite her lower lip, trying to think of something appropriate to say, Delores Ryan took matters into her own hands.

Spying Marianne's troubled expression, the judge's wife quickly rose and hustled her from the room. "Men and their politics," she clucked, her eyes twinkling. "I've half a mind to forbid the word in my house, except the judge would likely move out if I did. At least in here we can talk about more important things."

It occurred to Marianne that there was nothing more important to her than her husband's uncertain future, but she remained silent and followed Mrs. Ryan obediently. They entered a small parlor that reminded Marianne of her uncle Matthew's cluttered study. Books and papers lay everywhere, covering tabletops and a large desk at one side of the room. Only one corner, which contained a love seat and two small chairs, appeared to have escaped the riot of reading material.

"Calder hates to have me touch his things," Delores explained apologetically, "and I hate to sit alone in the evenings. So we compromise."

The two women sat down, and Marianne let her mind wander as she listened to Mrs. Ryan prattle on in a motherly fashion.

Compromise. Now there was a word she had always liked, mostly because she imagined there to be a promise lurking just behind it. But if there was some way she and Nick could reach a compromise on the subject of her return to New York, she couldn't see it. And if there was no compromise, she wondered dismally, how could there be any promise in their future?

It was highly possible, Nick pondered silently at that very same moment, that their future might well be decided by what Calder Ryan had to say to him. As soon as the ladies had gone, Nick had laid out to his friend the entire circumstances of their dilemma. Calder had listened with meticulous attention, interrupting only twice to ask pertinent, probing questions. Now he stared unblinkingly at the salt cellar in the center of the table, his fingers steepled in thoughtful contemplation.

"What exactly," Calder inquired, "do you want me to do?"

Nick replied swiftly. "Use your connections to find out where Marianne stands with this thing. From what she's told me, Adam Pemberton is a formidable enemy. I can't protect her if I don't know what weapons he has in his arsenal."

"You should leave it to the law to protect her."

Nick uttered a harsh sound. "Ideally, yes. But if the law were working, she never would have been forced to run away in the first place. Now that she's here I intend to keep Pemberton and his cronies far away from her."

"You'd take the law into your own hands?" Calder prodded.

Nick's voice was deep and resolute. "I would."

The judge knew all too well why his young friend was adamant on this point, and he also knew with absolute certainty that there would be no changing Nick Fortune's mind. He could, however, do what Nick asked of him and hope for the best. Information was what they needed, and information was what they would get. Calder grunted and filled his glass again from the decanter at his side. "You said this fellow who threatened your lady is one of Pemberton's men?"

"I don't honestly know," Nick admitted, relieved that the judge appeared to have relented. It was bad enough that Marianne was fighting him on this; it eased his conscience a bit to know his friend understood. "Horace Squiggs is checking Rhys Hartley out now."

For the first time since the beginning of this conversation, Calder Ryan allowed himself a craggy smile. "In that case," he grunted, "Hartley better pray he's got a damn good explanation."

The alley was as black as cinder, lack of light adding a gruesome touch to an atmosphere that was already hair-raising. Deputy Marshal Phil Owens, however, hardly noticed as he crept with his back pressed against the dank brick wall. Excitement at being in on his first interrogation made his breath come in quick gasps. "There's a light," he whispered over his shoulder. "Think we ought to rush him?"

Behind him, Horace Squiggs strolled forward with a calm that he knew was maddening to the younger man. " 'Course there's a light on," he chuckled. "That's how most folks see after dark."

Nonplussed, Phil moved closer to the door. "Should I break it in?" He eyed the pine planks, measuring their strength, then gauged the distance to the other side of the alley. Not much room for a running start, he thought worriedly.

Holding back a grin, Horace stepped to the door with his fist raised high. "No need ta git yerself hurt. Knockin's a dang sight easier." He rapped sharply.

Phil Owens backed into the shadows, preparing for the possibility of an ambush. He sure wished the marshal wouldn't act so damned nonchalant. What if the bastard resisted? Fingering the butt of his gun, Phil tensed, but to his further chagrin the door swung open smoothly—no ambush, no resistance.

From the doorway of his rented room, Rhys Hartley peered into the alley, blinking rapidly as his eyes grew accustomed to the dark. Under one arm hung his wooden crutch, now swinging uselessly several inches above the ground. In his other hand, a cocked pistol aimed at the shadowed figures. He waited until the shorter one stepped into the light cast from the room's single lamp.

"Mr. Hartley?" the lawman stated unflinchingly.

"Marshal Squiggs," Rhys returned. He relaxed his hold on the gun, letting the barrel drop to his side. At the same time, he eased his weight back onto the crutch, stifling a sigh of relief as the throbbing in his leg began to subside. "What can I do for you?"

Horace jerked his shoulder toward his deputy. "We come ta ask ya some questions."

Rhys stared hard at them both, weighing his thoughts carefully before allowing his decision to show itself in the form of a grim smile. "Come on in, then," he acknowledged, taking a short hop backward. Only young Phil Owens seemed surprised by his next statement. "I've been expecting you."

"What did Judge Ryan have to say?"

Nick couldn't blame Marianne for bursting out with the question the minute they stepped into their hotel room. All the way from the Ryans' she'd been patient, mincing around his terse phrases tactfully. No, he couldn't blame her one bit, but that didn't make it any easier to give her an answer.

He shrugged his shoulders out of the gray coat, letting it drop to the chair behind him. "He said he'd help," Nick replied without looking up as he tugged his shirttails out of his trousers.

"And?"

"And he'll let me know what he finds out."

From the corner of his eye, he could see Marianne standing next to the bed, her slender form poised and tense, just waiting for him to continue. Now there was no avoiding her anxious gaze. He raised his head. "Calder expects it to take at least a week, maybe two. But he knows enough people in New York and in Washington, D.C., to get to the bottom of it eventually."

"But what happens then, Nick? Surely he'll be able to make certain that I get a fair trial."

The soft pleading note in her voice tore at his resolve like a sharp-edged saw, but he steeled himself against the desire to bend to her on this. He'd known that it wouldn't be easy to convince her, but he'd let himself get soft the last few days. "You shouldn't be the one on trial at all," he protested gruffly, moving to stand in front of a tall dresser, his back to her as he removed the jeweled studs from his cuffs.

Marianne's irritation grew as she stared at the wrinkled fabric stretched across his broad shoulders. Wasn't he even planning to discuss the matter with her?

"If you're so sure of that," she declared, "then why don't you want it proved to the rest of the world? The scandal of my trial won't harm your reputation nearly as much as the disgrace when people find out I hid from the law!"

As soon as she said them, Marianne wished she could recall the bitter words that made Nick's head snap upright so fast she could hear his neck crack. He turned to her then, and she flinched a little at the hardness in his expression.

"You know damned well it's not my reputation I'm worried about! If it were we wouldn't be here now."

Marianne could only nod, blinking back the tears that threatened to blur her vision of him. His features looked as if they were etched in stone, and she longed for things to be as they were just a day before. "I do know that," she whispered. "But I don't understand why you're worried. Won't you tell me?"

Nick opened his mouth as if to speak, then his jaw clamped shut again even tighter than before. He almost wished he could tell her, but that would be giving too much, and he'd already given far more than he'd ever intended.

Marianne recognized the stubbornness in his expression, yet she was unable to surrender without one last attempt. "Perhaps we should go back to Tacoma right away and find out from Rhys Hartley exactly what Adam sent him to do. He might know—"

"We're leaving tomorrow for the lumber camp."

"But, Nick—"

Turning abruptly, he grabbed his coat from the chair, hooked his thumb under the collar and slung it over his shoulder. "I've got business to attend to. I can't waste any more time here in Olympia."

Stunned by his sudden change, it took a moment for Marianne to realize he was about to leave again. Her frustration grew, and with it not a small measure of anger. "Now look who's running away!" she blurted. "What are you afraid of, Nick? I thought you said we could face anything together!"

He met her challenging stare, wanting nothing more than to gather her close enough to feel her heartbeat through the blue taffeta dress. But that, he reasoned bitterly, wouldn't answer her question. He strode to the door, pausing to look back at her with one hand gripping the brass knob. "Maybe I was wrong, Marianne. Maybe I was wrong."

Chapter 20

Barney Clawson hesitated before knocking on the door to Adam Pemberton's bedroom. The telegram that had come that morning sure had his boss riled up, and Barney wasn't sure he wanted to know the rest of what Pemberton intended to do about it.

He raised his hand, but before he had a chance to rap his bony knuckles against the oak panel the door was yanked open from the inside.

"Get in here," Adam Pemberton growled menacingly, not waiting for his assistant to enter before he turned and strode back to the bed. A portmanteau had been thrown open across the dark velvet bedspread, shirts and cravats and handkerchiefs piled helter-skelter inside. Barney quickly recognized the extent of his boss's agitation; such disorder was highly abnormal for Adam Pemberton.

"I got the tickets as fast as I could." Barney handed his employer the three cardboard slips with an ingratiating smile, but Pemberton snatched them from his hand without looking up.

"You didn't use my name?"

"Nope. Told them I was Neil Dugan—that's my brother-in-law—and that I was taking my wife and ten-year old son to Philadelphia to visit relatives. You can buy the rest of the passage from there. Ticket agent believed me, because I showed him the daguer-reotype . . ." The evil glare in Adam's eye effectively halted Barney's monologue, and he gulped apprehensively as his boss slammed the traveling bag closed with a vicious blow.

"That bitch!" Pemberton's words bore the force of an explosion, though they were spoken barely above a whisper. "I don't know how she managed to stay alive, but I'll see to it she doesn't last long enough to testify."

"But boss," Barney protested. "If you get caught—"

Adam spun at him, rage turning his face to a deep shade of crimson. "You think I don't know that, you imbecile! I have no intention of getting caught!"

You never do, Barney thought irreverently, hoping that none of his disdain showed in his carefully controlled expression. Even though a part of him would miss the financial rewards of working for Adam Pemberton, another part took grim satisfaction in seeing the powerful man brought down. During the past few weeks, Senator Collins had continued his probe into the matter of the missing bonds, and Barney had watched his employer turn from a cool-headed businessman to a raving lunatic with frightening speed. Now, something had pushed him clear over the edge.

"Did she have the ledgers, boss?"

Pemberton shook his head, clearing his mind from the fog of madness that threatened to overwhelm him. "Apparently not, or that bastard Collins would have had me arrested by now. All the more reason why I can't take any chances with the girl. Without her *or* the books, Collins can't prove a damn thing. He'll have to let it go."

Barney nodded in mute agreement, his mind clicking over every possibility. "What if he gets suspicious when he finds out you're gone?"

"He won't. Tell him I'm sick—hell, tell him I'm dying, if he gets too insistent. You can even pay that old Dr. Schmidt to corroborate your story if you must. Just don't let Collins know that I'm gone, or I'll kill you, too."

These last words were spoken with such deceptive ease that Barney nearly missed them, but when he glanced up, he saw that Pemberton's eyes were glazed with a deadly calm that made his bowels turn to water.

"Y-you can trust me, boss," he said with false affability. "My lips are sealed."

"Indeed," Adam sneered. After donning the coat that lay at the foot of the bed, he hefted the bag into his strong grip and strode to the door, forgetting, for once, that Barney Clawson was paid primarily to perform such tasks. Almost as an afterthought, he snared a gray bowler hat from the highboy and placed it firmly on his head. "I'll wire from Tacoma when it's done."

As Pemberton disappeared through the door, Barney allowed himself to relax, but then Adam's final threat drifted back to him, slicing through his ease like a double-edged sword, sickening him with fear.

"I'll make that bitch pay! I'll make Julia pay for leaving me!"

He was gone then, leaving Barney alternately shivering and perspiring in his wake, feeling like a man who has just come face-to-face with the devil and knows without a doubt that it will not be for the last time.

Chapter 21

Nick was calling her.

Opening her tear-swollen eyes, Marianne struggled to wakefulness. Immediately, she looked to the far side of the bed, and could tell by the rumpled condition of the sheets that Nick had joined her sometime during the night, but now he was up and dressed, leaning over her without touching.

"We'd best get a move on," he said. "It's a two-day trip and I'd just as soon get there before nightfall tomorrow."

By the time Marianne had pushed herself to her elbows, he had turned his back and was cramming the last of his gear into a canvas bag. Her own things were already piled into the small trunk he'd brought with them from Tacoma. She watched as he closed the lid with a resounding thud. Hoisting the trunk to his shoulder, he strode to the door without looking around.

"I'll be back."

After the door slammed behind him, Marianne scrambled from the bed, her heart beating fast. He'd decided to leave immediately because of what Judge Ryan had said last night; that was all but an admission that she was right. Surely it would be only a matter of time before he recognized her need to see this done. His surliness, she hoped, would pass.

She dressed swiftly, donning the split skirt and sensible blouse that Nick had unpacked for her. A carpet-bag lay open on the dressing table, and in it she found her hairbrush and other toiletries. After pulling her hair up into a loose topknot, Marianne shoved the brush and her nightgown into the bag and snapped it shut.

She was ready to go when Nick returned for her, and she followed him down the main stairs silently, wishing she could make him talk to her without waking the other occupants of the hotel. Outside, the horses stood patiently in the traces while he tossed her bag into the wagon with the rest of their things. She quickly pulled herself to the seat.

Without a word, Nick moved to the other side, absently patting one of the animals on the nose as he passed. He hauled himself up beside her, untied the reins and released the brake.

Marianne had hoped that the morning would bring an end to the rift between them, but she was soon to be disappointed. Several minutes passed before she gathered the courage to speak, and then only enough to voice a meek question. "Where is your lumber camp?"

"East."

She threw him a startled glance, but his lips remained taut as he explained, "We'll make Fort Lewis tonight for more supplies, then finish the trip up the mountain tomorrow."

"Will we have to walk then?"

"You wouldn't last a mile in those shoes."

"If I'd known where we were going, I'd have brought proper footwear," Marianne retorted.

Nick's arm went rigid where it brushed against her shoulder, and he stared ahead obstinately, his jaw set at a stubborn angle. "From the very extensive wardrobe you arrived with, no doubt," he drawled.

Stung by his sarcasm, Marianne blinked back the angry tears that sprang to her eyes. "I know quite well that I have nothing to call my own. Nothing except my pride, and you would have me relinquish that, too."

"How much pride do you think you'll have after a few months in a jail cell?" Nick ground out from between clenched teeth. "Or worse yet, at the end of a rope?"

She lifted her chin a notch higher. "And how long will it last if I allow myself to hide behind your name for the rest of my life? What will your friends, your family, say when they find out about me?"

"They won't have to."·

"But they might!" she insisted. "It'll always be hanging over us, over you. Every time you hired a man or met a business associate you'd wonder if he'd take one look at me and *know*. We'd be forever on our guard against men like Rhys Hartley."

Nick gripped the reins hard. "I said I'd take care of him."

"But what about the next one?" Marianne beseeched. "Or the one after that? And if you were to run for a government office we'd be forever in the public eye."

"Damn Calder Ryan!" Nick exploded violently. "I never said I would run in the first place."

Sighing heavily, Marianne placed her hand on his tense forearm, feeling the muscles bunched beneath her fingers. "But don't you see?" she pleaded. "You won't have any choice now."

"That," he said gratingly, "was my decision."

The sky was a misty gray that perfectly matched Marianne's mood once they'd lapsed into an uncomfortable silence. She could barely make out the edges of Mt. Rainier beneath the blanket of clouds swathing it completely. The air had a heavy, trapped feeling, as if it lacked the energy to move about, but wished only to sink to the earth in utter dejection.

Marianne knew exactly how it felt.

How had everything, she wailed silently, gone so wrong in so short a time? And how could she have believed that it wouldn't?

Her memory of their wedding night still had the power to make her blush, even while it made her senses sing with remembered caresses, bold touches. Nick had treated her with gentle patience, eliciting responses that poured from her soul with all the fervor of a summer storm, and then he returned her passion with his own. So loving were his actions that she had soon forgotten to wonder whether he would someday regret his impulsive proposal. She had looked forward to the time when she could walk into his warm embrace as a free woman, clear of the charges haunting her. She'd even thought he would help.

Nick wanted to help, all right, she thought glumly, but not in the way she had anticipated. Instead of offering his support, he was stifling her with his protectiveness. Instead of trusting in the law, he had arrogantly decided he knew better. It was almost, she sighed dismally, as though he believed if she returned to New York she would never come back.

Could that be? Marianne forced another sigh back by holding her breath until her lungs burned. Nick continued to stew at her side, and the urge to reach up to touch the harsh line of his shadowed cheek whipped through her like a gale. Of course that was the explanation, she admitted silently, even though her heart shuddered at the knowledge. He didn't think she'd come back, and there could be only three reasons why.

One was that he believed her guilty, yet did not wish to see her stand trial because of the shame it would bring to him. Though the very thought made her throat constrict with agonized tears, she forced herself to examine the possibility. Nick was too honest to harbor a criminal, and too immune to the gossip of others to be bothered for his own sake. Besides, she reasoned, the ardor of his lovemaking, if not his love, was real. Thankfully, she dismissed that idea.

Which left only two other likely explanations, each one equally conceivable. Either Nick believed her love was false, an emotion she'd contrived to save her own skin, easily shed once she was safely away, or he truly cared for her well-being, but thought her too weak to face her accuser and win.

With a heavy heart, Marianne realized she had given him ample reason to suspect either. Her cowardly escape from New York and her refusal to reveal the truth to Horace Squiggs indicated the latter; her lack of confidence in him gave credence to the first. It was no wonder he didn't trust her enough to let her go.

But no matter how much she regretted her part in making him feel that way, she couldn't change her mind.

She would simply have to prove him wrong on both counts.

Trapped within the uncertain confines of his own thoughts, Nick was unprepared for the soft touch of her fingertips upon his arm. He jumped, clamping his jaw tight against his body's treachery when she gazed up at him with irresistible appeal.

"Please, Nick," she asked quietly, "can't we forget all about this argument for today?"

Normally, he was not one to give in easily, but her eyes shone luminously with a glistening light that made him want to lose himself in their depths, and he'd been more disturbed by the lonely silence of the past few hours than he let on. He was more than ready to make up. Of its own volition, one corner of his mouth curled upward, even while the anger that had clenched his heart into a tight fist fell away. He realized he hadn't given her much of an explanation for his behavior, so it was no wonder she defied him. Now, however, she was offering him a truce of sorts. "Just for today?" he asked with mock gravity.

"Well . . ." Marianne's spirits lifted considerably. So he wasn't going to sulk forever! He still didn't look quite ecstatic, but for right now, friendly would do. It would be far easier to prove her love to him if he acted the willing recipient. Marianne had no idea how to learn to be a stronger, more determined person, but she would surely think of a way in time. "We could try it for one day," she continued solemnly, "and if it's just too difficult, we can always fight again tomorrow."

Nick saw her lips twitch, erasing any doubt in his mind that she was teasing him in her own, delightfully gentle way. "That's a deal I can live with." His mouth relaxed. "Shall we seal the pact?"

She nodded happily, thrusting her small hand toward him.

"Unh-unh." Wagging his head, he hauled back on the reins until the wagon slowed to a complete stop.

"Married women don't shake hands with their husbands. Especially," he added thoughtfully, "when you've so much more to bargain with."

Watching his gaze turn from one of gentle humor to a hungry look that burned through to her very soul, Marianne breathed a shaky reply. "What did you have in mind?"

His throat grew suddenly dry as he ran his thumb over the back of her hand with a slow, sensuous motion. "I guess," Nick said raspingly, "I'll just have to show you."

Marianne would come to look back with longing upon that one brief interlude many times during the day, and not just because of the pleasure Nick's kiss had given her. By the time he halted the wagon for lunch, every muscle in her body was screaming to be stretched. The hard seat and uneven roads had turned the ride into a jolting ordeal as soon as they reached the outskirts of Olympia, and she almost wished she could have slept through this trip like she had on the way in. But if she were ever going to make Nick see that she didn't need to be pampered and coddled, now was the time to start. Gritting her teeth, she stepped down from the wagon without waiting for help.

"Are you hungry?" he asked unnecessarily, for her stomach had just left off with a most unladylike rumble, causing him to grin down at her.

Smiling sheepishly, Marianne bobbed her head. "No more than you, I suppose."

His response was a deep chuckle that made her already flushed skin tingle hotly. At least he was no longer angry; that would have made the trip completely unbearable!

"There's a stream somewhere through there," Nick said, gesturing toward the thick forest that edged right up to the road. "Why don't you see to lunch while I get some water for the horses. It'll take me a good twenty minutes. Will you be all right?" He dug a pair of tin buckets from the rear of the wagon, then turned to her.

"Of course," Marianne assured him, quelling the apprehension that belied her words. Naturally, he had to consider the animals' welfare first. Besides, she reasoned silently, he wouldn't leave her if there were any real danger in these woods. Would he?

"You should be safe enough," Nick was saying, as if he read her panicked thoughts. "If anyone comes by, just pull the team to the side of the road and let them through."

"All right. Anything else?"

He was already striding away from the wagon, but he returned long enough to place a gentle kiss on her forehead. "Shotgun's in the back," he added softly. "But you won't need it."

He had almost disappeared through the heavy underbrush before it struck her that if she wouldn't need it, why had he mentioned a gun in the first place! "Nick!" she called out, stopping herself from blurting that she was frightened, and that she didn't know how to shoot the damn thing anyway!

"What is it?" he hollered back.

She could hear the amusement in his voice even though she couldn't see his smile. It made her feel silly for acting so cowardly. She wouldn't let on. "What do you want for lunch?"

There was a pause from the woods, then the same resonant laughter she had grown to love. "Anything you can dig up."

She stood still beside the wagon for a few minutes, until she could no longer hear the swish and crackle of his movement through the trees. Then, with a resigned sigh, she began to study her surroundings.

Even to her inexperienced eye, she could tell this was virgin timber. The rough trail that Nick called a road was the only indication that men had passed this way before, and from the looks of the wild tangle that nearly spilled onto the track, it wouldn't take long for the forest to reclaim her own, healing the man-made scar until it disappeared completely. The thought filled Marianne with awe. It also brought back the disquieting knowledge that she was completely alone.

Mentally shaking herself, she concentrated on Nick's final words to her. "Anything I can dig up," she said aloud, frowning thoughtfully. Was this Nick's way of testing her, to see if she could measure up to life in the wilderness? Casting a despairing glance around her, Marianne sighed. She hadn't expected an opportunity to prove her competence as a frontier wife to come so soon, and she surely wouldn't have chosen this as the way. She supposed, however, that meeting unexpected challenges was part of what she would have to learn.

Fifteen minutes later, the determination that spurred her to action had very nearly dissolved, and in its place was a sort of helpless surrender. She had tramped as far from the wagon as she dared, pulling up every kind of plant she could find, but none of them bore roots that came even close to looking edible—unless, of course, Nick favored unwashed weeds for lunch. Her searching had, by luck, discovered a thorny bush heavy with overripe blackberries, but ten minutes of rapid picking had resulted in a few scant handfuls of the mushy fruit.

At least, Marianne thought disparagingly as she spread the fruit atop a clean handkerchief on the tailgate of the wagon, they would have fresh water, thanks to Nick.

It wasn't long before crackling footsteps signalled his return. She remembered then, with grim amusement, that in all her haste to provide a meal, she hadn't once thought about the potential threat of lurking beasts or dangerous men, though she might have preferred dealing with one of them to facing Nick with her meager pickings. Straightening her shoulders, she dredged up a brave smile.

"That didn't take long," she chirped ridiculously when he stepped out of the woods with a full pail in each hand.

Nick detected a note of false cheer in her voice but attributed it to weariness. "Right where I thought it would be," he answered. "Almost lost the water, though. Nearly fell over a branch, hurrying because I'm so hungry. How'd you do?"

She watched his broad, capable shoulders bend to the task of watering the horses, and she was unable to keep the dejection out of her voice. "Not as well as I hoped."

"Were you scared?"

His tone was gentle, and so sympathetic she wanted to cry. She shook her head. "No, I was too busy to be scared. Oh, Nick," she said sadly, "I'm afraid you're going to stay hungry."

This time, he couldn't ignore the unlikely words. He straightened up, running a soothing hand along the length of one of the horses as he approached her. "What is it, Marianne? Did something happen while I was . . ."

Stopping short, Nick stared down at the propped tailgate decorated, not by the meal he had anticipated, but by the forlorn little mound of fruit that she'd placed there. He raised a puzzled gaze to her.

"I'm sorry," she murmured, her chin quivering slightly, though she had lifted it as high as her damaged pride would allow. "It's all I could find."

"How hard did you have to look for these, girl?" Nick struggled to keep his mouth from twitching as he gathered her purple stained hands in his.

Encouraged by the way his eyes had softened tenderly, she replied, "Not hard enough, I fear."

"Too hard," he countered, allowing a rueful smile to surface. "I'm the one who should be apologizing. I walked off without even telling you."

Bewildered, Marianne watched him reach into the wagon and rummage beneath a pile of blankets and equipment destined for the lumber camp until he came up with a covered basket the size of a hatbox.

"I had the hotel pack up a lunch," he explained sheepishly. "I forgot . . ." He let the words trail away as she lowered her face into her hands, her frail-looking shoulder shaking so hard, he thought she would break into pieces. But when he reached her, enfolding her into his arms, she raised her head so he could see that it was laughter, not tears, that filled her eyes.

"Oh, L-Lord," she stammered. "I feel like such a fool. But I'm so very glad!"

"Not a fool, sweetheart," he countered, finally letting his own amusement join hers. "But definitely not a mind reader."

Her eyes were shimmering pools of blue, twin mirrors of the sky, sparkling with warmth and humor and something indefinable that wrapped around his heart like it was made to fit. This was a kind of sharing that he'd never asked for, not missing what he'd never known. It only made him hunger to learn what other joys they would discover together.

He gave her one tight squeeze and spoke in a voice that was hoarse, partly from laughter, partly from longing. "I'm starving, woman. Let's eat."

The rest of the afternoon was spent in a companionable exchange of banter and endearments that left Marianne wondering if God were somehow making up to her for all the aching loneliness she'd suffered as a child. It was wonderful, in a very different way, as the physical intimacy they shared. Even if Nick never loved her as intensely as he had Alicia, Marianne felt sure that this would be enough. She quite forgot the vow she had made to herself to guard her heart. It was simply too late. Now it belonged to Nick.

"Tell me about where we're going," she said once, when their conversation had taken a serious turn. "I feel as if I'm forever asking you that very question, but then," she laughed softly, "we've been doing a lot of traveling lately."

"Tired of it?"

His voice tinged with tender concern, making her heart swell with renewed love for him. "Not at all. I suppose this is a kind of . . . well . . . honeymoon."

Nick grinned down at her. "I suppose so. That is, if you're not particular about where you sleep or what you eat. I warned you we'd be camping out tonight."

"Hm-hmm. But at least we don't have to survive on blackberries." She paused. "Do we?"

"No," Nick answered, chuckling lightly. "We'll hit

Fort Lewis in about an hour. We can get something to eat, then set out again to make the most of any daylight left. There's a spot where I usually camp about five miles past the fort. We'll spend the night there."

Marianne could sense his eagerness by the way his eyes lit to flashing silver as he looked out over the trail ahead. "You make this trip often, don't you?" she asked, her words less a question than a statement of fact.

"Often as I can," he confirmed. "The mountain's my second home. It's where I grew up . . . where I learned to be a man. It's the first stake of land my father owned, and for five years he lived for it. Eventually," Nick murmured, "he died for it."

Not knowing how to respond to this, Marianne merely waited for him to continue the story. He had rarely mentioned his father's death, but now that they neared the mountain that was a part of his life's blood, she wondered if Nick would share the tale with her. Instead, he glanced down at her swiftly.

"You wanted to know about the lumber camp?" he asked, a wry smile touching his lips. "The surest way to do that is to tell you about the folks there. Some of them have lived on the mountain all their lives; a few even before Joshua Fortune made his claim. It's a hard life. Raw weather, dangerous work, crude conditions . . . it's no wonder most loggers get itchy feet after a season or two."

"But you said many of these people have stayed."

"They have," he confirmed, "though we still get our share of transients. My father was one of the first lumbermen to establish a permanent settlement, instead of relying on portable camps. We just keep harvesting the timber in a circle around the camp, going a little farther every year. That way, the men with families have a home of sorts."

Marianne lifted her head with sudden interest. "You mean there are women there?" It was a bonus she hadn't anticipated, but one which was more than welcome.

Nick smiled at the way her eyes shone with in-

creased confidence. "Only seven, last time I was up,"
he nodded, "though you never know when one of the
men'll bring a wife back with him after a week in
Seattle. Nine children, too. And one on the way," he
added, almost as an afterthought.

"Will I meet them right away?"

"I'm sure you will. There's not a lot of excitement
on the mountain, except when the occasional mountain lion sneaks into camp." He eyed her teasingly. "I
expect you'll raise near as much of a stir."

Marianne pondered this last thoughtfully. What *would*
these people think of her? she mused. Would they
scorn her for her sheltered upbringing, or would they
accept her as she was? Probably, she sighed inwardly,
a combination of both. After all, she had no reason to
expect instant liking from anyone, least of all from
Nick's employees. She supposed she would have to
prove to them, as well, that she was no hothouse
flower ready to wilt at the slightest hardship. She only
hoped she wouldn't be put to the test too soon, she
thought, remembering her dismal attempt at lunch
time.

"Don't worry," Nick said quietly, interrupting her
silent reverie. "You'll like them."

What he really wanted to say, he admitted to himself, was that they would like her. But he didn't want
to increase her self-doubt by letting on that she needed
such assurances. Besides, he wasn't all that certain
how his friends would react to news of his second
marriage.

Especially since some of them would have bitter
recollections of the first.

Firelight winked cheerfully throughout the tiny clearing like thousands of fireflies darting to and fro, de-
lighting in their playful game. Beyond the ring of
flickering orange light the night edged closer, darkness
and deathly silence threatening ominously, impervious
to the taunting dance of the flames as if it knew that
soon, when the fire faded to glowing embers, the
black forest would reign once more.

These were the vague thoughts that skirted the bound-
aries of Marianne's mind as she peered into the campfire, but any sense of unease she might have felt
disappeared in an instant when Nick settled down
behind her, drawing her back into his embrace.

Leaning into the solid comfort of his chest, she let
the blanket she had clutched around her fall from her
fingers, clasping, instead, the muscular forearms that
wrapped her in a warmth that far surpassed that of the
thick wool, or even that of the crackling flames. It was
a heat that radiated from deep within her soul, and it
was fed by the knowledge that she had found her
home at last.

"Still sore?" Nick asked gently, his voice a rasping
whisper against the heavy silence of the night.

Marianne shook her head. "Not anymore. The fire
feels wonderful . . ."

"Especially after the cold water," Nick finished for
her. He tightened his hold on her, cradling her
slim form against him. "I'll guarantee, though, now
that you've taken your first bath in a mountain
stream you'll never be satisfied with a plain old tub
again. You'll crave a dousing of ice water everyday."

Marianne laughed. "I doubt that, but I will admit it
wasn't as bad as I expected. Especially getting back
out."

Stirred by the memory of the way her skin had
shone with moisture, and of the freezing water cascading over her shoulders, making the tips of her breasts
darken and grow taut, Nick breathed raggedly against
her hair. "I agree."

Her own breath quickened now, the heat spreading
rapidly to a place low in her abdomen, urged on by
the need to demonstrate to him, in the way only a
woman—only a wife!—could, the depth of her love.
Despite their argument, or perhaps because of it, the
desire to affirm what was fine and good between them
coursed strong through her blood. Shifting so that one
muscular arm bolstered her, Marianne lifted her lips,
offering to his a mute welcome. His firm mouth, his
gentle hands, the hard evidence of his desire pressing

against her hip: all contrived to send her senses spinning beyond the realm of control.

Nick, too, was fast approaching the point where passion rules, though he had promised himself that this would not happen . . . not tonight . . . not out here. Tearing his mouth away from hers long enough to draw a shaky breath, he raised his head and forced his hands away from her luscious curves. "We'd best get some sleep," he said gruffly. "We'll have to leave at dawn again if we want to get there by nightfall."

Marianne could feel the red heat wash over her cheeks, and not all of it was due to their close proximity to the fire. Longing blazed through her like a smoldering ember that has been fanned to flame, burning more intensely for the discord that had threatened to dampen their fiery passion. Kneeling toward him, she let the dark wool blanket fall away from her as she raised searching fingertips to his face. "But I'm not tired," she murmured, gazing into the charcoal depths of his eyes, searching for the answer to her unspoken question. A muscle jumped beneath her hand, then his jaw relaxed slightly, turning so that he could place a kiss on her palm. His eyes softened, too, offering her the reply she had been seeking. A gentle laugh rumbled low in his chest.

"I had every intention of acting the considerate husband tonight," he explained, "instead of taking you in the woods like some kind of wild animal."

"A considerate husband," she replied with sweet intensity, "would never deprive his wife of the pleasure of sharing his bed, even if it *is* only a pile of blankets. Besides, you won't be *taking* me. Not when I give myself freely."

Now, instead of emptiness, the surrounding darkness became a cocoon, shielding them from the world, enveloping them within its protective embrace. In the amber glow of the fire, Nick spread the pallet that would be their bed, taking care to clear the ground beneath of any rocks as Marianne looked on. Her heart swelled with emotion as she watched him perform this loving task, knowing what great control it took for him to place her comfort over his own considerable need. Her heart took yet another turn when, as he stood across from her on the other side of the blankets, he gazed at her with an expression filled with a combination of longing and hesitation, and she realized that even after nearly a week of marriage he still did not know that her need matched his.

Though the blood raced to her cheeks, she lifted her head proudly, wanting him to see that she felt no shame or regrets, only joy at their union. She stepped forward and reached for his hand, tugging gently until he knelt with her on the pallet.

That was all the encouragement Nick required. Boldly now, he placed his hands on her hips and drew her toward him, then let his palms wander upward until they cupped her breasts. He inhaled sharply when she moaned out loud, and his narrowed gaze captured hers as he impatiently unbuttoned her blouse. Now his fingertips played upon the soft fullness, memorizing the curves, the textures, the look of her. His thumbs circled and teased the twin peaks of her breasts until they budded tight and hard, then he let his lips and tongue continue the exquisite torture.

Marianne gasped and shuddered forward, her fingers finding their place in the thickness of his hair, her cheek brushing its softness as she drew one unsteady breath after another.

He lowered her to the blanket, and she smiled at the rapid ease with which he removed the rest of her clothing, reveling in the intimacy it implied. Eagerly, she unbuttoned the clean flannel shirt he had donned after washing up, pushing it over his shoulders slowly, letting her hands absorb the smooth heat of his skin. When he turned his back to her to tug at his boots, she lifted herself behind him, wrapping her arms around his waist. She felt the huge tremor that racked his body as her breasts grazed his back, felt too, the muscles of his abdomen contract beneath her touch.

With a brazenness she could not fathom, her fingers searched for the row of buttons that would release his manhood, her heart pounding wildly when he caught and held his breath, but did not put a stop to her exploration.

Her hands trembled, fumbled, unwittingly drawing out his agony of waiting. When he could stand it no longer, Nick hissed through clenched teeth, clasping her hand convulsively, pressing it hard against him so that her fingers curved automatically to fit his throbbing need.

With a cry that was part surprise, part exultation, Marianne let him pull her around so that she rested across his lap. His mouth trapped hers in a kiss so breathlessly demanding that she arched upward, her lips and tongue responding wantonly to the wet, hot sensation she craved. It seemed that he covered her, his hands and mouth loving each inch of her, touching her everywhere at once, and yet not nearly enough.

His voice was a low, pleading growl. "I want you, Marianne. I want you so damn bad."

She never knew when he shed the rest of his clothing; suddenly he was over her, around her, inside her . . . and the pleasure and pain, the hardness and softness, all blended together in one endless, mindshattering moment that made her cry out joyously, "Yes! Oh, Nick, yes . . .!"

Chapter 22

They arrived at the camp the next day just as dusk began to veil the mountain in shadows. Marianne could make out the shapes of several cabins nestled back into the black-green forest, their sloped roofs merging with the trees that hovered over them like guardians. Some cabins were no more than one room, others boasted several, but all looked sturdy and homey with the welcoming glow of lamp light pouring through glass windows. A dog barked a sharp warning as they approached, but otherwise there was no sign that they had been noticed. All else seemed strangely quiet.

But not to Nick. The sound of the wind soughing mournfully through the treetops was like a song of gladness to him, and beneath the steady rhythm of the wagon's progress and the dog's lusty greeting, he barely detected the low, buzzing undertone that was like a beacon to a timber man. It was an atonal, discordant thrum, but it was the song he'd known since his first summer on the mountain at age twelve. It was the music of the mess hall, and like a well-trained animal, his stomach began to rumble in accordance. He grinned.

"Looks like we're just in time for supper," he said, pleased that Marianne's expression was one of anticipation. "Let's go on in. I'll leave the wagon here for now."

They had stopped in front of a long, low building that had a wide set of double doors hinged right in the center, with rows of small, high-set windows running along the side. At one end was a huge chimney, and even in the growing darkness she could see smoke billowing from the tin flue. Nick jumped from the wagon and hurried to her side to help her down.

Smiling at his unabashed eagerness, Marianne was not as calm as she supposed she appeared. Would she fit in here, or would her inexperience with this kind of life be more obvious than ever to Nick? Without realizing it, she let a sigh escape her.

As if reading her thoughts, Nick leaned over to kiss her on the cheek. "Don't worry if no one says much at first. They're not used to getting visitors way up here, and especially not a woman. You'll be fine once they get to know you."

Heartened by his words, Marianne forced down the nervous lump that had gathered in her throat and hastily straightened her skirt and blouse as best she could in the dim light. Sure that her hair was a tangled mess by now, she wished she had a mirror and someplace to wash before meeting Nick's men, then decided they were unlikely to set much store by her appearance anyway.

"Let's go in, then," she said bravely. "I'm hungry, too."

Squeezing her shoulders tight under his arm, Nick led her inside, swinging the doors open wide as he pushed through. And the sight that greeted them made him laugh out loud.

Thirty heads snapped upright, thirty pairs of eyes riveted fast on the familiar man in the doorway with the very unfamiliar companion, and thirty mouths now moved with varying degrees of surprise: some were shocked wide open, some fought grins of pleasure and embarrassment, and some continued to chew thoughtfully, pausing only long enough to stare at the unlikely sight before returning to the business of eating.

"What's the matter, boys? Beans too hot?"

Only one man answered, and he after hesitating so long that Marianne wondered if she'd suddenly grown another head.

"How ye doin', Neeeck?"

French, Marianne decided quickly, and then knew

she was correct when the man stood. He was a giant—taller than Nick and carrying far more bulk—but it was the unruly mop of jet black curls peppered with gray and his deep-set, black eyes that marked his nationality.

"Bass!" Nick tugged her forward with him, his hand outstretched toward the man, who wrapped it in a paw that looked to be the size of a dinner plate. "It's good to see you, Bass," Nick said, laughing.

Marianne could tell by the sound of his voice that this man was more than a mere employee; he was someone of whom Nick was truly fond. Her interest piqued, she studied the lumberman intently. He was massive from head to toe, with shoulders that were as broad as an oxen's and a chest that reminded her of a fish barrel. He wore black broadcloth pants with wide suspenders, and a flannel shirt that was so old it was nearly white with washing, which was none too frequent from the way her nose wrinkled involuntarily when he stepped closer.

"Marianne, this is Bass—Se*bas*tian Valliers. He's the best boss man in the territory."

Extending her hand, she smiled upward shyly, struggling hard not to be intimidated by the lumberjack. It might have worked, too, had he returned her smile. Instead, he peered down at her with an expression that was chilling.

"Bass," Nick said proudly, "this is my wife."

A frisson of fear shook her when his grip tightened menacingly, but then Bass Valliers dropped her hands and nodded curtly. "I am pleased to meet you, Meez Fortune."

Nick seemed not to notice that his friend's greeting was hardly heartwarming, for he swept Marianne toward another group of men, leaving the hulking Frenchman to follow or return to his dinner, as he pleased. She soon forgot him as new names swirled through the air, new faces grinned widely, new hands pressed hers. For the most part, the men seemed eager to be introduced, though quite a few blushed profusely when she murmured her pleasure. One thing they all had in common, however; they were the largest men she'd ever seen in her life. In Tacoma, Nick's height stood above the crowd. Here, he was just average.

"Nick Fortune!" A booming voice commanded their attention, and it wasn't until Marianne turned around that she realized it was a woman who had spoken. Standing with her hands on her hips at the entrance to what was obviously the kitchen was the oddest-looking female Marianne had ever laid eyes on. Her steel gray hair was chopped haphazardly to a point just above her collar, and she wore the same uniform of work shirt and pants as the men. Only the snow white apron tied around her waist looked slightly feminine, and only because it was cleaner than anything the timberjacks were wearing. "Ain't ya gonna introduce me?" she demanded loudly.

"Marianne," Nick conceded, grinning, "this is Matilda Yates. As you can see, Matilda fancies herself cook around here."

"I am 'cause otherwise ye'd all starve," the woman declared, but then she turned to Marianne, adding, "Ah don't set no airs by my chow, though. Ye'll eat worse pizen, ye'll eat better."

"I'm sure you're a wonderful cook, Mrs. Yates, or Nick wouldn't have been so anxious to arrive before dinner was over."

"Oh, pshaw!" Matilda waved a beefy fist, but she smiled nevertheless. "Man's hungry enough, he's like ta eat anythin'."

"That's right, 'Tilda, so dish it up!"

Nick's laughing words sent everyone back to their own plates, and it wasn't long before he and Marianne were seated at one of the long tables themselves. Matilda carried out two steaming bowls of stew and a plate of biscuits, disappeared into the kitchen, then returned with a platter of thick potato pancakes and two plates of beans. She slammed them on the table with friendly gusto and ordered, "Now eat!"

Aware that she was being watched carefully, Marianne eyed the heaping plates with a perplexed frown.

Certainly she was hungry, but did they expect her to eat all that! Tentatively, she speared a piece of meat from the stew with her fork and popped it into her mouth.

Nick saw her expression of surprise, then pleasure, as she chewed the tender morsel and swallowed, eagerly dipping her fork for another. He knew this was all strange to her, but she was facing the new experience with the same tenacity that had brought her to him in the first place. His heart swelled with pride, and he would have embraced her then and there if it weren't for the eyes that still regarded them with curiosity. Smiling warmly at her, he returned his concentration to sating his *other* hunger.

When their places were cleared half an hour later, Marianne realized she had been hungrier than she thought, and the cluck of approval from Matilda was proof she'd passed *that* test.

"You'll meet the others tomorrow," Nick told her as he downed the last of his coffee. "Only the unmarried men eat here; the ones with womenfolk generally go to their own places."

"The cabins I saw on the way in?"

"Uh huh."

"Where will we sleep?"

"My cabin." Nick's sly grin made her flush hot, but it was a happy blush that left her feeling warm and secretive and loved. She looked at him sideways.

"On pallets again?" she asked with mock innocence.

"Didn't you like sleeping on the ground?" he teased.

Marianne shook her head saucily, amazed by her own boldness. "It wasn't the sleeping that made me sore," she breathed. "I think I have bruises in several unmentionable places."

Nick's face registered surprise, then melted into rumbling laughter as he leaned toward her, scooping her hand off the table. "This may require close inspection . . . just in case you are in need of medical treatment."

"Don't tell me you're a doctor, too!" she exclaimed in a hoarse whisper. His thumb was tracing circles on the inside of her palm, sending delicious tremors up her arm and beyond.

"Not officially," he murmured, unable to keep the roughness from his own voice. "But I guarantee you'll feel better in the morning."

Marianne's breath caught as she glimpsed the startling passion in his glittering, steel gray eyes. Her own grew wide as she gazed back at him, caught up in the roiling storm that seemed to catch them both in its frenzied grip, leaving them unaware of anything but the current that raced between them. And so it was that neither of them noticed Bass Valliers until he cleared his throat noisily.

" 'Ere's some things I must say, *Neeck*. We talk. Alone."

The same disquieting feeling crept over Marianne as when she first met him, for Bass refused to look at her; he kept his eyes trained on Nick with solemn regard.

"Can it wait until tomorrow, Bass? The trip has been long and exhausting for my wife, and I still have to open the cabin."

Silently, Marianne wished Nick hadn't used her as his reason. She had a feeling she would have to earn the huge man's respect, and having him look upon her as a drain on Nick's time and energy wouldn't serve her well at all. Bass merely stared straight ahead, then grunted before turning to leave.

Despite Marianne's belief otherwise, Nick *had* noticed his friend's curt behavior, and it troubled him more than he cared to let on, though only for Marianne's sake. Bass Valliers knew him better than any man alive, and for that reason alone the Frenchman had plenty of cause for suspicion. In time, Nick felt sure, he would come around. He only hoped Marianne wouldn't be too bothered by it in the meantime.

"I'll show you the cabin, sweetheart, and you can get settled while I take care of the team." Slipping a protective arm around her shoulders, he brushed his mouth against her temple and whispered, "Don't fall asleep before I get there."

Marianne couldn't help but be warmed by his tender concern, not to mention his final suggestive comment. In less than a moment she felt anticipation return, and with it the knowledge that nothing else—not Bass Valliers, not even Adam Pemberton—really mattered. A smile blossomed on her lips, full and sweet and tempting, for it was born of the love that bloomed in her heart. "I won't fall asleep," she promised as they walked out the door and into the darkness.

Nick stopped suddenly, swinging her around in front of him so he could wrap his arms around her slim form. He felt as if it'd been years since he held her like this, instead of just a few hours. Only the thought of the hours to come made it possible to release her at all.

"I'll hurry," he said, his voice low and husky and his eyes hungry and bright. "I said I'd make you feel better by morning, and I always keep my promises."

Marianne woke to a world that was quite different from her impression of the night before. Then, the camp had been low-keyed and somnolent. Now, shouting voices roused her from a deep, restful sleep, urging her awake with sounds that portended a day of excitement. Behind the booming commands of the men, she heard softer, higher tones calling out cheerful good-byes and last-minute pleas, and even a few lighthearted jests. When she peered through the small glass window of the cabin's single room, hugging her nightrobe tight around her shivering, nude form, Marianne overlooked a scene of bustling energy.

From directions they came—lunch buckets swinging, axes propped high upon broad shoulders—converging onto the central road like individual streams feeding into a river of red flannel. Children darted like silverfish, the little ones begging rides, the older boys swaggering in an attempt to match the footsteps of their fathers, dropping away only when the path turned right at the mess hall. There the young ones gathered, tiny arms waving madly. At each cabin, too, handkerchiefs saluted until the last man disappeared into the woods, fluttering back into apron pockets as farewells to the men were exchanged for good mornings to neighbors.

Entranced, Marianne forgot to wonder where Nick was already, for his place beside her had been long cold by the time she awakened. She dressed hurriedly, anxious to find him and to make the acquaintance of those citizens of the camp she had missed the previous night—the women.

Smoothing nervous hands down over her most serviceable dress, one of heavy twill the color of pine needles, Marianne paused on the single step in front of the cabin, wondering where to start. As soon as she appeared, the voices of the other women dropped off as they froze in their doorways, studying her with guarded expressions. Marianne's throat tightened, and she dredged up a smile, praying fervently for courage.

"Good morning," she said clearly, directing her greeting to the occupant of the stoop closest to hers. A colorless woman of indeterminate age nodded once, muttered something to the woman on her other side about having work to do, and then retreated into her cabin.

Momentarily speechless, Marianne didn't see the younger woman who approached from the opposite direction until she was almost directly in front of her.

"Mrs. Fortune?"

The voice was soft and lilting, tinged with an accent that Marianne didn't recognize. "Yes," she replied. "I'm Marianne."

To her great relief, the woman offered a shy smile that was blessedly kind. She looked to be a few years older than Marianne, but a small baby squirmed in her arms, and two golden-haired toddlers clung to her skirts. Her own hair was a muted, honey brown, parted into braids that had been wound around her head. She was plump, but attractively so, and her complexion bloomed with the clarity of youth and good health.

"My name is Alna," she said. "Alna Hanson. My man told me of you. He helped—" She hesitated, blushing profusely.

"Go on," Marianne urged, unwilling to let this first tentative friendship falter.

"He helped Mister Nick when the train . . ."

"When the train crashed?" At first Marianne wondered if the woman simply did not know enough English to find the proper word, but Alna's sympathetic eyes told her that her uncertainty was due to compassion. Marianne smiled with genuine gratitude. "Then I owe your husband a great debt," she replied gently. "I'm afraid I don't remember, but I hope you'll introduce me so that I may thank him properly."

Again, Alna's face lit up with a smile, a little less shy than before. "Ja," she bobbed her head. "You vill meet him later. When the men come home from the big trees."

As if drawn by Alna's example, one by one the other women walked over—all but her next-door neighbor—and introduced themselves to Marianne. She counted eight as they chattered quickly, describing their husbands and houses and families. She was certain she would never keep all their names straight, let alone the names of the children that had gathered as soon as they realized there was someone new in camp, but she knew now they wouldn't hold that against her. What she had first taken as caution she now understood was shyness. It was as Nick had said; these women were unused to strangers.

When Nick returned an hour later, he found his cabin swarming with women wielding dust cloths and brooms, and children doing their level best to stay underfoot. In the midst of the commotion, his wife conversed happily with one or another of the women, oblivious to his presence until Alna Hanson's blushing silence caused Marianne to look over her shoulder.

"Nick!" she exclaimed. "The ladies were helping to clean the cabin. I forgot all about breakfast."

"Don't worry, I ate at the mess," he replied, grinning. "I thought you'd like a tour of the camp, but if you're busy . . ."

As if by mute agreement, the other women made their excuses and departed quickly, so that within a few minutes Nick and Marianne were alone. He continued to grin as he studied her from her dishevelled hair to her dust-covered toes, taking in her high color and pert expression. "I could have had one of the women do this," he offered.

"We were *all* cleaning," she reminded him. "And having a wonderful time. They've been very friendly." She couldn't, however, hide the flicker of disappointment at the thought of the single exception. Nick was quick to sense her uneasiness.

"Problem?" he asked quietly.

She sighed and nodded. There was no use hiding it from him; he'd see for himself soon enough. "There is one woman who did not introduce herself. Perhaps she was just too busy today." But Marianne knew that was not true; the cold disdain on the woman's face had been too similar to what she'd seen on Bass's.

Moving over to give her a quick hug, Nick placed a kiss on the top of her head as she snuggled against his chest. He knew immediately to whom she referred. "Megan Walters. I'll have a talk with her husband—"

"No!" Marianne pushed away fervently. "That wouldn't be right. Maybe she's shy . . . I should go over myself."

Admiration, as well as a little puzzlement, filled him at her show of spunk, though he knew that shyness wasn't the problem with Megan, and told her as much. "I expect she has her reasons for not wanting to get to know you," he cautioned. "It might be best left alone."

Marianne let it go at that, but as she scrubbed her face and combed her hair out before going with him, her mind continued to slide back to the problem. Two people, she mused, who had reacted to her with overwhelming distrust. Were they just naturally unfriendly? She didn't think so, or else Nick would have offered that as an excuse for the woman's behavior. And Bass was someone of whom he was obviously fond. All the more reason, she determined, to win the man over. And if she could manage to do the same with Megan Walters, then better still. What she would not do was allow Nick to intercede on her behalf.

And as for her husband eating breakfast in the mess hall, she vowed with a lifting of her chin, well, that would not happen again, either.

Despite Nick's advice to the contrary, when she returned to the cabin after he showed her around the area, then left to join one of the cutting crew higher up on the mountain, Marianne advanced on Mrs. Walter's cabin with a zealousness that was fed more by her desire to get the confrontation over with than any great need to garner for herself yet one more friend.

The door was opened to the late morning breeze, allowing her a glimpse of a spotless cabin similar to Nick's, though with many additional homey touches that were evidence of a woman's hand. A bright-colored braid rug was centered on the cabin floor, starched white curtains framed a pair of small windows, and an intricately designed quilt hung from a rod along one wall. It was a cheerful room; quite unlike its owner, who stepped in through a back door with a basket of laundry just as Marianne raised her hand to knock on the doorframe.

"H-hello," Marianne stammered, taken by surprise both by the woman's sudden appearance and the look of unconcealed suspicion that masked her plain face. "I thought I would come by to introduce myself. I'm Marianne Bla—, Marianne *Fortune*," she quickly corrected.

"Mrs. Walters," the other woman acknowledged abruptly, not offering the familiarity of her first name. "My man is Jake."

Marianne briefly wondered if that was supposed to mean something, then dismissed the idea. "I'm pleased to meet you, Mrs. Walters. Since we're going to be neighbors, I wondered if you could tell me where I might find cooking supplies. My cabin isn't stocked . . ." She paused, letting her words drift away as helplessly as she felt. The woman obviously was not moved by her plight, and her expression showed no sign of relenting long enough to assist.

"How long ya stayin'?" Megan asked curtly.

"I'm not sure. At least two weeks, I think."

"You and yer man can eat at the mess."

"Oh, I wouldn't want to impose on Mrs. Yates. She seems to have enough to do!"

Ever so gradually, the tight lines around Megan's mouth began to grow more shallow. Her breath, which had been held tightly within her skinny chest, now hissed through her nostrils slowly. "She'd do it, if'n Nick told her to."

Marianne smiled gently. "I know," she explained. "But we've only been married a few days and . . . well, I *want* to cook for him myself."

"Hmmmph." Megan Walters had by no means given in, but her guard began to relax slightly. She had no mind, however, to mince words. Her narrowed gaze raked the younger woman from head to toe, missing nothing. "I knew the other one, ya know."

Marianne frowned. "I beg your pardon?"

"The other one. Nick's first wife."

Silence extended between them like a rope pulled taut in a game of tug-o'-war. It occurred to Marianne that here might lie the source of the problem. "You must mean Alicia," she nodded. "Were you and she friends?"

Again, Megan Walters answered with a curt "Hmmmph," giving Marianne little clue as to the answer to her question. She decided to ask one more.

"Did she visit here often?"

Now Megan's response was closer to a snort. "Never did, to my knowledge. Jake used to work in one o' the mills in Tacoma."

"I see," Marianne replied, though she didn't really see at all. And now that she thought about it, what kind of woman mentioned a man's previous wife the very first chance she gets to talk to the new one? It seemed it was time to end this difficult conversation. "Well, it was nice meeting you, Mrs. Walters," Marianne said evenly. "I'm sure I'll be seeing you soon."

Turning to leave, she had taken only a few steps when Megan's harsh voice stopped her. "Matilda'll give ya all ya need to git started." At Marianne's questioning gaze, she added, "We all git our fixins from the one storehouse. Jist ask her."

Unsure whether she had met with success or not, Marianne could summon only a tentative smile. "Thank you kindly, ma'am. I'll do that."

Megan watched the slender young woman until she disappeared around the bend in the road, not even stopping at her own cabin on the way to the mess. There *was* something likable about Nick Fortune's new lady, she thought grudgingly. Even though she 'peared to be as out o' place as a frog in a desert, there was something about the way those pretty blue eyes looked straight ahead, like she weren't afraid to let a body know she knew what she was up against.

Shame for the way she had talked—or rather, not talked—threatened to cause Megan Walters to regret her actions, something that had rarely happened in her fifty-one years, but she quickly thrust it away with a jerk of her graying head. She never gave her trust freely, and even less for the past seven years, so she was justified in keeping her guard up with this one. With that thought, she turned her attention back to the basket of laundry still propped on her hip. Two weeks would tell, she decided glumly. Two weeks would tell.

At nightfall the next day, which was a Saturday and therefore an evening preordained for revelry, Marianne witnessed a transformation of the lumber camp that she wouldn't have believed possible had she not seen it herself. A great triangle of paper lanterns had been roped from the mess hall to Nick's office to one corner of his cabin and back again, and the gaily patterned lights now rivaled the stars hovering so close that it seemed one could snatch them from the sky as mementos.

On the ground, a foundation of smooth planks had been laid in the center of the area, nailed together quickly to form an impromptu dance floor. But most amazing of all, Marianne thought as she clapped her hands to the rowdy music, was the change in the people. Gone were the somber men and work-weary women she had watched go about their daily routine with cheerless precision. Like players on a stage, they had taken on new character, except instead of employing costumes to work the magic, it was the expressions on their faces that transformed them: they smiled because they were glad to see one another, they laughed because the workday was behind them, they grinned because they were celebrating the boss's marriage.

But they danced because it was Saturday night!

"Do they always do this?" Marianne shouted to Alna over the din. The two women, along with all the others, had cleared the floor for a group of men who were involved in a series of contortions that were a cross between a Russian folk dance and a kicking contest. The floorboards shuddered under the relentless pounding of their considerable weight, adding to the general noise of loud music and a great deal of friendly shouting.

"Oh, yes!" Alna exclaimed gleefully. "It is tradition. My Anders, he is the best!"

Watching the brawny blond man continue the rigorous exercise, while other men around him dropped with cheerful exhaustion, Marianne had to agree. Nick, however, ran a close second. Her lips twitched delightedly as he grinned and whooped, looking at that moment more like a devilish boy than the owner of half the mountain. His dark hair fell across his perspiring forehead and his face bore a fixed smile of concentration, broken only when his legs gave out, sprawling wide in front of him. A cheer went up from the crowd as Anders Hanson stopped, raising a victorious fist into the air before offering his other hand to Nick.

When the music had returned to a comparatively sedate reel, Marianne felt her pulse step up its beat as Nick approached. "I hope you're not too exhausted to dance with your wife," she teased gently, pleased when he refuted her statement by swinging her up onto the wooden platform with ease.

"Never," he growled playfully. "Just holler when you get tired of dancing with me."

"Never," she repeated, gazing at him with all the happiness her heart could pour forth without bursting wide open.

Unaware of the admiring looks they were collecting as he spun her effortlessly through the steps, Nick centered all his concentration on the woman whose essence radiated such joyful exuberance that he would have happily died just watching her. Except that living with her, he resolved, would be much more fun.

Marianne's thoughts were amazingly similar, though she would have been surprised to know it. After Megan Walter's cryptic comments—which she had refused to think about anymore, she reminded herself hastily—she had decided that the woman's coolness, and Bass Valliers's as well, was probably more of what she had experienced with Elizabeth. They had known Nick when he was married to Alicia, and were concerned because they had also known the agony of his loss. And she could not, she thought while gazing at her husband lovingly, fault them for that.

She briefly wondered what they would think if they knew that, though she loved him with all her heart and would willingly give her life not to see him hurt, just the fact that he had married her could result in scandal and disgrace, if not his ruin.

Determined not to let such dismal thoughts spoil her evening, Marianne resolved to have a good time. One by one, the men stepped in to claim their share of the dances from Nick, and he obliged by relinquishing her hand with a grin and claiming another of the wives for a spin around the floor. Even a red-faced Anders Hanson, after much prodding from Alna, had taken a turn. With just a little effort she was able to help him past his tongue-tied awkwardness by telling him how grateful she was for his wife's friendship. They were much the same, shy, sweet-faced Alna and her big, shaggy-haired man, whom the others had nicknamed "Swede".

Strangely enough, Marianne had been able to place each of the husbands with ease after having known their wives for just a day. Only Jake Walters stumped her for a while, until she saw him standing behind Megan with one large hand on her skinny shoulder. Jake was short for a logger, being only a head taller than his wife, and as solid and round as his wife was thin. His face was plain, his hair nearly nonexistent, but his eyes twinkled merrily with a vitality that matched the shine of his glossy pate. A friendly sort, Marianne decided as she watched him converse with some of the other men. When he'd been introduced to her, however, she could have sworn there had been a touch of anxiety in his expression. He had shaken her hand perfunctorily, then moved back to where Megan stood, silently studying Marianne's reaction. Not knowing what she expected, Marianne had smiled at them both, laying her hand on Nick's arm.

And then there was Trig Jones. Fair-haired and glib, he was as different from the rest of the men as a sleek panther from a group of playful bears. His name, he'd explained to her as he held her hand far too long, was short for trigger, because in other parts of the country he was well known for his fast gun. Marianne didn't doubt that his reputation extended to other areas where he was considered fast, and she was quick to hustle away from him when she spotted Alna approaching.

All that had happened before the dancing had begun, and now Marianne noted with curiosity that, though Trig Jones had pressed her into joining him for a reel, neither Jake Walters nor Bass had claimed her for a dance. Which mattered not a bit because it meant she had more to share with Nick.

And it was a sharing. It was slowing down and speeding up, it was giving and taking, joining and parting. They would touch, then they would not touch, but always their eyes were locked together as they danced. It reminded her of the night of the mill opening, except that then her love for him had been a thing of soul-shattering longing, a taunting, teasing emotion that made her ache because she had thought it in vain, where now she had tasted the sweet pleasure, and only longed for the richness, the ripening that would come with weeks, with months, with years of loving.

She wanted this night never to end, though she knew that it must because sooner or later the sun would rise, lighting the sky with ribbons of crimson and gold. She wanted this honeymoon trip to last forever, yet she knew that eventually Nick would be needed back in Tacoma. But most of all, she wished that their silent truce would shield them both from heartache, though she was sure it would cease to exist when she brought up the subject of New York and Adam Pemberton again, as she knew she must.

Tingling with awareness as Nick's gaze enveloped her, his eyes growing dark with desire as he held her close in the final waltz of the evening, Marianne vowed to cherish these days, to let them burn into her mind and her heart like a brand, so that she would remember them always.

Chapter 23

Though Sunday was a great deal quieter than the previous night had been, Marianne found it was still a day devoted to fun and relaxation, luckily with less tiring activities. Alna had invited her and Nick to join them on a picnic, and Marianne had risen early to fry a batch of chicken for lunch. It was good that she remembered the few simple dishes she had been taught to cook at the orphanage, at a time when she had believed it would be necessary to know such things. Once she went to live with Uncle Matthew, she was never allowed to step foot in the kitchen except to discuss menus with the cook, but now she was happy to recall the pleasure of preparing their meals. She vowed to ask Claire to teach her more when they returned to Tacoma, for she knew her mother-in-law was proficient in the culinary arts, enjoying an occasional stint in the kitchen despite having plenty of competent servants.

"Mmmm," Nick sniffed, slipping his arms around her waist from behind her. "Smells good."

Domesticity had its advantages, she decided, taking a moment to lean back against his broad chest, one hand caressing his bare forearm as the other waved a fork through the air. "None for you until lunchtime," she chided lightly, shivering as he nibbled on her sensitive earlobe.

"Lunchtime, eh? What if I can't wait that long?"

Marianne's shiver had turned to a full tremor, for his mouth now trailed a moist path down her neck.

"But you must," she insisted, laughter shaking her voice, "or there won't be enough left for Swede, and he looks to have a healthy appetite."

Nick's grasp around her waist tightened and he chuckled against her hair. "There'd better not be. I wasn't talking about the chicken!"

A loud commotion from outside interrupted what promised to be an interesting appraisal of Marianne's accomplishments in the kitchen. Nick lifted his head with a rueful sigh, and they both hurried to the door.

"Better come, Neeck," Bass called from the mess hall. "Mateelda ees hurt."

Marianne followed in Nick's wake, aware that others from the surrounding cabins were hurrying forward as well, though most of her neighbors had already left the area for picnics of their own. She nodded toward Alna, who watched from her own doorway with her youngsters in hand. Megan Walters fell in step beside her. Soon they arrived at the scene of the accident.

Matilda Yates, as dishevelled as ever, but now looking decidedly sheepish, sat at the large worktable in the mess kitchen, a blood-soaked towel wrapped around her hand. A bloody paring knife lay on the table next to a kettle of potatoes, half of them peeled. Several men gawked at the growing stain, but none moved to lend assistance. Instead, they all looked up with relief when their boss entered.

"Gawd-awful sorry, Nick," Matilda said loudly. "Jest a damn-fool accident."

"Let's have a look," he grinned, relieved that whatever the trouble, she had retained her sense of humor.

Marianne swallowed hard as the stout woman began to unroll the cloth. "Isn't there a doctor?" she whispered over her shoulder to Megan.

Nick heard her and looked up, shaking his head. " 'Tilda here generally takes care of such things, but she'll be hard put to stitch up her own hand. Can you, Megan?"

The scrawny woman shrugged apologetically. "Not with my rheumatism, Nick. I don't reckon I can hold a needle."

Returning his gaze to Matilda's wound, which was now exposed as a deep gash across the fleshy part of her palm, he smiled grimly. "Guess you'll have to settle for me, 'Tilda. I never sewed anything except for a torn saddle, but that skin of yours must be near as thick as leather anyway. All right?"

"I-I can do it." Marianne was nearly as surprised as everyone else to hear herself speak, but once the words were out she had no choice but to continue. Feeling herself grow hot with a mixture of embarrassment and fear, she lifted her flushed face as determinedly as she could manage. "At least I can try. I'm good with a needle."

"Sewin' flesh's different 'n sewin' cloth," Megan interjected. The woman's expression was as suspicious as ever, but her voice had taken on a new tone, a gentler one that Marianne hadn't heard before.

Nick raised an eyebrow in his wife's direction, but his smile had broadened to one of pride. "She's right, darling, though you probably will do a better job than I ever could. Are you sure you want to try?"

Marianne wasn't sure at all, but with several pairs of eyes watching her expectantly, she wasn't about to demur now. "Yes," she said firmly, risking a glance at the prospective victim of her impending attempt.

Matilda grinned up at her gamely, nodding her gray head with vigorous jerks. "Ye're a spunky one, I'll give ya that. Bring me a bottle o' rotgut, Bass," she bellowed over her shoulder. "Don't reckon it'll hurt ta have some fun 'til all the pokin's over with." She eyed Marianne gleefully. "Ya look like ye kin use a belt yerself, girlie. Reckon ye'll git woozy if'n ye takes a swaller?"

Despite her fears, Marianne couldn't help returning Matilda's smile. "I'll wait until I'm done, for your sake."

At that moment Megan reentered the kitchen, having gone to fetch her sewing bag. After shooing all the men from the room—all but Nick, whom she wisely decided might be needed for moral support—Megan set about pouring a small bowl of steaming water from the kettle on the stove. "I cain't hold the dang needle," she said briskly, "but I've stitched up a few cuts in my day. I'll help how I can."

Relieved and surprised by her offer, Marianne looked at her and nodded. "Thank you, Megan."

"Enough o' this jaw-waggin'," Matilda barked. "Let's git started."

Once she got over the trauma of taking the first stitch, Marianne found that, if she centered all her concentration on the task, clearing her mind of the fact that it was live flesh she was tugging together, it wasn't as difficult as she first thought. Matilda had helped herself to a generous amount of whiskey, handing Megan the remainder of the bottle for pouring over the cut, both before and after Marianne finished the job.

"Well done," Nick said proudly, once Matilda's hand was bound in a clean bandage.

Marianne offered him a weak smile, grateful that he'd stayed nearby during the arduous half-hour. Knowing he'd been there had made the ordeal much easier.

"Let's get you to your cabin, 'Tilda. Marianne, why don't you go ahead with Swede and Alna. I'll meet you at the lake."

Despite her previous resolve to show Nick how strong she could be, at that moment she was quite willing to let him shoulder the rest of the responsibility. She didn't even realize how truly shaken she was until she and Megan reached her cabin. Stumbling on the single step up, she would have fallen forward if not for Megan's firm grasp on her elbow.

"Ya got some tea left from breakfast?" the older woman asked. Marianne nodded. "Then let me heat some up fer ya. Ye'd best sit down."

Marianne would have liked to protest, but her hands were shaking so badly and her throat was so constricted with sudden tears that she could only obey Megan's gentle command. She reached trembling fingers for the straight back of a chair, lowering herself with care as Megan bustled familiarly over the stove.

Before too many minutes passed, a steaming mug of tea was pressed into Marianne's grateful hands.

As she sipped slowly, allowing the soothing warmth to work its charm, she couldn't help but notice that the older woman was again staring at her frankly, now with an approving expression.

"Ye're not what I thought ya were," Megan said bluntly, her keen eyes assessing. "I reckon ya think I'm a might rude one, the way I talked the other day, but I'm as quick ta say I'm wrong, too. I 'spects I owe ya the reason why."

"Oh, Megan, you don't owe me an explanation—"

"Mebbe not, but I'll give ya one anyhow. That way, there won't be nothin' keepin' us from bein' friends."

Curiosity—and a certain feeling of triumph at knowing she had accomplished one of her goals—virtually wiped away the last of Marianne's own attack of nerves. She waited patiently for Megan to continue.

"We come up here about seven years back, me an' Jake. In some ways it was like startin' over, and we'll always be beholdin' to Nick Fortune for givin' us a second chance."

Marianne didn't quite understand, but she smiled anyway. She was learning that Nick had a way of instilling a sense of loyalty in people.

Megan Walters saw that smile, recognized it for what it was, and in that split second decided that she could not, in good conscience, reveal the entire story to Nick's new bride. "It wasn't just the job, either," she said gruffly. "We was in bad need of a chance to git away. There was . . ." she paused, gathering her words, and then spitting them out like bitter seeds. "Jake had woman trouble."

Comprehension dawned on Marianne like the sun. Naturally Megan was immediately suspicious of other women; wouldn't any wife be? Nevertheless, she couldn't help but admire Megan for her honesty. It had to have been a difficult admission. Smiling, Marianne stood and placed her hand on the older woman's, gently squeezing the work-roughened fingers. "I think

I understand now," she said quietly. "Thank you for telling me. We'll not speak of it again."

Relief spread through Megan's features, but not the relief that Marianne thought. Inside, Megan's heart twisted guiltily for her sin of omission, even though she was glad she had decided to spare Marianne the details. After all, there was no real *need* for her to know the truth, Megan decided firmly. And what the girl didn't know couldn't hurt her. Could it?

Later that night, as Marianne snuggled into Nick's arms, she very nearly mentioned Megan's confession, but then she stopped before the words were more than a hint on her lips. Discussing it with Nick might be too much like betraying a confidence, even though Megan had clearly implied that he already knew the story.

"Did you say something?" As if reading her mind, Nick peered deeply into her eyes, satisfied when she shook her head.

"No," she replied softly. "I was thinking about today."

Nick tightened the arm that circled her shoulders, stroking her cheek with his free hand. "You were wonderful today. Even Megan thought so, and she's a tough nut to crack."

Hiding her startled expression against the wall of his chest, Marianne silently agreed. She didn't know many women who would willingly begin a new life with a man who had shamed himself as Jake must have done, but she felt a quiet bond of kinship with Megan. The woman had salvaged a marriage with a husband who abused her love, while Marianne was determined to forge one with a man who would never return hers completely. Was it so different?

The sigh that escaped her lips fluttered over Nick's skin like the wings of a butterfly, and his blood quickened at her nearness. He'd been so damned proud of her today, he'd wanted to shout it to the world, but it had been almost as good to see the others look at her with admiration and growing respect. Then later at the picnic, when he had watched her playing with the Hanson children, had seen her shining head lowered over the tiny, squirming bundle she'd held in her arms, he'd been overwhelmed with emotions he had thought never to feel again.

He felt them now, though, and that feeling and giving and taking and loving was something he would never give up. His hands, stroking her bare, satiny skin from shoulder to hip, conveyed his need, and as he rolled to his side, his lips joined in the silent communication that molded them together into one.

Marianne knew, too, the quiet desperation in wanting to share every thought, every emotion, and yet knowing that words would never be enough. Her flesh responded to his tantalizing kisses with a passion fueled by love, and her last thought was that she would love him enough for them both.

After that there was no more room for thinking.

In the next few days, Marianne learned that bearing a reputation for handling emergencies well was not without its price. Despite Nick's assurance that no one would think less of her if she refused, Marianne agreed to take over the task of helping out in the mess kitchen during Matilda's convalescence. Fortunately, she was not obligated to test her limited knowledge of cooking; Matilda was perfectly capable of ordering her through each and every procedure of "whippin' up a meal," so long as Marianne provided a pair of willing hands.

It was exhausting work, she quickly realized, mostly because it was never-ending. Breakfast preparations began before dawn, and after flipping nearly three hundred pancakes, frying a hundred sausages or so, and boiling twenty pots of coffee, she could relax with a mound of dishes that topped her head.

Then it was time to start lunch!

To his credit, Nick helped all he could, but he was scouting out a new stretch for next winter's cutting, and so was gone from camp most of each day. Megan stopped in occasionally when she had time away from the laundry she took in for the unmarried men. Each of the other women had too many small children to be of much assistance, and so the duty had fallen to Marianne.

Of course, she thought to herself as she reached for another apple to core for baking, there were advantages to being needed. She was quickly becoming familiar with the routine of the kitchen, and now the thought of matching her skills against Claire's was less daunting. Also, she had earned a fast—if unlikely—friend in Matilda, who had even taken to curbing her language to a degree of mild profanity in Marianne's presence. Best of all, however, was the feeling of accomplishment, knowing she was helping Nick in a way that astonished even him.

This was exactly the kind of example she had wanted to prove, though when the pile of apples yet to be cored seemed to grown higher at every glance, she wondered if there mightn't have been an easier way. Neither of them had mentioned last week's argument since arriving at the camp, but Marianne had not forgotten it, and she doubted Nick had either. She still could not completely understand why he took such a dim view of her intention to fight Adam Pemberton, but she hoped that her actions of late would reassure him that she would no longer let the man frighten her off. And if he worried that he could not hold her affection once she was far away, well . . . Marianne felt the familiar knot tighten low in her abdomen as she recalled some of her behavior during the nights, and a rush of hot blood flooded her cheeks, even though there was no one in the kitchen to witness her thoughts. She was completely captive to the rapturous tides of passion that he aroused in her, and if he didn't know that . . . well, she couldn't think of one more way to show him that she hadn't already tried!

There must have been another reason for his reluctance then, she decided, though she had no idea what it could be.

Over the next days, Marianne found little time to

wonder about anything except how thirty men could possibly eat so much food, and how Matilda had ever managed on her own. The woman's hand was healing well, and she would be ready to take over the job by the following week, which was when Nick hoped to be ready to leave. Marianne looked forward to the day with mixed feelings. On the one hand, it would be nice to return to what she now thought of as home, to see Claire and Elizabeth again—not as benefactors, but as family—yet she was loath to leave the isolation of the forest, where time had little meaning and thoughts of Adam Pemberton could be shuffled back to the farthest corner of her mind.

And she couldn't help remembering there was one last beast for her to conquer.

Bass Valliers still viewed her with suspicion and coolness, though Marianne had taken pains to be as friendly to the man as she was to the younger swains who were abnormally gallant in her presence. If anything, she saw Bass more often than anyone except Matilda, for he was always in Nick's company, saying as little to her as possible and watching his boss's frequent displays of affection through narrowed eyes.

So it was that on a day when Marianne was alone in the kitchen, she pounced upon the opportunity to force Bass into a frank discussion when the man wandered into the mess hall.

"Hello, Bass," she greeted him boldly, staring him straight in the eyes.

He bent his huge, grizzled head once, then muttered, "Where eez Mateelda?"

"She took a pot of stew up to one of the marking crews. If you've come for something to eat, I've got more simmering now."

Again, Bass barely lifted his head, but Marianne had no intention of letting him escape. She knew he had missed the lunch hour today, and must certainly be hungry. "Sit down," she demanded gently. "I'll get you a plate."

To his great discomfort, she figured somewhat gleefully, Marianne slipped into the place opposite him at the table after she'd placed his meal before him. He glanced up, grunted, then began to eat as if she didn't exist.

She waited.

When he emptied his tin mug, she poured him more coffee. When he finished his three biscuits, she buttered him two more. The silence, marred only by the sound of his chewing and the clink of cutlery against stoneware, drew around them like a heavy cloak, its ominous weight making her grow more irritated with every passing minute.

"You don't like me very much, do you?" Marianne asked bluntly, unable to bear his stubborn silence any longer.

Bass grunted in surprise, raising one shaggy eyebrow as he scraped his chair back. "A woman makes a man soft. Especially," he added pointedly, "a soft woman."

Having no suitable defense against his not-too-subtle accusation, Marianne could only stare at her adversary until he reached the door. "Doesn't it matter to you that he's happy?" she finally asked.

Bass seemed to pause then, as if giving her words thoughtful consideration, but then she realized he'd only been gathering a mouthful of saliva, which he spat into the yard with deadly accuracy. "Won't last," he predicted glumly, then tramped out.

Marianne bit back a venomous retort, partly because she didn't want to tangle with a man who looked as though he could flick her aside with no more than a finger, and partly because she feared he wasn't so far from the truth.

Not that she believed loving a woman was a sign of weakness in a man, but it *was* true that few men wanted to be saddled with a totally helpless female. And despite all evidence to the contrary, that was exactly how Bass Valliers saw her. What did he expect her to do, she wondered angrily, go with the men and chop down a few trees to prove herself? He was the stubbornest man alive, bar none! But she could be stubborn, too.

Gathering up the dirty utensils with less than tender care, Marianne stalked to the kitchen, determined to show Bass Valliers what she was made of. With vague thoughts of unmovable objects connecting with unstoppable forces, she picked up a cleaver and began to chop a dozen onions to add to the beans, satisfied that at least she had *something* to whack at!

The subject of Bass Valliers was still uppermost in her mind several hours later as she brushed her hair vigorously while preparing for bed. It was not until Nick stayed her hand with a gentle grip, his gray eyes laughing silently, that she realized she'd been practically snarling with each vehement stroke.

"I know I haven't been spending much time with you lately," he murmured, amusement erasing the lines from his face, "but I hope to heaven it's not *me* you're angry with."

Laying the brush aside with a shaky sigh, Marianne stood and wrapped her arms around his waist. "I'm sorry. I didn't mean to work myself into a snit, but . . . really, Nick. That Bass!"

Stroking her back through the thin batiste of her nightgown, Nick felt the tension as tight as a bowstring between her shoulder blades. "Bass?" He hid his smile in the silkiness of her hair. "What has he done?"

"He's just . . . I don't know! He doesn't like me at all!"

Hearing how childish her complaint sounded when voiced out loud, Marianne leaned back in Nick's arms, peering up at his face searchingly. What she saw there was more indulgent laughter, and not one whit of concern.

"Isn't it enough that you've won every other heart in the camp?" he asked, his words laced with mirth. "Must you have his, too?"

Marianne frowned. "You know that's not it at all, Nick Fortune! I don't care what anyone else thinks. In fact, I could do with a little *less* attention from some quarters," she thought briefly of Trig Jones, but let it pass without further mention. "Really, Nick. Bass is rude and sloppy and not at all friendly. I don't even see how you can *like* him."

All trace of humor disappeared from his face, and he trailed his hands down the length of her arms with gentle tenderness. "He was my father's best friend, sweetheart, and now he's mine. He held this place together for my mother when I wasn't old enough to do it myself, and then he taught me everything I know. I owe him more than I can tell you."

Chastised, Marianne touched his cheek softly, dragging her finger down the rugged planes of his face. He was trying to tell her that nothing she said would change his opinion of Bass, and she could not find the words to tell him that was the only reason it mattered.

For a moment, Nick considered confessing to her the whole extent of his debt to Bass, knowing that it might help her to understand not only why the gruff man felt it his duty to remain aloof from her, but why it was imperative that she give up the notion of returning to New York. But when he would have spoken, she placed the tips of her fingers against his lips.

"I'm sorry I brought it up," she apologized sweetly, her breath whispering across his chin like a caress. "Please forget I said anything."

She stood before him clad only in the sheerest of gowns, for she had packed the first thing that came to hand and he had decided, with gleeful wickedness, not to buy her anything warmer in Olympia. The night-gown clung to her body like dewdrops to a silk-spun web, catching the eye and drawing it to the intricate beauty beneath, yet hiding none of her loveliness. He could see the budding swell of her breasts and reached for her, rubbing the fabric until its gentle friction made the rosy peaks harden against his palms. He loved knowing that she was as aroused as he, and that her body conveyed that message in ways as visible, if slightly more subtle, than his own.

Marianne watched him through eyes heavy-lidded with desire and she whispered his name, her tongue edging around the inside of her lips as he drove her wild with his hands. Her own fingertips fluttered lightly over the broad expanse of his chest, trailing lower across the hard plane of his abdomen to where the silky soft line of dark hairs disappeared into his low-slung trousers. She felt his muscles grow taut beneath her hands as she deftly unfastened the buttons that stood in the way of her quest, then heard his shuddering groan when her fingers encircled his velvet heat.

Nick could take no more. Lifting her high against him so that their faces were on a level, he kissed her, his mouth grinding into hers. His hands grasped her soft buttocks, pressing her hips against his swelling hardness, inciting her to the same frenzied passion that was burning through him with uncontrollable rage.

Nick walked with her across the room to the bed and fell down upon it, raining hot, wet kisses on her face and breasts and belly with such fierce intensity that she moaned and dug her fingers into his shoulders. He tugged at the wide neckline of her gown until her breasts swelled free and proud against his mouth, then slid his hand up the side of her leg, feeling the smoothness of her skin beneath his palm, the nightgown's feathery weight brushing the back of his hand.

She wanted to join in the gentle assault, to touch him, too, to drive him to the heights of pleasure where she was beginning to soar, but the gown was pushed down her arms, and she could not lift them free from its bond. Helpless, she arched higher when his mouth trailed downward from her breasts to her thighs, scorching a path of delight that made her quiver like a sapling in a windstorm. Another moan escaped her, this one when he found the hot center of her and loved her with his mouth and tongue, searching and teasing and drawing on her until she felt a knot of incredible fire mount deep inside her core. She writhed wildly, at once begging him to stop and urging him to go on, and somehow, he must have heard her wordless shout, for he filled her then, powerfully and completely.

"Ah, love," he groaned, clutching her to him, struggling for the control to prolong their ecstasy. Her hands flicked his sides like caged birds in a frenzied quest for freedom, the quick, erratic movements nearly sending him over the edge of the abyss. With deliberate slowness, he withdrew until she cried out against his leaving, then plunged back into her secret heat, making her shudder with the final throes of her climax.

Only then did he drive her to the brink again with the pounding rhythm that ended in his own, quaking release.

Their descent was a long, slow spiral from heaven, punctuated with murmuring kisses that tasted like nectar to Marianne's lips, and sweet, whispered words that fell on her ears lovingly. Nick had finally freed her arms by removing the gown completely, and now the cool night air danced pleasantly across her moist flesh, nearly as tantalizing as the soft, caressing motion of Nick's hands as he drew invisible patterns on her skin with his fingertips.

While her limbs still bore the heavy lethargy of satisfaction, weariness crept over her, threatening to steal her away from him. Nick watched her muffle a yawn against his shoulder and he gathered her tenderly and rolled to his back, taking her with him. "Good night, my love."

Somewhere in her groggy mind she remembered that he had never called her that before, but before she could respond with more than a tremulous smile, she was fast asleep.

Chapter 24

Barney Clawson shuffled his feet impatiently, wondering for perhaps the thousandth time what in hell he was doing here. Ever since the day, over a week ago, that Adam Pemberton left New York, Barney had vacillated between feelings of incredible relief and ominous dread. The only thing that *had* been certain was that with Adam gone he was free to make a choice that'd been floating about in the back of his mind for years, just waiting for the opportunity to come forward.

The boss was crazy, Barney told himself repeatedly, though repetition wasn't necessary to further convince him; only to enforce the necessity for action.

Pemberton's parting statement about someone named Julia had puzzled him at first, and except for the disquieting fear that had hovered around him for the next few hours after Pemberton left, it had been easy for Barney to attribute the error to anxiety. But then he had returned to Adam Pemberton's room later in the evening with the intention of hiding all evidence of his boss's departure, just in case . . .

What he found had made Barney's armpits grow clammy and his balls shrivel up like two dried acorns. In the top drawer of Pemberton's dressing table had been a folder full of newspaper clippings, the latest of which had been dated less than a month before. A prostitute had been murdered in shantytown, it said, the perpetrator unknown. After a cursory glance at the rest of the articles, Barney established that each told of a similar incident, with only the names of the victims differing.

So his boss liked to collect reports of dead women? Barney had tried to shrug. He knew, however, with horrified certainty, that if he checked the dates of the murders against Pemberton's appointment book he would find that those were the nights his employer had gone out with no explanation.

Driven by a sense of morbid curiosity, Barney searched further in the drawer, not even certain what it was he looked for.

And what he found was exceedingly disappointing, at first.

A portrait miniature in a gold filigree frame, small enough to fit in the palm of his hand, showed a golden-haired beauty with flawless white skin, and eyes—like Adam's—the color of pale blue ice. So the bastard had a mother, Barney thought, giving it a preoccupied glance before tossing it aside to continue the search. It fell face down upon a stack of laundered handker-chiefs, and that was when he caught sight of the in-scription on the back.

It was only a date—March 12, 1867—and a single name engraved in scroll letters, but its impact on Bar-ney Clawson was such that he clutched the edge of the dresser top, suddenly dizzy with recognition. *Julia!*

He had known then what he had to do—what he had *wanted* to do for a long time—for he no longer considered Adam Pemberton merely dangerous. At that moment Barney had known the man was insane.

Now, a week later, clutching a sheaf of folders in one sweaty hand, Barney gave a thought to fleeing. But as before, he discounted it quickly. If he ran away and Pemberton somehow escaped the law, his life and the lives of his sister and her family wouldn't be worth a damn. A man willing to travel across the country to exact vengeance wouldn't think twice about crossing New York to do the same, and if Adam *had* killed all those prostitutes . . .

Barney shuddered. No, what he was about to do was the right thing—for once in his life, he added

ruefully. If the man he was about to see had any sense
at all, Barney'd walk out of here a free man. He'd
only have to hide as long as it took for the authorities
to find and arrest his former employer, because once
they did, there'd be no chance of parole.

Not with the evidence Barney was prepared to give
them.

A door opened behind him, causing Barney to jump
nervously and utter a short, barking laugh.

The man in the doorway looked him over without
comment, then stepped aside and waved Barney in.
"I trust this visit won't be a further waste of my time,
Clawson."

Barney laughed again, but this time relief welled
into his throat, making his answer sound almost gleeful. "It won't, Senator Collins. You can count on
that!"

Chapter 25

The trouble with Trig Jones began the next day, but Marianne was so gloriously happy that she didn't notice until it was almost too late.

Trig and the rest of his grading crew had arrived in camp the day before, tired and hungry but filled with the kind of desperate rowdiness that comes from balancing too long on the edge of danger. Only once since the night of the dance had Marianne allowed herself to remember the feral light that came from Trig's small, dark eyes, but she had quickly brushed aside the uneasy feeling that accompanied the thought, trusting that she would never have to deal with the man again. The same watchful gleam marked his gaze as he followed her across the grassy triangle to the kitchen that morning, but her mind was too full of memories of the previous night to pay attention. It wasn't until she was all the way into the kitchen that she realized she wasn't alone. Turning quickly, she stifled a small gasp when she saw Trig's wiry form blocking the doorway.

"Oh, Mr. Jones!" she said breathlessly. "I didn't hear you behind me." Disgusted by the uneasiness that crept over her unbidden, Marianne determined not to let her feelings show. She lifted her chin. "Breakfast was over an hour ago, but I expect I can find you something. Go on into the dining room."

Trig Jones grinned, letting his gaze wander lazily from the modestly buttoned neckline of her dress to her breasts, rising and falling just a tad too quickly for normal. She was frightened, he could tell, but most women of his acquaintance found a little scare now and then exciting—at least, that was what he figured from the way they were always asking him to come back again, no matter how rough he got.

"My, my," he drawled smoothly, the words sliding from his lips as if on well-oiled skids. "You're even prettier than I remembered. One thing I'll say for Nick, he sure knows how to pick 'em. Two beautiful wives is more'n most men deserve."

A sudden twinge of curiosity nabbed her heart, and Marianne nearly asked Trig if he'd known Alicia, but then she caught the flash of evil intent glittering beneath his hooded eyelids and she forgot everything but her desire to get him away from her.

"If you don't mind," she said, lifting a heavy kettle from the iron rack overhead and holding it in front of her defensively, "I have a lot of work to do. You can leave the door open on your way out."

His grin openly taunting, Trig Jones took another step into the kitchen, releasing the catch on the door as he did so that it swung closed behind him. "Now why would I want to leave," he crooned ruthlessly, "with such a tasty little morsel waiting for me right here?"

Now a smidgen of fear shivered down her spine, but Marianne stood unmoving, confident that she was safe while within shouting distance of half the people in camp. She stared at him with an expression of withering disdain, hoping he would need no more discouragement than that.

To her surprise it seemed to work, for Trig Jones merely watched her for a long moment, then jerked his muscled shoulders carelessly. "Of course, this isn't the best place to have a taste," he said, turning to the door and pushing through.

Marianne watched him go with a mixture of dread and relief. Even without knowing that Nick didn't trust the man, she wouldn't have had any liking for Trig Jones. He was arrogant in a cunning, sneaky way, and she hated the way his eyes grew narrow and contemplative whenever he looked at her.

Shrugging away her fear like an unwanted cloak, Marianne forced her mind back to filling the kettle she'd been clutching so tightly to her middle.

Before long she forgot about Trig's disturbing behavior. It wasn't until much later that she realized he mistook her silence for an answer—and not the one she would have given.

Nick entered the darkened cabin hurriedly, not pausing to wonder why Marianne hadn't bothered to set a match to the lantern. In his anticipation, he could picture her waiting for him in the wide, featherbed, and that was the direction his eyes shifted the moment he closed the door behind him.

Empty. Where was she? he questioned immediately, quelling the impatience that rose in him like a flooding stream. He'd been kept later than usual out at the cutting site, checking over some of the equipment with Bass long after the other men had come in for supper. It hadn't been easy, especially when memories of last night kept slipping in front of his eyes, distracting him so that he had to retotal a figure more than once. Only the knowledge that if he finished that particular job today they could start back for Tacoma tomorrow kept Nick working when he only wanted to hurry back to her waiting arms.

And she should have been here, Nick thought with a worried frown. The mess hall had been dark and silent when he'd passed by, so he had known she and Matilda were finished cleaning up. From the bunkhouse, laughter and the squeaking chords of a harmonica had cut through the night air, and the muted sounds of gentle voices had floated from the other cabins, increasing Nick's longing to reach his own.

That's where she must be now, he calculated rapidly, returning to the starlit night. She was visiting with Megan, or perhaps Alna Hanson. Standing on the single-stepped porch, he glanced from the cabin to his right to the one across the wide dirt path, figuring which one was the most likely choice.

Megan, he decided, recalling the friendship that had

sprung up between his wife and her nearest neighbor. But Megan soon turned him away, saying she hadn't seen Marianne since before the supper bell. Alna, too, was of no help to him.

For just one instant a thought sprang unbidden to Nick's mind, the cold dread it brought with it quickly replaced by scorn as he shook himself free from its momentary paralysis.

No! he scolded himself, dredging up a forceful smile. Shouldn't he know that history did not always repeat itself? The difference between Marianne and Alicia was like . . . like the difference between heaven and hell. He had to stop letting his mind churn over memories that had no place in his life now.

With a lighter step, he headed across the center of the camp toward the mess hall and Matilda's cabin just beyond, wondering what his beautiful wife would have to say when he told her they would soon be going home.

Marianne tugged her shawl tight around her and hurried faster along the darkened path, her gathering basket full of ripe blackberries swinging against her hip, keeping time with her rhythmic gait. That afternoon when she had laughingly told Matilda of her first wifely attempt to prepare a meal, the other woman had been quick to point out what a triumph it would be to present Nick with another offering of fruit, this time baked into a succulent pie. Eager to comply, Marianne had set off right after supper with explicit directions and high hopes, leaving Matilda to finish cleaning up.

Trouble was, Marianne thought as she scurried toward the distant lights of the camp, she hadn't reckoned on Matilda's "just a mite past the ole camp" turning into several miles, or her "mought have ta scramble up the hill a speck" to mean she would climb halfway up the mountainside.

But once she found the site Matilda had steered her to, Marianne discovered, not a small patch, but nearly two acres of clearing covered with the brambly bushes.

It hadn't taken her long at all to fill her basket to the brim.

Now the lengthening shadows had turned into full dark, and she realized, with a sense of anticipation that sang high and sweet in her thoughts, that Nick would be down from the mountain soon. She probably wouldn't have time to bake the pie tonight, but she could always hide the berries until tomorrow. She wanted to surprise him.

The foot-worn path twisted down through the trees, breaking open as it reached the cleared space between the bunkhouse and the mess hall. Matilda's cabin was a hundred yards on the other side of the mess, and Marianne paused a moment to catch her breath, wondering if she should let the other woman know she'd made it back all right.

As she stood, one of the bunkhouse doors opened quietly. Light spilled out like a fall of golden water, cut off abruptly as the door swung closed again.

Marianne started to call out, then quickly decided it was probably just one of the men stepping out to catch the night air. Nevertheless, a tiny shiver whipped through her, making her tug her shawl a little higher on her shoulders. Matilda could wait. Right now, thoughts of Nick's snug cabin held far more appeal. She'd taken no more than three steps when a hand grasped her arm just above the elbow, tilting the berry basket so that most of its contents spilled to the ground. Marianne gasped. "What . . .?"

"Shhh." Another hand snaked out of the darkness, clamping around her mouth with just enough force to make her wince slightly. "It's me," a voice whispered. "Don't go rousin' everyone in the camp."

Marianne jerked back wildly, the unfamiliar touch sending waves of revulsion rippling over her skin. "Who—?" She never voiced the question, for she could see, even in the dim starlight, just who had accosted her.

"I knew you'd be here sooner or later," Trig Jones gloated, his dark, animal eyes glistening narrowly.

"Didn't think you'd be quite this impatient, though. Hasn't been dark an hour yet."

His low chuckle grated through Marianne like a dull sawblade, almost painful in its implied malice. "You must be mad!" she blurted, her heartbeat escalating crazily. In some distant part of her brain she remembered saying those words to a different man in a different situation, but just now the shock and anger felt remarkably the same. Trig's viselike grip on her arm tightened.

"You ain't gonna start teasin' now, are you?"

His voice was deceptively gentle, but Marianne could sense the malevolence just below the surface. Stiffening, she clutched the basket in front of her and tried to step away from him, but his hand never loosened its hold.

"Somehow, Mr. Jones, you've gotten a very wrong idea. You'd best let go of me immediately, or you'll be in a great deal of trouble." She only hoped her tone carried enough conviction, for inside she wasn't at all sure that mere words would convince him. They didn't.

He yanked her closer to him, unmindful of her gasp of pain. "Wrong idea, huh?" he growled. "You're nothin' but another slut, happy as long as you're prancin' around in front of a bunch of woman-hungry men, and then cryin' off virgin the minute one of 'em expects you to keep a promise. But I ain't like the rest of 'em, sugar."

With one quick motion he knocked the basket from her hands and dragged her toward him, locking both her wrists in a manacle hold. She managed to wrench a hoarse scream from her throat, but couldn't draw enough breath to let out another yell before his mouth covered hers brutally, grinding into her clenched lips until she tasted blood.

"Give it up, girlie," Trig demanded, his hot, musky breath nearly suffocating her. "That's what you came out here for, ain't it."

"Nooo . . ." Marianne wasn't even sure if she'd been able to speak the word out loud, for all her concentration was centered on fighting her way out of his persistent embrace. She squirmed and twisted, but he only tightened his arm around her, his free hand roaming boldly over the curve of her hip, thrusting upward to squeeze her breast unmercifully.

Throwing her head back and away from his smothering kiss, Marianne managed to draw a ragged gasp of air into her lungs.

"Don't scream," he said savagely, his hand jerking away from her breast and coming up hard and fast against her open mouth. "If you scream, I'll have to slap you. Now come with me."

Her cry as he yanked her arms high behind her back was muffled against the clammy palm of his hand. Spinning her around toward the forest path, he shoved her ahead of him, keeping tight hold of her aching wrists and her mouth. He only let his grip falter once, when she pretended to stumble, but it was all the slack Marianne needed. She opened her mouth wide, biting down as hard as she could on the fleshy part of his hand between his thumb and forefinger, not releasing him until the taste of his blood nearly made her gag.

"Ow! You bitch!"

She regretted her action almost immediately, for he snapped her arms back so far she could almost feel the tendons ripping. Then, mercifully, he let go of her wrists, allowing her arms to drop. Marianne nearly wept with relief as blessed feeling returned to her limbs, even though the momentum of their forward progress made her fall to her knees. With her hands pressed to the cool, thick loam of evergreen needles, she gulped several harsh breaths, too stunned to wonder why he'd let her go.

"Bastard!'

It took an instant for the word to penetrate her dazed consciousness, but with it came a sense of deliverance so overwhelming that hysterical laughter bubbled from her, though in the cold night air it sounded more like sobs. Nick was here!

Pinwheeling backwards, Trig Jones was held upright by his shirt balled up in one of Nick's fists, while his belt cut into the soft part of his belly, pulled tight from behind.

Blinding rage lent power to Nick's already considerable strength, so that when he threw Trig to one side he felt as though the man weighed no more than a scrawny boy. His fury abated somewhat when he saw that Marianne was unharmed, then rose again when she lifted her face to him, her cheeks shining wet in the moonlight. He turned back to Trig.

"You have until dawn to clear out of here, Jones. If you have any sense at all, you make sure I never see your face again."

Marianne heard the frigid sound of pure, unadulterated loathing in Nick's words, and she felt a shudder of inexplicable foreboding cascade through her. "Nick?" she said, her voice little more than a rasping whisper.

He went to her then, and the mask of anger was replaced by tenderness as he dropped to one knee before her. The scuffle had roused some of the men from the bunkhouse and light poured over them as the doors and windows were thrown wide, allowing the false cheer of lantern light to escape its cozy haven.

"What's goin' on?" someone shouted.

" 'T's Nick an' his woman," another man answered.

At that, Matilda appeared on the scene, hustling from her cabin with an ancient horse pistol banging halfway down her leg. "Bear?" she grunted, then followed Nick's fierce gaze to where Trig Jones was hauling himself up from his undignified crouch. "Hmmph," she acknowledged. "Worse."

Recovered from the ordeal enough to be embarrassed by the undue attention, Marianne let Nick help her to stand. The warmth of his hands gently circling her waist was comforting, and for just a moment she laid her head against his chest, absorbing his strength.

"Did he hurt you?" Nick choked over the rage that still burned in his throat like acid, though he tried to shield her from it by cupping the back of her neck with one shaking hand as she leaned into him.

Marianne uttered a trembling sigh. "N-no. I'm all right."

"Best git her inside, Nick, afore she gits a chill." Matilda's command bore the desperate tone of one who is trying to avert trouble, and Nick recognized her attempt to divert his attention from Trig's slow progress toward the bunkhouse. She was right, he knew, feeling the tremors shuddering through Marianne's slight form. There was nothing to be done now.

With one arm still draped protectively around her shoulders, he scooped up the now-empty basket, noticing for the first time the blackberries scattered and crushed beneath their feet. His questioning gaze searched Marianne's face.

"Oh, Nick," she whispered sorrowfully. "Your . . . your pie!"

He tensed, and she knew his anger had returned anew. Quickly, she laid her hand to his cheek, feeling the muscle in his jaw grow rigid against her palm. For some reason she could not fathom, she was nearly as frightened of his anger as she had been of Trig's assault. Probably, she realized with a flash of insight, because she had known Nick would rescue her from Trig, but against the power of Nick's rage she was completely helpless, though it was not directed toward herself.

"Let's . . . let's go home," she breathed, drawing herself upright in an attempt to show him she was unaffected by the near tragedy, even while her nerves screamed silently.

The voices from the bunkhouse had died to a low murmur and Matilda was already headed back for her own cabin when they reached the clear area in the center of the camp. A swaying lantern approached them from the direction of the rest of the cabins, and soon Swede's tall form materialized.

"I heard noise," he said slowly, raising the kerosene lamp until its ring of light enveloped Nick and Marianne. "I come to see—"

His explanation was cut off by a loud commotion from the bunkhouse.

"Nick, look out!"

Marianne never did know who shouted the warning, but it was enough to spur Nick to action long before she had a chance to reason out the meaning. He thrust her toward Swede, dropping to a crouch as he spun around.

Obeying the unspoken command from his boss, Swede wrapped his huge arm around her waist and lifted her bodily, not setting her down until they had cleared the area by several yards. Only then could Marianne see what had caused such alarm.

Just at the edge of the circle of light formed by Swede's lantern, Nick faced Trig Jones. They were both positioned low, knees bent and arms spread out, circling one another as if caught up in some bizarre dance. It was not until the other men poured from the bunkhouse, forming a ring of light around the two combatants, that she saw a fiery glint of steel flashing in Trig's hand.

"No man knocks me down and gets away with it," Trig said, his voice grinding. "No one."

Skirting around the rest of the men, Bass took a step into the light. With a flick of his hand, Nick waved him away. "He grabbed the knife before I see him, Neeck," Bass rumbled. He spat on the ground. "Son of a beetch."

Nick raised one hand in a conciliatory gesture. "Don't be a fool, Jones. Put the knife down and you can walk out of here now. If you kill me, you won't get twenty feet from this camp."

Marianne felt her limbs grow cold at the sound of Trig's maniacal laughter. Unthinking, she lunged toward Nick, but Swede's massive arm held her tight.

"Pretty damn sure of yourself, ain't you, Fortune?" Trig taunted. "Just how sure are you that your woman there won't up and off with me soon as you hit the dirt? What's got you riled?" he continued. "Me touchin' her, or her meetin' me out back?"

His next words were spoken so low Marianne couldn't be sure she heard them right, but from the way Swede sucked in his breath she knew Trig had hit a sore spot. What she thought he said was ". . . like the other one."

Nick's jaw tightened as cold fury turned his veins to ice. It was easy to see what Jones was getting at, and that he was forcing him to make the first move, but he wasn't about to stand here and listen to much more, especially with Marianne within easy hearing. "Better shut up, if you know what's good for you," he warned.

By now the women had gathered around the circle, which was lit as brightly as daylight. The shadows of the two men in the center were painted in sharp relief against the hard-packed earth, distorted by the varying angles of light that turned them into scarecrow images. Megan sidled up, and Marianne felt a bony hand clamp protectively over her shoulder. In morbid fascination, they watched.

Trig did not advance on Nick, nor did he retreat, but his jeers continued to provoke as surely as if he had waved his knife in front of his opponent's face. "What's the matter, Fortune? Don't tell me you don't mind everyone knowing what a slut she was?" He paused, considering for a moment before chuckling evilly. "I guess you don't. If'n you did, you wouldn't keep Jake around to remind you. 'Course maybe you like thinking about what a great, forgiving kind of fellow you are."

Marianne's gaze darted frantically from one to the other as she tried to understand the meaning behind Trig's obvious insults. She didn't even notice that Megan's hand had dropped from her shoulder, or that Jake had moved behind his wife.

"You don't know what you're talking about," Nick said in a threatening voice, circling to his right, away from the seven-inch blade that glistened in the light like a long, deadly tooth.

"Oh, but I think I do," Trig crooned. "And it's time the rest of these folks learned the whole story. It's no coincidence I've been working here for the past six years. Alicia told me all I had to do was keep my mouth shut and you'd hire me. She said you were an easy one to fool."

Lurching forward, one arm swinging wildly as the other grabbed for the knife, Nick let out an angry roar. But Trig sidestepped quickly, slashing downward as he did, his blade narrowly missing Nick's shoulder.

"The truth ain't pretty, is it?" Trig goaded, beads of perspiration just beginning to gather on his high brow. His once-handsome face was twisted into an expression of malice, making Marianne wonder how any woman could think him attractive. A violent shudder racked her body and she uttered a low moan as Nick regained his balance and crouched again.

"But I bet even *you* don't know the whole truth, Fortune. I bet they told you she was alone when she died, didn't they?" Trig didn't wait for an answer, simply nodded as he went on with his crazy litany. "I paid out my last dollar for that favor, but I was with her at the end, and I can tell you, Mister High-and-Mighty Fortune, it was a sight worth seein'. Yessir. Never knew a body had so much blood in it, 'specially a woman as dainty as 'Licia. But I didn't kill her, if that's what you're thinking. I had her . . . maybe I even loved her a little . . . but I didn't kill her. You did."

Though no one witnessing the scene made so much as a sound, Marianne could feel shock reverberate through the throng of timber folk like a tidal wave pounding the distant shore. Her mind, numb from the terrible events of that night, stored away these bits of information like so many meaningless tidbits. Later, however she would ponder them well.

For now, her frightened gaze was riveted on Nick.

She thought he would go wild at Trig's final accusation, but instead he seemed to grow calmer, though his eyes still glittered with ferocious rage. His feet stopped moving in that incessant circle, his hands fell lower, and he stood up as if he had called a silent halt to the confrontation. For just a moment Trig's eyes flared in sudden panic, but then he grinned again, his wrist twisting slightly so that the blade of his knife caught and reflected the light as it waved.

"Drop it now, Jones," Nick issued a final command. It was not obeyed.

Trig lunged forward, catching the razor-sharp tip of the knife on Nick's forearm, but Nick jumped backward before the blade could do any more serious damage. Hefting the weapon in his hand, Trig returned to his crouching stance.

"Nick's not armed," Marianne whispered to no one in particular, her voice rising hysterically. "He hasn't got anything to fight back with!"

Some irrational part of her mind must have hoped the encounter would end with her enlightening pronouncement, but her heart plunged in despair when someone from the crowd tossed a blade to the ground next to Nick's feet. With a swift movement he snatched it up, feinting to his left to avoid Trig's next assault. What followed was a scene that would burn itself into Marianne's brain, promising to haunt her for the rest of her life.

It was as if it finally dawned on Trig that he had pushed Nick as far as he could with words, and now he would have to complete the job he'd begun. And Nick, in turn, ceased trying to talk Jones out of his foolish attempt. The hard determination masking his face made it clear to all who watched that he was done with reason; only force would triumph now.

Nick dove in low, thrusting his hand upward toward Trig's exposed belly, just missing as the other man jumped back, flailing his arms for balance. Retreating, Nick panted lightly, no more than if he were merely catching his breath after a rousing dance. Trig, however, was showing signs of wear. Large patches appeared beneath his arms and across the back of his shirt, testifying—not to his lack of stamina—but to the amount of emotion he'd spent during his tirade.

For a second his muscles seemed to go slack. It was a trick. In the next moment he sprung forward, his blade whistling through the air with lightning speed. Marianne felt the collective gasp before she heard it, but it was not until Swede swore under his breath that she noticed the thin line of blood welling from a tear in Nick's sleeve. She started forward again; again she was pulled back.

Despite his wound, Nick made the next move, grappling with the smaller man, their arms locked in deadly combat. Trig, with his wiry frame, had had the slight advantage of speed, but now that they stood wrist to wrist, chest to chest, it was apparent that Nick's strength would soon overpower him. Trig spun away quickly, but not before feeling the sting of Nick's weapon as it sliced across his chest.

"Son of a bitch!" he exclaimed softly, as if amazed that he'd been injured. "You cut me!"

Nick did not waste his breath with an answer. His agile movements were as deft and smooth as a magician's, and just as deceiving. As Trig raised his head from where he stared at the blood dripping down the front of his shirt and dove toward his opponent, Nick, too, closed in.

Horror engulfed Marianne as she watched them come together in deadly battle, as she dimly wondered if one of these savage beasts was the man she had married. Trig raised his knife-hand over his head, prepared to bear down on Nick, but in doing so he exposed himself to attack. With a motion so deliberate there was no mistaking his intent, Nick plunged his knife into Trig's chest.

True surprise registered on the younger man's face and he dropped his own weapon, raising his hands to the place where the dark, leather-covered hilt stuck out from his body like some bizarre ornament. He looked up at Nick, opened his mouth once, and fell forward.

It was over.

The lumberjacks surged forward as one, one body in celebration, one voice shouting victory. Even the women, clucking noisily as they trailed their husbands, contributed to the congratulations that were morbidly cheerful. Only Marianne stood back, abandoned by Swede, alone and shaking from the shock of seeing a man killed.

Nick felt the adrenaline wash out of him, leaving him bone weary and sickened by what he'd had to do. All around him his men spoke in grim voices, but more than one expression was lit with excitement. Turning from the body, he searched for the one face that might help ease the bitterness that burned in his gut.

Watching him walk toward her, Marianne tried to summon feeling to her heart, tried to will her limbs to respond to her brain's command to run, but she could only stand submissively, numbed by what she had witnessed. She saw the lines of struggle etched across Nick's face, saw the pain around his eyes as his gaze sought hers, but she could not bring herself to acknowledge his agony. Just now, hers was too great.

Nick saw her eyes grow dull with shock, but it was not until he reached for her hand, hanging limp and bloodless at her side, that he realized the extent of her distress. Thinking it was concern for him that had driven her to this state, he drew her into his embrace. She remained stiff and unyielding.

"Marianne . . .?"

Arching back, her eyes focusing on some distant point as if she dared not meet his gaze, she uttered a strangled cry, unable to bear his touch.

Confusion tore through Nick, along with a mixture of fear and anger. He stared at her blankly, too tired and hurt to try to understand. He lifted his hands imploringly, unsure what to say, but needing some kind of response from her.

She was dimly aware that her voice, when she finally spoke, was as flat and emotionless as he had been when he stabbed the life from another man. It was no more than a whisper, and yet its impact on him was a blow like no other he'd ever known.

"You murderer . . . you killed him."

Chapter 26

Nick's expression first registered disbelief, then his look turned to granite. He nodded slowly. "Would you have preferred he killed me first?"

Now Marianne felt her blood begin to rush through her again, pounding at her temples and flooding her face with dizzying heat. A part of her wanted to call back the words that had changed Nick's eyes from gray warmth to cold steel, but her mind was so foggy she could only shake her head dismally.

Nick did not answer. He pushed past her, heading into the darkness surrounding the cabins, away from the confusion, away from the stench of death that hung over his head like a cloying mist. Behind him, Matilda called his name gruffly, and he was aware, too, that Bass lumbered in his wake, but beyond that he had no thought but to reach the relative comfort of his cabin.

As if she had no will of her own, but was drawn by invisible threads that bound her to him, Marianne fell in step silently. In the background she heard Swede's calm, commanding voice take charge, ordering some of the men to carry Trig's body to the bunkhouse. Occupied with that task, no one else seemed to notice that Megan had slipped away from the others, tears filling her deep wrinkles, or that Jake had followed his wife.

When Marianne reached the cabin, Bass had already placed his kerosene lamp on the shelf nearest the bed. Nick was seated on the feather mattress, trying to ease his shirt from his shoulders. When he grunted audibly from the pain, Matilda stepped forward, wielding a knife similar to the one Trig had used. The sight of the ugly blade caused Marianne to gasp out loud.

Matilda glanced up, then turned her attention back to Nick. "Have to see that cut," she said, slicing cleanly through the fabric so that his shirt fell away from the wound without further injury. A jagged line ran down his blood-smeared arm from his elbow to his wrist, the edges showing nearly a half-inch gap in the worst places. It made Matilda's accident of two weeks ago look like a mere scratch.

Marianne stumbled into the cabin, all three pairs of eyes turning to her questioningly. "Let me see," she demanded softly, hurrying to the bed. Bass stepped aside and reached for the lantern, holding it higher so she could inspect the wound. Her breath caught in her throat at the sight of the torn flesh, and she gritted her teeth in order to keep from crying out.

"Least it 'pears ta be clean," Matilda commented. "But it'll need stitchin'."

Hearing a challenge in the words, Marianne straightened. "I'll have to get hot water and a needle from Megan." She bent to inspect Nick's arm more closely, aware of his ragged breathing as she drew near. He shifted slightly when she touched him, but his expression remained as stony as ever.

Only his voice gave the slightest hint of softening. "One of the other women can see to it."

Marianne could not yet meet his eyes, for the shock and horror were still too fresh in her mind, but her heart felt as if the frigid hand that gripped it had loosened its hold just a little. "I'll do it," she murmured, her intention firm. "After all, I've done it before."

Matilda uttered a soft snort, then offered to trot over to Megan's herself. When Bass departed to find a bottle of whiskey to use as a disinfectant, Marianne and Nick were momentarily left alone.

The silence was profound.

"Does . . . does it hurt much?"

Nick glanced up sharply, his eyes gleaming angrily. "Nothing I can't handle, considering the alternative." His voice was tainted with sarcasm.

There was absolutely no way for her to reply without adding to the desolation already choking her, but she was too upset to guard her words. "You could have stopped it!" she said, her voice so tight it quivered in the air like brittle glass.

"I tried. You heard him. He was beyond reason—crazed. He would have killed me."

"And you think killing him first was the right thing to do?" she asked, incredulous.

"It was the *only* thing to do!" Nick exploded. "It's the only thing some men understand!"

Folding her arms across her chest against the violence in his answer, Marianne gave her head a stubborn shake. "No!" she protested. "I don't believe that. We're human, for God's sake! Not animals who must kill to survive. There are laws—"

"And what good has the law done you!" Nick surged to his feet, towering over her with his fists planted on his hips. "Thanks to the law, your Adam Pemberton is free to hound you, while you spend the rest of your life trying to avoid his disreputable henchmen."

Marianne willed herself not to cower. She didn't even stop to wonder how the argument had circled back around to her, merely jerked her chin a notch higher. "Not if I go back to testify against him! Otherwise, I *will* have to hide away from him for the rest of my life."

"Not if he, or any of his men, crosses with me."

"I trust that justice will win out!"

"I don't!"

"Then you're no better than he is!"

The words were flung at him in anger, past her lips and irretrievable before she had a chance to fully understand what she had said. She understood well enough, however, when she saw the shutter of pain and anger close over his eyes.

The air in the cabin, which had many times echoed

with the sounds of their love, now bore the ominous weight of disillusionment. Even when Matilda slammed the door open, admitting a gust of fresh wind, the tension and bitter disappointment did not leave, only shifted to allow for the job that was yet to be done.

Bass returned with the bottle, first offering it to Nick, who upended it greedily. He felt like it'd been a long time since he'd wanted to get drunk, but tonight it was more than the dull ache from his arm that needed drowning.

Marianne, too, wished that there was some easy way to erase the evening's tragedy and its painful repercussions, but, as much as she longed to lay her head down and let sleep take her to blessed forgetfulness, until Nick's arm had been tended to she could not afford the luxury of rest. Tomorrow, when daylight cast its bright sheen upon the night's terrors, then she would think about what had transpired between Nick and herself. Now, she must concentrate on his wound.

It wasn't easy.

It wasn't easy to sink the needle Megan had sent, thick and long so that she could grip it with her thumb and forefinger, into flesh that she had caressed lovingly. It was even harder to keep from weeping each time she drew the thread through the edges of the cut, making him flinch as she pulled the wound together. And it was impossible to stop the regret from tearing at her heart, for with every passing minute her anger lessened, leaving her feeling empty and shamed.

By the time Marianne was finished, perspiration had soaked through her dress, the thin calico plastered to her skin. Though Matilda had moved back to stay out of her way, Bass stood near, holding the lantern with a steady hand to light her way. She knelt away from the bed where Nick now dozed fitfully, overexertion and alcohol having worked their effects upon him. Gazing at him wistfully, she wished she could lie down beside him and snuggle close. But his injured arm, not to mention his injured pride, would never allow it.

Nothing remained but to clean up the messy, blood-stained cloths she'd used to stem the bleeding and then watch over him for the rest of the night. Marianne knew that infection posed the worst danger now.

Matilda helped her, gathering up the soiled cloths and putting away the needle and thread. Bass assisted in removing Nick's boots, then helped to roll him aside while Marianne put clean sheets on the mattress. That done, she covered him with a warm blanket, her hand automatically brushing a lock of dark hair off his forehead with a loving, lingering touch.

When she looked up, Bass was watching her, his eyes narrowed to a piercing, black gaze. Her first impulse was to snatch her hand away with embarrassment that he had witnessed such an intimate gesture, but she lifted her head and met his look with a challenging one of her own.

Then his lips twisted into a parody of a smile. "You deed good," he said, unintentionally echoing Nick's praise when she had stitched Matilda's hand. "You are a good woman for *Neeck*."

Marianne was dazed by his sudden admission, even while a sense of triumph surged through her. It was short-lived, however, for the smile dropped away from Bass's face and was quickly replaced by a studied frown.

"You love him, *non?*"

"Yes," she replied softly. "I love him."

"Then why are you not happy when he stop the man who would dishonor you? It is proof he loves you, *n'est-pas?*"

Marianne sighed, then shook her head dismally. "That isn't proof of love. It's only proof that violence begets violence."

"Pah!" Bass's dark head swayed back and forth. "You are good woman, but *très stupide*! A man such as Neeck takes no pleasure in killing, but what must be done . . .?"

He shrugged his massive shoulders in a typically Gallic way that made Marianne smile, despite his unintentional insult. "Now I know why Nick thinks the way he does. He said he learned everything from you. Did you teach him to fight, too?"

She had meant her words to be light and humorous, but they had the opposite effect on Bass. His thick brows drew together in a forbidding frown, his eyes grew sad.

"Oui," he nodded.

The silence stretched between them, broken by Matilda's raw voice. "Didn't ya know, honey?"

"Know what?" Marianne's glance darted from one to the other.

" 'Bout how Nick's pa died."

When it was obvious from her quizzical expression that she did not, Matilda drew a deep breath, cast a resigned look in Bass's direction, then said, "Best sit down. This could be a long 'un tellin'."

Obeying, Marianne settled into the rocker that she'd pulled close to the bed. Bass retreated to the shadows on the far side of the room, but she was still aware of his presence there, no longer disquieting. Matilda pulled one of the ladder-back chairs from the small table in the corner, swinging it around so she could straddle the seat, her arms crossed over the back. "Joshua Fortune weren't no lumberman when he first came up the mountain," she began, "but he had the timber in his heart and soul, and sometimes that's more'n enough. He'd made a big profit sellin' his boat, and his dream was to start a loggin' crew up here and build his own mill down on the river, so's to not be relying on one or t'other. Nick was just a little tyke then, those big gray eyes o' his'n starin' straight up at the tops o' these trees like he wanted to fly clear on over the biggest. I 'us jest a young gal myself, newly married ta Red Yates. My Red was the biggest, orneriest cuss this side . . ."

Despite her disparaging words, Matilda's face took on a faraway expression that made Marianne wonder about the man she had once loved. But the older woman waved her hand suddenly, as if clearing the air around her head of troublesome insects.

"Never mind that," she said gruffly. " 'Cept for

me'n Bass, there's a whole new set o' folks here,
though in some ways, they's the same ones as back
then.

"Joshua built his mill, and then he started cuttin'.
We was a lot farther down the mountain in them days,
an' it didn't take so long to git into town once in a
while. Tended to git more drifters, too, fellas that'd
work a few months fer a grub stake, then set out fer
greener pastures." She shook her head incredulously.
"Didn't they know it don't git no greener than this?"

Marianne silently agreed, entranced by the story as
Matilda continued.

"Two years or so went by, things was lookin' fine,
and Joshua Fortune set his sights a little higher. He
risked everythin' on a part o' the mountain they said
could never be cut, on account o' being so far up. He
nearly went broke hirin' enough men to finish the skid
road, and still keepin' the mill busy enough to make
money. But he had a lot ta work for. Nick was growin'
by leaps and bounds, already stickin' his nose into
everythin'. And Claire was expectin'.

"One night he was ambushed on his way home by a
murderin' thief name o' Grundy. Bass, here, knew
Grundy had a hankerin' fer Joshua's gold watch, but
even we was surprised that the fool was stupid enough
to go showin' it around less'n a week after the funeral.
He bragged it was his reward, fer doin' a favor.

"The nearest law back then was in Seattle, 'cept fer a
circuit judge that'd come 'round ever' few months. He
was due that week, so some o' the men trussed Grundy
up tight an' waited fer the chance ta tell their tale. We
reckoned the watch was proof enough, but no'un
figgered on the judge bein' bought off by the men
who'd hired Grundy."

"He went free." Marianne spoke softly, not asking a
question, but stating the facts that were bringing a lot
of things to light.

"He did," Matilda nodded, pursing her lips. "Leastways, fer a few days. Folks 'round here took Joshua's
death mighty hard, an' it didn't set well that his killer
was let loose. Claire held up purty good—she's a tough

one—but the whole mess hit young Nick like a boulder smashin' down the mountain. He was thirteen or thereabouts, burstin' ta be a man, but still young enough ta think the sun rose and set on his pa."

Marianne was rocked with unexpected grief for the people she now loved so well. Unconsciously, she slipped her hand to Nick's brow, as if her touch could somehow erase the sorrow from his mind.

"Nick swore he'd kill Grundy himself—even set out ta do it, 'cept Bass stopped him. It woulda ended there, but Grundy was too big a fool ta let it. He showed up in a saloon in Tacoma, boastin' agin. The town was smaller then, an' word spread fast where he was. Nick heard, an' it was all me an' Red could do ta keep him in camp. He was a strong 'un, and Red ended up lockin' him in the cold cellar so's he wouldn't git himself killed."

"And Grundy?"

Matilda paused, gazing steadily toward the shadows where Bass was hidden. There was a movement there, a heavy shifting of weight, and then silence that was broken by Bass's voice, low and grim.

"Tell it."

Matilda nodded, then turned back to Marianne. "He disappeared that night, and when he washed up in the sound a few days later, folks jest figgered he got likkered up and drowned. No one paid much attention to the fact that his neck was broke like a pine twig."

Matilda rose, signalling that she'd said all she intended for one night. To Marianne, who's mind still reeled from the implications, it was quite enough. She joined the other woman at the door, quietly thanking her for all her help.

Matilda eyed her steadily before stepping down into the darkness. "What Nick did tonight weren't easy, no matter how much that fella needed killin'. Don't think so hard on him, come mornin'."

Marianne watched her go until nothing remained of her in the black night except the lingering sound of her words on the chilly wind. Then a movement behind her brought her attention back to Bass, who now stood in the middle of the room, looking sheepish and defiant and fearsome all at once.

Some of the contention she felt toward Nick earlier surfaced once more. It *wasn't* right, Marianne thought sadly, but she couldn't bring herself to hold it against the man who had killed for Nick's sake, any more than she would hold it against Nick, who had killed for hers. Her voice shook, but not with fear.

"Thank you, Bass."

He shuffled his huge feet and glanced over at Nick. "Joshua Fortune was my very good friend. Ze men of the woods, we look after our own."

After he had gone, Marianne let her mind go over Matilda's story again and again, letting her imagination play with the details until she could hear and feel and smell every instant as if she had lived it. She could picture Nick as he must have looked then, her heart swelling with love for the boy/man who had been forced to grow up practically overnight. Until now, had she ever truly understood what he meant when he told her how hard and cruel this land could be?

The realization brought with it a further revelation. In Joshua Fortune's case, the law had not been enough to ensure that justice was done. Was that why Nick did not trust that it would be in hers?

She inched her chair closer to the bed so that she could check him for fever without rising. Before settling down for the night she pulled the blanket up higher over his bare chest, leaving only his bound arm on top of the cover. The stark white of the bandage emphasized the bronzed hue of his skin. Marianne was gratified to see that his face had returned to its normal color. He had finally slipped into a deep, restful sleep.

After finding another blanket in the sea chest beneath the bed, Marianne wrapped herself up like a cocoon and sat down with the intention of getting some much-needed rest herself.

Sleep, however, would not come easily.

Night sounds that she'd never noticed when in Nick's embrace enveloped the cabin, adding their haunting voices to the troubled thoughts that flitted through her mind like bats, dark and elusive and terrifying. Had she done something to cause Trig to single her out? What had he meant by those awful, taunting words? What if Nick had been killed?

This last nearly made her moan out loud, but she gripped the arms of the rocker until her knuckles ached. *Dear God,* she prayed, *I couldn't bear to live without him.*

No, she told herself firmly, she could not think about it tonight. Tomorrow, after she'd had a chance to make peace with Nick, she would feel better. Right now her nerves were taut wires, ready to snap at the slightest provocation. She had to clear her mind, to empty herself of everything but that which brought her comfort. Nick.

She gazed at him through bleary eyes, watching the rise and fall of his chest, matching her own breaths to that steady rhythm, feeling the tension slip from her body as she imagined her heart beating with his. She did not touch him, but she loved him with her eyes: his dark hair, feathers of black gossamer upon his brow, his face, relaxed and looking younger in repose than when daylight touched it with harsh reality, and his lips, which were often a single slit carved in stone, yet could touch her as gently as the spring sun.

The image of him embedded itself in her brain, so that even after her eyelids had drifted closed, her mind still wandered over each beloved feature.

She found her ease, and slept.

It was the aching that woke him. Not the throbbing, pulsing ache of his arm—though that was considerable, too—but the dull remorse that made his heart feel as if it'd been ripped into pieces. He had killed, and something inside Nick had died as surely as if Trig Jones had clutched at a part of him with his lifeless hands, tearing away what was good and clean, exposing that which was not.

Murderer. That was what she had called him, and even with his lids squeezed tight against the memory,

he could still see the shock and revulsion that had
filled her eyes.

Murderer. The sound of her voice knifed through
him, bludgeoning him until he was racked with doubt
and self-disgust.

Murderer. He hadn't wanted to be, but as of last
night, that was what he was.

Slowly, Nick opened his eyes. Sunlight filtered
through the window's thick pane, lifting shadows from
the room as it came. Speckled with dust motes, it
poured through the uneven glass in yellow streaks,
falling indiscriminately upon furniture and floor, bed
and chair. Painstakingly, Nick turned his pounding
head to follow the ray's path across the room, his gaze
halting when it reached Marianne.

His heart lurched crazily.

She hadn't stirred yet, despite the light that bathed
her from head to toe. She looked, Nick thought, as
bad as he felt. Dark crescents dipped beneath her
eyes, the shadows made more prominent by the strong
light. Each delicate bone in her face seemed to stand
out in sharp relief against her skin, which was colorless
except for a smudge on her cheek that Nick recognized, with a slight start, as his own blood. Her hair
was lying over her shoulders in a tangled mess, her
clothes rumpled and dirty.

Unspoken misery, and longing so great it rivaled
every emotion he'd ever known, warred with each
other until he had to close his eyes again and swallow
hard.

She couldn't have heard him, and yet when he opened
his eyes again it was to meet hers, liquid pools of blue
that shimmered and filled with tears.

Tears, he decided, of disillusionment.

Tears, she recognized, of relief.

Marianne rose quickly to kneel at his side, ignoring
the muscles that protested over having spent the night
cramped into an uncomfortable chair. Her heart
slammed against her ribs again and again, stealing her
breath away until she could manage only to whisper,
"Oh, Nick!"

"Good morning," he said thickly, steeling himself against the desire to haul her into his arms. He closed his eyes as if the effort of facing the light was too much for him, though in actuality it was the sweet concern trembling around her lips that drove him away.

Marianne forced a smile, knowing he would not see it, and laid her hand to his scratchy cheek. When he flinched at her touch, she removed it rapidly. "You . . . you haven't got a fever. That's a good sign. Matilda said if you rest it for a day or two, you'll be able to use your arm soon. I don't know much about these things, but it didn't seem to have gone through to the muscle, though you lost a fair amount of . . . Oh!"

She stopped abruptly as he rolled to the other side of the bed and sat up, presenting her with a view of his broad shoulders, bare except for the creases made by wrinkles in the bed sheets. His pants, which she'd unbuttoned but had not removed, hung low on his hips, and she noticed for the first time the line of fine hair that dusted his lower back when he leaned forward, planting his elbows on his thighs, his forehead resting against his good hand.

"Maybe you shouldn't be up yet," she offered, biting her tongue to keep from prattling on nervously. There was nothing to be nervous *about*, she scolded herself. Nick was her *husband*.

He pulled on his boots and staggered to his feet. "Nothing wrong with me now," he muttered. "Too much whiskey . . ."

Marianne hurried around the bed as he took one swaying step forward. "Nick, I don't think—"

"Leave me alone," he grumbled, even while clutching her shoulder for support.

Marianne didn't know whether to laugh or cry, so she pressed her lips into a thin line and helped him walk to the table. Once there, he let go of her and braced his good arm against the pine boards, leaning heavily. From the way he held his bandaged forearm tight against his body, she could tell it was hurting him dreadfully. "Nick, it's too soon to be up."

"I know what I'm doing."

"You'll make yourself ill, pushing this way."

"I believe," he said, swiveling his head enough to pin her with an agonized gaze, "that I can get to the outhouse and back without doing any permanent damage."

Taking a step backward, Marianne let him pass, bewildered by his disparaging tone, but hoping that it was the pain that made him talk so. He crossed the small room with slow deliberation, pausing only to hook a clean shirt from the nearby rack when he'd reached the door. Again he swayed, again he reached out to bolster himself, this time finding the doorjamb.

Marianne sighed and shook her head. "You're the most stubborn person I know, Nick Fortune. You'll be lucky if you don't fall flat on your face out there."

He shot her a look that made her feel as if a cold hand had squeezed the blood from her heart. "If I do," he said, uttering a short, mirthless laugh, "I'll know exactly where to come for sympathy."

Demoralized, Marianne watched him go out the door. He was even angrier than she'd expected, and he had every right to be. Last night she'd behaved like an hysterical child, not even trying to understand what he'd gone through. And after Bass had explained about Joshua Fortune, she understood more than she cared to. The only thing to do was apologize when he returned.

But when several minutes passed and Nick had not come back, Marianne went to the door to look for him, spotting him talking to Bass near the bunkhouse. As if sensing that she had seen him, he glanced up, bridging the distance with a look that was as devoid of emotion as one of the towering trees, then turning away without acknowledging her.

Her heart sank another notch. Would he even give her a chance?"

A low greeting sounded through the fresh morning air, and Marianne turned to see Megan and Alna crossing over from the Hanson's cabin. Though Alna approached with her familiar slow smile—and a baby on one hip—Megan wore an expression laced with concern, and what looked unbelievably like shyness.

"Can we come in?" the woman asked without her usual brusqueness.

Marianne had already ushered them inside before she realized that her cabin still bore the signs of the previous night's wear. The bedclothes were in complete disarray, chairs were pulled out haphazardly all over the room, and the empty whiskey bottle lay overturned on the table. Megan took one look around and began setting things to right, apparently glad to have something to occupy her hands.

"It'll just take a minute to get the coffee ready," Marianne offered, bending to stoke the fire to life.

"We were worried for you," Alna said quietly, shifting the babe onto her lap as she settled into the rocker. She wagged her head sadly. "He was a bad man."

"It was a horrible thing to happen. Horrible." Megan's bony shoulders shook vehemently.

Marianne straightened, tears of gratitude stinging her eyes. If they only knew that strangely enough, this morning she had hardly thought of the trouble with Trig Jones. What was bothering her was Nick's reaction today. "You mustn't worry over me," she choked. "He didn't hurt me."

Megan gazed at her with steady eyes, then turned back to the task of making the bed. "Not bodily, he didn't, but we were afraid you might be frettin' over the things he said."

For the first time since last night, Marianne remembered Trig's puzzling accusations, and she was stunned by what she recalled. Had he said something about Jake . . . and Alicia?

"Oh, Megan. He couldn't have meant . . ."

"He did," the woman said abruptly. She met Marianne's gaze unflinchingly. "The woman trouble I told you about was with Alicia. I didn't say anything before 'cause I thought you might take it hard, seein' as how Nick didn't tell you himself. But we figgered you might be wonderin' today. It's only fair that you know what she was."

"She was a whore."

Alna's voice was barely above a whisper, but she spoke with such simple sureness that Marianne knew, without being told, that shy, gentle Swede had also been prey to Alicia's charms. No wonder Elizabeth's description of her deceased sister-in-law had been fraught with discrepancies! It would have been easy for an eight-year-old child to misread the undercurrents beneath Nick and Alicia's marriage, but there was no mistaking the distaste in Megan's eyes, nor the sadness in Alna's.

"But why," she blurted angrily, "did Nick put up with this?"

"He didn't. That's why she left him." Megan's explanation made so much sense that Marianne wondered why she hadn't realized the truth sooner.

Alna rose from the chair. "Nick is a good man, but he had no use for women after what she did. That's why we were surprised when he brought you here."

"You're as different from her as night and day, but we were worried that Nick would blame you for what happened last night. If he does," Megan said, placing her hands on her hips, "at least you'll understand why."

Reaching her hands to her two friends, Marianne squeezed them tight, grateful that they had put aside their own pride to help her. "I don't know how to thank you," she said, blinking back tears. "But I promise everything will be all right from now on."

If only, she thought resignedly, she could be as sure of that as she sounded.

Chapter 27

Megan's revelation continued to haunt Marianne for the rest of that day and the next, and since Nick spent as little time as possible in her presence, she had plenty of opportunity to mull over what she'd learned.

Elizabeth was wrong. Alicia had *not* been a lady. That much, Marianne decided, was irrefutable, given Megan's and Alna's confirmation and Trig Jones's arrogant claims. What was still unclear to her was how Nick felt, not only about Alicia, but about *her* now that Trig had accused her of leading him on.

Nick couldn't possibly believe that, could he?

Her thoughts returned to the dilemma she'd faced when they first left Olympia. She'd wondered then if Nick were so unsure of her love that he wouldn't risk letting her go to New York. Was his faith in her so fragile that a lowlife like Trig Jones could shake it?

On the other hand, now that she knew how his father's murderer had nearly escaped punishment, it would seem that Nick had reason to doubt the methods of justice. That would explain his reluctance to let her confront Adam Pemberton in court.

Sighing heavily as she packed the last of her belongings into a carpetbag, Marianne wished she could simply *ask* Nick which it was, but for the past two days he'd been busy making the final arrangements for their departure. Despite his wound, he'd gone back out to the cutting site with Bass on the previous day, returning long after she'd gone to sleep. The next morning, staying remotely silent while eating the breakfast she'd prepared for him, he had announced they would be leaving for Tacoma at dawn. When she attempted to engage him in light conversation, he answered her questions but volunteered nothing. When she offered to see to the packing of their personal belongings, he acknowledged her with a smile that did not touch his eyes.

It reminded her, she thought sadly, of the way he had behaved in the first days after she'd arrived at his home. Just a few weeks ago, she realized suddenly. It seemed much longer.

A few weeks ago he hadn't known who she was, and she hadn't understood why he'd been so stingy with his emotions. Now her identity was no longer a secret, but she was no closer to figuring him out than she had been before. Intimacy had not changed that, nor had love.

Maybe he'd be more himself once they were home, she hoped fervently. But deep inside, she recognized that returning to Tacoma only meant resolving the problem that was at the root of all the others.

If not for Adam Pemberton, she reminded herself, she would never have come to Washington, never met Nick, nor fallen in love with him.

It was utterly perverse that the question of how to deal with Adam Pemberton was now driving them apart.

What should have been a joyous homecoming was marred by two things; Nick's consistent stubbornness and Claire's urgent announcement, which came before they'd even stepped foot into the house, that Horace Squiggs had been a frequent guest during their absence.

Nick frowned. "Did he mention Hartley, the man who threatened Marianne?"

Surprised that Claire seemed to know so much about the troubles precipitating their trip to Olympia weeks ago, Marianne merely listened with keen interest.

"No," Claire shook her head. "He only said he wants to talk to you both. I told him I wasn't sure when you would be home."

She didn't have to add that whether they informed him or not, Horace would soon know. Tacoma wasn't *that* big. Besides, Marianne reasoned silently, she couldn't avoid him forever. Talking with the marshal represented the first step toward establishing her innocence, and one she would doubtless have to take no matter how unsure she was of her path from there on. And she knew that Nick must realize it as well, or he wouldn't have brought her back to Tacoma. Her attention drifted back to what Claire was now saying.

". . . terribly disappointed, I fear. Who would have thought, after all that fuss, that she *wanted* to be a bridesmaid." Claire spoke with the resigned air of one who has sacrificed willingly, but not without regret. Her green eyes flickered over her son, then rested lovingly on her new daughter-in-law. She embraced her lightly. "*I'm* just glad you've settled everything now, fancy wedding or not."

Marianne smiled in return, aware that their silence was beginning to grow awkward. If Nick was unwilling to share their happiness with his own mother, then she would make up for it herself. "I wish you could have been there," she told Claire sincerely. "You and Elizabeth were the only things missing to make it perfect."

"Oh, dear," Claire laughed, pulling a handkerchief from her pocket to wipe the tears that clung to the creases at the corners of her eyes. "I *never* cry," she exclaimed, then laughed at herself while wagging her head back and forth. "Besides, as long as the two most important members of the wedding party are in attendance, the rest are just extra baggage. Let's go in and sit down. I've so much to ask you!"

When Claire linked her arm in hers and began to draw her toward the parlor, Marianne glanced back helplessly at Nick, who had not moved from the open doorway. He met her gaze with a guarded one of his own.

"I have to see to the stock now, Mother. I'll be in for supper." He paused before leaving, as if to say something else, but then his mouth clamped tight as a sprung bear trap, and he turned and strode out the door.

Marianne watched him go with a mixture of anger and longing that must have shown in her expression, for Claire sighed and patted her arm comfortingly.

"By all the saints," she said, her voice trembling, "I wish I were still bigger than him. 'Times I think he could use a good thrashing."

The mental picture of tiny Claire taking after Nick with a switch was more than Marianne could bear, and her shoulders began to shake with unsuppressed laughter. All the worries of the past weeks seemed to weigh a little less now. There was a bond between Claire and herself, a bond of friendship made stronger because they were two women who loved the same man, even though they each recognized his obstinacy. It was a blessing Marianne hadn't expected. It was a comfort.

And by that evening, she was sure it was the only comfort she would have for a long, long time.

Nick trudged out toward the barn, his sore temper matching the ache in his arm. What in hell, he wondered angrily, was the matter with him?

Jan had already begun unloading the wagon, dividing the cargo into two neat piles just inside the barn doors. One consisted of his and Marianne's bags, the other was mostly worn or broken equipment from the camp that he'd replaced with items purchased in Olympia. What could be repaired would be returned on his next trip up, what could not would be sold or discarded. Normally Nick made quick work of the sorting, but today he turned his back on the task, knowing he would be unable to concentrate on anything but the memory of Marianne's valiant attempt to put up a good front.

Her smile, puzzled but genuine, had softened her lips in a way that made him feel as if a fist had slammed into his gut. It was not a pleasant feeling, but one that forced him to examine his own troubled emotions.

As Jan looked on curiously, Nick stepped into the

tack room and lifted a brush from the table, then strode toward the far stall where his favorite saddle horse was kept. That the animal had already been tended to that day was obvious, nevertheless, Nick began to curry with vigorous, mindless strokes.

He loved her.

He hadn't realized quite how much until that moment when he'd stood over Trig's body, heartsick and spent, and knew only Marianne could restore him. That she had turned from him at that moment wasn't even the issue now. He understood her shock and revulsion, and probably would have felt the same way had he been a witness.

No, what really bothered him was the *needing*. It ate at him, a living thing, gnawing at his soul like an animal that, once tasting human flesh, consumes with an insatiable appetite. Was that what loving someone should be? Marrying her had been an admission to himself how much he desired her, but even then he hadn't wanted her to become the center of his life. No one, he believed, should wield that much power over another person.

Power, the wanting and the having of it, destroyed. Alicia had wanted it, and nearly ruined him and finally killed herself seeking it; Adam Pemberton had it, and now Marianne was threatened by his evil greed.

Nick's hands flew over the horse's silky hide—brushing, smoothing, brushing, smoothing—working independently from the churning and erratic impulses of his mind. Once, when he thrust just a little too hard, the animal turned a pair of liquid brown eyes on him, as if to say, "Take it easy. What did I do to deserve this?"

"Sorry, boy," Nick muttered, easing up a little. His thoughts turned back to Marianne.

It seemed he had a remarkable tendency for taking out his frustrations on the wrong people, but he knew of only two ways to prevent himself from hurt. One he'd demonstrated to Trig Jones. The other was to hold on to his own heart. The rational part of him argued that Marianne would never willingly cause him

harm, but the well of bitterness Alicia had dug into
him was deep, and there was still the chance he would
lose Marianne, not by her own choice, but irretriev-
ably, just the same.

Old habits, he acknowledged to himself grimly, died
hard.

True to his promise, Nick showed up in time to
change for dinner, but he was startled when he entered his room and found Marianne seated on his bed,
doubled over as she rolled one stocking up her slim
calf. She didn't see him come to a halt just inside the
door, nor did she notice the hungry look that came to
his eyes when she lifted her skirt halfway up her thigh.

"That," he said dryly, "is the most welcome sight
I've seen in days."

Marianne jerked her head up, surprised more by his
conciliatory tone than by his presence. "It's one you
could have seen anytime . . . if you wanted to," she
added, her cheeks growing fiery hot at her own boldness. It struck her then how incongruous that she
should blush now, when just a few nights ago she had
joined him in unchecked passion with nary a doubt.
The difference was he'd desired her then; now she
wasn't sure.

He stepped further inside, shutting the door sound-
lessly behind him. He crossed over to the bed, his gaze
locked on her eyes, which shimmered like liquid sky.
Reaching his hand to her hair, he sifted his fingers
through the honey gold waves. The pulse at her temple jumped beneath his hand like that of a frightened
animal.

"I've been a fool," he said.

Her throat thick with unshed tears, Marianne shook
her head. "'No, I was wrong to say what I did. I'm so
sorry."

He sat on the bed, sweeping her into his arms as he
did, heedless of the warning bells that sounded in his
head like clanging alarms. Keeping his emotional distance was difficult when he stayed away from her;
when he held her in his arms it was nearly impossible.

"You were in shock," he murmured against her cheek. "It was a normal reaction."

"Then why—"

Slanting his mouth across hers, he silenced her with a kiss, enjoying the feel of her graceful curves molding into him. He shifted, lifting her onto his lap without breaking the contact of his mouth against her soft, parted lips. The pleasure of coming home was nothing compared to the joy of holding her again. Her answering kiss was a sweet nectar that revived him, that fed his spirit.

And yet, were he given the chance, he would have denied that it was so.

His arms held her like steel bands wrapped around a precious cargo, not easily relinquishing their hold. Only when Marianne wriggled closer to him, winding her fingers through his hair, her breasts thrusting against his chest impetuously, did he relax his embrace enough to let his own hands wander over her delicious curves. He pressed her hips tight against his own, wanting her to know his need.

With one hand he stroked her breasts, teasing first one nipple, then the other, into eager hardness. He felt her gasp, and seized the opportunity to deepen the kiss, tasting, exploring, suckling.

She tore her lips away. "Oh, Nick!" she breathed. "I've missed you so!"

"Then let's not waste any more time with words."

"But dinner . . ."

"It'll wait."

His eyes were hot, smoking coals that set her on fire everywhere his ardent gaze lingered, and as she moved away from him to unfasten her dress, that was nearly everywhere.

"Here, allow me," he growled, turning her so that she faced away from him on the bed. The dress, one from Millie that she'd never worn before, was of a blue and green plaid taffeta that made her eyes change like the sea, from sapphire to turquoise and every hue in between. The nape of her neck flushed pink, so enticing that it was harder on him than it should have been to work the buttons that stretched all the way to her narrow waist.

Only halfway down, he couldn't resist the lure of her exposed flesh any longer, and slipped his fingers beneath the gaping dress, savoring the warm temptation of her skin. She moaned when his hands pushed around to cup the sides of her breasts through the filmy lace of her chemise, and she lifted her own hands to press against the backs of his. With his fingertips, he could just reach the turgid centers without tearing her garments. He flicked over them gently, and when she moaned again it was all he could do to remove his hands long enough to finish undressing her.

She lay back against the plumped-up feather pillows on the bed, watching him as he removed his own clothing with feverish haste. Any lingering shyness was gone as she surveyed him proudly, loving every inch of his long, lean form—hard muscles covered by smooth flesh, strength tempered with gentleness.

When she lifted her hand to him he took it, lacing his fingers through hers, answering her silent, eternal plea. His knee sank into the soft mattress as he lowered himself to her side, drinking in the sight of her as if she were a vision he were seeing for the first time.

Her hair spread across the pillows like a silky fan, a mantle of softness that beckoned to be touched. Her face—loving, eager eyes, skin as fragile and soft as butterflies' wings, lips full and moist with the lingering taste of their kisses—and then her body, delicate yet womanly, slender and resilient and perfect, all waited for him.

When he caressed her, his hands covering her with long, slow strokes that aroused and taunted, it was as if she had been waiting forever for the blissfulness of his touch. When he spread his fingers, hot and searching, over the soft flesh of her belly, Marianne's insides quivered as if rising to meet him.

Nick felt it, too, and his own reaction was as strong and urgent as hers. He rolled over her swiftly, his mouth slanting across her in a kiss that matched the tender violence of her nails raking his back. With his leg he parted her thighs, shuddering from the controlled effort it took to woo her slowly, but when she surged upward to meet him and he found she was as ready for him as he was for her, he could no longer hold back. He filled her then, majestically and with a force that pushed them both to the limits of ecstasy and beyond.

Afterward, when they lay heart to heart, his pounding sure and steady, hers adding a gentle syncopated beat, she thought again of the question that she'd never had a chance to voice. Now it seemed pointless.

Nick, however, did not fail to see the bewildered flicker in her eyes, and he hastened to explain before she asked him questions for which he had no answer.

"If this is your response every time I neglect you for business for a few days, perhaps I should make it a habit."

She opened her mouth to protest, then clamped it shut on a grin when she saw the teasing glimmer that lit his eyes to gray lights. "Business! Hmmph! I'll just have to think of ways to keep your mind *off* your work!"

Nick's deep chuckle set Marianne's mind at ease. Rolling to his back, he pulled her with him until she was sprawled across his chest, her fair hair cloaking them both. He cupped her round buttocks in the palms of his hands possessively, nipping at her lower lip with bared teeth. "You can try," he quipped dryly. "In fact, you can begin right now."

But despite his playful teasing, Marianne was stunned when Nick announced at dinner that he would be leaving for Olympia that evening.

"Tonight?" she exclaimed incautiously, unaware of Claire's curious glance or the amused snicker from the girl who was serving them generous slices of beef. Even Elizabeth, who was so raptly admiring the dress Marianne had bought her in Olympia that she'd barely spoken of anything else, looked up with a quizzical frown at the outburst.

"If I travel through the night I can be in Olympia for business hours tomorrow. I'll rest up a bit and then head for home the following day."

Marianne felt her heart plummet to the bottom of her feet, but she smiled brightly, hoping she wasn't beginning to sound like a nagging wife already. "Can't it wait a few days? Then I could go with you."

Nick peered at her thoughtfully, but his eyes did not show any sign of his feelings. "This is something that needs to be done tomorrow."

"All right then, I can be ready as soon as you want to leave."

"No."

Though he hadn't raised his voice at all, it seemed as if his forbidding tone echoed through the dining room with a resounding boom. Marianne's throat tightened, but so did her resolve. "Nick—"

"I'll be travelling fast." The corners of his mouth lifted, and she thought she saw a flash of something behind his eyes, but just as quickly it was gone, nothing remaining on his face except for the cool, unrevealing smile.

"Will you bring me back a bonnet to match the dress, Nick?" Elizabeth's piping voice broke in, dispelling the tension.

"That's a lovely idea, Elizabeth. Why don't you, Nick?" If a child could accept his decision without pouting, Marianne braved, then she would do no less. He was watching her carefully, and she realized, with a sudden smug satisfaction, that he had *expected* her to protest. Well, she could show him a thing or two about covering up feelings. After all, she'd been practicing at it all her life!

Difficult as it was, she did not even follow him upstairs for a more private farewell, but waited to say good-bye in the parlor with Claire and Elizabeth. The book she clutched in her lap remained unread, and she caught herself more than once losing track of her mother-in-law's attempts at conversation, but otherwise, she thought she had done a creditable job of appearing unconcerned.

Not so, in Claire's estimation. The volume Marianne had chosen randomly from the shelf was in Latin, and unless she was gravely mistaken, that language was not taught in any orphanage she'd ever heard of. Nor was she fooled by the pinched smile that Marianne was trying to pass off as genuine. Her suspicions were confirmed when Nick's saddlebags thudded to the hallway floor, nearly sending Marianne springing from her chair like a jackrabbit. And after he was gone, by the way she blinked back tears that made her eyes shine like forlorn jewels.

"Elizabeth," Claire said quietly, but in a tone that would brook no disagreement, "you'd best go to bed now. It's been a long day."

The girl's head snapped up, but when she saw the determined set of her mother's chin she did not argue, only glanced at Marianne's bowed head and nodded. She was not so young that she couldn't see *any* of what was going on.

On the mountain, Marianne recalled miserably, all would be silent by now. None of this incessant ticking from the foyer clock, not the titter of servants finishing up in the kitchen, not even the intermittent squeak of Claire's rocker as she swayed back and forth, stopped, swayed again, keeping up an irregular rhythm that nearly drove Marianne to distraction. On the mountain, the wind shuffled through the treetops like a ballerina pirouetting around one partner after another, creating a music that lifted one's soul clear up to the sky.

Holding back a sigh, she was about to excuse herself when Claire began to speak in an offhand way. "I recollect when I was a young bride, nervous and unsure and skittery as a colt. Joshua used to sail off for months at a time, and every time he left, I swore by the saints it'd be different, that I'd think on all the good things that came of his going: the nice things he'd bring back, the profit from the sale of the cargo, the way he always looked when he came home, refreshed and proud and handsome as the devil. But it was like the faeries, it was, the way thoughts'd come spinning into my mind, picking and poking and making me wonder if he would ever come home, or if I would ever see him again. It wasn't until after wee Nick was born that I stopped wondering, and even then I thought it was the babe that'd keep him." Claire chuckled. "Funny thing, how a lass can get notions like that, though I had good enough reason. Joshua didn't marry me for love, so I didn't think it'd ever be otherwise. Sure 'n I was wrong."

Marianne tried to smile, to show Claire that she appreciated what she was trying to do, but instead her chin quivered desperately and tears sprang to her eyes. "It's not the same."

"It's not so different either, child. The trouble with you young people is you don't want to give yourselves time to let the changes settle in. You've never been a wife before, bless your heart, and it's been a long time since Nick's been a husband. Time, and a few wee ones, will see a difference."

Frustration and despair welled inside of Marianne until she thought the pressure would tear her apart. She gulped, wanting so badly to pour out all her woes, but to do so seemed a betrayal of Nick's fragile trust in her.

"Suppose," Claire said softly, "you tell me what happened up on the mountain."

Her gentle invitation was more than Marianne could bear, and as suddenly as the tears swelled over her eyelids she began to stammer out the events since the night she'd fled with Nick. Claire made no response during her outpouring, except to offer an occasional sympathetic nod or a derisive cluck of her tongue. Which was why, when she finally did protest loudly, her reaction had such an impact.

"He said what!" she exploded

"Trig Jones said that Nick had killed Alicia. I'm not sure what he meant by that, but when he said she bled to death, I thought perhaps she'd killed herself with remorse for having turned away from Nick's love."

Claire jumped from her chair with the agility of a much younger woman, driven by anger reborn. "That's not true," she sputtered. "Alicia wouldn't've known remorse if the good Lord Himself set it right on the end of her spiteful nose. And Trig Jones must've been daft not to know that what she did was her own sin, not Nick's!"

"So she did kill herself," Marianne breathed.

Claire paused in mid-stride, then dropped down onto the sofa beside Marianne. Her green eyes blazed with disgust, yet underneath the fury was a sadness the depth of which transcended all else. "She did, though it was unintentional. She bled to death after letting some back-street butcher give her an abortion. She died killing Nick's son."

Chapter 28

The buggy wheels clattered noisily despite the soggy weather that drenched Marianne's shivering form and everything else in sight—and even a few places that were not. She'd been warned, she thought disconsolately, that the dry, summer days would not last long in Tacoma. Now the clouds wept mournful drops that plunked down on the buggy's roof and slithered over the sides, only to be blown against her each time the wind gusted, which was often. She couldn't have been more wet had she jumped headfirst into Commencement Bay, but it was her own fault that she'd volunteered to run several errands for Claire in an effort to keep her mind occupied, and her own fault that she hadn't stopped long enough to don the short jacket that went with her dress. Not that it would have done any good.

Her thoughts were as dreary as the day, and she wondered why it often seemed to be so. The sky that had dawned as clear as crystal had turned dark well before noon, then the clouds had broken up a little, taunting, just before developing into a full fledged storm. Just plain confused, Marianne decided.

Why in God's name hadn't Nick told her about Alicia? With a tiny shudder, she remembered accusing him of having had so much love in his life that he had no room for more. Now she knew the bitterness he must feel, not because Alicia had left him, but because she had taken their child with her.

Marianne's stomach churned, acid rising high in her

throat as she swallowed back her disgust. How could any woman not want a child? she puzzled. Not want *Nick's* child? It was a concept she could not fathom, any more than she could understand how her love for him had grown and expanded to include this new knowledge of his past.

The last stop of her journey was just ahead. She sniffled. Thankful that at least she could dry out at the orphanage, and sure that Ruth would have a warm fire and hot coffee waiting, she urged the horse on with a quick snap of the reins.

Marianne was anxious to reach the old mansion, but not only because of the welcome she was sure to receive. It was easier, she had learned, to forget her own problems when she remembered the children who had nothing at all. She was eager to start back to work, and secretly hoped that Ruth had not replaced her at the school, though it was unlikely since she'd been gone nearly a month. Still, there must be something she could do.

It turned out she was correct on both counts. Ruth *had* replaced her with another teacher, Marcus's wife Kathleen. And there was plenty for Marianne to do.

Two of the children, boys who would turn eighteen soon, had left to join the crew of a steamer, and six new children had arrived that week, necessitating a change in the room arrangements. When Marianne arrived, Ruth was supervising the moving of several beds. Her raucous voice sounded throughout the house, commanding, curt . . . comforting. Marianne smiled.

"Well, blessed if you aren't soaked to the skin, young lady," was the greeting bellowed from the top of the stairs. "Get along into my room this instant and strip out of those clothes. You'll find an old robe—wrap around you twice, it will—hanging inside the closet door. Hurry now. I'll be down as soon as I finish with this muddle."

Marianne obeyed, and she was just folding the sides of the flannel robe across her breasts and tightening the sash, which she'd doubled around her waist, when the door burst wide open and two tiny figures flew at her.

"Mith Mary, Mith Mary!" Leigh cried, her lisp intensified by excitement. "Gueth what!"

Dropping to her knees, Marianne scooped the girls into her arms, overjoyed to see them looking so happy and well. "I guess . . . that you're glad to see me," she finished in a rush, hugging them tight.

"*Nooo,*" Leigh squealed.

Gracie, ever the oldest, shook her head furiously. "Oh . . . yes . . . we . . . are!" she pronounced.

"And I'm very glad to see you. Now what is your big news?"

"We're getting a new mama and papa!"

"Leigh!" Again, Gracie frowned. "I wanted to tell."

Completely flabbergasted, Marianne looked up to see Ruth watching the reunion with a knowing grin. Clasping a tiny hand in each of hers, Marianne stood.

"It's true," Ruth confirmed, flashing Marianne a look that said, *I'll explain later, everything's fine.* Several minutes passed, and after a reading demonstration from Gracie and several sweet, wet kisses from Leigh, the two girls scampered away when Kathleen poked her head in the kitchen and called them to a lesson.

"They've done so well!" Marianne exclaimed once they were out of earshot. "How did you do it?"

Ruth laughed hoarsely, then shrugged. "It was *that* one," she said, indicating Kathleen. "They adore you, but they took to her like a couple of newborn kittens latch on to their mother's milk. What surprised me the most, however, was Marcus. It turns out they were only afraid of tall men with dark hair—"

"Like . . . Nick?"

"Like the man who hurt them. They were a little shy of Marcus at first, but he's fair-haired and shorter, so I guess he was okay in their eyes. Besides, there's something about him that makes him easy to like, don't you think?"

Marianne nodded, recalling Marcus Knowles and his quick smile and easy manner.

"It seems they can't have children of their own, but it wasn't until Kathleen took over your job that she considered adopting. They're giving the girls a few weeks to get used to the idea before making it official."

Marianne thought it was wonderful how things had worked out and told Ruth so, then hesitated before revealing her own news. It wasn't just her marriage to announce; fairness dictated she reveal the entire story to her friend. "I have something to tell you, as well," she began slowly. "I've never been a teacher."

Ruth nabbed Marianne's hand, shaking it peremptorily. "I knew that the minute you walked in here—you were too much in awe of the young ones—but I didn't know the whole tale until after you'd gone and Claire drove over to tell me you wouldn't be back for a while. She suggested Kathleen take your place."

"I'm sorry I lied to you."

"You did what was necessary. I generally hold with telling things as they are, but you had good reason to be cautious, *Marianne*."

Marianne cocked her head. "Then you *do* know everything."

"Don't blame Claire too much, dear," Ruth cautioned. "She couldn't be more worried for you if you were her own daughter. Under the circumstances, it was better for *her* sake that she unburden herself on someone, and she knew she could trust me."

Marianne hadn't even considered her mother-in-law's health throughout this ordeal, but now she was doubly grateful that Ruth was a willing friend. Overwhelmed with emotion, she marveled that, after nearly twenty years in New York, she hadn't had anyone to turn to, but in less than two months here she'd experienced more sincere friendship than she'd ever thought possible. This truly was the start of a brand-new life for her, and very soon the old would be behind her completely.

"Anybody here?"

The familiar voice rang through the kitchen, sounding just as cheerful as always. Marcus Knowles burst into the room like a cyclone.

"I heard you were back," he said to Marianne, planting a smacking kiss on her cheek before settling himself into a chair. "Where's Nick?"

"Hello, Marcus." Marianne paused to catch her breath before answering him. "Nick had to go back to Olympia. He'll be home tomorrow evening."

"Without you?"

With no comment other than a shake of her head, Ruth poured him a cup of coffee, spooned three lumps of sugar and a generous measure of cream into the mug, then pushed it across the table at him. "Drink," she commanded.

He obeyed, grimacing slightly as he held the cup out to her. "Needs more sugar."

Obviously, Marcus had become as much of a fixture around the place as his wife, for he and Ruth quickly became involved in a discussion of the plans for repairing the roof, which had been postponed due to the change of weather.

Marianne listened with half an ear, letting her mind drift back toward Nick again. If he remained insistent that she only bear him one child—his son—then perhaps he would have no objection to adopting more later. Better yet, when they had settled the problem of her trial once and for all, he might change his mind altogether. *If*, she thought decisively, her love was enough to help him forget the past.

"By the way," Marcus said, interrupting her thoughts, "who was your visitor?"

Ruth frowned. "Visitor? Today?"

"Yes. The fellow on the broken-down nag. At first I thought he was looking for something, but when he saw me he started riding back toward town. I thought he must have stopped here. There's nothing else up this way."

Fear worked its way up Marianne's spine. "What . . . what did he look like?"

"It was hard to tell in the rain." Sensing her dismay, Marcus peered at her intently. "Should I have known him?"

"N-no, I don't think so."

Marcus shook his head. "This fellow appeared to be tall, though it's hard to tell on a horse. Reddish hair, good clothes. That's about all I could see."

It was enough. As much as Marianne longed to deny it, there was no doubt that the man Marcus had seen was Rhys Hartley.

"Good Lord, child! You look pale as new snow!" Ruth's barking voice roused her a little. "Is that the man Claire said was following you?"

"I-I think so."

"Following you? What's this all about?"

She could do nothing but listen as Ruth launched into a detailed explanation for Marcus, including elements that made Marianne's cheeks flush so hard she knew she couldn't possibly be pale anymore. How had Claire known so much about their feelings for one another before either Nick or herself? And apparently, she smiled wryly, Marcus had made a few assumptions of his own, because he didn't seem the least bit surprised by anything Ruth told him, except when it came to her explanation of Rhys Hartley.

"He's probably one of Pemberton's men, sent to take Marianne back to stand trial," she concluded angrily. "But he's *not* going to succeed!"

"Damn right!" Marcus chimed in. "Is there another way into town from here?"

Marianne brightened a little. "There's a path through the woods. The children and I found it one day when we were berrying. I think it leads to the main road about a half mile from here, but if I can get around without him seeing me . . ."

"I'll distract him. When I went by earlier he pretended he was leaving, so he'll probably do the same again, assuming he hasn't hidden himself better. Kathleen and I'll leave like we usually do, but I'll keep a lookout. If we spot him we'll act like something's wrong with the wagon. That ought to keep him hiding long enough for you to get home."

"But what if he follows her anyway?" Ruth's voice was gruff with concern.

"Don't worry," Marcus replied, his cheerful face grown grim. "I'll stop him somehow."

Katey Muldoon grinned at the two ladies sitting in

her gold parlor and wondered at the vagaries of life that forced such odd friendships. Ruth Lyons was responsible for the moral and physical upbringing of Tacoma's orphans, yet thought nothing of marching into the most notorious saloon on the bay whenever the mood struck her. And now, she'd brought with her a woman Katey had secretly admired and publicly avoided for years. Claire Fortune sat primly upon the velvet-covered loveseat, but her emerald eyes gleamed with eagerness and excitement as she spied out her surroundings, albeit surreptitiously.

"May I offer you more tea?"

Claire smiled widely at her hostess, taking care not to pay too much attention to the way her satin gown plunged scandalously, or the jeweled ornaments that clung to her hair like so many artificial raindrops. "No, thank you . . . uh . . ." She paused, uncertain how to address the woman she'd seen on many occasions, but had never met.

"Katey, please."

"Don't you think we'd best say what we came for?" Ruth interrupted, knowing that the situation was awkward for both her friends, however sure she was that the awkwardness wouldn't last once they got down to business.

"Yes . . . yes, of course," Claire hastened, setting her empty teacup down upon its delicate, hand-painted saucer. She wondered briefly why Nick had never told her how charming Katey Muldoon was, then smiled secretively when she remembered that sons were not supposed to tell mothers about their women friends, charming or not.

"I need help," she began without preamble, "and Ruth suggested we come to you." Quickly, she explained about the problem with Rhys Hartley.

Katey nodded, frowning slightly. "But why hasn't Horace taken care of him?"

"We don't know," Ruth burst out. "Horace hasn't done anything, and now Nick's gone to Olympia. This afternoon that man followed Marianne to the orphanage and waited outside all day. She was frightened to death!"

"The poor wee thing had to sneak out the back and run home through the forest," Claire continued. "I suggested she start carrying a pistol with her, but she refused."

Katey studied Claire Fortune, knowing at once that though Nick did not resemble his mother in the physical sense, there was a great deal of strength hidden inside this tiny woman that had carried over to her son. Suddenly, the idea of being friends with her didn't seem strange at all. She leaned forward intently. "How can I help?"

Ruth and Claire exchanged a wary glance, then Ruth frowned. "Mary . . . Marianne has some foolish notion about turning herself over to Horace. Nick made her promise not to do anything until he gets back, but he didn't know this man Hartley was still around."

"So we have to take care of him!"

Silence followed Claire's statement, so profound that she wondered if the idea was as ridiculous as it sounded. Within moments, however, Ruth was bobbing her head in agreement.

"He'll be sorry he ever set foot across the Mississippi," she declared gleefully.

Katey pondered the situation. "How do you propose we 'take care of him'?"

"We thought you might have an idea," Claire said truthfully.

"Then let me think." Katey stood then, clasping her hands behind her back as she always did when either upset or deep in thought. She was aware of the other two women watching her pace the length of the small sitting room; was aware, too, that a proper hostess would not ignore her guests so. These, however, were extraordinary circumstances.

Ruth's weathered hazel eyes followed Katey's progress back and forth, her brow furrowed with concern for her young friend.

Claire's bright green eyes closed prayerfully as she willed her heart to be strong for just a little while longer, for just as long as Nick and his new bride needed her.

And finally, Katey's warm brown eyes flickered with hope, then rested upon the ladies who waited for an answer. "Here's what we'll do," she announced firmly. "But we'll have to work together."

Nick strode through the rutted mud, irritated that he'd been unable to procure a room at a decent hotel. The streets in the better part of town were paved with local brick, but out here on the edges of civilized living, muck was the norm.

He cursed aloud, but not because of the atrocious condition of the road. Right now he was wishing he'd waited long enough to talk to Horace before rushing out of the house like a hotheaded fool. Lord, if he wasn't acting like a fifteen-year-old kid, too shook by his first kiss to stick around for another! Only this time there was more at stake than a quick feel in the dark; it was love he was afraid of, and never more than now, when he realized how very strong a hold it had on him.

Strong? he thought disparagingly. Strong wasn't enough to describe the knot that clenched his gut like a vise when Calder Ryan told him Adam Pemberton had disappeared from New York, presumed to be trying to find the missing witness on his own.

Marianne was in danger. Horace probably knew it, but Nick hadn't given him a chance to tell them. Self-disgust warred with tormented worry for the upper place in his thoughts. What if Pemberton got to her? Why hadn't he stayed?

When he reached the shabby facade that fronted the boarding house, he paused before entering. *Cool down,* he told himself. *This isn't the time to lose your head.*

He could saddle up and leave right now, but he was dead tired and so was his horse. Even if he could hire another animal at this time of night, by the time he got home in the morning he'd be so exhausted he'd be no use to anyone. On the other hand, there was a train leaving at 7:00 A.M. that would arrive in Tacoma by noon. Three hours. Would it make any difference? Cold logic began to return to him.

He'd asked Marianne to stay at the house until he got back, and since Horace knew she was in danger, he likely was keeping an eye on the place already. That's probably what the marshal had been doing all the times he'd called on Claire while Marianne and he were gone. Too, Calder had mentioned that there were federal agents on Pemberton's trail, and at least one already in Tacoma. Chances were, the bastard'd be caught before he got near Marianne, *if* he was headed this way at all! No one knew for sure, but one of his employees-turned-witness seemed pretty certain that's what Pemberton would do.

So, did he go now, or wait for the train?

Torn by his dilemma, Nick forced himself to admit there was more than fear for her safety urging him back to Marianne. There was something he wanted to tell her; something he should have said to her a long time ago, but had been too stubborn or too blind or too crazy to see.

He loved her.

It was as clear now as Marianne's eyes when they looked at him with all the bright promise of a cloudless sky; it was as sure as the mountain, majestic and proud and forever.

He loved her so much it hurt him.

He loved her so much it healed him.

Nick Fortune stood in the rain, fists clenched and aching to touch her, muscles rigid with wanting, and made up his mind.

His boots sloshed through the mud, but the wet, sucking noise was a livelier one than when he'd trudged in the opposite direction just a few minutes before. Smiling for the first time all day, he hurried back to the livery.

Chapter 29

Rhys Hartley, happy to be rid of his crutch at last, yet still victim to the wrenching ache in his leg that made walking uncomfortable, yanked on the reins of today's hired nag, optimistic that *this* mount would be better than the last. It couldn't be much worse.

Yesterday, when he'd spotted Marianne Blakemore slipping into the trees behind the orphanage, he'd hurried to the strawberry roan that was costing him two dollars a day plus feed, only to find that the beast was sound asleep and decidedly *dis*inclined to giving chase. With nothing more than curses to spur the animal on, having disposed of his switch once the doctor removed the splint from his leg, Rhys could only bounce along in frustrated agony as the horse moved into a stiff-legged trot, obviously with no intention of going any faster. Just as well, because he'd not got more than a hundred yards down the road before he was stopped by a young couple having trouble with their carriage. They waved him down, calling for his help, and his purpose would've been quite transparent had he ignored them and continued after the girl.

It was no wonder she'd slipped away. Again!

Now Rhys studied the path very near to the spot where he'd first accosted his lovely quarry and contemplated the changes wrought in the past few weeks. He'd been baffled by Marianne's sudden disappearance, though his state of confusion lasted only a few short hours, for Horace Squigg's visit had cleared up many of the questions that had plagued him. The marshal—Rhys chuckled at the memory of how surprised *he* had been—had quickly filled him in on the missing details, once it was clear who's side they each were on.

That they were on the same side came as no shock to Rhys. After all, wasn't he a lawman, too?

The clatter of wheels rumbling over the corduroy road quickly gained his full attention, and he set aside his thoughts in anticipation of the task ahead. He'd be able to return to them soon enough, he had no doubt, for now he played a game of waiting that would most likely produce no more than extreme boredom and a few saddle sores. He was, however, under orders, and as determined to follow this new set as he had the old.

He melted back into the trees as the buggy approached. It was the same vehicle she had driven the day he'd first accosted her; a light two-seater with plenty of room in the back for packages and such. He recalled that yesterday she had taken several bundles of clothing to the orphanage, but now he could see nothing behind the seat. All his attention was focused on the slight figure perched alone in the front.

She'd never worn a bonnet before. Rhys frowned. He had no business wishing he could see her face, or the shining glory of her hair, but there it was. One of the things he'd had to deal with in the last two weeks was his overwhelming relief upon learning that Marianne Blakemore was *not* a criminal. That particular emotion attested more to the attraction he felt for her than he liked to admit. Perhaps it was better that she remained covered from him: following another man's wife might have been part of his job description, but lusting after her certainly was not!

The buggy drew even with his hiding place. Rhys gathered the reins, prepared to follow at a discreet distance once she'd driven past, but to his great surprise he watched as the vehicle slowed to a stop not twenty feet away.

"Mr. Hartley?"

The voice that called to him was not the one he

expected, though he honestly hadn't expected any-thing like this at all. Uncertain whether to answer—how the *hell* had she known he was here?—he remained silent, hoping the woman had not really seen anything and would soon give up trying to find him.

"Mr. Hartley, are you there?"

Rhys furrowed his brow in concentration, trying to place the voice. He was sure he had never heard it before. Did he know her? Did she know him?

"Mr. Hartley, please come out. It's Claire Fortune. I need to speak with you."

Rhys started. Claire Fortune? The mother? His mind churned, trying to figure out what she could possibly have to say to him. Obviously, Nicholas Fortune hadn't kept anything from his family—Horace had told Rhys they thought he'd been hired by Pemberton—but did she now know who he was really working for? And if so, who had told her?

Realizing there was only one way to find out, Rhys nudged his heels into the horse's flanks, gratified that this mount responded after only a few seconds' hesita-tion. Picking the way carefully over rotted stumps and beneath low-hanging branches, Rhys moved out onto the road. He dismounted.

"Mrs. Fortune," he nodded in greeting, eyeing her carefully. She was wearing a dress of the same light blue that Marianne favored, and it was clear to him now that Claire had purposely attempted to deceive him into thinking she was her daughter-in-law, at least at first glance. There was trepidation in her sparkling eyes, which shone with the verdant hue of the sea, but that did not arouse his curiosity as much as the trium-phant lift of her chin as she stepped down from the buggy.

"I thought you might be here," she said, "but I wasn't sure until I saw the place where you went into the woods. You're a city boy, aren't you?"

Chagrined, Rhys could only agree. "I am. On a busy street, you would have walked right by me, ma'am. I guarantee it."

Claire stared at him for a long moment, then nodded stiffly. "I have no doubt."

Rhys waited for her to explain why she had sought him out, but to his consternation, the woman turned to study his horse, appearing to be fascinated with the borrowed mount.

"I hope you're not paying much for her," Claire sniffed. "Ethan has a tendency to overcharge strangers."

"Then I've most certainly been bilked," he replied pleasantly. Rhys knew what she was doing now, and it amused him that she would think such an obvious ploy could work. He was perfectly willing, however, to go along with the game for a time. After all, if Marianne were going to the orphanage via the back road again, he would certainly know soon enough.

Claire edged closer to the horse, patting the animal's thick neck with her tiny hand. Rhys stepped nearer. "You probably won't trust me," he said, "but I only want what's safest for Marianne. Perhaps it'd be best if I called on her to explain."

Claire looked up, her gaze flicking over his shoulder once before settling on his generous smile. For one brief moment she almost believed him, but then she remembered what Nick had told her of Marianne's past and the man who was responsible for all her woes. Quelling the tremor that passed through her heart, she tightened her lips. "You're right, Mr. Hartley. I don't trust you."

At the moment she spoke, he heard the snap from behind him that warned him, too late, that she had not been alone. Roaring pain shot through his neck, paralyzing him instantly. The last thing Rhys saw was her eyes widening slightly.

Then he saw nothing at all.

"Staring out the window won't help, you know. He won't be home until after dinner."

Marianne allowed the fringed curtain to drop back to the window, startled by the sound of Elizabeth's voice close behind her. "It's not Nick I'm watching for," she said quickly, regretting her words the mo-

ment they left her mouth. There was no point in
getting the entire household in an uproar just because
Claire was late getting back from a round of calling
. . . for the second evening in a row.

Elizabeth joined her at the window then, peering
into the growing darkness before turning to Marianne
and saying in her most adult tone, "It's very sweet of
you to be concerned about Mother, but she always
comes back. I used to worry that she wouldn't, after
. . . well, when I was small," she amended. "But now
I know all that worrying was silly."

Marianne wished with all her heart she could pass
off as "silly" the apprehension she felt, but the fright
of having seen Rhys Hartley yesterday afternoon still
had her jumping at every sound. And now Claire was
long overdue for dinner. She wouldn't, however, let
Elizabeth see how truly anxious she was. Only the fact
that her young sister-in-law was making an obvious
effort to distract her was enough to channel her thoughts
away from the darkening sky. "You're right," Marianne agreed. "I'm not doing any good standing here.
Shall we sit down?"

"If you'd like." Elizabeth's carefully arranged expression broke into an impish grin as she plopped
down onto a footstool near the sofa. "It's too bad
Nick didn't take you on this trip with him, but I
suppose the honeymoon is over."

"What makes you say that?"

"Only that you seem lonely without him. On the
other hand, waiting by the window is rather romantic
too, don't you think?"

Marianne smiled gently. "It all depends on how you
look at it. When I was your age I was entranced with
the story of a girl who was taken far from her lover by
strangers, and they pined away for each other for
years. I thought it quite romantic at the time, but not
now."

Elizabeth, eyes wide with rapt attention, leaned forward eagerly. "Mother says I have *too* many foolish
fancies. Did you?"

"Yes."

"Tell me about them."

Pausing to consider, Marianne let her mind wander back to the time, not so very long ago, when she had dreamed of something very different from this. "There was one—I suppose you could call it a fancy—about the man I would marry someday. He didn't have a name, or even a face, but just the same I knew he was wonderful."

"And now you know that it's Nick!" Elizabeth's tone was triumphant. Marianne couldn't help laughing at her pleased expression.

"I didn't think so at first . . . but yes, it is Nick."

"I didn't think so, either," Elizabeth confessed, lowering her head just a little. "One of *my* fancies was that my brother would love Alicia forever and ever. That's why I was so mean to you when you first came, because you were spoiling everything." She hesitated, swallowing hard. "I'm sorry I acted that way."

Reaching for her hand, Marianne gave it a quick squeeze. "It must have been hard for you, too. Let's forget it, shall we? Pretend we've only just met?"

"Okay." Elizabeth's face brightened immediately. "You want to know what else I think is romantic? Eloping! I thought and thought about having a big wedding, and for a while I even wished you and Nick had had one so I could be a bridesmaid, but I decided when I get married I'm going to elope, just like you."

"Oh, darling, people don't elope because they want to. They do it because they have to."

"I know *that*." Her voice clearly said she wasn't born yesterday. "I'll just think of a reason why I have to."

They were still laughing when Sue Kim hesitated at the parlor door. "Missies eat now?"

When silence ensued, Marianne realized with a start that *she* was expected to make the decision. "As soon as Mrs. Fortune arrives, Sue Kim. Hopefully, it won't be long now."

The servant fidgeted, lowering her eyes. "Missy Claire say not wait. She say not set place for her."

Marianne exchanged a glance with Elizabeth, who

shrugged once more. Frowning, she tried to puzzle out Claire's odd behavior. The older woman had been strangely quiet the previous evening, secretive that morning, and now this. Something was definitely going on. She only hoped it was not Claire's health that was the problem, and that her mother-in-law was not making clandestine trips to see her doctor.

Rising, Marianne linked arms with Elizabeth, the warmth from having made their peace dispelled by her growing concern for Claire. Now, she thought ruefully, she truly did hope Nick would hurry home.

Horace Squiggs dragged himself one-armed across the floor of his office, unmindful of the blood that pooled beneath and around him, darkening nearly to black as it soaked into the worn planks. It was not his blood, but the agony that ripped through him made him feel as if it was; just a few feet away, Phil Owens stared at him through sightless eyes, watching Horace's halting progress with an eternal smile frozen on his face.

"Goddamn," Horace muttered, unable to think of anything better to say, but needing to say something to break the awful silence. Ignoring the pain in his shoulder, he pushed himself to his knees next to Phil and placed two fingers beneath the still man's throat. It was an automatic, though useless gesture. His deputy had died instantly.

Again, Horace was racked with an anguish he had rarely known, for his success as a lawman had stemmed, in part, from his ability to remain dispassionate from most situations.

From most, but not from this.

Gently, the way a father would lovingly caress his sleeping son, Horace replaced a lock of Phil's hair that had fallen across his forehead, then brushed his eyes closed. Only then did he look around.

The office had been ransacked, probably during the hour—according to his pocket watch—that Horace had lain unconscious. He knew what the bastard had been looking for, though it gave him little satisfaction to know the books hadn't been found. For the first time, he was glad that Rhys Hartley had convinced him to give over the ledgers.

"Goddamn," Horace repeated weakly, surveying the wreckage of his office. At least it was a little easier than looking at the mortal remains of a life.

He tried to remember exactly how it all happened, and though he was dizzy from the loss of blood and his own wound, he could still picture how it had been . . .

It was no coincidence that he and Phil had been discussing the case of Marianne Blakemore, for it had been much on Horace's mind lately. Owens, too, was intrigued by the case, and he never tired of extrapolating the possibilities out loud whenever the two had a few minutes alone at the end of a busy day.

"Only thing I can't figure out," Phil wondered idly, "is why Nick hightailed it back to Olympia so fast without waiting for you to tell him what's been going on here?"

Horace had pondered the same question himself, and from his knowledge of Nicholas Fortune and conjecture based upon years of experience, he thought he had that one figured out. "Nick still isn't sure what'll happen to her if she goes to trial, and he doesn't know yet that she likely won't have to. It's a matter of weighing his feelings for her against trusting us—"

"And we lost," Phil replied, grinning knowingly. "Can't say as I blame him. Funny thing is, assuming he believes in her story, why *wouldn't* he want her to stand trial?"

As briefly as it was possible to tell the rather complicated story, Horace filled his deputy in on the events of over fifteen years ago that had resulted in his becoming a deputy himself. He paused before revealing the last part of the tale. He'd never told anyone of the deal made with Bass Valliers, but he reckoned it was time Phil knew the truth. The past few weeks had put them through a lot of tricky situations, but the end result was that Phil Owens had matured a lot, a fact that made Horace strangely proud. It also helped make up his mind.

"There's times—not often, but frequent enough—
when seeing justice done and following the letter of
the law don't mesh together. *Sometimes*," Horace
stressed the word, "a man has to do what his conscience says is right, though now, with statehood just
around the corner, it'll be harder and harder for a man
to make his own private stand. In more'n fifteen years
I only bent the law a few times. Letting Bass Valliers
go free was one. Not arresting Marianne Blakemore
was another. I expect you'll run into a few times
yourself."

Phil nodded, his expression properly sober, even
though his eyes shone with delight that his mentor
was sharing secrets such as these. He opened his mouth
to comment, but a sharp rap at the door cut him off
abruptly. "No one knocks when the light's on," he
said, puzzled.

"Must be a stranger," Horace grunted in agreement, but swung his legs off his desk as Phil strode to
the door.

The man who entered was definitely one he'd never
seen before, but he was just as unquestionably one he
would never forget. His blond hair was slicked back
with a heavy dose of oil, his broad shoulders and tall,
slender frame clothed in a suit that probably cost him
as much as Horace earned in a month. The smile on
his face was just as polite, just as polished as the rest
of his appearance, but it didn't quite reach his eyes.
Within them, Horace sensed a well of passions that
were hidden by the rather unctuous exterior.

"Can I help you?" Phil asked, hooking his thumbs
in his belt with a smug air.

"I certainly hope so," the gentleman replied smoothly.
"I'm looking for someone, and I've reason to believe
she was last headed in this direction. I heard of the
railroad tragedy, and since I've had no word . . ." He
shrugged disarmingly.

Horace remained seated behind his desk, but spoke
for the first time. "Who're ya looking for?"

The man settled his gaze on the marshal, a mixture
of contempt and supreme confidence filling his expres-

sion for one swift moment. In that instant Horace was swept by a feeling of dread so frightening that it told him, as surely as if he'd been handed a calling card, that he was face to face with Adam Pemberton. The man fit the description Hartley had given to him not long after they learned Pemberton had disappeared from New York. They had feared he was headed this way, which was why Rhys was now standing guard over Marianne. Horace *hadn't* figured on the fellow walking right into his office, but then, perhaps Pemberton didn't know yet that he was a wanted man.

"She's a friend of mine," Adam Pemberton finally answered. "Miss Marianne Blakemore."

Phil drew his breath in sharply, and Horace wished he could've somehow signaled his deputy to stay calm. It was too late, though. The younger man had already taken a step closer to Pemberton, eyeing him suspiciously.

"What do you want with her?" Phil asked. "Who are you, anyway?"

To Pemberton's credit, Horace thought, the man appeared as unruffled as ever, though he must have been sweating bullets. He watched him smile at Phil.

"Then she *is* in Tacoma. Where is she?"

Horace noted that Pemberton's control had slipped a notch, but not enough that he could be easily fooled. "She's dead," the marshal said bluntly. "Died in the train wreck. She's buried up in the churchyard with the rest of the victims."

The look that passed over Pemberton's face was one of such rage and frustration that Horace nearly reached for his gun then. Later, he would wish he had, but instead he waited for his visitor's next words.

"No!" Pemberton's voice ground like cut glass. "I know she's alive. I saw the report . . ."

As if he realized he'd said too much, Pemberton reached inside the front of his coat, his pistol flashing out before either of the other men could react. Phil Owens, who was unfortunately the nearest, took the first bullet in his chest.

Horace managed to get off a single shot himself before his shoulder exploded with pain and he was thrown off the back of the chair, landing on the floor behind the desk. He had a vague notion that he'd hit Pemberton, but the last thing he'd heard before blacking out was the sound of heavy footsteps approaching where he lay . . .

Now Horace struggled to keep from passing out again, knowing that if he did he would likely bleed to death before anyone found him. Unless Pemberton decided to make trouble tonight, it'd be morning before anyone came around. By then it would be too late for him, and maybe for Marianne, as well.

He thought about Claire and her weak heart, wishing for the first time that he'd put aside his hesitation and spoken to her about how he really felt.

He thought, too, about Nick, and wondered if his friend—strong as he was—would be any match for a man as crazed as Adam Pemberton.

But most of all, Horace thought about Marianne. He couldn't get the image of her out of his mind, face glowing as she smiled up at Nick in front of the mill. Thinking about what Pemberton would do to her revived him a little, anger surging through his veins, making up for the blood that was no longer there.

He had to get to her first, warn her of the danger and alert Rhys Hartley to take protective action. He *would* make it, Horace determined grimly, if it was the last thing he did.

Chapter 30

Craziness is nothing more or less than an altered state of mind, Adam Pemberton thought as he slogged through the rain-wet forest with his pistol clutched to his chest like a cross intended to ward off evil. The fact that in his occasional lucid moments he *knew* he was going insane did not bother him. During those times he experienced a heightened awareness that rushed through his senses like an electric current, clarifying every detail of his life, slotting each event in such a logical sequence that he could see, as he'd never seen before, how he was only doing what had to be done—what he'd been *born* to do.

The only thing that did bother him—and that only a little—was that there were parts of the past few days he could not remember at all.

For instance, he could not recall leaving the marshal's office, though his mind retained an image of the weasel-faced marshal and his impudent deputy. All he knew was that he'd awakened—it felt like waking up anyway—inside a dingy, boarded-over cabin, with blood splattered upon his coat and his head reeling with the knowledge that he was on Fortune's property, and that Marianne was less than four miles away.

Now that he was thinking clearly while pushing through the underbrush, heedless of the low branches that whipped his face and hands and hair, he could even understand *why* his desire to confront Marianne was so great that he risked certain arrest to see her. It wasn't only *she* whom he needed to confront.

Memories assailed him, tiny barbs that viciously ripped at his brain. Adam didn't mind the pain, because as long as it was there he knew he was still in control. Not like when the madness began to ooze through his head, sucking him into its shuddering blackness like quicksand.

When he was thinking clearly, he sometimes wondered what it was that had marked the beginning of his madness. It wasn't the killings, he knew. He'd done that before, with never a twinge of the helpless frustration, the surrender to destiny that ruled him now. No, it wasn't the killing.

His lips pursed in concentration even though the lower one bled profusely from where he'd bitten through it. *Perhaps*, he thought, *I was always a little insane.*

This rare appearance of conscience, however, did not last long enough to make an impression. By the time the idea was formed, it had already been squashed from his mind like a troublesome insect, to reappear no more.

He would not think about that, Adam vowed silently, pausing just long enough to get his bearings. He still wasn't sure how he knew where to find Marianne, but he wasn't overly concerned with such an insignificant detail. Probably, he had seen a map of some kind in the marshal's office, or perhaps the skinny little man had even told him before he died. Adam didn't know, nor did he care. The important thing now was to reach her while he still had the capacity to act out his final deed with a modicum of rationality. The *last* thing he wanted was to accidentally kill her before he'd had the opportunity to make her pay for her sins.

With that, Adam Pemberton smiled a wide, demented grin that pulled at his cut lip, starting the bleeding all over again. He didn't feel it.

After all, insanity had its advantages.

*

"There's no use trying, Mr. Hartley. If you ever do manage to untie those knots, I'll simply have to blow your head off."

Rhys glared over at the figure who watched him

from the far side of the room. "How you can call this tangle of ropes a knot is beyond me," he said stiffly. "No self-respecting boy would acknowledge such a shoddy piece of work."

"Unfortunately for you, Mr. Hartley, I was never a boy, so I don't care how a knot looks, only that it holds." Ruth Lyons smiled. It was hard not to like a fellow as charming and good-looking as Rhys Hartley. But what she liked most about him was his sense of humor. Despite his every effort to free himself by means physical and otherwise, there was still that feeling that he found the whole situation amusing. It was in the way his green eyes twinkled every time she and Katey and Claire discussed what to do with him, and in the way he teased them about the ineptness of three old ladies trying to play kidnappers. Yes, he was an easy one to warm up to, she nodded, which was all the more reason to be extra firm.

"When will Miss Muldoon be back?" he asked, reluctantly ceasing his attempts to unfasten the fist-sized ball of rope that held his wrists together behind him. There was no way in hell he could get out of it, and though he didn't *think* the schoolteacher had it in her to shoot him, he wasn't willing to put her to the test.

"She'll be here soon enough," Ruth replied calmly. "Mrs. Fortune went downstairs to fix us some dinner. Are you hungry?"

"I don't suppose there's a chance you'll let me feed myself this time?" Rhys said disparagingly.

"Nope."

"Or that you'll let me go even if Miss Muldoon *can't* find the papers?"

"Nope."

Rhys grimaced. "Then I'm afraid it'll be all the more embarrassing for you ladies when Marshal Squiggs tries to find me."

Ruth looked up from her knitting long enough to send him a measuring glance. "Be that as it may, Mr. Hartley, I have no intention of freeing you until we're sure. Embarrassment is something I've lived with before. I daresay I can live with it again. What I couldn't live with is letting anything happen to Marianne."

"Then you must believe me!"

Startled by the force of his words, Ruth jumped, dropping a stitch as she did. "I'll believe you when I see proof," she remarked, seemingly unperturbed as she returned to the place of her error and picked up the missing stitch. Inside her mind, doubts were flinging back and forth, clamoring to be heard. What if he was right? she wondered. What if that Adam Pemberton fellow she'd heard about really was coming to hurt Marianne? Had they left her completely unguarded? Her hands flew over the needles automatically, keeping time with the speed of her troubled thoughts. Were they doing the right thing?"

No such doubts were bothering Rhys. He knew exactly what the three women were up to, and also knew it was just a matter of time before they realized their mistake. The question was, would that time make any difference?

With nothing better to distract himself, he studied the room with the same scrutiny he would have given to the scene of a crime. In a manner of speaking, he thought wryly, a crime *was* being committed here, though it was a crime of good intentions, if there was such a thing. Ruth Lyons, Katey Muldoon, and Claire Fortune were a most unlikely threesome, joined by their common interest in protecting the people they loved. It was merely his poor luck that they thought *he* was the one who threatened Marianne's safety. Though he had attempted to goad them into releasing him by pointing out that they were each ill-equipped to carry out their plan, in truth they hadn't done a half-bad job of it.

That he was here now was proof of that.

Muffled laughter drifted up from beneath the floor, confirming his belief that he was being held prisoner somewhere inside the *Golden Lady*. The meals he'd been fed—spooned into him as if he were a baby, no less—had been well-prepared and steaming hot, obviously cooked on the premises. Despite the comfortable bed and cheerful decor, the sloped ceilings told him he had been relegated to an attic room, and he wondered briefly how the women had gotten him up here without help. He decided they could most likely do anything they set their minds to.

From the minute he'd awakened that afternoon, his head throbbing as if a lumberjack were dancing on it with spiked shoes, he'd gained grudging respect for members of the opposite gender. Katey, her voice hard and commanding, had been in charge of interrogating him, and her relentlessness would have earned her accolades from law enforcement agents the world over.

Claire Fortune, organized in her decisions, had quickly assessed what was needed in the way of personal amenities, both for him and for his jailers, and then saw to accumulating them. Before he'd been conscious long enough to make sense of what was happening, she had blankets on his bed, food in his stomach, and a chamber pot stashed behind a folding screen in one corner.

Ruth Lyons was the only one of the three he hadn't recognized on sight, but since Claire considerately performed the introductions, he now knew she was the headmistress of the orphanage where Marianne worked. Levelheaded and calm, Ruth was charged with standing guard over him, armed with the small derringer that Katey owned but had confessed to never firing. He'd heard Ruth say once to send a message to someone named Kathleen to stay at the orphanage until she returned, but other than that, she appeared as comfortable watching over him as she undoubtedly was at any task.

More voices from outside the room, this time closer and quite distinctly female, alerted him immediately. After a sharp rap at the door, followed by three slow knocks, Ruth Lyons rose and slid the bolt—brand-new that morning; he'd watched Katey install it herself and had smirked at the way she'd handled the screwdriver as if it were a scalpel—admitting the owner of the house. Katey hadn't bothered to discard her cloak, so quickly had she rushed up the stairs. Her cheeks were flushed with the effort, her ample bosom heaving rapidly as she gathered her breath. Behind her, Claire Fortune entered, setting another steaming platter of food on top of a small desk without a word.

"Well?" Ruth Lyons searched her friend's face, knowing by her troubled expression that their efforts had been for naught.

"He is who he claimed to be," Katey stated breathlessly. She turned toward Rhys. "I found the papers, Mr. Hartley. I only hope we haven't made things worse."

Releasing a lungful of air he had unconsciously held, Rhys nodded consolingly. "No one can blame you for trying to help," he said. "The chances are good that nothing has occurred more serious than allowing Marianne an afternoon's peace of mind."

"Marianne doesn't know about this," Claire said. "We didn't want to worry her any more."

"Then I commend you all for your thoughtfulness, though perhaps it's best she understand the danger she's in now."

"You're right, of course." Claire stepped forward, wringing her hands apologetically as the other two women looked on. "Mr. Hartley, is there *anything* we can do to make up for this misunderstanding?"

Rhys studied them one at a time, suddenly wishing he didn't have to return to New York as soon as this assignment was over. He would have liked to get to know these women better. He chuckled. "One of you," he said lightly, "can cut this rope off. I seriously doubt you'll ever get the knot untied."

Marianne's head snapped up, her ears instantly tuned to a strange thumping sound on the porch. That's funny, she thought. She hadn't heard a carriage or horse at the front of the house. Had she fallen asleep?

A quick glance at the mantel clock confirmed that she had not. Ten minutes after eight. Just five minutes later than the last time she'd looked. Quickly setting aside the embroidery she'd taken up only to occupy her hands, she rose, smoothing the wrinkles from her skirt as her anticipation grew. Claire must be home, or perhaps . . .

She dared not hope it was Nick, knowing that her disappointment if it wasn't would surely be apparent by her expression. If Elizabeth came down and saw her, she'd be in for more of the teasing to which she'd been subject all evening.

Marianne smiled. Nick, and Claire too, would be pleased to learn how easily Elizabeth had shed her resentful behavior now that the two had made their peace.

Moving impatiently to the parlor's arched opening, Marianne placed a hand on the looped-back drapery that lined the entrance. Her gaze riveted on the front door, she waited for it to open.

Nothing happened.

With a slight frown, she started forward, only to be stopped in her tracks by another sound, this time from outside the French windows in the parlor. She spun around, her mouth turning cotton-dry as she stared at the door latch barely visible through the closed curtains. Her mind whirled, random thoughts springing to and fro. Why would Claire come in this way? she questioned, even while a more tranquil part of her mind provided the answer.

Claire would not, nor would Nick.

"Elizabeth?" she asked, her voice no more than a croaking whisper. No reply could be heard, but the latch moved slowly downward, soundless, and Marianne prayed it was locked tight.

It would do no good to run from the room, she thought, amazed by her own rationality. There were no parlor doors to bolt behind her, and few of the upstairs rooms had locks either. The servants had all retired to their quarters located on the far side of the house, so there would be little help there. Besides, Elizabeth would soon return. Marianne couldn't let her walk into an intruder unsuspecting.

The door latch rattled again, and her mind flew to the memory of Rhys Hartley's threats on that day so

long ago. What would he do to her once he got in?
There was no doubt in Marianne's mind that he could
if he wanted; all that lay between them now were a
few strips of thin wood and fragile glass.

Her gaze darting frantically around the room, she
searched for something to use as a weapon. Marianne
wished she'd listened to Claire's pleas that she carry a
pistol, then reasoned that she probably would not
have kept it with her inside the house anyway.

The tinkling, silvery sound of breaking glass muffled
by the heavy curtains spurred her to action. Marianne
rushed to the fireplace, clasping the iron poker in a
firm grip as she spun around to face her tormentor.
The vision she saw, however, was not the one she
expected. No green eyes or copper-colored hair. No
gentlemanly bow or rakish smile.

Instead, she stared at the man before her as if he
were a spectre from some hellish dream.

Adam.

It was a long moment before she realized she hadn't
said his name out loud, and perhaps he thought she
didn't recognize him, for he spoke as he raised the
pistol from his side.

"Don't you know who I am?" he asked, his voice a
chilling parody of its former self.

Frozen with shock and fear, Marianne could only
gape at him, willing her limbs to move, to somehow
help her live past this moment. Slowly, sensation came
back to her hands and feet and she remembered she
was still holding the poker over her head.

"I suggest you put that down," Adam said, motion-
ing toward her with the gun.

Automatically, Marianne obeyed, letting the pointed
rod drop to the floor with a loud clatter. Satisfied,
Adam circled around her quickly, glancing out into
the foyer to make sure they were alone before he
turned to her again.

"How . . .? What are you doing here?" She could
hardly believe this was the same man she'd last seen
standing over her uncle's still-warm body. Even then
he'd been as composed, as meticulously groomed as

ever. Now he was positively unkempt; filthy and wet
and staring at her with a wild-eyed gaze that frightened her beyond thought.

"You didn't think I'd find you, did you? That's
because you *always* underestimated me, from the time
I was a boy. You thought I was a child, but I've come
to prove you were wrong. Wrong, I say!"

Beneath the terror that clutched at her chest like a
giant, clawing beast too heavy for her to bear, Marianne wondered dimly what he was talking about. She
recognized the disjointed ramblings of a crazed person, but was too aware of the Adam Pemberton she
remembered, the one capable of cool, emotionless
murder, to think how this new information might help
her.

"What do you want from me now?" she asked
hoarsely.

"What do I want. . .?"

Adam's face twisted into a grotesque mask, and she
realized with sickening horror that he was trying to
laugh.

"What I want," he said finally, "is to collect what
you *owe* me. But first I think I'll deal with the bastard
who took you from me. Where is he?"

"Wh-where's who?"

"*Where's who?*" His voice high-pitched and mimick-
ing, Adam repeated, "*Where's who?*"

At that instant, Marianne knew just how bottomless
was the depth of his madness, and she was filled with a
hopeless dread that made her heart sink to the soles of
her feet. She could not even respond to his taunting,
could only stand motionless before his power, watching his expression harden once more.

"Who do you think I mean, you bitch? I want to see
the man you married, the man you've been screwing
for the past twenty years!"

Twenty years? Elizabeth paused in the foyer, unsure
what the man who was yelling at Marianne meant, but
determined to defend her new sister-in-law. Hands
thrust against her hips, she lifted her chin high despite
the blush that spread across her cheeks like liquid fire.

She knew what screwing meant, because she'd heard boys use the term when they thought no one was listening. She also knew Marianne was only nineteen years old, and besides, gentlemen just didn't *talk* that way to ladies!

Marianne's eyes widened fearfully as she spied Elizabeth's approach at the same moment that Adam took a step forward. "No!" she shouted, raising her hands as if to push the girl back. She saw Elizabeth stop, furrowing her brow. "No, get back! Go away!"

Adam seemed not to notice that Marianne's horrified gaze was focused over his shoulder, for his grin only intensified at her display of fear. "You can't rid yourself of me so easily again," he said. "No more running away, no more hiding yourself from me. I've spent a lifetime searching for you, and this time you won't escape until you're dead."

Marianne's eyes were locked with Elizabeth's in silent communication, and she saw the young girl stiffen, felt her shock at these last words. With a stifled gasp that was covered by Adam's maniacal laughter, Elizabeth spun away, disappearing from the doorway. Marianne nearly sobbed with relief, but Adam's threatening presence proved stronger than any momentary consolation she might have felt. Brandishing the pistol, he waved her toward the broken glass door.

"Let's go, bitch. I don't want to raise an alarm before I've had my chance at you. I'll come back for your *stud* later."

Again, Marianne stood rooted to the spot, unable to move until he clasped her arm roughly and slammed the barrel of the gun between her shoulder blades. She opened her mouth to protest, but no sound emerged except a pitiful whimper.

"Move, I said."

As if sleepwalking, yet knowing that this was a nightmare from which she might never awaken, Marianne stepped out into the cold, wet darkness. Dimly, her heart mourned for the glimpse of heaven she'd shared with Nick, and grieved because she might never know it again.

It *had* been heaven, she thought numbly as she stumbled on the brick porch, because she felt as if she was walking into hell now, and surely it was the devil at her back.

Nick urged his mount faster with a regretful slap of the reins, sorry that he had to drive the weary animal so hard, but mindful of how late it was already. He'd make sure Jan gave the horse a good rubdown tonight along with an extra measure of oats. *After* he saw that Marianne was all right.

Grimacing, he tried not to let impatience make him careless. The road was strewn with small branches and debris knocked down by the heavy rainfall, and this part of the road was already thick with mud. Best to let the horse find his own pace, he thought resignedly, slackening his hold just a little. He'd had enough delays since last night; there was no sense in asking for another. Not when he was this close.

The first holdup had come when he'd found the livery stable closed, and had wasted precious time waking the disgruntled owner and bargaining with him for a mount. Nick had gone no further than the edge of town when the damned horse had turned lame, so he had ended up starting all over with the irate liveryman, who had accused him of pushing the animal too hard.

Heavy rains had prevented him from making the speed he would have wished, but the final blow had been when he reached the DuPont bridge—or rather, the place where the bridge should have been. He had searched two hours for a suitable spot to cross before bedding down under a tree until morning. Which had not, he thought ruefully, come soon enough.

All that was behind him now, Nick tried to tell himself, but the needless delays grated at him like salt in an open wound, difficult to bear and impossible to ignore. Now it was dark already—not that it'd been much lighter even in the middle of the day—and he was more anxious than ever to be home. The only blessing was that the rain had finally stopped.

Nick knew as soon as he dismounted in front of the house that something was wrong. The outside lamps hadn't been lighted, nor was there smoke curling from the chimney. It was a rare evening, and then only in midsummer, that Claire did not have her fire. Striding toward the house, his eyes trained on the broad, double doors, he quelled the panic that threatened to burst his chest wide open.

"Nick!" Elizabeth's scream tore through the air like the piercing cry of an osprey, her slight form hurtling out of the house and into his arms. "Oh, N-Nick! It's so awful. It's Marianne! Y-you've g-got to h-help her!"

"Where is she?" Clasping Elizabeth's shoulder hard so that he could hold her away slightly, Nick struggled to keep his voice calm. "Slow down and tell me what happened."

Gulping back tears, his sister repeated what she'd heard of the confrontation between Marianne and her abductor. When she was done, Jan, the stableboy, limped from the house, one hand steadying his head as he added his own version of events. Whoever the man had been—and Nick knew from Elizabeth's description that it hadn't been Hartley—he had knocked Jan a good one before stealing a horse for his and Marianne's getaway.

"I didn't know what to do, Nick," Elizabeth sobbed. "I was so scared. When Marianne told me to go, I started to run for help, but then I was afraid it would take too long. By the time I got back they were gone. Sue Kim went to the Delaneys' to ask them to send for the marshal."

"How long ago, Elizabeth?" Nick's voice was cold steel, slicing through the air with a murderous edge. "When did they leave?"

Before his sister could answer, another horse approached, this one moving slowly, picking its way carefully toward the house in an effort to keep its rider from toppling over. It was not until the animal stopped just a few feet away that Nick recognized Horace.

"Nick," Squiggs rasped, wheezing hard. "Pemberton's here . . . in Tacoma. . . shot Phil."

Helping his friend down, Nick was dismayed when his hand came away wet and sticky. At that moment Horace began to sway, and Nick rapidly lifted the smaller man in his arms and strode into the house, Elizabeth trailing. After lying him on the sofa and sending Jan for the doctor, Nick bent over the injured marshal.

"Tell me what you know, Horace. He's got Marianne. I have to find her."

Eyelids flickering with the effort to maintain consciousness, Horace Squiggs summoned the last of his strength to answer. "The map," he gasped. "It was on the map."

"What? What map?"

"On . . . on my wall. Your land . . . marked. The cabin too . . ."

Gripping Horace's hand, as if to lend him strength to continue as well as to convey his own desperation, Nick ground out his words. "What cabin, Horace? What cabin?"

"Y-yours. I've had it labeled since . . . since you built it out there in the w-woods. It had . . ."

The marshal stopped, squeezing his eyes tight, drawing his last words from some inner region. When he opened them again, it was to peer up with an expression so fearful that Nick felt his gut twist violently.

"There was a bullet hole . . . right through the map . . . right where your place is. Try there, Nick . . . that's where he'll be."

Nick stood, letting Horace's hand drop to his side as the marshal appeared to have lost his hold on consciousness. He looked around, surprised to see Claire standing behind him. What startled him even more was the man who stood beside her, cupping her elbow gently.

"What are you doing here, Hartley?"

"It's a long story . . . too long to start now. I'll ride with you."

Impatient to be off, Nick peered at the other man suspiciously, then glanced at his mother, who nodded her confidence. "All right then. Find your own horse, then try to follow me. I can't wait for you now."

"Nick."

Horace's weakened voice stopped him as he hurried to the door, and Nick turned to see the marshal struggling to lift himself on one elbow. "Take care, boy," he whispered, a trickle of blood escaping the corner of his mouth. "He's worse than . . . he's not . . ."

Collapsing back onto the couch, Horace waved his hand feebly as Claire rushed over to him. His eyes widened slightly and he coughed, yet somehow managed to gasp his warning once more. "Take . . . care."

Chapter 31

A night bird screeched just outside the cabin, its raucous cry shattering the silence, the swoosh of its heavy wings beating the air as it homed in on its prey. Marianne cringed at the high-pitched squeal that followed, weeping inwardly for the poor animal that suffered within the hold of the bird's talons.

She knew exactly how it felt.

Huddling closer to the stove to absorb the meager warmth it gave, she risked a glance toward her captor. Adam Pemberton sat hunched over the table not three yards from her, his head buried in his hands. He hadn't moved for several minutes, making Marianne wonder hopefully if he had fallen asleep. But then he lifted his eyes just enough to pin her with a bleary glare.

"Are you warm yet?" he asked thickly, his voice heavy with sarcasm and something she could not identify, something that sounded oddly like despair.

She stared back at him without blinking. "You can't get away with this, Adam. If you kill me, you'll hang."

"Don't you think I know that?" he whispered. For just a moment, his eyes flickered, losing the vacant stare that he'd worn since arriving at the cabin. She saw intelligence there, and pain and sorrow as well. For just that moment, a tiny measure of hope thrust into her heart, then withered away like a dying flower when she saw his expression grow blank again. "So what?" he muttered. "So I'll be dead, too."

And that was what terrified her. He didn't care, so

how could she stop him from carrying out what the demons in his head were driving him to do? A couple of times during the harrowing ride to the cabin he'd shouted over his shoulder at her, and she thought he'd called her Julia. The name meant nothing to her, but it obviously did to Adam, for his voice reached a deeper level of hatred each time he said it.

The only consolation, Marianne thought desolately, was that he probably would not carry out his threat to harm Nick. The same instinct that warned her he was completely insane also told her that once he'd killed her—and by killing her had also killed "Julia"—he would be finished.

Jerked from her thoughts by the sound of his chair scraping across the floor, Marianne followed his movements with a horrified gaze. He rose from his chair slowly, as if his every muscle and joint were stiff and aching. After shuffling toward the stove like an old man, he groaned and stretched his hands out toward the weak flame just showing through the open grate. "Just look what you've made me do," he murmured, his words gruff and whining. "I could've had everything—I *did* have everything!—but you took it all when you went away. I should have known you were a slut."

Marianne held her breath, uncertain whether answering would mollify him or draw his anger. In a few minutes he continued.

"Pa never should have let you go. He should have choked you to death before letting you make a fool of him. *I* would have, but then, you knew that, didn't you?" He cocked his head sideways, watching her with a malicious gleam in his eyes. When she didn't respond he spoke up again, his voice gaining strength with every word. "You didn't want me to hurt you, so you decided to make me love you instead, isn't that right? You used your body to snare my soul, and you tried to use me to satisfy your own selfish lust."

Stunned, Marianne could scarcely believe what he was saying. Some woman—his father's woman?—had seduced him, and now Adam had her confused with the one who had hurt him. Was that who Julia was?

Her mind swirled, desperately trying to think of a way out. It was painfully obvious that Adam no longer cared about the ledgers, and yet, if she could steer him toward a subject that was tangible, concrete, and keep his thoughts away from whatever memories haunted him, then perhaps she could buy some time.

"I—I'm sorry I took the books from you, Adam. I . . . shouldn't have done that. They're lost now."

Pemberton pursed his lips, his gaze intensifying as he struggled for concentration. "Books?"

"The ledgers . . . yours and Uncle Matthew's account books."

Understanding dawned on him, changing his expression to one of gleeful malice. "Ahh, the ledgers," he said, bobbing his head like a child. "Don't worry about them, Marianne. It doesn't matter anymore."

"Then why did you hire Rhys Hartley to follow me?"

Adam looked puzzled. "Hartley? I don't know anyone by that name. I told you, the books aren't important."

"But isn't that why you came here? To get them back?"

Adam stared hard at her, trying to fixate Marianne's image long enough to explain before she turned into Julia again. Was she stupid? Hadn't he told her why he'd come? "I could have loved you," he said, enunciating his words as if to clarify his thoughts. "I *did* love you. You looked so much like her that sometimes I imagined you were Julia come home. I was happy when Matthew sold you to me, and I would have been a good husband. I would have given you everything in the world. I had the money."

Money you stole, Marianne thought bitterly, though she knew better than to say it out loud. "And I might have married you," she lied, "but I couldn't after what you did to Uncle Matthew. Can't you understand?"

His eyes narrowed. "That's when it all started. I had everything under control until you left, but after that it began slipping through my hands like water. I tried to hold on. I tried to make it work out, but you ruined it, you and Julia."

"But I don't know who Julia is!" Marianne protested gently.

Adam's eyes clouded over, leaving her with the sinking knowledge that she had pushed him too hard. But instead of sliding back into the fog of madness that threatened, he shook his head, his lips curving upward into a strange smile. "I suppose it's only fair that you know," he replied. "Julia was my mother." His chin dropped, and his final words came out in a hoarse whisper. "*You* are Julia."

And now Marianne understood, though she wished with all her heart that she didn't. Only a woman who was half-mad herself could seduce her own son, and only a man who had carried the same madness in him would spend his life seeking vengeance. Pity for Adam welled in her, but she knew she could not allow sympathy to temper her will to live. She could not let him believe she was Julia!

As if he sensed her unspoken denial, Adam lurched closer, clutching her arm through her damp dress so hard she could feel the bruises forming already. She reacted automatically, pulling away, but his grip tightened, his eyes narrowing to evil slits.

"You laughed at me, you bitch," he said acidly. "I'll never forget the way you laughed when I couldn't do what you wanted. I could have strangled you then, *would've*, except you got away and never came back." He flung his head back as if to laugh out loud himself, but the only sound that emerged from his throat was a half groan, half cry that rent the air in two.

It ripped through Marianne, making her quiver like a rabbit caught in a snare, but it also released her from the paralysis that had turned her limbs to lead. "No!" she screamed, surging backwards hard enough to break his hold. "Let me go! I'm not Julia . . . I won't let you hurt me!"

With a feral growl, Adam lunged for her, falling to his knees in front of the stove as she spun away, but catching the hem of her skirt with one hand. The lethargy, the listlessness that had lulled him just a few minutes ago was gone now, and in its place raged a beastly wrath that pulsed and pounded and consumed him. He yanked hard on her skirt, watching her bounce back toward him like a lifeless puppet. Leaping to his feet, he wound one arm around her, trapping her arms ruthlessly. With the other hand he grabbed a fistful of her long hair and snapped her head around so that she faced him.

"You're mine now," he spat, his eyes raking her with a deadly gleam. "You're mine and you will be forever, because you'll die begging for more."

Marianne closed her eyes when she screamed, not wanting to see his twisted face looming over hers, not wanting her last glimpse of the cabin to be tainted with darkness and cold. She wanted to remember it as it had been, bright sunlight streaming through the windows, her heart warmed by Nick's love.

Desperately, she struggled to free herself again, but Adam's arms were locked around her, squeezing the breath from her lungs. Now his laughter, coarse and ugly, filled her head, and she felt his hand free itself roughly from her tangled hair.

"I want to see your eyes, slut!" he said at the same moment his fingers clutched her left breast. "Open your eyes!"

Of their own volition, her eyelids flew wide, more in reaction to his mauling hand than to his spoken order. She cringed inwardly, but could not move even a fraction of an inch within his insane hold. He laughed again, this time fondling her more painfully.

Marianne's eyes drifted shut again, only wanting this nightmare to come to an end. And it really was like a dream, she thought distantly. A dreadful, endless dream, eased only by the sound of Nick's voice . . .

"Let her go, Pemberton."

Her heart thudded against the wall of her chest, threatening to leap right out of her. She felt Adam's arm grow taut, then his hand dropped away from her. She slumped against him, knowing there was something she should remember, but only wanting the dream to go on if she could just see Nick one more time . . .

"I said, let her go!"

Marianne allowed herself to look for him then, and the cold fury in Nick's eyes dragged her shocked senses back to reality with all the force of a blow. He was here! Her soul leapt upward, a strangled cry of joy jamming in her throat.

"Son of a bitch!" Adam cursed, swinging her around so that she blocked his body from the deadly aim of Nick's rifle. The same arm still clasped her to him with an iron grip; his other hand fished around somewhere between her back and his chest. She couldn't think . . . couldn't remember . . .

"Nick, he's got a gun!" The words ripped from her mouth, raw but effective. Before Adam could draw the weapon from his coat, Nick raised the rifle barrel and sprang forward, bringing the heavy wooden stock down with a staggering blow against the juncture of Adam's shoulder and neck. Now when Marianne pushed away, Adam's arm slackened just enough to let her slip free.

She took one step forward, then tripped over the hem of her gown and stumbled, sprawling across the floor.

Ironically, that fall saved her life, for at the instant she dropped, Adam fired his gun at the center of her back. The bullet whistled harmlessly above her head, shattering one of the blue china plates on the shelf above the table. Marianne watched the slivers plunge hopelessly to the floor as if a bright summer sky were breaking into a thousand pieces.

Nick reacted to the blast of the gunshot and the sight of Marianne's limp form tumbling to the floor with an agony that swept him from head to toe. His mind did not register the fact that she had begun to fall *before* Adam pulled the trigger; he only remembered the helpless pleading in her eyes. With an angry roar, he clubbed Pemberton once more with his rifle, already too close to turn it around and fire. Adam grunted at the blow, but did not waver. Instead he turned toward Nick, his head lowered as he barreled into his chest like a raging bull.

Marianne watched in stunned horror as the two men rolled back toward the door, locked in mortal battle. Both Adam's gun and Nick's rifle had flown into the air on impact; both now lay on the floor near the stove. On her hands and knees, she crawled toward them. She had no idea how to handle the rifle but the small pistol looked simple enough. Holding it with both hands, she crouched on the floor and took aim.

Except that there was nowhere to point it without endangering Nick. Bound by arms and legs, the two men clutched at one another, each struggling to gain the advantage.

Nick felt as if his breath had been knocked clean out of him when Pemberton rammed him with his head, but anger and fear for Marianne gave him more power than he'd known possible. Adam, too, was possessed of herculean strength, but its source, Nick knew, was in his madness.

Marianne felt as if they'd been grappling on the floor for hours. With panic filling her heart, she saw signs of Nick tiring. Her lips moved in a silent prayer for him, rounding to an O when Adam clutched at Nick's injured arm, causing him to grunt painfully. Nick lost his balance then, rolling to his back with Adam on top of him.

"I ought to kill you," Adam raved, as if unaware that he was already doing just that. His hands were clenched around Nick's neck, his thumbs pressed tightly to his windpipe.

Straining, Nick pushed with all his might against Adam's shoulders, his slightly longer arms the only thing that stood between him and certain death. He was vaguely aware of Marianne watching them with the pistol clutched in both hands, and the thought of what would happen to her if he failed gave him the impetus he needed. He ground his heels into the floor and heaved upward, flinging Adam over his head in a grotesque somersault. Twisting rapidly, Nick pounced on the madman before he had a chance to regain his equilibrium.

"Oh, God," Marianne murmured, unable to bear much more. It seemed that just when she thought Nick was gaining the upper hand, something went wrong. And whenever Adam was on top, she couldn't get a clear shot at him. Would this ever be over?

It nearly was, for in that final throw, Nick had slammed his knee into Pemberton's groin at the same moment his hands found the man's throat. Dazed and weakened, Pemberton's resistance began to ebb in direct relation to the pressure Nick was applying to his air passage. The cords stood out on his neck as he struggled for breath.

The bastard had touched Marianne. That thought, that vision raced through Nick's mind like a recurring nightmare, relentless in its torture. He wasn't seeing Pemberton's eyes bulge or his face turn blotchy red beneath his hands; he saw the man's paw on Marianne's breast, his mouth gaping cruelly over hers.

The muscles in Nick's hands twitched, warning him that they had reached the limit of their strength, and still he squeezed, not wanting to let go until every ounce of rage was gone, yet knowing it would never leave him completely. Pemberton jerked spasmodically, his fingers clawing helplessly at Nick's shoulders, at the backs of his hands. It was almost over, Nick thought, his mind singing in a tuneless litany. *It's almost over. It's almost over . . .*

And then he stopped.

His hands grew limp around Pemberton's neck, and the only sounds left in the room were his own harsh breathing and the mewling noises that escaped through Pemberton's lips. Nick pushed himself up slowly without taking his eyes from the man's shuddering form. Now it *was* almost over, but not quite.

He hauled Pemberton to his feet with a brutal grip and spun him around, twisting one arm behind his back. Coughing and wheezing, Pemberton sagged, his weight propelling him forward as Nick shoved him toward the stove.

Marianne scrambled out of the way, but not so far that she couldn't see the pure loathing that etched every line of Nick's face, nor did she miss the sound of his voice, deep and merciless, as he grasped Adam's right hand.

"This," he said, "is for my wife."

Time paused then, like a giant clock that is slowly winding down, each second passing inexorably while events stretch out beyond their normal reach. Marianne saw what Nick was about to do, was shocked by what he was about to do, and yet, when he forced Pemberton's hand against the side of the stove she felt a rush of some emotion—triumph? exultation?—that surprised her more than the grim determination on Nick's face.

And when it was over, when Nick turned to her with sorrowful eyes and Pemberton lay sobbing on the floor, she could only stare back at him mutely, shock having taken over her senses.

Nick spoke hoarsely, but without regret. "I'm sorry you had to see that."

With a cry muffled behind her hand, Marianne felt the sobs of relief billow through her, shoving past all her resolve and leaving her quivering and weak. She tried to stand but the starch had gone out of her knees, so she plopped back to the floor, the pistol gripped tightly in her white-knuckled fingers.

"I'm not," she finally managed to whisper.

He lifted his head, gray eyes meeting blue. "When I thought of him touching you, I . . ." Nick glanced down at Pemberton, whose once evil expression was now blank, and then returned his gaze to Marianne.

"Y-you didn't k-kill him," she stammered. "Why?"

It was a question for which he had no answer, but the realization of the choice he'd made rolled over him like a life-giving breath. Despite his weariness, despite his pain, Nick felt stronger than ever before in his life.

"I'm not sure." He nodded down toward her hand, asking gently, "What did you plan to do with that?"

Marianne's gaze followed the direction of his eyes, coming to rest on the gun she still held. Her stunned gasp only made him smile, and she matched it with a puzzled one of her own as she tossed the weapon aside. "I guess," she said meekly, "I've learned a lesson in survival."

"So have I," Nick said. He peered thoughtfully at Adam Pemberton, who was staring at the wall with vacant eyes, clutching his burned hand to his chest.

"There was a minute there when I knew I could kill him," Nick continued slowly, "when I knew all I had to do was hold on just a little longer. But then I remembered what you said that night after I fought Trig, and what Ryan Calder said yesterday. Some men *are* no better than animals, but not all of us." He looked back up at Marianne, his expression warm and loving and victorious. "Not all of us."

Gazes locked together in a wordless mating, their hearts bridged the distance between them as he stood guard over the man who had threatened their peace and she watched him with pride and joy chasing away the last vestiges of fear.

I love you, his eyes told her.

I love you, hers answered.

Her insides were still quaking like jelly but she stood, surveying the damage to the room, her eyes sliding evasively past Adam, then returning to him when compassion overruled the disgust in her heart. "What will we do with him?"

"Don't worry!" Rhys Hartley's voice broke the quiet. He staggered bowlegged through the door, grinning as he returned his gun to its holster. "I'll take care of him now."

After Rhys had gone and Nick had found a few dry logs at the bottom of the woodpile just outside the door, Marianne watched him light the fireplace in the bedroom with a hot coal from the stove. They had already straightened the furniture and cleaned up the broken china, as if by setting the room to rights they could erase some of the horror that had taken place there. When that was done they stared at one another for a long moment before coming together, not speaking, not breathing, only daring to hope that it could all be over. Neither knew who took the first step, nor who uttered the first murmurs and joyful cries as they found each other's arms.

Nick's mouth sought hers, sought release from the pent-up frustration and fear and longing that rippled through him with a force as strong as the wind whipping the treetops.

She pressed her body the length of his, wanting, *needing* to feel him warm and hard and solid against her. Wrapping her arms around his neck, Marianne matched his urgency with a driving desire of her own. It was the desire to heal, to hold, to blot out everything but this. Her blood danced through her veins as his hands skimmed from her hips to the sides of her breasts, desperately gentle, fiercely possessive.

"Ah, love," he whispered, then could say no more as she drew his head down for another kiss; caressing, thrusting, until they both knew that kissing was not enough.

She broke away first, smiling shyly as she gripped his hand in her trembling fingers and tugged, elation filling her when he grinned in response and followed willingly into the other room.

Dust lay thick on the floor and furniture, marred only by Nick's footprints leading from the door to the fireplace. The top of the vanity table was thick with it too; the bedspread, once white, was nearly gray. Nick hesitated at the door.

"Would you rather go home?" he asked, his voice as rough and beautiful as an unpolished gem.

Marianne stepped toward the four-poster, whisking the bedspread back with a quick, decisive motion that shook up a cloud of dust, yet trapped most of it in the folds of the coverlet. The single blanket and sheets that had lain beneath it were clean. "No," she said, her eyes happy and shining with want. "I want to stay here with you."

Nick stifled a groan of pure gladness as she came to him again, this time wasting no time tugging out what little of his shirttail remained in his pants and smoothing her hands up and around to his back, his shoulders, sliding under his arms and spreading across his chest.

"I've missed you," she whispered, unable to get enough of him with only her hands to absorb the sensation. Hurriedly, she pushed the shirt down his arms, easing it over the injured one, pulling impatiently at the other.

"I can see you have," he teased, but it was he who was tormented anew by the hunger, the longing that surged through him like a living force whenever her hands brushed his flesh. Her scent rose to fill his nostrils, swirled around his head like a drugging mist as her own clothing slid down to the floor, billowing around her in colorful folds that were *nothing* when compared to her own beauty.

"Come," she said, leading him carefully, then dropping his hand as she scooted onto the center of the bed.

For a long moment he stood still, his gaze sweeping her from head to toe, drinking in the sight of her greedily. But when she raised her arms in sweet welcome, he could wait no longer.

He shed the rest of his clothing as fast as he could, and it was not fast enough.

She raised herself to meet him, pulling herself close, and it wasn't close enough.

He kissed her and caressed her until her flesh rippled and her blood pounded, and it wasn't hard enough.

She opened herself to him, drawing him home with all the womanly instinct and trust and heat that throbbed through her and through him, until what was empty was full, empty and full, then full and full and full . . .

And then, quite simply, it was enough.

It was a long time before they could speak, and when they did it was in low whispers, murmurs lost in the taste of one another's flesh that led to more touching and tasting and filling . . .

After an eternity of loving there was silence again, this time punctuated by Nick's slow, rhythmic breathing and Marianne's shallow gasps. Finally, after her pulse slowed to a pace only twice as fast as normal, she was able to smile at the knowledge that they had succeeded in chasing the shadow of evil from this cabin. She might remember at times what had occurred here, but mostly she would remember the love. But she still wanted to understand. She sighed.

"Are you okay?" Nick asked, his voice rough, yet, with emotion.

She shivered and he reached for the blanket that had been kicked to the foot of the bed and covered them both, then gathered her close again.

"I'm fine," she said. "I was just thinking . . . Half the time he didn't even know who I was!"

Nick held her protectively, his jaw clenching tight as it rested on the top of her head. "I know. Hartley explained most of that when we were out tying Pemberton to the horse. It seems he's been on a steady downhill path since killing your uncle. When he learned you were alive it was the final straw, and in his own sick way he blamed you for the problems he'd brought on himself. The trouble was, he'd already been blaming his mother for so much that his mind couldn't differentiate any more. He wasn't sane, darling."

"And Rhys?"

Nick held her shoulders away and grinned. "That's the strangest part of all. To think, if we'd only known he was a federal agent, we would have saved ourselves a lot of trouble."

"He couldn't tell us who he was when he believed I was guilty," Marianne said thoughtfully, "and then Marshal Squiggs never had the chance to tell us after we got home."

"Hartley would have saved *himself* a lot of trouble if he'd only come straight to you instead of trailing you in secret," Nick replied, chuckling. "I have a feeling he's not much of a rider. He confessed to being a little saddle-sore after the past few days. It also must have been some blow to his ego, being bested by three women."

Marianne laughed along with him at the mental

picture that Rhys had described to them of Ruth, Katey Muldoon, and Claire holding him captive. Then her expression grew serious again. "So many people have been hurt by Adam Pemberton: Uncle Matthew, all those women, Deputy Owens, and Marshal Squiggs . . ."

"Horace'll be all right," Nick assured her, pressing her tight to him. "He'd lost a lot of blood but his pulse was strong when he passed out, and it looked as if the bullet went clean through his shoulder."

"I'm glad," Marianne whispered. "To think I was so frightened by him that day, and then he risked his life for me."

"People aren't always what they seem," Nick said, murmuring into her silky hair. With great care, he lifted her face, his hands cupped around her cheeks as if they were delicate flowers, his eyes searching hers. "I was wrong about so many things," he admitted gently, "but mostly I was wrong about you. You're much stronger than I ever thought possible."

"But I'm not strong at all." She pushed back against his arm. "When Adam threatened me I ran away, and when Marshal Squiggs questioned me I lied, and I should have stood up for myself before I let you marry me just to protect me from Rhys."

"I married you for more than that," Nick replied, his eyes glowing embers in the darkened room. "I just wouldn't admit to myself how much I needed you. That night in the forest, when you came to me with passion even though I'd acted like a beast all day, that's when I first started to know how deep was your love, and how much it meant to me. But until tonight, I didn't realize how empty my life would be without you."

Tears trembled on her lashes as she gazed at him, all the warmth and hope and passion in her heart combining to engulf them both. She swallowed back the lump in her throat. "I loved you so much that I didn't care whether you loved me back, as long as I could stay with you forever. But Nick, I was wrong about some things too, and I blamed you for things I never should have. I understand now about Alicia. Megan told me a little about how she was, and Claire told me what she did to you. All that time I thought it was Alicia you loved."

"I should have told you about her myself, but I thought the one thing I couldn't bear from you was pity—"

"Pity," Marianne interrupted, "is for those weakened by misfortune, not for one who learns from it, who grows stronger."

"Like you."

Amazement filled her as she looked at him, meeting his loving gaze with a puzzled one of her own. "Me?"

"Yes, you. Your love *is* your strength, my darling. And it'll only continue to grow, because I'll love you forever."

Her eyes glistened brightly, drifting closed when he lowered his mouth to hers in a kiss that sealed them together for all time.

Heart to heart, soul to soul, they joined as one, knowing that nothing, *nothing* would separate them again.

About the Author

Robin LeAnne Wiete was born and raised in New York State. After marrying her college sweetheart in 1976, she lived in Cincinnati, Ohio for several years, where she worked for a national investment firm. It was largely through the enthusiasm of a co-worker there that she discovered a deep and abiding passion for historical romances, and decided to write one of her own. *Fortune's Lady* is her second historical romance.

Ms. Wiete has recently returned to Cincinnati with her husband and two children. She spends her nonwriting time enjoying her family, reading, and working with other writers.

She welcomes comments from readers at the following address:

P.O. Box 58608
Cincinnati, OH 45358